SOMEWHERE

IN

LORRAINE

A NOVEL
BY
CAPIO

For Beth, Drew, Tina, family and my encouraging friends: Ace, Speedy, Jon, Suzanna, Clip, Pat, Jay, Grace, the Leaskians, to Val, to the dear memory of 'Curly' Howe and to fallen ones over there, somewhere in Valhalla. – Capio

Somewhere in Lorraine is a work of fiction. Characters, places and incidences are inventions of the author. A resemblance to any person is entirely accidental.

Published by Capio's Camp LLC
Hopkins, Minnesota, USA
ISBN 978-0-9826-1520-1 (pb)
Library of Congress Control Number: 2010902150
16 15 14 13 12 11 10   2 3 4 5
www.capioscamp.com

ଞ୍ଚଷ

Introduction

Dusk's dim purplish hue leaked past Everett's eyelids. He lowered a blanket from his sweating head after dreaming that a single-engine reconnaissance plane circled his farmhouse bedroom. He aimed an ear to his alarm clock's bee-like drone and focused on its glowing green hands. In fifteen minutes the buzz would crescendo to a pealing meant to wake the dead. He set it himself like a loaded gun for his appointment with Doc.

He dragged a sheet across his face and slipped back into the warm depths of his bed where he would wait for Huan. She would sail right in, past the sunset, past his radium-tipped clock, straight to his heart, with her slight smile and ripening Korean idealism. It was time now. He lifted as cold eddies spilled over his wings. He circled like an eagle above a nest of fifty silvered eggs arranged along an oval-shaped street, trusting he might remember its name when he woke.

The eggs nested in an Iowa cornfield by the university, each globe protected a family from the cold winter, each complete with a mother, a baby or two and a father who slept with a book in his hand, not the weapon from his war. The Quonset, a shell of galvanized steel, kept them safe as Everett descended upon 'Bird Nest Lane'.

His feet ripped sheets as his talons gripped the quiet night's snow and he trotted from his dormitory past the fourth row and Quonset number four-thirty-nine, where a warm yellow light glowed. A baby wailed inside. His claws retracted into boots as he transformed and slipped quickly past, frigid and wingless, towards the bus station on the next block.

Frozen tears stippled at his cheek as he shuffled his boots in long strides for the white vapors rising from an idling bus nearby. A driver lifted a small suitcase to a doll-like oriental girl and helped her up the steps into the four-wheeled aluminum cocoon.

He watched from the curb as she made her way down the aisle and sat in a seat by a frosted window. Her small finger traced a transparent line through the thin crystal. The window opened a few inches. Her once, youthful, oriental face, so intense while delightfully deriving mathematical proofs of continuity and existence while he worked his slide rule on engineering problems, held tears at bay. She looked old now as the clock droned and the hand's green radioactive tip crept electro-magnetically towards another minute.

"You promised not to come. You wait. I come back when papasan better." She waved her tiny bare hand in the sharp sleet as the bus spun its tires in the snow.

Her parents had whisked her safely away to college six years ago, just before Pearl Harbor. She had but the one photograph, black and white, dated 1940 – in which she posed inside a pagoda, grey in the photo - but she said it was bright orange. It stood like a shrine in their garden with the Taeback Mountains in the background. The once forested river valley, home to her mother's family, cut through the Taeback's to the south. Huan's mother, in a wedding magoja coat, stood next to Huan who said it was once bright red or maybe blue. Huan wore a cowboy shirt and her Japanese father, out of uniform, wore a sports coat. She stood proud then as a girl, with the same small cloth suitcase in front of her that the driver had just heaved into the bus.

Huan's father, no longer the proud out-of-uniform Japanese soldier, was ill. Her little hand retracted into the bus' cold metal shell as its tires turned snow to steam. The silver shell crawled east across the Mississippi to Chicago to fly home, to Yangu. The clock groaned six-twenty-five.

He could fly her now - he knew the way as he lifted back into the air above Bird's Nest Lane. If only he were there, but Everett was here, alone in his bed, dripping wet in sweat as he woke again. His clock roared its nuclear brilliance to the dark night. He'd be late. Doc would wait. Doc was all he had in the whole world.

◆ ◆ ◆

It always felt a little strange to see Doc professionally like this, Everett thought as he rushed late into Doc's office. Doc pointed to the patients' chair beside the grey metal desk. Everett remembered the chair brand new when he first visited Doc over a year ago. He eased himself into the leather, and curled his feet under himself on the big soft cushion and stretched out. Too expensive a chair for the veteran's hospital to afford, Everett partly believed Doc bought it for him.

"Are you comfortable living there alone on your dad's old farm?" Doctor Hershey asked, "Is there anything you need, son?"

"I'm fine, Doc."

"I spoke with your professor," Doctor Hershey said, "he agreed to meet with you once again about you continuing your graduate work after your winter semester struggles. How do you feel about that, Everett?"

"I don't think I like studying Aeronautics, Doc. I took French and German as you suggested but I never dream of flying anymore, just those nightmares."

"So we're back onto the long hard road. Are you sure I can't find you another doctor? I'm not really a psychologist."

"I need to talk to someone I trust, like you, Doc."

Doc reminded him of how they would start, where they left off last.

"Captain, have a seat. Please forgive me, I keep thinking of your dad, Russell, he was a Captain, you look like him."

"That's all right, Doc," Everett said as he ran his hands back and forth across the leather arms of the cushioned chair.

"Do you think we're really close?" Doc asked.

"Yes, Sir," Everett said, knowing that addressing Doc Hershey, as Sir, allowed Doc to ask him the tough questions.

"Good, Everett. Today we'll finally come to the difficult part, won't we?"

"Yes Sir, - I'm rather nervous, as you can see."

"How long have you been coming for your visit, Everett?"

"Every week since the incident last year, Sir."

"Why, Everett, do you think it's taken us so long?"

Everett bent forward to Doc's desk, as he always did before they started, and ran his fingertips across Doc's nameplate for luck. Dr. Robert Hershey, MD.

"So now, back to this incident when you returned home to Iowa from Korea, tell me again what it was - I know of course, you've told me before, but I want you to tell me again."

"We're here because of," Everett stammered. "That pig roast last year in town where I had to make a speech."

"We talked about that other pig business before, do you remember?" Doc asked.

"Yes, in school after father's funeral, I think. The class bully from town whispered to me that it runs in the family. He said he heard that my mom slit her wrist over the pigsty and fell in. I punched him before he knocked me out."

"And you know now it's not true," Doc said. "Because I told you that I was there at the hospital when she died just after you were born. Kids can be cruel."

"It just stayed with me so long, Sir," Everett said, aware of his shoulders slightly shaking and hoping Doc didn't see.

"Alright then, we're past that. Now back to this end-of-the-war gathering. There were others too from here, in your Korean war. Why did they want you to speak and not someone else?"

"Well," Everett said as he again ran his hand across the leather arm of the chair, "it's because I was probably more educated than the rest - I suppose."

"You've said all this before Everett, what else?"

Everett tapped his fingers on the chair.

"I think," he started.

"Yes?"

"I think it's because, I was the most presentable - I mean they thought I spoke well and I didn't have wounds that might repel the public. You hadn't had time then to look me over yet."

"There were so many discharged at once, Everett."

"I know, Doc."

"Do you remember how we started our first session last year, Everett?"

"I didn't say much."

"Just sit back and tell me like it was then. I want to see how far we've come. Would that be OK, Everett?"

Everett looked out the window towards the town.

"It was last year, you remember, Doc, in the park in the middle of town - the church set up chairs, banners waved from telephone poles, a band, speakers from town and a big fire pit - well you know what happened, of course. It was that fire pit where they were turning a pig on a spindle. The pig caught fire from its own fat dripping down into the pit. They just sat there watching it burn."

Doctor Hershey swiveled in his seat and moved closer.

"They all just sat there watching it go up in flames," Everett repeated. He curled his legs under his seat on the couch.

"You were about to give a speech, as I recall," Doc said.

"Yes, I guess I must have snapped at someone to go over there and take care of that pig, but nobody moved. I must have said a few inappropriate things before I decided to get down from the stage and take matters into my own hand. I picked the pig up and set it in the river."

"And you burned your hands," Doc said.

"Yes, you wrapped gauze around them, Doc."

"Of course - but that was a year ago, Everett. Now, where have we come, where are we now on your long walk? Can we go there now? Would it be all right with you?"

"Yes, Sir. Tell me where you last left me."

The doctor ran his thumb over the stack of papers on his lap quickly coming to the last page. He paused to review it while Everett moved his hands, trembling and sweating, under his seat.

"Oh, yes. Here we are. You were telling me about the briefing in the map room with the other pilots. We had to stop our session then because you weren't sure if it was still classified information, but I think you just started to feel anxious and wanted to leave - is that right?"

"Yes, Sir. I'm not as nervous today."

"It was towards the end of the war, wasn't it? Tell me, if you can, what happened in the map room."

Everett closed his eyes and tried to picture the big detailed map on the wall of a dark smoke-filled room. He could see his old wingman, Bender, sitting beside him, screwing the cap back onto the small flask of medicinal whiskey to which Bender had grown attached.

"Do you remember me talking about my old pal, Bender?"

"I'd like to meet him sometime," Doctor Hershey said.

"Bender was just assigned back to our wing. He was sitting next to me. I could smell whiskey on his breath. They pointed to a target up along the front line in the foothills of the Taeback's in a little river valley where Bender would be shot down by ground-fire in a few hours."

"I see," Doctor Hershey said, making a few notes.

"They told us an enemy command post was in a house that was never hit before, in an area we flew over every day, right under our noses. It looked like a temple."

"Were temples off-limits?"

"No, we targeted them before," Everett said, "but Bender always seemed to find a way to go long or short."

"Did you ever intentionally miss one?"

"No, I was always right on the money."

"You were always a good pilot," Doc said. "Go on."

"I had become more than a pilot by then, Sir."

"Go on."

"They wanted Bender's flight to drop napalm, so he wouldn't miss this time," Everett said, puckering his face as though he had swallowed milk gone sour.

"You don't like using napalm do you?"

"Not many did."

"What happened next?"

"Bender stood up and said that single houses were always tough to sort out on a flight, especially flying west to east against the grain of the valleys and ridges. We didn't want to fly with the grain either, because if we went short, we could hit our own troops. They told Bender he couldn't miss this one."

"Do you mean if Bender missed this one he would be court-martialed?"

"Maybe, but I think they meant he couldn't miss the house because it had an orange pagoda in the yard and he had napalm under his wings. Intelligence indicated no AA in the area, but after Bender unloaded on the target he took a round of thirty-seven millimeter that brought him down."

"I'm sorry," Doctor Hershey said. "Did they recover Bender's body?"

"Yeah, someone from close range put a bullet through his brain, probably after he gathered his chute."

"Well this sort of thing happens in war, Everett. It'll stay with you for a while, but Bender wouldn't want you stewing about it. In a way, it was probably best for Bender - he must have felt awful about hitting the pagoda."

"That's just it, Sir. Bender missed it again. The next day my flight was ordered to take it out, and I did - Oh, boy, did I ever set that thing on fire for him!"

"Then you should be feeling somewhat relieved, Everett, to avenge Bender's death."

"That's not it, Sir," Everett said, as he wedged his hand between the cushions.

"Tell me you're not looking for coins," Doc said, pointing to the cushions.

"Bender knew I didn't want to bomb the place, because I told him I knew someone who once lived by an orange pagoda." Everett pulled his hands free.

"A Korean woman?" Doc asked. "Why didn't you tell me this before?"

Everett's hands dove into the comforting cushions.

"Front and center, here Everett!" Doc said, grasping Everett's arm. "I knew a few women in France and so did your dad. A man misses that soft touch."

"That's not it, either Doc," Everett said. "I didn't want to get you into trouble."

"How in the Sam Hell can you get me into trouble?" Doc snapped.

"When I first went to college, before the war, I dated this Korean girl," Everett said. "She returned in 1947. She said her Japanese father was sick, but she might have been a communist. I'd hate to see you forced into taking a loyalty oath."

"Mass hysteria," Doc said. "The cure for that is blinding truth. Now, I appreciate your concern for my position, but even if she were a communist, I don't see how this would cause you to see her inside every damned orange pagoda in Korea."

"I think she was pregnant when she left college," Everett said.

"Oh." Doc combed his thinning hair with a quick plow of his hand.

"On our outbound flights," Everett said, "we would pass through the valley over the pagoda and she would be out, early in the morning hanging clothes with a little boy at her side. A little boy, with red-hair - just like mine."

Doc smiled.

"That shouldn't be funny, Doc," Everett said.

"Let's take a walk by the river," Doc said.

It was dark, except for white glowing lamps above the brick walkway near a long stone-arched bridge. An attendant pushed a man, wrapped in a tattered combat jacket, who hummed without taking a single breath, across in a wheelchair. Doc stopped Everett in the middle to watch the river flow.

"It's time to toss it for good into the river, Everett. Tell me, how many pagodas in Korea?"

"Tens of thousands."

"And what color are they?"

"Orange, they're all orange."

"Out of all the beautiful colors in Korea, they only chose orange? You've seen all these pagodas?"

"Well no, but I know they're all orange."

"Someone told you this? You didn't learn this in school."

"I know Huan's was orange."

"And therefore, they all had to be orange, and this particular orange pagoda, out of the tens of thousands, just had to be this Huan's? Come to your senses, son."

Everett listened to Doc trying to inhale a lungful of heavy river air.

"Are you alright, Doc?" Everett asked, knowing Doc hadn't taken a full breath since the Great War.

He felt Doc's arm lay across his shoulders. Doc pointed to the wide and swollen river in the moonlight. A tall elm broke free from a snag and took to the current.

"You should let it go, son," Doc said, pointing to the drifting elm.

"You're not very good at this, Doc," Everett said.

"I know," Doc said as he laid his big hand on Everett's shoulder, "but let me ask you one more thing."

"You don't think I killed them, do you?" Everett asked.

"Oh, you most definitely killed the one in that pagoda," Doc said, "and if she was a communist she would have definitely killed you or someone, like you, had she survived – and it's hard to kill an idea, as you know, that's for sure. That's not what I was going to ask you."

"What then?" Everett said.

"What was your major in college, before the war?" Doc asked.

"Aeronautical engineering, like now, you know that," Everett said.

"Well, you should have majored in genetics then," Doc said.

"But I always loved flying, until now," Everett said. "You think I should go back to farming like Father tried to do – maybe with hybrid corn? Is that why you say genetics?"

"No. Because if you understood genetics, Everett, you would realize, how nearly impossible it would be for a Korean woman to give birth to a red-haired boy like you."

"No shit?"

"It's the blinding truth, son," Doc said as he caught Everett's sleeve. Doc led him down from the bridge, along a path at the river's bank. The elm bobbed in backwater, out of the current.

"Don't you ever have nightmares of your war," Everett asked, "the one you and Father were in, the Great War?"

"You don't remember much of him, do you?" Doc said.

Doc put his foot in the crotch of the tree and pushed it back into the river.

"Not much. I was nine," Everett said. "Did he have nightmares?"

"He had what we called, 'consumption', from the gas, and," Doc stopped.

"What," Everett said, "what else?"

"Well," Doc cleared his throat and spit into the river, "your dad carried a lot of guilt about losing his regimental band over there. We never did find out what killed them, it happened the night before we were ordered forward."

"I never heard of this before, Doc. Did he have nightmares?" Everett asked.

"Probably," Doc said.

"Couldn't you just tell him the blinding truth about war?"

"No," Doc said, eying the tree, snagged against another.

"You don't know what it's like to wake up like that, Doc," Everett said. "Why couldn't you help him with his nightmares like you helped me?"

"Why don't you wade out there and free up that tree," Doc said, then turned to walk back up to the bridge.

Everett's shoes sunk in the mud as he made his way out into knee-high water, testing each step and trying not to think about why Doc put him off. He lifted a branch and pushed the tree on its way.

He found Doc grasping a lamp pole when he returned. Doc coughed. His eyes welled-up in tears in the lamp light.

"Damn gas," Doc said. "You've never been to France have you, Everett?"

"I always flew west."

"Did you ever wonder why you have such an unusual name, Everett?"

"Why did father pick it?"

"You're named after a French painter, Evariste, from the Great War," Doc said.

"Do you think it will do me good to look him up?" Everett said.

"No, don't waste your time, son," Doc said. "Évariste disappeared before we arrived. One night, he chased the enemy in the trenches with a paintbrush. He's famous. Your dad liked that story. If you're really interested, I think I can get you in contact with Évariste's widow, Madame Lambert, she was with your dad and me over there."

"Will I stop having these dreams?" Everett asked.

"Probably not, son."

"Why go then?"

"To find out what happened to that band for your dad," Doc said. "To find the blinding truth."

"How would I know where to start?"

"Go through some of your dad's things, there's got to be something," Doc said. "You might even remember certain things about him too – his voice, his face, his smell. You always called him 'Dad', not 'Father'. You'll find him again, 'Over There' - somewhere in Lorraine."

On their walk back to the office, Doc described the country and the war that he and Everett's father fought in long ago; the long, frigid marches, endless drills, brutality and compassion, power and helplessness, the devastation and the beauty of France. Although no longer a game of villains and heroes, Everett felt the riptide of his father's war drawing him in like a nine-year old.

Everett thought about France and the Great War all the way home to the farmhouse, not once dwelling on the orange pagoda. He thought too, of his father and Doc, when Everett was young, never once mentioning anything at all about his father's regimental band disappearing.

In the farmhouse cellar, Everett sorted through his father's old war chest. He emptied it of his father's fishing gear, hoping to find maybe a letter written in his father's own hand to Everett's grandmother or to his father's Iowa sweetheart. Maybe a letter might still carry the fragrance of his father's cologne, or shaving cream, or maybe the sweat of fear. He smelled only mold as he searched for anything about this regimental band or this person, Madame Lambert.

He found military maps of France near the bottom of the chest. He saw them as a child but was never interested then - they described the area in Lorraine as a quiet sector. As he pried the maps loose, careful not to tear them, he found a stack of bluish envelopes beneath, tied in a rotted string that crumbled like burnt ash when he touched it.

The first letter, addressed to "The Family of Jim Crabshaw", carried the name of the town, his town, and street where he sat on a curb watching marching bands pass in review. The letter began, "Dear Norton and Matilda, I only wish I had a moment to write more, so I could tell you what a fine young man your Jim was and what it meant to us here in France to hear him play that trombone."

The next too, "Dear Charlie and Ethel, I truly join you in this moment of sorrow. I only wish I had a moment to write more, so I could tell you what a fine young man your Lester was and what it meant to us here in France, to hear him play those drums."

Twenty-six letters to the loved ones of the saxophonists, the trumpets, clarinets, flutes and the tuba player, Stephen Collins and each with "From Somewhere in Lorraine" written in the return address, each scrolled in a similar cursive style to Everett's own hand.

Like his own grandmother, Charlie and Ethel, Norton and Matilda and all the other parents had passed on years ago. He decided that nobody needed to know about his father's letters - not even Doc.

He ruffled the envelopes under his nose for a hint of Father but all he caught was a fishy smell and it came not from the letters but from the bottom of the chest where an old army tunic lay flat to cushion the letters. An ordinary doughboy's jacket but adorned with colorful fishing lures and a rainbow colored patch. He fluffed it up trying to picture the man filling it out then folded it up in triangles like a flag and set it at the bottom again.

He took the maps he needed and packed them with the letters in his small traveling bag with only enough room for a few changes of socks and underwear.

At least he knew now exactly where he was going and why - to finish twenty-six letters from somewhere in Lorraine, France.

Doc's big black Buick rolled up the gravel road to the farmhouse as Everett, on the porch, checked his back pocket for his train ticket from Chicago to New York. Doc would drive him to Chicago and bring him the ship tickets to Le Havre. Everett swung his bag into the front seat and then watched his father's old farmhouse disappear in a cloud of lime dust as Doc drove them along the river. He rolled his window up and it quieted inside the big car.

Doc chewed at the side of his cheek.

"I finally tracked down Madame Lambert," Doc said. "She's still alive. She wants to meet you."

"When do I meet her?" Everett said, turning to Doc.

"That's just it, I've already got your tickets," Doc said, looking out across the river. "She'll be in Strasbourg for a few weeks before she returns to Lorraine."

"I'll just meet her in Lorraine," Everett said. "Where exactly in Lorraine were you and father – that's where I want to go."

"Ville Negre," Doc said. "You'll never find it alone."

"Doc, I'm twenty-six years old. I've flown combat missions over Korea so many times I didn't even need a map. You must think I'm really a mess."

"Not any more than me," Doc said. "I wouldn't allow you to travel if you weren't in good shape, but Madame Lambert has seen to it that someone will show you around. Your boarding ticket is in the glove compartment."

Everett caught the ticket as he dropped the door to his knees after it nearly caught the wind. He felt a little better as they crossed the Mississippi into Illinois with ticket in his hands.

"This ship, the Excalibur, it's putting into Marseilles, not Le Havre," Everett said.

"Madame Lambert's daughter docks in Marseilles aboard the ship Pasteur from Indochina when you do," Doc said as he nervously tapped his fingers on the steering wheel. "You're supposed to meet her at a café called the Port-du-Chien. She'll escort you by train to Ville Negre, southeast of Nancy in Lorraine. Madame Lambert made all the arrangements."

"What's Madame Lambert doing in Strasbourg?" Everett asked.

"She's a kind of a retired nurse, still," Doc said as he raced the car past fields lined in a dizzying pattern of sprouting corn. "She's volunteered to help the returning French soldiers at the hospital there."

"I see," Everett said, slapping the tickets against his thigh and shaking his head. "And what exactly is her daughter doing in Indochina?"

"Like Mother, like daughter," Doc said.

"How's a nurse supposed to help me find out about this band?"

"Madame Lambert was there the night they all disappeared, near Ville Negre," Doc said, gripping the wheel.

❧ 1 ☙
Marseilles, May 1954

Everett dragged his knuckles across the wall behind his bed, expecting the comforting patter against the soft pine wainscot of his farmhouse bedroom. He knew, even asleep, it was the cold steel wall of the ship but he wanted it to be Quonset four-thirty-nine in his dreams and so it was. Behind those three tin numerals, they made love to the random patter of sleet, falling like mayflies from the night sky and turning by morning to dry, light flakes against the windowpane. He dragged his knuckles across the corrugated Quonset wall as he walked past, outside in the cold.

He missed the companion footsteps of his light-footed Huan, scrunching and squeaking in the snow beside him as he passed by four-thirty-nine - Bird Nest Lane to his dormitory to the solitude of his bunk bed.

A damned durable dream, he knew, as it came to his head aboard the ship; an aluminum airliner lifting Huan into the black sky to that little Korean hamlet and her pagoda with its orange-painted wood rendered in cold grey ash and sifted by winds running down the Taeback Mountains.

◆ ◆ ◆

Everett woke crosswise in his rumpled bed. He sniffed the sea air from his opened porthole for a trace of ozone left by the night's thunderstorm. He looked out his cabin door and waited for the storm to clear so he could take a walk on deck and get this nurse off his mind.

The end of night had been the best time to walk when only André, the late shift steward might happen by, off-duty, with Everett's cognac. To Everett's surprise, the French he had taken in college proved adequate and the ever patient André never bothered Everett with too many questions about Korea while they drank.

Inside the iron drum of his cabin, caressed by the churn of the Excalibur's huge propellers, he lay back on his bed sorting fickle memories for small talk to bring on deck for André, afraid the alcohol might loosen a nightmare in front of the innocent steward.

The Excalibur gently heaved and rolled. The propellers slowed as they had done before docking, first at Cadiz, then Barcelona. The low rumble in his cabin changed pitch. He waited for tugboats to bring the Excalibur to a full stop then guide it to its berth in Marseilles, but he felt the ship coasting as if it were a puck on a frozen pond. The random, uncommitted motion coaxed him back into a brief twilight sleep until the startling tremble and ratcheting of the falling anchor brought him onto the darkened deck with his pants and shirt in hand.

The ship, no longer under power, swayed unsteadily beneath his feet as he dressed. The air, still and damp as he stepped to the rail, carried the fragrance of lavender. Below, the Mediterranean slapped the hull. Behind him squealed the main deck's bar door as it opened. It would be André, coming off duty. André would know why they stopped before coming to Marseilles. The distant light of the port and city glowed through the fog.

André stepped out still dressed in his uniform - a red blazer and an oversized cap, always cocked unnaturally and covering his right ear. He carried a pair of tall crystal glasses, one full, the other nearly empty, teetering on a tray with the name of the ship etched into the silver, S.S. Excalibur.

"Good evening, Monsieur Taylor. Your morning cognac?"

"Merci, André. Will we be late docking tomorrow?" Everett asked. He reached for the full glass.

"No, Monsieur."

André sipped then set his glass on the deck with the tray. He pulled a small towel from inside his blazer, wetted it with his mouth and began to clean the front of Everett's shirt.

"Is that really necessary, André?" Everett said. He took another drink and looked overboard, thinking he heard something in the water.

"Drinking alone is acceptable in France," André daubed the stain. "However, eating alone each night in your cabin is considered rude. If you had only joined them in the dining room even once, you would have seen the other passengers not paying much attention to your trembling fork - the way this old ship shudders and shakes. Still, I will miss cleaning your clothes."

"I don't need a nursemaid, André."

"Well most other passengers, especially Americans," André said, "bring along more clothes than you.

"I brought several pairs of underwear and socks," Everett said. "I was unaware of a dress code requirement to enter France."

"What is the American expression, 'Put the best face forward', I believe it is," André said. "May I please launder your clothes tonight? I give you my word - I will have them ready before you disembark tomorrow."

"As you wish, André, but first, do you know why we've dropped anchor?"

"Listen." André bent over the deck rail to look astern.

Two tugboats growled below. A searchlight panned to the port side out from where they stood, projecting a long narrow carpet of light onto the sea to a spot below. Fog boiled and whirled as the bow of a large white ship, with the name La Pasteur, passed slowly in front of them at a safe distance. Everett's heart quickened at the name.

On the darkened upper deck of the Pasteur, night people lounging in recliners quickly shielded their eyes from the Excalibur's panning spotlight. The Pasteur's stewards looked better dressed and more numerous than those aboard the Excalibur. Wearing immaculate white uniforms and caps, they bent strangely, nearly reverently, to the feet of the Pasteur's passengers. Then it struck Everett - they were nurses caring for patients, but not ordinary patients - Gods it seemed. Someone aboard La Pasteur cursed the light and it panned instantly away towards the aft section of La Pasteur. The bright light glinted from tall neat stacks of stainless steel caskets until someone again shouted. The lamp went dark.

"It is the hospital ship, La Pasteur, returning the last of our wounded officers from Indochina. I was just told of our defeat," André reached for Everett's glass to take a sip. "We must allow them to pass before we dock tomorrow."

André bowed to the ship as though it were royalty, but kept his cap in place. After instinctively lowering his head in respect, Everett raised up to gaze more directly at the Pasteur for a while until he became aware of André watching him.

"Is there someone you are looking for?" André asked as he handed Everett the glass.

"I'm so sorry, André," Everett said. "It must have appeared impolite for me to stare at them. I'm to meet a nurse who, I believe, is aboard that ship."

Everett ran his nose over the top of the glass then tipped it to his lips and let the thick liquor pool on his tongue. It burned as he swallowed it. Soon, fresh sea air, cooled his throat.

"Is she pretty?" André said after he found his glass on the deck and drank. "A soldier may have already fallen in love with her, even if she is not pretty. She will, no doubt, soon return to Indochina aboard Le Pasteur for more."

"I've never seen her," Everett said. "I'm to meet her at a café, Port-du-Chien, in Marseilles."

"The Port-du-Chien – it is a bar, not a café. I hope you do not plan on keeping her to yourself in such a place."

"We're to take the train immediately to Lorraine," Everett said, wondering for a moment why she chose to meet in such a bar. "I hear she always takes the train back home near Nancy between tours."

"The train north leaves from Gar-St. Charles at exactly 2 PM," André said. "The trains are very dependable, just as this nurse must be to sail La Pasteur."

"How long do you think La Pasteur has been at sea?"

"Over three weeks." André lifted his long nose into the wind towards the Pasteur. "Just long enough to discharge the wounded Legionnaires from other colonies before bringing our own soldiers and Legionnaire officers back as it always does. Most stop at the Port-du-Chien."

A pair of tugboats urged the white Pasteur into the harbor like ushers leading a perfumed old woman to her box seat at the opera.

"Your nurse aboard the Pasteur, what is her name? Perhaps I know of her"

"Mademoiselle Lambert."

André adjusted his cap.

"You know her?" Everett asked.

"Nurses returning from Indochina are given special names, like Nightingale, Jeanne de Arc or Brunnhilde, but never last names or one might be tempted to seek their angelic solace at home. I do not know of a nurse named Lambert - though I never returned on the Pasteur, thank God."

"I didn't know you were over there," Everett said.

"Marseilles!" André said, as Marseilles glowed behind a veil of fog as the Pasteur passed by. In the distance, a hill jutted through the fog. At the top, a cathedral glowed with a golden crown illuminated from below. André pointed to it.

"It is the Notre-Dame-de-le-Garde," André said, "The last war ruined the harbor and parts of Marseilles, but the church was spared. I can arrange a visit, if you wish to pray there."

Everett raised his hand in protest.

"Thank you all the same, André."

"Monsieur - it was presumptuous of me to assume you are in need of prayer - it seems we all are today. Please tell me, if I am not being too personal, why you have come to France - to visit our beautiful Lorraine with your pretty nurse?"

Everett raised the glass again, taking his time to let the cognac disinfect the inside of his mouth. As André took in the view of the harbor, Everett caught himself staring again at André's huge cap, always tilted over an unseen ear.

After all these nights on deck, Everett had hoped to resurrect something of his past that might interest André, but all André ever asked about was New Orleans and Charlie Parker, not Davenport or Bix Beiderbeck. Tonight, Everett felt André wanted more than small talk about Iowa.

"I've come in the stead of father. He lost something out there in the Great War," Everett said, aiming the drink to France, north and east. Surprised at himself, he handed the glass back to André, who sniffed it then tipped it back and emptied it in a single long swallow.

"Ah, tre bien, Everett. A perfect reason to visit France," André said. "He is merely lost in time, as nothing is ever lost in France."

"Perdu dans le temps?" Everett said.

"Your French has improved a great deal since you began your voyage and you will soon need it in Lorraine," André said. "Please allow me to show you through customs in the morning. I should escort you to the Port-du-Chien - only certain people like me are allowed inside."

"I can take care of myself, my friend," Everett said as he eyed potato soup spots still on his shirt from last night.

"I will launder your things, Monsieur. You shall have fresh clothes in the morning to meet your nurse, Mademoiselle Lambert."

After returning to his room, Everett handed André his soiled clothes around the cabin door. André whistled as he disappeared down the deck with one arm full of clothes and the other with his drink.

Everett stumbled back to bed thinking of the ship, La Pasteur, with its honeycomb of cold metallic coffins. It made his cabin feel like the cockpit of his Sabre, cold and lonesome after his last flight. He wondered about his father having trouble sleeping aboard the Leviathan, an iron transport ship Doc Hershey said had carried them home from the Great War – that too had been stacked high with caskets, only of wood, yet short twenty-six bandsmen, whose names he knew not only from the letters, but from the lore of his small Iowan town.

What most kept Everett awake was the daughter of a wartime acquaintance of his father's and Doctor Hershey – this nurse, who returns each month like the moon with the wounded to escort the dead.

✦ ✦ ✦

Half awakened by a motion in his ears – an imbalance Everett knew as the familiar feel of tugboats in control of the Excalibur, he lay in bed as the sun warmed his cabin. He flattened his small pillow to his head, throbbing from cognac. He rose to a riveting, painful knock on his cabin door.

Falling to the floor, he searched for his clothes and found only underwear and socks. He panicked, thinking he might need to enter France this way, until he remembered André taking his laundry. Outside his door, a fresh string-tied bundle sat on a deck chair.

A bright sun glinted on the smooth harbor water and shimmered against the white hull of the Pasteur docked alongside in the next berth. On the aft stern, now clear of caskets, a dark-skinned crew scrubbed the deck with mops as grim-faced nurses and doctors disembarked. One nurse bent down to the clean deck of the Pasteur to pray. Everett wondered if the nurse he was to meet today had done the same, maybe it was Madame Lambert's daughter.

He sank against the door thinking of her as the smell of flowers from dock vendors filled the air. He stepped back inside to wash. As he changed, he found that even his laundry smelled of flowers. He packed the dirty socks and underwear into his small bag, cushioning his maps and stack of letters, then stepped outside again.

On the pier below, the Excalibur's passengers pushed through customs on the pier. There in a stream of black felt hats and feathered bonnets, floated André's cap, like a big red duck, paddling its way forward.

André paused to speak with one of the officials before returning to the Excalibur. On the gangplank just below Everett, André looked around then tipped his cap in the hot sun to wipe his brow. He quickly propped it up again, cocking it to the side then headed up the gangplank. He turned around to see if anyone had noticed that he had but one ear.

Everett looked away, towards Marseilles, catching glimpses of rebuilt white stone buildings, but many others in need of repair. He wondered if there was any place in Europe, or the Far East, where a tourist might casually venture into a past untouched by a war.

The sun had a drug-like effect on the nightshift customs officials. One yawned while the other tottered to life and waved Everett forward. One impatiently held his hand out, speaking in French to the other, while waiting for Everett to find his passport.

He always kept it in his back pants pocket, but he didn't remember removing it before André had them cleaned. He must have, though. It must be in his bag. He leafed through the letters and finally the maps, whose sight, he feared, might cause the officials to think he was leading another invasion. No passport. He spanked the seat of his pants in desperation and found the rectangular outline of a passport, whose pages must certainly be paste by now.

"Francois," the older one said, in a nasally, Parisian French. "Our American has obviously concealed his passport between his buttocks for keeping safe. Help the poor man."

Everett reached in his back pocket for the passport, at once surprising the official. Everett was amazed to find it dry and unlaundered. Such a friend, André, had become.

"André asked me to point out the Port-du-Chien," the one named Francois spoke in English. "Many pardons. André asked me also to expedite your entry to France, but first, if you could please give your passport to my crass Gaullist superior – he speaks not a word of English and has never been to Paris in his whole life, although he loves to pretend."

"I'll not inconvenience him. I'll speak French," Everett slapped his passport into the Gaullist's hand. Francois looked over his boss' shoulder at the passport.

"Everett?" Francois said. "An unusual name for an American, closer to French - were you named for someone French?"

"My father named me for a French painter named Evariste," Everett said. "He went missing while charging the enemy with a paint brush during the Great War. I guess he's a legend."

Francois simply shrugged, suggesting it was common.

"Now, I must ask, Mr. Everett Taylor - what is your business in France, to find some old girlfriend of your father's? Many come now to search."

"I'm here to find something of my father's."

"I must warn you about removing treasures. France is been looted and plundered far too often. There are serious penalties even for our friends, the Americans. Are you staying here in Marseilles?"

"No, I'm traveling by train this afternoon with a nurse to the area near Nancy. We're to meet at a bar called Port-du-Chien."

"Yes," Francois said. "André asked if a Mademoiselle Lambert passed, but no one of that name. There was Sister Beatrice, of course. She passes through each month, but I am certain she would pray as she walked past Port-du-Chien. I am told only one woman is allowed inside, Brunnhilde, whom we have never seen entering France, or leaving, for that matter."

"Strange name, Brunnhilde - sounds German," Everett said.

"More than that," Francois said. "Brunnhilde is a pagan name, a "near-goddess" - a Valkyrie who reclaimed from the fields of battle, souls of worthy, slain soldiers. I am told that this Brunnhilde disappears with soldier's who are never seen again. Be careful, Monsieur."

Francois handed the passport back to Everett and pointed to the head of the Pasteur's pier where a round of horrendous barking rose above the quiet lapping of the sea.

"I'll steer clear of her," Everett said, looking towards a dirty, white stucco bar apparently filled with harbor seals from the sounds.

"I do not mean that, Monsieur. There has been trouble with the Algerians again today, so be careful and welcome to France, Everett. Bienvenue."

ಏ 2 ಎ

Brunnhilde

Never come between a hungry dog and his chow', Everett thought while approaching the pier. Military guarded the seaside of the bar, but dogs guarded the street-side - not just a dog or two but a mangy pack. From Port-du-Chien's high balcony, drunken soldiers threw meat left and right. The dogs dove like seals, clearing the pier.

As he put his shoulder to the heavy oak door of the Port-du-Chien, an odd blend of mercurochrome, formaldehyde, tobacco and a guitar trio's fandango washed past his head. The bar overflowed with regular French soldiers and a few officers of the Legion, all entranced by the sparkling eyes of a young belly dancer as she wiggled across a small stage, whirling before each of them. It had the feel of a Geisha bar his wingman once dragged him to in Japan, except for the language and the music.

As she turned to Everett at the door, he found himself moving to her hips and unable to take his eyes off her. She motioned him in to sit. The men turned, and with their heads, looked him up and down as though he was a tourist and when Everett glanced down at his floral scented shirt and pants, he understood. Rather than recite his wartime résumé, he opened the door with his hands behind him and stepped backwards, outside to a table just around the door, close to the street.

He sat back in a wicker chair, stretched his legs out to his bag and listened to the music and the sounds of dogs along the pier still diving into the water for scraps of food. After several minutes, a waiter escaped to lean against the sunny side of the stucco wall next to Everett.

"This is your first visit to the Port-du-Chien?" the waiter asked.

"You're an American," Everett said, relaxing his shoulders.

"Not quite," the waiter said. "I'm Canadian; I was captured in 1942 in the Battle of Dieppe. I like it here where it's warm. What brings a Yank to the Port-du-Chien?"

"I'm looking for a woman named, Lambert," Everett said, as he barely recalled the first invasion of France during its long occupation by the Germans.

"A dancer? She needs a better stage name than Lambert," the waiter said.

"She's a nurse," Everett said. "We're to take the train to Nancy."

"No Lambert here, only Brunnhilde. She's the only nurse who ever returns to the Port-du-Chien," the waiter said. "It is early for the train to Nancy. It leaves in a few hours from the north rail-station, Gar-St. Charles."

"Brunnhilde," Everett said, "that's a pitiful name for a nurse."

"Not if you've seen her work," the waiter said.

Everett slumped in his chair as sweat formed across his forehead, wondering why Madame Lambert's daughter would pick such a whore-filled bar.

"You look ill – I'll get you something."

The waiter ran inside as Everett shook with a slight chill in his back. Trucks of medical supplies drove past him, down the dock towards the Pasteur as he waited. He wondered if the nurse had gotten the message to meet him at all.

The waiter returned with a small cube of ice rapidly melting in a glass of water.

"You better surround your little bag with your arms and legs," the waiter said. "The place is thick with thieves. You still look bad, take this."

He gave Everett a fan made of bamboo and silk, much like those that he and other American soldiers brought back from Korea and Japan.

As Everett slowly opened it, he shook his head and laughed. The chill disappeared as he unfolded the image of a woman's vagina, surrounded with flesh, colored pink as Huan's, delicate and fair. He waved it across his face in the hot and humid air. It smelled of fish. The small wedge of ice slid down his throat as he gulped the water down.

"I don't know if Brunnhilde ever worked a Yank before," the waiter said.

"What do you mean?" Everett asked.

The waiter shrugged as he recovered the fan from Everett.

"I mean Brunnhilde visits the Port-du-Chien every new moon," the waiter said. "She always carries a wounded soldier home with her. You don't fit the bill."

Everett held the back of hand to his forehead in disbelief.

"I will bring something stronger to drink."

The waiter cracked open the bar's door to a blast of music and smoke. The dancer pushed a big Legionnaire outside and swung him onto the chair beside Everett. She jumped onto the man's lap, picked up Everett's fan and waved it - to give the man some air.

Judging by the lieutenant's epaulet on his shoulder and his age, Everett guessed the old Legionnaire was passed-over and now succumbed to a combination of drink, foul air, and her dark eyes. With a few passes of the fan and her whispering in his ear, the Legionnaire slumbered, maybe to dream of his last fight, Everett thought. It didn't last long.

Everett jumped from his seat as machine-gun fire ricocheted from the distant white walls of Marseille. The dancer flashed the fan past Everett's face to distract him. The Legionnaire casually raised his head, pulled a knife from a leather sheath at his belt then jammed it straight into his own leg where it stuck, quivering.

"If it were not for this leg, I would join a squad this very afternoon and take care of that little business," he said in German before collapsing into the dancer's arms. She pulled the knife from his wooden leg and slid it back into his sheath as Everett considered that even a Nazi could become a Legionnaire. Everett felt strangely at ease.

The dogs returned, shaking themselves dry near the table then stood before the old Legionnaire, as though on roll call. They came up one by one to taste the salty sweat of Everett's hand until more machine-gun fire startled them. Meaty bones flew from the balcony and they dove once again.

The waiter wavered at the door with a glass of wine before stepping outside.

"I feel much better now," Everett asked. "How do I get to Gar-St. Charles? I don't want to miss that train."

"Aren't you going to stay for Lambert, your nurse?" the waiter said. "The train doesn't leave for a whole hour."

"An hour? What if it gets in early?"

"Come now, Yank – this is France. It leaves in exactly one hour."

"If she shows, tell her I've left."

"You should at least take the Lieutenant along," the waiter joked, as he opened his arm to Marseilles in the direction of the gunfire.

He pointed beyond the ruin of the old city – "Past Le Panier", he said, aiming up as though Everett could merely fly above the narrow streets and assembly of tongues, faces, costumes and smells of Marseilles to the one place he needed to be in a few hours - the rail station called the Gar-St. Charles.

Le Panier. He walked first towards a church steeple to the east. The "Cathedral-de-la-Nouvelle-Major" a freshly painted sign said, held by the shaking hands of a beggar who spoke a language Everett never heard before. Everett unfolded his wallet and gave him a Franc note. It only seemed to attract others.

Everett's nose twitched as it translated the smells of the district's old streets. He hustled towards a bazaar in the middle of the street ahead, thinking he might assimilate into the mass of humankind who dragged their goods to market. Surrounding him on tables, hooks and baskets were fruits, spice, fish, fabrics and animal skins to eat and wear. Nearby, he smelled perfume – and found neat rows of jars filled with iridescent insects, oils and flower essence.

The strange new language surrounded him, spoken more from the back of the tongue, Arabic - like the Pasteur's deckhands had used. Faces from dark corners appeared like targets in a carnival's shooting gallery and seemed to follow him everywhere.

Soon, it seemed, the whole street flowed behind him in a river of bobbing felt hats, turbans, skullcaps and fez. The swelling voices surrounding him carried scents of anisette and tobacco to form a strange chorus as hair, flesh and fabric pressed against him on all sides. His feet hurt as his shoes bent above enormous cobblestones.

Contortionists, flame-throwers, sword-swallowers, snake charmers and fortunetellers mingled in a carnival, beyond comparison to anything in Iowa.

As he basked in its delirious clutter, he caught the bright noon sun reflecting from a blade drawn from a man not more than ten yards away. Everett wondered if it were a Damascus blade – one so sharp, it would cut a falling veil in two before touching the ground. Other foreigners shopped about, but he seemed be to the focus of the swordsman's intentions and the man's Muslim following.

He decided his dissection would only double his misery, and quickened his step to a peculiar tune in his head. Not knowing its lyrics, its rhythm alone propelled him effortlessly. With his bag swinging at his side, he ambled down the narrow street, Rue Casserie. His cadence only seemed to draw more strangers with knives.

He breathed easily as he came at last to the Rue de La Republique. A column of black smoke rose near the rail station, not far away. He ran towards the smell of burning fuel and tires and found the station ringed with police shouldering automatic rifles, still hot from their last bursts.

The robed crowd swarmed to an over-turned car in flames. They chanted and prayed while the car's small external gas-tank produced towering balls of flame. A child's voice squealed inside while the mother hovered above the flames like a moth. The crowd pulled her away as Everett found himself drawn to the stench of burning hair.

He felt his hand immediately against the hot metal door, now alone with the tiny voice yelping inside. He followed his arms inside the car, waving about, hoping for the soft touch of tender living flesh rather than the crumbling of thin cinders of carbon.

A tune broke free in his throat amidst the crackling of flames and fabric. He liked its sound. The small voice inside the car, in return, peeped like a chick as a rush of hot fumes from the rear seat filled the car, about to burst into flames. He reached in, humming the comforting, rhythmical tune. He felt the child coil around his arm. He gently pulled the light, wreathing body and snuffed out the flames bursting around its long white shirt.

The child's eyes opened - it was a little girl. Her big eyes, Mediterranean blue, glistened with tears in the bright afternoon sun of Marseilles. Everett let her roll delicately into her mother's arms. She ran her fingers through the baby's thin black hair, removing burnt strands. She plopped a small roll of candy on the little girl's tongue, then placed one to Everett's lips. The child rubbed its eyes as she turned to smile at Everett and touched his burned hand. He was too happy to notice the pain as the sweet soft candy dissolved in his mouth and the girl laughed.

A train whistle blew. Everett turned, not wanting to miss the nurse a second time. As he kissed the child, he tried to step away, but felt a cold steel blade against his shoulder and neck. The man with the turban waved his broad sword and blessed him before escorting Everett to the awaiting train to Nancy.

"A kiss from heaven, Monsieur," the man said in English.

Everett sat in his window seat and waved to the crowd following him, still cheering and envious, he thought, for the moment he had waited a lifetime - the moment of which he had robbed them.

He felt tired and believed he was close to falling to sleep with this decent thought on his mind, when the train jerked forward. A conductor swayed as he walked down the aisle, grasping the backs of seats for support as the train gathered speed. Everett rose to remove his wallet to pay.

A tall nun, wearing a white habit, stood solidly behind the conductor, unaffected by the abrupt jostling of the train as it switched tracks. She held a small vial to her lips, glanced around, then corked it before slipping it into a large white purse, sheltered beneath her armpit as though it were a plump chicken.

She caught Everett's eye then carefully opened the purse again, producing two tickets, saying she had paid for Everett's ticket already. She tried closing the bulging purse then set it on the floor before sitting next to Everett. He wondered if maybe she didn't trust him near it. She gave him a pleasant smile and a gentle nudge with her hip.

"I have seen children burned before, Monsieur, you saved her just in time - thank you," she said in perfect English, "I assume you are the American I am to meet, Monsieur Taylor - Everett, am I right? Most American's I have met are rather tall, but then you are a jet-pilot."

She looked tired, but pretty - too pretty for a nun.

"Mademoiselle Lambert?" Everett said in carefully annunciated French.

"Please, Monsieur. Your command of my language is excellent, but not so loud," she whispered. "I am Sister Beatrice. Did Mother not tell you? When I heard the crowd, I just knew it must be you. You Americans do love the grand entrance."

"Sister Beatrice? I expected just a nurse. I didn't know you were going to be a nun."

She bent to his ear. He caught a hint of vanilla on her breath as she whispered, "I did not know I was to be a nun either."

Everett flinched as the person he was to meet, the one who was to resolve all of his father's conflicts, was a nun, a rather worldly nun, who after a night at the bar, sanctified her breath with a drop of vanilla extract.

"I won't be here longer than a few days," Everett said, struggling for words.

"Mother said you have come for the trenches and the dead," she said, "but I see you have already saved a new life in this old world. I expect you will stay longer than a few days."

She sat back and closed her eyes. Her stomach rumbled.

"Didn't the Canadian get you something to eat at the Port-du-Chien after your aperitif?"

"He said you were rather nervous about missing the train," Beatrice said.

"So, you did go inside. What is it exactly that you do that requires you to cover your breath with vanilla, not that I don't like it – I do, but I'm just curious."

"I'm only a nurse on the hospital ship Pasteur. After twelve days steaming to Saigon to load the dead and wounded then twelve days caring for them as we steam to Marseilles, most make the journey, but many linger and tragically expire only minutes before we dock after my attempts at resuscitation. My lungs are filled with their last breaths."

"You must be exhausted," Everett said, ashamed at his suspicions.

She nodded and with a long blink, her head slumped and rocked gently to the train's motion. She probably hadn't slept in days, Everett thought. Bloodstains on her white shoes told him she had her hands full on the Pasteur. She stirred once more, swinging her foot to and froe. Her head bobbed against his shoulder as she slept. He shrugged off a random notion that the stains were not those of the wounded, but hers. A truly saintly nun, would need neither menstruation nor sleep. Those were the stains of men's blood, he was certain of that.

While she slept, Everett stretched his arm to his bag and carefully pulled a map from his bag, setting his stack of letters between himself and Beatrice. He traced their path from Marseilles with his finger, tapping each station they passed. The movement tightened the singed skin on top of his hand from the burning car. It hurt a little, yet reminded him of the touch of the young girl's hand. He craved something sweet in his mouth.

No matter where the train stopped, cicadas would sing. Through lines of olive trees and vineyards, the hot bright afternoon sun amplified their mesmerizing buzz. The lingering scent of gardenias and jasmine near the Mediterranean dissipated in the cigarette smoke of the car as it carried them further north, past Roman arches and aqueducts, and the deep canyons and gorges along the Rhone River. He wished Beatrice would wake for a moment to describe its beauty.

The train's gentle rocking nearly lulled him to sleep with the map in his hand. With each shimmy and shake, or the soft touch of the nun shifting against his side, he found his hand had slipped from its place on the map and rested instead on top of hers. He lifted it gently each time back to the map to retrace their progress, reciting villages like sheep. He ran his finger north on the map over Chateauneuf-du-Pape and Lyon, up the Rhone Valley then past Macon to Dijon.

According to Doctor Hershey, Everett's father and the doctor arrived in France at the northwestern port of LeHavre, not Marseilles, in November of 1917. They traveled with the band by narrow gauge train in small boxcars called, 'forty-and-eight', with each carrying either forty men, or eight horses across France, west to east from battle to battle. How the villagers must have marveled at the vitality of his father's regiment as they stepped off to stretch their legs and for the band to tune their instruments and play to keep limber. Yet the villagers must have seen every fresh strange face and musical phrase in the world by then only to watch them return in caskets atop horse-drawn carts.

This rail was wide. This car was not a boxcar; it held at least sixty humans and didn't feel like it was skating on a pair of narrow rails. It was comfortable. Even though he couldn't experience the discomfort his father and Doc had felt, it was satisfying to look at the rolling hills and know from the map, that he rolled towards the front as they once did.

He thought he might sleep with this on his mind rather than the smell of the burning car and the screams of the child from earlier in the day, but instead his thoughts were of the nun next to him, Beatrice. He reached for his father's letters that he had forgotten to replace in the bag. They wedged ever more tightly between Beatrice and him as she settled against them. He wouldn't bother her for them just yet .

At his side, her face turned up to him as though she were about to say something, but she was fast asleep. A small thread of saliva dangled from the corner of her mouth. Everett delicately captured it with his shirt cuff, provoking a benign response - she snored.

Her eyelid fluttered open like a leaf about to lift in the wind, exposing a large emerald, wet with a tear. Her beautifully chiseled face lay beneath red curled hair bound in her wimple. He guessed she looked thirty although her face carried complicated and intricate marks and lines of an older woman. Her soothing voice, an odd marriage of German and French had a caring, yet sultry tone.

She shifted in her seat, unconsciously re-securing her purse against her side while squashing Everett's letters with her other – still, he refused to disturb her sleep.

Her long white habit flowed to thin-boned ankles covered in smooth white socks. Her feet toyed with her white canvas shoes, precariously balanced at her toes like a pair of puppets, both freckled with tiny red spatters of dried blood from the Pasteur. She turned her head to the open window. Curls of auburn hair escaped her wimple, rippling in currents from the window, as the train sped from the Dijon station. He wondered if they should be changing trains soon to Nancy.

"Louis," she murmured the name to herself in French, then German, passionately, affectionately. Someone she must love very much, Everett guessed, because of the way she laughed when she said it, as though this phantom, Louis, were kissing her neck. She giggled for him to stop. Her vanilla-scented breath lingered warm and moist next to his ears, but her habit smelled of tobacco and sweat - Louis's tobacco, Louis's sweat. If he looked hard, he thought he might find a long black curly hair from the Legionnaire's beard. He must be a giant soldier too, to match Beatrice's size. He wondered what infirmities could attract Beatrice to such men. His burned hand throbbed with pain.

She woke for a moment, looking to him as though she maybe expected Louis to be there beside her. When she unconsciously turned away to the aisle to stretch her legs, he found himself waiting for her to turn back to him. Each time the train rocked, her shoulders lifted briefly but with disappointment on her face, always falling quickly asleep against his shoulder while bending and pressing his letters.

It irritated him that Doc so doubted his recovery to have sent him this nurse. But, Doc would have never sent a nun, even if he knew she was wayward.

Everett retraced the villages on the map as she twisted minutely in her seat. Her long nose, with its slight but majestic asymmetric cant, lifted as it drew in the countryside's ever-changing character then lowered as she spilled it from her lips in narrow, vanilla-scented streams. After all of these monthly trips, Everett guessed, she knew the route in her sleep, guided along by the scents in the air.

She would hear the bell chime in Orange, the loud call of the vendors of Lyon selling fruits and flowers at the station, and the diminishing shouts of the Indochina war protesters at the station in Dijon and she would always know exactly where she was, even in her sleep.

He felt his hand slip away from the map, hoping to sleep and dream he was on a journey with Huan at his side, not this Sister Beatrice. At least Huan had been a devout communist.

As the train slowed, he woke to the smell of mustard and menthol. A thin coat of a soothing lotion covered the burn on the back of his hand.

"The salve will toughen your sensitive skin," Beatrice said. "That burn must be hurting."

"How long have I been out? Did I say anything?"

"No," she said while freeing his hand. "But, you have been twisting in your seat since leaving Dijon. I did not want to startle you, as you were not entirely sleeping, but we have crossed the Marne and must change trains soon to take us to Vittel. We are near the Lorraine, from where these letters were addressed."

Beatrice handed the stack to Everett.

Everett quickly wrapped them in the map and stuffed them into his bag, wondering if Doc hadn't instructed her to be so intrusive as to have read them all.

"Mother wrote that you are coming to France to find a band which disappeared."

Everett fidgeted in the seat, certain she read all twenty-six letters while he slept.

"Yes," he said. "They were under my father's command. I'm told that their deaths disturbed him a great deal."

"You are fortunate the thieves in Marseilles did not run away with this," Beatrice touched the bag once with her toe.

"I'm told that it's your mother who has all the facts," Everett said.

"I am sure she does," Beatrice said as she pointed her crucifix like a small sword to her head, deep in thought. "She was a hypnotherapist during the Great War."

"I thought she was a nurse," Everett said, trying to control his anger over Doc's additional manipulation, but he felt comfortable beside Beatrice. Warm currents raced through his veins. He stared out the window to the foreign countryside.

"She is also a nurse," Beatrice said. "Although she has retired, she volunteers her skills to the wounded. She is bound by many vows of privacy, but perhaps she can help."

Everett laughed to himself, wondering exactly what vows a nun upheld these days in France.

Beatrice lifted the crucifix from her neck. It swung once past his face, by accident. She wrapped the cord around the tiny figure, carefully opened her already bulging purse and wedged it to the side.

"Does Madame Lambert remember much of the Great War?" Everett said.

Beatrice worked at adjusting the wimple on her head, crumbled against Everett's shoulder during the ride.

"Well, I would have to say," she said as she unpinned her hat and placed it on top of Everett's bag, "that Mother is more remarkable in her ability to extract memories from others than of actually recalling her own."

"I refuse to be hypnotized!" Everett said, again suspecting Doc Hershey's meddling.

"I am so sorry – not you, of course not you, but my friend, Sigmund – the old General. Mother once told me she hypnotized him - but I think then it did no good."

"Sigmund, sounds like a German General," Everett said.

"We once called him, Le General Allemand. He was in the Great War but never completely returned from it - he is, how do you say, a recluse.."

"I'd like to meet this recluse."

"Sigmund leads a dangerous, solitary life," Beatrice said while examining his burned hand. "However, Mother is the one you want to speak to - she will tell you what you need to know, I am sure of it. She needed to visit the hospital in Strasbourg; otherwise, she would be traveling with us. There are so many wounded from Indochina, even hypnotism is popular again. And this trouble with Algeria, when will it ever end?"

"When can I meet her? I'm anxious to learn what happened to my father's band although, I must tell you, I'm not keen on spending much time with a hypnotist."

"Tomorrow. She and my brother, Philippe, are to meet us with the car in Schirmek and drive us to her home where his small family lives, just north of the town, Ville Negre. You need not worry about Mother; she will be more occupied with Philippe. I did not know you were averse to hypnotherapy, like Sigmund."

"I've been known to be reclusive too," Everett said. "Why does Madame Lambert need to spend so much time with your brother?"

"Philippe was a political prisoner during the occupation," Beatrice said as she smoothed her hand over the form of the crucifix, bulging from the side of her purse.

A chill raced from Everett's feet through his groin and up to his chest and hands. His lips quivered. The countryside, which looked and smelled so genuine a moment ago, now boasted a tragically beautiful fantasy that he traveled through, with that red and painful sore on the back of his hand throbbing. He focused on a quiet place in Iowa, by a river, for relief.

He felt a bird perch on the bridge of his nose, flapping its wings ready to take flight, but it was only the sunlight piercing through the quickly passing trees and hedges from the window of the train. A gentle pressure on his hand woke him.

"Are you alright?" Beatrice asked.

"Yes," Everett said. "Well no, not exactly."

"Mother did tell me you suffered from nightmares."

"It doesn't surprise me that she knows," Everett said, again becoming irritated at Doc.

A dark, fly-sized ash from the window landed on Beatrice's shoulder. A touch of her finger, transformed the ash into a smudge.

She wetted her finger with her tongue and daubed the stain.

"I become so filthy when I travel. This habit - I am afraid I have worn it out, perhaps I no longer need it."

Everett shook his head in disbelief. She lowered her voice.

"It was given to me for protection."

"Oh, for the love of God!" Everett said, as his disgust grew.

"God had nothing to do with it, Everett," Beatrice said with such a bewildered look that Everett considered maybe she was posing as a nun for the resistance.

"It's hard to imagine living in France, occupied by the enemy," Everett said.

The train passed over a newly built bridge, whose previous iron skeleton, bombed from the last war, lay twisted, rusting in the field beside it, in memorial.

"It was a different war in Indochina when I first arrived in 1944," Beatrice said. "The Japanese were the authorities."

"That's even more reason not to return," Everett said, recalling long lines of sullen Korean refugees leaving their villages. He shook inside, realizing Beatrice had left France during the occupation. Everett closed his eyes and felt his cheeks drop to a frown.

"I had to leave France then, you see," Beatrice whispered.

Everett sat back in his seat, stunned at the prospect that Doc had sent a traitor to help him. Beatrice's face hung low. She tugged at the habit as though it were prison garb.

"It is not what you think," Beatrice said.

"How did you ever get inside Indochina?"

"Can I trust you?" Beatrice said.

"Do you trust recluses?"

"I do, if they are like Sigmund," Beatrice said.

Beatrice carefully opened her purse, removing her passport. She opened it and handed it to him. He felt a raised seal. A Vatican seal, signed in 1944, allowing 'Sister Beatrice' unrestricted travel. Everett's disgust doubled, until he noticed the date and place of birth - February 27, 1919, circa Ville Negre, Lorraine.

"You must know someone special to get this, and" Everett stopped to do some arithmetic.

"And, what else?"

"Your father, this great Evariste, charged the trenches well before you were conceived." Everett startled himself. "My father and Doc would have been here at the time."

"You must think I truly am your sister - Beatrice," she laughed.

"That's not funny!"

"Sigmund, the General Allemand, is my father," Beatrice whispered.

Everett breathed a sigh of relief.

"How am I supposed to learn anything about this band, if nothing here is what it seems," he said. "Are you really Madame Lambert's daughter, Beatrice?"

"Yes, but Beatrice is not my Christian name – Sigmund liked Brunnhilde."

"I would have guessed Beatrice would be more Christian. I suppose the men in the Port-du-Chien prefer Brunnhilde," Everett said, still thinking of her with Louis.

"You must understand what it was like during the occupation to have a name like Brunnhilde. The soldiers in the Port-du-Chien or the wounded on the Pasteur do not use names or titles at all. I can be myself there. Away from the Port-du-Chien, and particularly at home, in

Lorraine, you must always call me Sister Beatrice. There, you must refer to my father, as Sigmund – or the General, if you prefer. I am simply a nun there, known as Sister Beatrice, who comes each month to tend the wounds of the great Evariste's only son, Philippe."

Everett wondered why she didn't just go straight to heaven with the Vatican pass, but he let it go. He knew what a war could make people become, warriors and civilians alike.

"The waiter at the Port-du-Chien said you usually visit the wounded on your way home," Everett said. "They must be expecting you."

"Yes, every month on the new moon," she sighed. "I meet my old wounded friends in Lorraine - in the spa of a small village where Roman Legions once bathed."

"With the tides?"

"The Pasteur crew claims we arrive on the new moon because of tides, but I believe the captain prefers to arrive then because it is so very dark. It feels more like smuggling our wounded into Marseilles in the middle of the night, hidden from view. Can you imagine returning home as they do? I am happy it is over, but I shall miss my old friends. I think they would very much like to meet you."

She set her head next to the window, where the wind loosened the coils of her hair. It fell in sections, unfurling into a red-feathered wing on her shoulder. Everett found himself wanting to bathe beside her now, even if it meant sharing the bath with Louis and others.

"The Vosges are so beautiful and it smells so sweet this time of year," she said as she took a long ivory needle from her purse and formed her hair into a small tight bundle to run the needle through. She straightened out her wimple before placing it back on her head, put her forehead to the window, and slumbered as the train passed through deep woods.

Her purse, resting beside him, opened up like a fish's mouth. Crammed next to the coiled crucifix, rested a slab of chocolate wrapped in silver foil. His mouth watered as he recalled the sweet taste left in his mouth by the mother from Marseilles. He already felt guilty for what he was about do.

He pried the foil open another inch and discretely snapped off a small corner to satisfy his urge. Instead of the smooth light brown color of chocolate, the slab was darker than the richest chocolate he had ever seen. It felt tacky between his fingers. As Beatrice stirred, he popped it into his mouth and found its taste, tart and bitter. "Opium!" He remembered his wingman, Bender, forced him to taste it once in Japan, on a dare. Everett looked at the crucifix, wound in knots by his fidgeting in her purse, and thought it represented his own befuddlement to a tee, at this beautiful woman, posing as a nun to smuggle drugs for her beloved Louis. He pushed the bar gently into her purse.

"I know your hand hurts but that will not help," Beatrice said without even looking. "Where are we, exactly, on your map?"

Everett, caught in the act, raised the map to his face to hide and swallowed the little chunk of opium. He surveyed where he was while wondering if Doc knew anything about his old comrade's daughter, this nurse. They drew near the Vosges. The train slowed. Everett thrust his head out the window,

"We're coming to a switch, Chaumont one way and Neufchateau the other - Which way do we go?" Everett asked.

"Neither." Beatrice said. "We change trains now to the north and east."

"I don't see it here," Everett said, returning to the map.

"My little train is not marked on maps. If it were, it would run like this," she said as she drew her finger along a valley of a river named Semouse in an undulating curve, "all the way to Bain-les-Guerre - for our bath."

She rested her finger on a bare spot of the map in a valley with forests drawn in green to either side. She tapped the spot with her finger.

"But, there's nothing there," Everett said.

"It is where it has always been, right here," Beatrice said moving her hand gracefully from the map to the center of her forehead which she tapped twice, "never to be written down."

"It is reserved for all of us," Beatrice said. "Even Germans bathe there. I would imagine your father bathed here, it was used also by Americans during the Great War."

"But I'm not wounded like that."

She took his hand and smoothed more ointment over the thin, but already hardening skin covering the burn.

"Better?" she said. He nodded as he felt the heat leave the painful spot and wondered if it was the ointment or the effects of the opium, calming his nerves.

"In the morning, from Guerre-les-Bain, we travel here," she said, pointing with her greased finger to the map, "to Rothau then on to Ville Negre."

He found Rothau on the edge of the map, nestled beneath tall green ridges and covered in forest. The train line appeared as a long stitch, drawn along the valley.

"And where is this Ville Negre?"

Beatrice took his hand, moving it down south and west of Rothau, then up a small road to another blank spot on his map, which she tapped twice.

"Ville Negre," she said.

The train slowed and passengers began standing with their luggage.

"Please, Everett, let them pass. Can we stay sitting for a time?" Beatrice said. "There is something I was thinking of just now - something you need to know. The place you wish to find this band, near Ville Negre, is most likely in the Zone Rouge."

"There's nothing colored red on the map."

"It is the most dangerous place in all of France, we do not wish to attract tourists," Beatrice said.

"Marseilles would be first on my list. What is this Zone Rouge?"

"A very narrow strip of devastated land along the Western Front. The soil was never fertile, even less so now because it is filled with unexploded bombs and shells - millions of them." Beatrice moved her finger across the area, near the unmarked, Ville Negre," Everything here lies inside the Zone Rouge. If the whole band disappeared in one night, as you say, it would have been there, where it is now forbidden to walk."

Everett frowned.

"I can see you are disappointed, Everett. You must not think of walking in the Zone Rouge alone."

"Maybe Philippe can show me," Everett said.

"Not Philippe, but perhaps Sigmund can," Beatrice said. "My father lives there."

"In the Zone Rouge?" Everett asked. "You're joking."

"No. Father became a demineur after the Great War. He knows how to defuse munitions. I must even smell like him by now," Beatrice laughed, "musky and soiled."

Her emerald eyes glistened and her face reddened about her tight, weathered skin – it was an angel's laugh, light and lifting. Wrinkles disappeared from her brows as she laughed again, this time deeper and straight from the chest. Everett's face flushed to life.

He held her arm as she walked down the steps from the train into the bright afternoon sun shining through the glass windows of the train station's ceiling. Businessmen reading newspapers at the station, all shook their heads in disbelief that Indochina had fallen to the Communists. Mothers ripped fingers through pages in search of sons.

Beatrice guided him from the station until they came to a remote switch where a pair of slender rails ran off to the north and east. It seemed strange that the switch stood rusted in one position so a train on these tracks could not enter the station. Nearby fields lay planted right up next to the tracks. In another month, crops would completely cover it. A column of black smoke churned upwards in the distance, a train whistled.

"We must hurry to the Spa," Beatrice said as Everett felt her hand grasp his then firmly tow him to the waiting train. "My dear old soldiers will be wilting."

Steam shot from the side of a small, black engine. Behind it, trailed a coal car, two boxcars and a caboose, all of them resting on a pair of narrow, rusted rails. A bottle, hurled from the door of the first boxcar, crashed into a small mountain of broken wine bottles. A man inside the car smashed another bottle into tinkling bits, before jumping down. Dressed in the oily overalls of an engineer, he removed his official-looking cap and waved Beatrice forward, puffing his chest, as they neared, to display tarnished medals and ribbons.

"You better get rid of the opium." Everett fingered the bar protruding from Beatrice's purse.

"Nonsense," Beatrice said as she crammed it in deeper. "He is only our conductor, not the Gestapo."

The conductor, stepping back from the car, ambled to a short water tower where a young boy showered himself, clothes and all, with a hose. The conductor barked and the boy swung the nozzle to the engine's boiler.

The conductor wiped his forehead free of sweat then turned to the side of the track where a set of dilapidated wooden steps lay on its side. He tipped it up easy enough but then, grunting and groaning, he struggled to drag it to the door of the boxcar. Everett moved to help, but felt Beatrice grip him firmly about the shoulder.

"He will not appreciate you helping him," Beatrice said. "It is all he does. We must respect that."

Everett turned away, not wanting to watch the man work on his behalf, and listened to the steps croak as the man inched, first one side forward then the other. He couldn't understand how Beatrice could bear watching.

Everett focused on an older couple strutting from the station towards them. A smallish man, burdened with boxes and shopping sacks trailed behind an even shorter woman who strode with a degree of pomp that Everett didn't expect in the middle of an abandoned rail yard.

Everett turned as the wooden steps slammed against the edge of the boxcar's broad open door. The conductor placed a clean towel over his greased sleeve then offered Beatrice his arm, as though it were a ritual, to board.

"Quarante Hommes?" Beatrice said, aiming her purse towards the pile of bottles. "Forty men?" Everett thought, then realized he was about to step into the same forty-and-eight style boxcar that delivered his father, his father's men and Doc Hershey from the Atlantic port to the front.

"Huit Chevaux?" The conductor looked at Everett suspiciously. Beatrice laughed. She spoke with the conductor in a whisper and kissed the tip of his nose, nested in hair.

The conductor came to Everett with a broad, toothless smile. He grabbed Everett's shoulders, sighed a breath, stale with wine - about to administer a greeting kiss when the conductor glared past Everett's shoulder towards the caboose. A woman's shrill command penetrated the quiet afternoon lull.

"Stop! Stop that train at once!" The woman barked at her husband, trailing behind, teetering her shopping boxes on his knees.

The conductor quickly urged Everett aboard then stepped up himself before turning his attention again to the angry couple standing below the car's door. The woman pushed her husband onto the first step. The conductor thrust his arm out to stop them.

"Private!" The conductor said sternly and pointed them back to the station.

"What's going on?" Everett asked, standing in the car at the door.

The woman cursed then spit to her side, over the top of her husband's head until Beatrice stepped to the door. The woman bowed, making the sign of the cross and stepped back as the conductor pushed the little man off and kicked the steps away from the car.

The conductor slammed the door shut, throwing the car into darkness except for small shafts of sunlight from tiny postcard-sized windows.

"What does she want?" Everett asked.

"It is Madame Chauchat and her husband," Beatrice said. "They own the brasserie in Ville Negre. They want this train to travel to Nancy for more shopping. I am sure they would pay the conductor a considerable amount of money to take them."

"She seems a pushy type, one who would have just hijacked the train," Everett said. "Do you know them well? They seem to respect your habit."

The conductor shouted an insult at the couple before bolting the big wooden-door shut from the inside. Madame Chauchat's voice pierced through the thick wood then ceased after hurling a rock at the door. The conductor lit a lantern.

"They still do not recognize me," Beatrice said as she straightened her habit and adjusted her wimple. "These garments offer many forms of protection, but this train, at this time, with this conductor is more than enough protection, especially with you here at my side. At this time of the month you see, the train is reserved for those with special needs who travel to the Spa."

Before Beatrice could sit, the conductor removed his cap and cleaned the dirty wooden seat with a sweaty bandanna from his neck. An old scar ran from the man's ear to his forehead where Everett surmised a metal plate lay beneath the skin. The conductor nodded his head in disgust at the couple's rude attempt to board. He bowed slightly to Beatrice, and then opened the door, checking for the Chauchat's before jumping out.

The conductor grabbed an oilcan from the coal car, anointing spots along the engine before swinging himself up the engine's steps. With a quick twist of a valve, the engine gushed steam and nudged the small train forward with a ring of a bell and a whistle. In the distance, walking towards to the station, Madame Chauchat hoisted her arm in an obscene gesture as Everett closed the door again.

"The Chauchat's look like they've done well for themselves," Everett said. "They act like they own the whole train."

"It is not their usual train," she said. "I am certain they have difficulty understanding why a man and nun need a whole car," she said. "They probably believe I am, how you say, a naughty nun."

Everett thought of the one named, Louis, she had called out to in her sleep.

"But you're not a nun."

"And I am not naughty, either," Beatrice raised an eyebrow. "However, a long time ago in Remiremont the convent was run by powerful women - so powerful they refused to take the vow of chastity and the church let them have their way."

"How could they keep calling themselves nuns?"

"They could call themselves anything they wanted, they were very influential."

"That's a pretty good legend," Everett said.

"There are better legends here," Beatrice said. "Perhaps you will find your father was a legend, perhaps you will become one here - my Lorraine is most fertile for it."

The lantern swung from the ceiling as the train jumped forward. Their wooden seats squeaked and bent slightly as the boxcar, a forty-and-eight, rolled out. He let his head arch over the hard wooden back, listening to the grind of iron rails on iron wheels, and the wooden seat giving with each turn. He dwelled on the sour smell of the forty-and-eight, for it smelled of horse and man moving to war.

Beatrice described Lorraine to him like a bedtime story as the train carried them through rolling hills planted in grains and flowers, where wolves ranged, and King's mounted horses and knights killed dragons. The land was now scattered with broken down old carts and giant, rusted steam-powered tractors leaning like invalids in the shade of stone barns capped with red clay tiles. Every now and then, an old tank stood out amidst the junk piles of brown rusted metal.

"Nearly one hundred years before your country was discovered," Beatrice said, "Jeanne d'Arc was born not far north of here in Domremy-La-Pucelle. Although I am not truly a nun, I try not to be spiteful, but I cannot help but think that if Madame Chauchat were alive in those days, she would have, for her own gain, sided with the English and provided them manufactured evidence of Jeanne d'Arc's heresy."

"I guess, I always thought of Joan of Arc as more of a legend or myth," Everett said, almost ashamed of his ignorance. "It's still hard to believe men could follow a woman warrior like that."

"You will not want to mention that in Lorraine," Beatrice said. "The land roils in legends."

"For example," she continued, "the coat of arms of the Lorraine contains three birds, in flight, pierced by the same arrow. According to the legend, after Jerusalem was captured by the Crusaders, one of the leaders, Godfrey de Bouillon, son of the daughter of Godfrey II the Duke of Lower Lorraine, shot an arrow into three flying alerions, you would call them small eagles - but they have tiny beaks and are considered birds of peace. It was taken as a divine sign of the Holy Trinity - he was made King. If you take the word alerion and change its order, it will eventually read 'Loreina', as spelled eons ago. You will see my Lorraine during a rare moment of peace."

"Would the Chauchat's back there believe the story too?" Everett said.

"I am sure the story is much too tame for them," she huffed. "They would prefer to repeat the story of the naughty nuns of Remiremont, and pass along the many myths of fairies and pagan gods which still live in the minds and hearts of many in Lorraine and the Alsace."

"Do you think I believe in fairies and pagans?" Everett asked.

"I do not yet know. What do people in Iowa believe?"

"The Bible," Everett paused. "Oh, yes, the Farmer's Almanac too."

"I wish there were an almanac to predict what might happen here, near Lorraine," Beatrice said.

"The Lorraine sounds like a magical place," Everett said, opening the window to the woods.

"Alsace too," Beatrice added, "wonderful and so quiet now."

A yellow-white rectangle of light slowly moved from the right side to the front of the car as the train twisted around wooded hills, traveling eastward and leaving a long coil of dense, black smoke behind. They passed over several bridges then entered a large river valley, churning through dark and shadowy forests, then burst back into the low light of late afternoon.

"We are entering the Semouse Valley now, at the edge of the Vosges very near my Lorraine," Beatrice said, her arms proudly folded across her chest. Everett imagined her running its pageantry through her mind by the way she tilted her head back, sighing with her eyes closed. He wondered why she ever left such a place.

"The men from the Spa will be returning to their fields to finish planting after their bath," she paused. "And what do you do for a living? Mother wrote that you were in graduate school, studying engineering."

"Aeronautical engineering." He looked out the window.

"It sounds difficult," she said.

"I had trouble concentrating," Everett said.

She knew just the right questions to ask. He pretended to sleep, still wondering if Doc had coached them on his nightmares. He fixed on the bulge of opium in her purse for relief and it put him to sleep.

ℬ3ℭ

The Spa

He descended the public restroom's steep stairs. The cement steps, once clean and grey, lay caked in years of cigarette stains and dried tobacco spit. Other men, tonight, would simply use the river by the Legion Hall. He needed privacy, he didn't need to pee - he needed to puke. He made it as far as the sink.

Green bits of kimchi cabbage plugged the drain from his purging. After he cleaned himself, he staggered outside and clung to a streetlamp for a minute.

A gigantic circus-like tent billowed behind the Legion Hall, glowing like a Halloween pumpkin filled with lights. He struggled up the alley, wishing he had his tinted flight glasses. Outside, a fire raised burning ashes high into the still night air above a fat and well-done pig turning on an automatic spit.

He felt weak. Men who should be in charge, instead guzzled beer, traded stories and pinched wives and girlfriends, all the while ignoring the pig's skin, bubbling out of control on the spit. It didn't seem like a proper way treat an animal, even a dead one. Entering the huge tent, he wondered why this hadn't annoyed him before.

Families and friends chatted over the sound of big band music blaring from a public address system in the yard. Most who returned last week from Korea wore various parts of their uniforms. Some recognized him right away and greeted him - as he was the only jet pilot in town. He wasn't sure who they all were anymore.

A bell sounded from the stage. He felt the squeeze of the mayor's hand around his arm to usher him up, he didn't like the way the mayor did that.

Banners and strings of lights waved behind the stage with flags standing at each corner. Veterans took their seats at a long table beside white, half-folded postcards, serving as nametags, standing like a row of gravestones.

He brushed the mayor off like a fly and climbed the last few steps up to the stage to his place at the long table with the tag, "Captain Everett Taylor - USAF". A varnished wooden folding chair appeared as if by magic for him to sit. He watched the pig twisting slowly, unattended. Its dripping fat caught fire as it fell, flaring up in yellowish-orange streaks.

A band played the National Anthem, followed by a long prayer. Everett's collar tightened. The smell of the burning pig blended with the scent of candles in front of him on the table. The candle's flame lapped in the still evening air. He glanced once more to the pig.

Before he could sit, the mayor introduced him. The crowd looked up with a proud smile as Everett loosened his collar and his kimchi speckled tie.

He looked about nervously, wondering why someone wasn't doing something about that pig. Was it only him, he wondered, who could hear that awful popping as its skin exploded? The crowd quieted.

In unison, they shifted their feet in anticipation with heads bent like clusters of heavy sunflowers. In the yard, loudspeakers broadcast ever-deepening gasps of breath. He soon realized they were his own as he began to speak. He stopped.

The bright yellow flames from the spit drew his attention again as the pig sagged on the spindle, making it impossible for the small electric motor to take another turn. The motor seized as though the pig decided it had had enough.

A loud crack and some veterans, he knew which ones, fell to the stage floor as combat had taught them. The town went dark, except for the fire blazing beneath the pig. He leaped from the stage, ripped his shirt off and wrapped it around his arms. He dashed to the spit as others flared cigarette lighters looking for electrical shorts.

He grasped the hot metal spike with his shirt-wrapped hand and lifted the burning pig free. He carried it away in the dark towards the river, illuminated only by a small flickering flame still burning the pig's skin. Scalding grease oozed through the shirt to his hands before he gently lowered the pig into the river. The pig floated briefly in sputtering flames until the cool backwater snuffed them out. It bobbed and drifted, caught in the river's current, towards the bridge.

He stepped out of his clothes as the smell of pig overwhelmed him. He flung them into the river as the lights returned inside the distant tent. Someone gripped him around his naked arm. The smell of breath mints - it was Doc.

He felt the weight of Doc's coat hanging at his shoulders. Standing for a whole minute in the river, Doc held him and rocked him as the waves lapped against the calves of his legs. He sang softly above Everett's shoulder into his ear, a song Everett longed to hear as everything went black.

He felt himself lift into the air. Hands, a river of them, buoyed him while handing him off to the next pair. Doc coughed near his head and guided them. He looked down to their faces - the same as those who had fallen to the stage floor at the gun-like report before. Doc led them straight past the curious crowd to his black car, coughing, and pausing now and then to take a breath as he sang that tune in his ear all the way to the veteran's hospital.

◆ ◆ ◆

The train slowed. The lantern swung forward as the train screeched its wheels to a stop. Everett jumped; startled that such a vivid memory would try to spoil such a wonderful day. He wanted out of the closed car. He walked to the door and gave it a good tug, waking Beatrice.

"The conductor will do that in a few minutes," Beatrice said. "You really must be patient."

"I needed something to do," Everett said. "Where is he?"

"Probably walking back from the engine, he is the only one operating the train - it is his job and he loves it."

"Good for him," Everett shrugged. He slid the door open to the west and found another wall of glass wine bottles at their destination, filled with the setting sun, sparkling before his eyes. He wondered if the train hadn't passed through a tunnel of glass bottles.

"Why are all these bottles here?"

"Men have taken this train to the spa each month for decades," Beatrice said. "They like their wine, both coming and going."

He jumped down with his bag. Beatrice sat at the edge of the car door waiting for his arms.

She was heavier than he expected, but solid and muscular as he swung her into his arms. She let out a cheerful and delightful yelp. He gripped her firmly while turning her away from the train. She hadn't asked to be put down. Instead she looked up to him, smiling, yet shaking her head in feigned impropriety as he carried her a few steps.

She stretched her head up to his ear and whispered, "You are quite good at this!"

He held her up with his hands beneath her arms and tipped her slightly to stand. As she pulled away, he felt a sharp pain on the back of his hand. The skin that formed over his wound during the day, thanks to Beatrice's rejuvenating ointment, remained stuck beneath the sleeve of her habit. He moved with her to keep it from ripping away until, after a few steps, it was free of her clothes. She turned to him with a curious look as though he was being too possessive.

The conductor appeared from the other side of the caboose, and not noticing them standing, began tugging at another set of wooden steps. Everett apologized in French for jumping down without the steps.

The conductor noticed them still holding each other. He smiled and held out his arm with a clean towel, to escort Beatrice. Everett walked backwards a few steps to admire the forty-and-eight once more from a distance.

The train that had carried his father's regiment would have many more forty-and-eight's. The regiment had been two-thousand-five-hundred strong coming to the front. The train, towing maybe ten cars, would have probably carried two companies of two-hundred-fifty each. It would have taken days to assemble a whole regiment at the front. As he looked at the boxcar, he wondered if on the way home, the regiment might have left it just as empty as now, with its door open for the band.

"Come on along, Everett," Beatrice turned around to say. "He is escorting us on the walk to the Spa."

The old conductor led Beatrice and Everett on a short sunset walk to the little village, Bain-les-Guerre. A pretty place, Everett thought, with woods all around. The conductor urged Beatrice to quicken her step - they were running late.

"You will soon feel like you are home, Everett."

"But, I'm not from the city – I'm a country boy," Everett said, half in fun. "Didn't Doc tell you?"

Beatrice shook her head. For the first time, he doubted his suspicions that Doc had sent her to nurse him. He found himself swaggering a little bit on their stroll through town, feeling somewhat free.

Bain-les-Guerre. If the same-sized town were in Iowa, Everett judged it would have a single tavern and it wouldn't be on a map either. This town, though, had a few grand old stone buildings and houses along the street with neat hedges and plantings. Beyond their roofs, the sky extended to the green forest walls along a valley's fold. The valley ran broader and deeper than along the Iowa bluffs of the Mississippi, with smooth, clean green slopes of pine and beech rising like a swelling sea.

Taking both Everett's and the conductor's arms, Beatrice hurried between the two men down the long curvy street, lined with budding blue hibiscus, to a low building, dazzling unnaturally in the sunlight. Set in the ground like a multi-faceted ruby, the building seemed born to the earth like a crystal in the afternoon sun.

"Rather unique for a bath, is it not?" Beatrice asked.

"It looks almost Roman."

"Martian, might be more appropriate." Beatrice said with a grin, "a quiet place for Mars and his men to heal. But, you are correct, at the center of its Art Nouveau style, is an ancient Roman bath. Once, rather small, it grows with each war like a volcano."

A man sat high up along the spa's oval, reddish-glass cupola, washing the translucent ruby roof with water then polishing it to a high sheen. He rose and waved to Beatrice when he saw them, then shouted down.

"He said my friends are waiting for us in the spa."

"How did they know you were coming?"

"Everyone in Lorraine knows each time the Pasteur docks to bring their men home," Beatrice said. "Was it not the same when the wounded began to come home from Korea?"

Everett shook off the remaining smell of the burning pig, as Doc had so carefully taught him – think of a quiet place, Doc always said.

They strolled from the street through a small garden. A late afternoon rainbow stretched in the mist of a tall fountain, spraying water high in the air. Through the mist, the bathhouse took on a haunting but majestic appearance. Men sang inside. Not bawdy or raucous songs, but melodious and full of harmony and dynamics amplified by the building, which seemed more like a living instrument to be played, than a holy place.

Its tall white pillars stood with deep-blue mosaic tile, irregularly cut along its oblong oval-shaped base and topped with the single huge cupola of red and orange-colored glass. A guard, dressed in a faded spectrum of lost empires, stood outside a large varnished wooden door. The train conductor shoved past him, as though late. Pivoting on the heel of his tall polished black boots, the guard announced their presence. Men's voices soared inside.

Beatrice and Everett stood alone inside a vast, undecorated vestibule, except for a pair of stone gargoyles perched on ledges and streaked white with bird droppings. Blue mosaics, along the lower walls, shimmered in the light from the windows above. The air hung warm and humid with a slight scent of sulfur. Shoes, boots and socks lay in a neat line along the wall.

Beatrice removed her white, bloodstained shoes. She peeled her white socks from her ankles as she leaned against Everett's shoulder for support then set her shoes beside the others. Everett did the same. He noticed marks on the wall behind their shoes where other boots, boots with spurs, boots with real armor and mail, may have rubbed centuries ago.

On each side of the hallway, tall arches led to separate chambers. Red and orange-tinted light spilled from the glass-domed ceilings. Splashing water reverberated from a nearby chamber.

"This is your bath, to this side," Beatrice said lifting her arm to the one room, "I will take mine in this other, but first there is a pleasurable duty I must perform."

Beatrice let go of his arm and walked to the center of the hallway, bent to her knees, bowed her head and began to chant, sing or pray – Everett couldn't tell. One thing he knew, this Valkyrie had no gift for singing. He felt embarrassed for her, until he realized that she had no shame either.

At first, Everett thought the song was insincere, a joke or a crude ritual, but as the splashing in the next chamber stopped, low and humble sounds of men, filled the hall. Everett too, mumbled along before he realized there were no words - a fitting phrase, he thought, from a nun imposter – only haphazard rhythms and out-of-tune tones of a near song. The men knew it well.

After Beatrice finished, she stood, removed her wimple then undid her hair. Highlighted by the late afternoon sun projecting from the hallway's domed glass ceiling, the hair fell to her shoulder in a blazing avalanche of red. Everett turned to leave, in awe of the transformed nun's beauty.

"Wait there, I am not finished," she said, as she knelt to pray to the men. Everett folded his hands then, sensing the gesture insufficient, knelt and bowed.

She sang, hardly in a key he knew, with her head pitched to the sunset from the translucent ceiling. The men listened in silence until she finished. Everett's initial amusement with her singing turned to sorrow as she spoke to them briefly from the hallway. Everett felt her lifting his bowed chin.

"I told them, I have a friend from America, one who is returning home from war. I told them of your wound. They meet here because it is safe and sacred and the only place where they pass along their stories. There are no rumors here, only legends, and not a word spoken outside. I have never seen them in their chamber, but I know them all and sing for them each time the Pasteur arrives. Now, they are waiting for you - the waters are divine." She handed him a clean white towel from a marble shelf and disappeared into the other chamber.

Everett removed his clothes. He nearly tore, by accident, the half-dollar sized flap of skin from his hand that had hardened. He carefully stretched the sheet of skin back into place - it didn't seem to hurt. Naked, he felt neither warm nor cold, but exposed. He wrapped a towel around his waist.

The men continued to sing as Everett walked inside. He undid his towel then eased himself into the warm water. It rose slowly to his neck as he slid deeper into the large pool. The water felt odd, but comfortable. It found its way into pores he never knew he had, penetrating old cracks of his dried skin, finding hidden folds of flesh, diving deep into old scars from slivers, broken glass, and embedded fish hook wounds of his youth. There seemed no place it didn't seep to apply its restorative powers - except for his hand.

When the water found it, the wound reacted by glowing incandescently red, producing searing pain. Rich in salts and minerals, the water seemed designed to both enhance and elicit pain. Finding its way beneath the patch of skin, the current lifted it, and washed it away, floating from him like a manta ray or a willow leaf, thin and curled.

He held his hand in the air, steaming from the warm waters - the sulfurous air applied its corrosion to the open wound. The men's singing grew louder, as Everett searched for his patch of skin as if it were his soul in flight. The leaf of skin surfaced a few steps away, bobbing, white as birch bark.

The singing lifted to a bold fortissimo, now so strong that he could scream if he wanted, but all he wanted was that skin. As he walked to it, his waves pushed it further away. As he swam to it, his head throbbed as though he were a snail screaming inside its own conch shell. The patch of skin, he needed so much, floated in front of his face like a butterfly then sank, making one last little pirouette motion in front of him. His eyes stung in the salted water as his patch disappeared.

Beneath the water, he hummed to the beat of own heart. The colored mosaic tiled-floor, mixed with the blood-like hues from the domed ceiling that brought in the remaining light of sunset. He felt without body, density or need for air - a sunken ship.

As he rose, he grabbed hold of a man's leg to force himself back down. He felt hands all around him lifting him up where purple colors of sunset now intensified and glimmered on the water's surface. When after, it seemed, they had allowed him to deplete the blood-tinged water of its last molecule of oxygen, he lifted his head and took a breath at last - an easy breath. He cleared his ears of water to the sound of men in solos of song.

He arched his head back to float, keeping his ears clear so he could hear. His body felt more buoyant than he had ever known - like a thousand hands suspending him, finding exactly the right places to massage. The water moved from one man to the next, to purge, clean and carry a bit of each man's sorrow to the next. Pains and injuries diluted and passed around in the warm liquid until all the wars blended into one in the small cavernous pool.

When one finished singing, another began. Some, young enough to have fought in Indochina, others old enough for the Franco-Prussian war, and everything in between with strong and broken voices, they each sang then hummed to the other's song.

It grew still after a time, only a few splashes and some sighs and coughs which sounded hauntingly familiar, like Doc's or maybe his father. The light from the dome turned to violet as the sun set.

The men looked at him, smiling warmly and coaxing him to sing, some with hands, others with their chins. Some with skin so thin and fragile he wondered if they could ever leave. Some floated on their backs without legs and others with perfect bodies, smooth skin but wild-eyed - all waiting for his song.

"Come on along, come on along", he began the song as though he knew it, but didn't. He choked the moment his own words came back to his ears in the acoustically perfect chamber. Then he recalled the song that

Doc sang to him at the river. He wondered how he remembered even a simple phrase of the lyrics.

The men remained silent. He thought he should leave, but from the far end of the pool, a small, scratchy German voice began, "to Alexander's Ragtime Band. Come on Along, Come on along," Everett sang with him. Soon everyone learned the refrain and the pool nearly shouted its lively melody. He reveled in the thought that at least one man may have heard the band play it long ago. Yet, it was unthinkable to interrupt this majesty with such an inquiry.

When Everett finished, they applauded and proudly slapped him on his back as their naked and wounded bodies passed by in the water according to a certain order, each man assigned to another as though they were a string of blind brothers. Each one lifted the one before them from the pool. As they stepped from the bath, each admired the other's infirmity with a certain grace. After the water was still, Everett rolled like a seal.

"You must be getting tired and hungry," Beatrice said from the hallway. "Come out now, the water must be getting cold."

"I never want to leave."

"Come, Everett. My old room is ready here for you, with its two beds. You will sleep like a baby. Tomorrow you meet Mother. She will tell you what you need to know of the band."

That night, as the Beatrice snored in the bed next to him, the sound of crashing bottles came from the window, then a whistle and a bell. He smelled himself – an amalgamation of scents, pungent to floral, a rainbow bouquet from the Spa where a total stranger had finished his song.

ಏ4ೞ

Edge of the Vosges

The Jeep's engine groaned as it lumbered through the rough back roads from the flat plains of Suwon, to the northeast. Streams turned to rapids of white water and to waterfalls in the greening foothills of the Taebeck Mountains - the vertical uninterrupted spine of Korea.

"Tell me a story, Bender," Everett said.

"Say, what was the name of that pretty young gook you said you liked in college?"

"Tell me a story, Bender."

"She was a commie. Cripes, they say even Ike was a commie sympathizer. She had it coming."

The voice sounded as though funneled through his flight helmet's headset, over a radio, adding its own crackle, static and sizzle like flying through charged clouds.

Everett pulled the Jeep over to let a small family passing by - grandparents, and a pregnant mother with three complaining children. He looked for one whose hair was red as his own.

He turned away from them towards the hills ahead as they asked their mother, 'Why, must we leave!' The mother would say because it's not safe to live at home. Tears came to Everett for some reason, before he realized he had never walked in his own mess before. He rubbed his eyes with his hand and blew his nose while edging the jeep back onto the narrow road.

"Tell me a story, Bender, tell me a story."

"Mind control then? OK, mind control it is. Now, I'm a very religious man as you know and the professors at the university laughed at me for even bringing it up - but the Red's are controlling our minds, or rather slowly ruining them. The atheist fiends are tainting our water with sodium fluoride. I'm glad they didn't have time to brainwash me."

"Bender, the story."

"OK, buddy."

Everett listened as Bender went on to describe a communist conspiracy to turn America's minds into clay by deluding whole communities into believing small doses of sodium fluoride, the active ingredient in rat poison, could reduce tooth decay.

"You know, my minister would tell you a higher spirit is at work here. What in the world ever possessed you to fall for a communist? You know they don't baptize their kids. Pull over here."

"Tell it, Bender," Everett said.

"The guys who come back tell us you don't see the ground fire coming up at all, no streaks, no wiz-bang of the gun, just a black puff of smoke and the jet goes out of control for some reason - you think it's because you screwed something up, then you see your gauges - they don't lie. But I can tell you for a fact, when you squeeze that jettison trigger it's like being shot from a cannon, not like that little jettison-seat trainer in the hanger. Yeah, over here by that tree."

"Go on, Bender."

"Did you know there's a live thirty-seven millimeter charge under the jettison seat to lift us free of the jet? It's the same size of round as the ground fire. There's a certain balance in the universe. I perturbed it somehow. I didn't even have to look down for the jettison trigger; my hand went right for it."

"Go on."

"Do you know how long a prayer should last? I mean, you hate to take up His whole day, but the parachute took forever to land. I expected ground-fire right away, but nothing came. Funny, I don't remember praying at all. I sure hated to lose my jet. I followed it corkscrewing into the ground. A little red-headed kid, they all look five or six here, I kid you not, sauntered up John Wayne style, just like you, to help me gather my chute then pointed a pistol at me - Cripes, I thought it was a goddamned toy!"

The Jeep rolled to a stop just off the road where a lone tree stood. Everett ran to it, leaned against it and slowly found his arms wrapping around its small diameter. In a minute he walked uneasily back to the Jeep and steered it in the direction of a dark cloud of smoke in the distance.

"Another story, Bender."

"Sweet Jesus, this is a nasty road! You said there were beautiful places she wanted to show you here. God, look at it now. Oh, no! There's a sentry up ahead."

"Tell me a story, Bender."

"Too late. Dear Lord, I'm so tired now, yesterday just took it all out me. It takes something big to make that happen, to make the war, grinding on below us, suddenly jump into your face like a mad cat. I'm sorry about the temple, Everett. I thought I was the religious one. Here's the sentry now, buddy. Time to amscram."

♦ ♦ ♦

Sunlight glared through Everett's window from the distant crest of the Ozark-like mountains called, Vosges. He lay in his bunched-up shorts and sweaty T-shirt on a small bed, next to another rumpled bed. He unfolded his neck from the headboard and, for the first time, his head felt good. He guessed he hadn't hammered the wooden board with his head all night as he normally would.

He pulled off his T-shirt, underwear and socks. Beatrice's habit lay on the floor at the foot of the other bed. He felt somewhat relieved that there were two beds, but knowing he probably had the one normally reserved for her Louis.

From his bag, he quickly pulled out a fresh change of underwear wrapped in laundry paper from the Excalibur. He ripped the paper off and changed. A bowl of warm water, a shaving brush, soap and an old straight razor rested on a small table. He lathered his face, winked into the mirror and began shaving.

A knock on the door, followed by the creak of a door hinge then Beatrice, "Are you decent?"

"Mostly, please come in," Everett said.

Dressed in a sweater and a pair of slacks, Beatrice entered with a package tucked beneath her arm.

"What's that - breakfast?" Everett asked, trying to keep his eyes from focusing on her curvaceous form.

"It is my habit," Beatrice said. "We must hurry to catch the train to Rothau. Philippe and Mother will be waiting and Philippe hates to wait in Rothau."

"Why?" Everett resumed shaving, but watched her from his mirror.

"Philippe was imprisoned near Rothau."

From the map, Everett recalled Rothau near a larger town called Schirmeck.

The old razor tugged at his whiskers. As he cleaned it, other whiskers clung to the blade - Louis' whiskers, Everett guessed.

"Beatrice, who was that man singing at the spa last night, the one with the high-pitched voice?" Everett said, looking into a small mirror on a shelf to see her. He focused, though, on his own angular face and a hint of a dimpled smile that seemed his own.

"He is German, I think from the Great War," Beatrice said looking up from the table. "Why did you not ask him last night?"

"I guess I didn't want to disturb him, Ouch!" he said, nicking himself with the razor.

"My dear Everett," Beatrice laughed. "You could not disturb him anymore than he already is. He is probably, how do you say it, shell-shocked from the Great War."

"How could he possibly sing that particular song so well," Everett said. "He must have heard an American singing it - maybe even the band played for them!"

Everett quickly toweled his face and walked to the window where Beatrice sat with her red hair lifting in the light wind. She looked out across the yard, where a whistle blew - more like a child's than a train. She turned to the bed for her habit, wrapped in paper.

"We must run," Beatrice said. "The train is waiting for us."

"I didn't think French trains waited for anyone." Everett grabbed his bag and poked an arm into his shirt. She snagged his arm and led him away.

At the station, they walked past the heap of wine bottles along the narrow gauge rail of the forty-and-eight boxcars to a stack of timber. To the side, ten small, iron-wheeled cradles, rested empty on a track whose gauge was no larger than Everett had seen at amusement parks. The train's engine, towards the front, looked like Doc's big black car.

"It's a toy!" Everett exclaimed.

"No, it is the lumber train," Beatrice said. "It does not stop until it is high in the Vosges."

"But, Beatrice, there's no passengers, no seats!"

"Here, this car is the cleanest," Beatrice said as the train inched forward. "Can you lift me again?"

He held her up. It wasn't that high, he thought as he set her down, she could have easily stepped aboard. He swung his bag and jumped beside her as the train gathered speed.

With their backs against the wood and iron of the lumber cradle, they watched the sun finish rising as they crossed a river, the Moselle, Beatrice said. Everett pulled out his map. She guided his finger to the green arc.

Past Bruyeres, he glanced up from the map while passing through small sleepy villages with higher pitched roofs for snow and exposed wooden timbers between sections of stucco. The train weaved through several low ranges of beech and pine in tight turns, following streams and ravines. As they passed through smaller villages, people waved, yet Beatrice burrowed her head beneath Everett's arms.

Just as Everett wondered if she had traveled here before without her habit she asked, "Did you always wish to be a pilot?"

"I always wanted to fly."

"Have you ever considered anything more, well, more unworldly, Everett?"

"Unworldly?"

"A priest or a monk perhaps," Beatrice said.

"Why do you ask, Beatrice?"

"You come so driven to find this band, but I think inside your own heart you are looking for more than you can hold with your hands."

"Did you ever want to be a real nun, Beatrice?"

"No. I always wanted to be a nurse. I liked the way the nurses worked with Mother - always at her side."

"Do you think you might ever become a nun?"

Beatrice held the habit in its paper-wrapped cocoon like an old pet who had finally died and was about to be buried.

"No." Beatrice turned her head into the wind as the train picked up speed. She drew a breath so deep that Everett imagined only Brunnhilde's brass breastplate could contain her latent power.

The train labored a gentle climb into the mountains alongside a river. Tall, narrow pines lined the tracks. Slender rays of light, penetrating from above, made the whole forest floor, covered in soft needles, appear as an endless stage populated by legions of tall and thin toy soldiers, extending as far as he could see into the forest.

Sporadically, up steep hillsides, ran parallel tracks of logs, curving gently up the hill, with wooden pegs staked on either side. Beatrice said if it were not a weekend or a holiday, men, real men, would guide a wooden sled, called a schlitt, filled high with fresh cut timber, down the slopes. The big men, schlitteurs, were skilled in keeping it from getting loose and shooting down the track out of control.

Where lumber had been cut, there stood swaths of land with cattle grazing on hills above valleys, green with tall grass and, for a time, long narrow fields of ankle-high corn. Later, the forest darkened and ferns grew full and green.

Wherever they crossed a bridge, villages would appear and always dotted with tiny red-roofed houses and a church with a single, unglamorous spire.

"It's so beautiful," he said into Beatrice's ear over the noise of the train, growling into the climb along steeper slopes then idling down the valley.

The little train finally slowed then stopped at the river. The engineer quickly filled his engine with water from a hose on a water tower then shoveled coal, piled nearby, into the car behind him. A lush forest covered low peaks on both sides of the tracks.

"It is the Mortagne, our forest," Beatrice said. "Look ahead, next to the river - there in the field," Beatrice, pointed.

A new bridge spanned the river. Beside it, lay a crumpled remnant of the old one, as he had seen after Marseilles and much like the work his jet had done in Korea.

"We aren't at the Western Front yet, are we?"

"No," Beatrice said. "The bridge was destroyed by the German's who retreated in the last war after the Americans stormed up the Rhone Valley. They all followed nearly the same route as we have been traveling."

The train's bell rang and whistle blew. It soon groped back up the slow climb.

Everett nodded, recalling the second invasion from the south of France, not from Normandy, but from St. Tropez.

"St. Die is on the north side of the Mortagne, we will pass by it soon," she said.

As the train rounded the mountain, St. Die appeared. The height and perspective of the view, with the mountain on one side, the town in the distance below surrounded by the river Doubs, with low green mountains all around. It looked like many towns in the Taeback's of Korea - crouched behind the mountains along river valleys. He looked for the spire of a church. There was none. The small train twisted around the mountain, climbing the side, still in morning's shadow and leaving St. Die below.

"St. Die was mostly destroyed in the retreat," Beatrice said. "It is nearly rebuilt. We pass on through to the Vosges now. Sit closer, it will be getting colder."

Beatrice hummed notes, whose timbre and melody made no sense, but she smiled as her breath left her mouth in a condensing vapor, filled with the comforting scent of vanilla. Everett felt her body radiate as she sang. He warmed to her lack of shame as she randomly adjusted her pitch to the wandering tone of the little train's whistle.

Beatrice said they were traveling north along the edge of the western Vosges, following the river Bruche towards Rothau and, if he looked carefully, he could see where they would cross the old western front.

"It will not be much longer," she said, "then we will be home."

As they came through the Vosges, he noticed barren land among the trees where he expected to find maybe a cultivated plot a farmer had worked up from the forest floor. But, as the train rolled through, they only looked like rolling, naked hills covered in short shrubs and saplings.

"Did you feel that?" She said.

"What?"

"The old front, we just crossed over it. It is amazing how we have recovered so much of our Lorraine in most places," she said proudly. "One cannot even feel it anymore."

Her cheeks, now red and full, shone in the late morning light. It wasn't until they passed a narrow road, leading upwards, deeper in the woods, that her face turned somber. The train picked up speed after it crested a ridge with the village of Rothau below.

"What is it, Beatrice?"

"We get off here in Rothau, but back up that road was where Philippe was held prisoner," Beatrice said. "Up there past the woods. You cannot see it, but I can still smell it."

She didn't look away from the woods until Everett placed his hand on her steel-cold cheek.

"We must hurry," she said, as she turned. "Philippe will be at the station with Mother and the car. We do not want to keep him waiting so near to the horror that still haunts him, besides he will be in need of this, that is, unless you ate it all."

Beatrice smiled then felt for the bar of opium, bulging from the side of her purse. Everett pitied her brother, Philippe, for whom the drug seemed destined and relieved that it wasn't for her lover, Louis.

"I can see why you smuggle it in, but hasn't your mother been able to help Philippe, without the drug?" Everett said, raising his voice over the rumble of the cradle that now accelerated down the slight incline towards the station.

"The opium is for when Mother and I are not here to help Annette, Philippe's wife. Mother has only been marginally successful in applying her hypnotic treatments. She and Annette, sometimes get him settled down for a time with a cold therapeutical bath."

"Has he been to the Spa?"

"Even the Spa could not help Philippe - he is filled with so much hate."

"And Sigmund, your father?"

"After Philippe returned, Father tried to help by giving him some work, but Sigmund is Philippe's step-father and a German. Arbeit macht frei - 'Work will make you free' was the slogan Philippe muttered whenever Father came around."

"What does Philippe do with his time?"

"He tries to paint, like his father Évariste."

"I don't think it's too good of an idea for me to spend the night with his family now," Everett said, quickly assessing his situation as the train whistled its arrival into Rothau. "He might resent me for being named for his father."

"Nonsense, I would think Philippe might enjoy your companionship. Besides, Mother is here if Philippe has another spell. But, please, remember to call me 'Sister Beatrice' around the family, their son believes I am a nun – he is only nine."

Beatrice threw him the paper-wrapped habit as she stood on the lumber cradle, balancing herself on one foot to see.

"I see the car now!" Beatrice said. "The engineer will not stop for us. He will be starting his climb into the Vosges."

The train closely raced past an old convertible Mercedes - a German staff car with its top down. A woman and a small boy inside waved to them. A man rested his shoe on the chrome front bumper, leaning sideways against the grill, reading a newspaper. Everett judged, by his jutting chiseled chin, that the man was in denial of the defeat in Indochina.

"We need to jump, it is Philippe, but dear God - where is Mother?"

The train slowed into a climb, nearly stopping. Everett jumped then helped Beatrice step down. Her paper-wrapped habit tumbled to the ground. As Everett grabbed it, the boy's small hand lightly tapped his sensitive skin to accept the package.

The boy's deep blue eyes danced as Everett smiled. He snapped his suspenders then spread his arms like swept-back wings.

"Meester Sabray Chet?" The boy said with some excitement as he twirled with the habit then hurled it into the backseat of the convertible.

"Louis knows his jets," Beatrice said. "Speak French, Louis. Everett understands. But, Louis, where is your grandmother, Madame Lambert?"

"Louis?" Everett said, shocked by the boy and uncomfortable listening the Beatrice refer to her mother as Madame Lambert.

"Madame Lambert said you flew a Sabre jet," Beatrice said to Everett.

"An F-86," Louis interrupted.

"Louis?" Everett asked again.

"Louis?" Everett asked, looking into Beatrice's green eyes, sparkling with pride.

"Louis? Yes," she said. "You are surprised. He is a wonderful little boy. Did Madame Lambert not tell your Doctor Hershey? Everett, this is Philippe and his wife Annette."

Annette welcomed Everett with a wet kiss along the cheek – a little too close to the corner of his mouth. Flushing red, Everett glanced to Beatrice who raised her eyebrows and shrugged as though Annette were notorious for this introduction. Philippe rolled a wild, brown eye to the side then returned to his paper.

"You must pardon my husband," Annette said. "He loves bad news and is a slow reader."

Annette ruffled Philippe's dark, perfectly shaped hair. With a quick jerk of his head, Philippe straightened it without losing his place in the newspaper.

Louis tossed their things into the trunk then opened the heavy car door and helped Beatrice and Everett into the back seat. As Louis slammed the door shut, Philippe fluttered the newspaper. Louis leaped over the top into the back and crawled between Beatrice and Everett.

"Louis, you should make room for Madame Lambert. Where is she?" Beatrice asked.

Philippe turned from the paper, glancing sideways.

"She has been further detained in Strasbourg. We are to entertain her guest until she relieves us," Philippe said. He trained his penetrating dark eyes on Beatrice's clothes. "I see you have changed clothes, Sister Beatrice. It not wise, this close to Ville Negre."

"Father, Sister Beatrice is still my angel," Louis said as he snuggled next to her. "When she wears her habit into Ville Negre, it covers her nice smile. Look at her pretty face."

Beatrice flashed a smile to Louis and Everett, and bared her teeth to her brother as Everett wondered what crime had caused her to hide from her own village.

"Can I call you Beatrice if you are not wearing the habit?" Louis asked.

"No, she is Sister Beatrice," Philippe barked. "And she will always be Sister Beatrice."

Philippe folded the newspaper awkwardly, clasping it strangely until Everett recognized the metal pincers Philippe had for a left hand. Then, coerced by Annette, Philippe extended his good hand to Everett, shook it once, and then grunted to her that his duty was done.

Philippe focused on Everett's forehead then stepped back, snapping the newspaper open to the headlines. His brown eyes retreated into deep and dark sockets to finish reading while he slowly worked the squeaking levers and springs of his hand.

He wondered why Beatrice hadn't told him about her brother's hand. He guessed she must be embarrassed to point out all of Philippe's frailties at once - but this one was certainly the most obvious. The aged, stretched skin around Philippe's hand wasn't a recent accident. As a prisoner of the Nazi's in the last war, if Philippe's arm were a genetic defect, Everett knew the remedy would be castration or worse.

He wished Beatrice might have said something earlier, but after all these years, she might think Philippe's hand as familiar as his obnoxious manner.

Philippe drove south from the station on a winding road barely wide enough for one small car, let alone the Mercedes. He shifted the car clumsily with his right hand on the shift until he eventually found a faster gear. His mechanical hand on the left however, effortlessly twirled and twisted a special ball bearing mounted on the steering wheel.

Everett caught himself staring at the arm.

"It was to have been his painting arm," Beatrice reached across Louis and whispered into Everett's ear, "the left one, like his father, Évariste – the painter."

Beatrice drew Everett's attention to a prominent peak to the right and ahead of them, up high in the distance, marked by rising white puffs of the little train engine.

"You see there, it is Donon," Beatrice said proudly, "not high by your standards perhaps, but it the highest place we will see on this side of the Vosges. Druids once lived beneath its rock. You can see it all the way from Switzerland! Can we stop, Philippe?"

Philippe only drove faster, flicking his mechanical hand to passersby as the big Mercedes glided down the slopes of the Vosges. Everett sensed Philippe's apprehension, knowing these same people might have turned a cheek during the incarceration of fellow countrymen like Philippe, in such awful times, yet Philippe honked the horn, startling them rudely, as though to remind them that his integrity was intact.

After several minutes of driving through tall pine along the foothills from Donon, the big car slowed. The forest abruptly ended and a rock-strewn plain lay below them. The road, lined on each side with tall poplars, drew Everett's attention and extended in a gentle curve below before rising slightly to a ridge, running northwest to southeast. It seemed strange, finding poplars, purposely planted beneath the Vosge's pine wilderness.

Philippe cut the engine, steered to the side and braked the car just above the tips of the long, undulating string of tall, closely spaced trees. Without saying a word, Philippe stepped from the car, slammed the door and sauntered to a ledge. He struck a match and lit a cigarette stub that he held close with his pincers.

"The Lambert property is beyond the ridge," Beatrice said. "Philippe claims this is one of the few places where he can see the frontline trench where his father died, but I can see nothing."

"Dragons guard Évariste's bones," Louis whispered. "Father is afraid to enter the frontline trench to find him."

"Louis, that is disrespectful," Annette said. "Philippe has his spells. I wish Madame Lambert were here. Sister Beatrice, did you remember Philippe's medicine?"

"Yes, but is there nothing else you can do for him?" Beatrice asked.

"Of course," Annette smiled at Everett in the mirror as she checked her hair, "but, it is never satisfying. I will not be long."

Everett followed her lilting step until she snatched Philippe's hand at the ledge, leading him to the brush off to the side.

"I want to look," Louis said as he rose from his seat.

Beatrice snared his suspenders at the back.

"They want to be alone, Louis," Everett said.

"Not them, Sister Beatrice. I want to see the Zone Rouge from here. This is where the German cannons stood."

Beatrice rose slightly to check through the brush at the ledge where Philippe stood. Everett leered, as the Renoir-like landscape turned surreal.

A single mesmerizing line of trees cut through an un-cultivated patch of land. Along the ridge, hidden by the trees, ran a nearly invisible parallel stitch of trenches, the French on one side and the German's on the other, with no-man's land on the crest. The harsh features, subdued with overgrowths of moss, lichen, short shrubs and saplings, jumped out to Everett like ravaged hillsides of Korea, covered in a thin green blanket.

After the horror subsided, the nature of the deadly stalemate, known as the Great War, became clear in this small patch of Lorraine. The ridge was the line and because of the slope to either side, artillery would forever fall long or short. How adversaries convened at such a place, Everett thought, must have a stroke of luck.

"The Zone Rouge is a most dangerous place, as Louis says," Beatrice said, "but there is also Lac Noir."

"And General Sigmund's trench," Louis said.

Everett turned to Beatrice, puzzled.

"Sigmund," Beatrice said, "cleared an entire reserve trench so that children might come to visit him where he lives."

"This land will once be yours, Louis," Beatrice said quietly.

"What about the land, all around? It looks cleared too." Everett asked.

"It is the neighbors' land. It has all been recovered by the government after the last war by brave demineurs, even the Germans helped."

"That's how Philippe lost his arm?" Everett whispered.

"No," Beatrice said, then moved closer to his ears and whispered, "Sigmund, volunteered to clear the unexploded munitions by himself and the government, naturally was thrilled - not wanted to kill their own. I am afraid Sigmund has not made much progress since Philippe's accident after Louis was born. I cannot help but think that if Philippe could only find Évariste's remains it might ease his troubled mind. His father has been laying dead in the Zone Rouge since 1917. Philippe is too afraid to step beyond the cleared trenches, as he should be."

"Did his father, Évariste, really charge the Germans with a paintbrush?" Everett asked.

Beatrice and Louis nodded sincerely. Everett gulped out of both respect and astonishment.

"Where did Évariste live?" Everett asked. He knew his father's headquarters had been in Madame Lambert's home and that the band must have been nearby.

"In the tuilerie," Louis said, still watching.

"They lived in a garden, here, along the Western Front?"

Louis craned his neck to Everett and snickered.

"You are thinking of the famous Tuilerie in Paris, now a palatial garden, but it once produced tiles," Beatrice said. "Évariste's family, for generations, made red roof tiles in their tuilerie in Lorraine. Évariste only used it to fire pottery for painting. It is a miracle the tuilerie survived."

Everett imagined shards of red-tile raining down on his father and the band in the tuilerie where they headquartered and billeted.

"Can I see the tuilerie from here?"

"No." Beatrice said, "Below, this road, Rue Gambetta, lined in poplars, eventually leads south to Ville Negre. The road was named for Gambetta, our leader during the Franco-Prussian war of 1870. Before Ville Negre, past that crest below, you can see Lac Noir."

"The tuilerie rests intact, out-of-sight, near Lac Noir." Beatrice drew his hand to the glistening of a distant dewdrop.

"I don't understand," Everett said. "Even though the cannons standing up here had no line-of-sight to the tuilerie, couldn't they just train a few degrees to the left of Lac Noir, knowing the tuilerie was there?"

Everett focused on the distant trench works, trying to imagine a band of twenty-six bright-eyed boys, marching and playing alongside his father's riflemen.

"I think I can see General Sigmund gathering dragon eggs," Louis said with his hand shading his eyes.

Everett raised his brows, thinking it were a belated Easter egg hunt for elders or some sort of pagan ritual, enough so, that it drew Beatrice's attention.

"Sigmund makes his living selling unexploded munitions that lay about the Zone Rouge like eggs," she said with a note of pride.

"Like an opportunistic weasel!" Philippe, standing covertly at the side of the Mercedes, reached in and tapped Louis on the head with his metal pincer. Louis winced then ducked under Beatrice's arm.

"Philippe!" Beatrice looked to Annette who shrugged her shoulders helplessly. "Have you taken that hand to Louis while I have been away?"

"No, Sister Beatrice," Louis said, lifting her arm from his head. "Father has difficulty sleeping."

"The General would think the Zone Rouge surrendered long ago , just to to him," Philippe said as he nervously flexed his metal joints.

"Well, he did succeed in clearing the French reserve trench," Beatrice said.

A spring in Philippe's hand tensed to the point at which it might break.

"I have what you need," Beatrice said as she lifted her purse and showed Philippe the bulge of opium.

Philippe ground the gear around, shifting, until it took hold. The car lurched forward, pitching down towards the Zone Rouge and the unseen tuilerie as Everett wondered to himself what role he played in getting Philippe so upset, yet he understood restless nights.

After several minutes, the road progressively narrowed into a mere trail between the poplars. Green shrubs brushed the side of the car. Louis reached across Everett's lap and pulled a handful of leaves from branches flashing by. Philippe turned, shouting twice for him to stop. Annette shook her head hopelessly then turned to Beatrice to say something.

"Annette wonders if you are married. You seem so comfortable with Louis, she wonders if . . ." Beatrice said before Annette finished.

"Children?" Annette asked.

Everett turned to the Zone Rouge, thinking of a round-faced redheaded little boy and then gently squeezed Louis's hand. He no longer heard the whine of the engine as they stormed down the narrow and rutted Rue Gambetta, only the pulsing throb of his jet.

"Triste Américaine," Louis said beneath his breath.

"Sad, American," Everett understood.

Annette asked Philippe to slow as they passed a sign affixed to a small tree on their right. It read, "Non Interdit". Beatrice whispered to Everett that it was far too dangerous to speed - they were about to brush alongside the Zone Rouge, up close. A second later, she drew his attention to an old bomb crater, smoothed over and eroded by weather, then another.

"This place gives me the creeps!" Everett said. "What are you looking for?"

"This is where Madame Lambert's children played, Everett," Beatrice said raising her chin with pride. "I am looking for the old French reserve trench."

"How many children did Grand-mere Lambert have?" Louis asked.

Everett thought he would rather play on broken glass.

"Only one true, child." Philippe said, as he accelerated the big car.

Beatrice explained that the government constructed the road to breach the Zone Rouge beneath Donon, but Sigmund's trench was a short cut to the tuilerie.

"Philippe! Slow this car down!" Beatrice leaned to the front and slapped Philippe's shoulder. Philippe dragged the brakes.

An unsettled doom grew inside Everett's stomach as the car crawled along Rue Gambetta. It was clear to Everett why poplars lined the road, to obscure a frightening landscape that looked more like the high sea known as No-Man's-Land. Everett could see Annette sensing it too, as she glanced to Philippe, who seemed almost casual now.

"Make me fly like an angel, Sister Beatrice!" Louis demanded. He stood in his seat and offered the back of his overalls for Beatrice to grab.

"You have grown big, Louis," Beatrice said. "And we are moving too slow to fly."

"You show me then, Meester Sabray Chet!" Louis slapped Everett on the back.

Everett smiled, not knowing if Madame Lambert had told the family his war story or not, but it didn't matter. He felt better now, distracted by Louis' playfulness.

"So you want to be a jet pilot, 'eh Louis?" Everett slipped by mistake into English. "Sure, I'll show you how it's done then, if you think you're ready to take-off!"

"Sure, sure! Ready to take-off! Please speed up the car, Fatherrrrr," Louis said in English with a jet-like growl.

Everett, surprised by Louis' command of English, lifted him by the back of his overalls. Philippe ignored him while staring off into the Zone Rouge.

"We could be driving a fine Citroen, if only my father had not felt compelled to attack the invaders with his brush," Philippe said in perfect English. "It is one thing to be forced to drive this German monster through our, once beautiful, Lambert property. It is quite another misery to listen to yet another foreign tongue practicing French."

Louis's feet marched time on Everett's knees ready to leap into space.

"Please, Philippe," Beatrice said.

Philippe obliged with a surge of power. In the rearview mirror, Everett caught a glimpse of Philippe gnashing his teeth.

"Tre' Beau!" Louis said, angling forward, held there by the wind building against his chest and Everett's firm grasp.

The big, black Mercedes bounded over a swell in the road, with its tires leaving the ground. Louis lifted into the air. Everett gripped him, but found himself just as weightless.

"We just passed over the last of the French Front-Line Trench," Beatrice said, noticing Everett's concern, for the trench looked more like a meandering, trash-filled ditch.

"Faster, Father," Louis, pleaded. Philippe accelerated. A few hundred yards later, Everett felt the car lift again.

"It is the French reserve trench, the one father cleared," Beatrice said. "We are about to leave the Zone Rouge - thank goodness."

Everett turned back to what looked like a long-green terrace extending to the west, rather than the warped spectacle of the front-line trench and No-Man's-Land. As they left the mutilated land behind them, the land sloped sharply downward. A white horse stood on a side road, ready to enter the road with an old man and a cart in tow.

"I told you I saw the General," Louis said. "He and Gerta are taking dragon eggs to market again."

"Sigmund?" Everett turned to Beatrice.

"Yee!" Annette screamed as the horse bolted in front of the Mercedes. Philippe braked, sending the car into a skid to the side of the road.

The old horse raised its head, snorted a white plume of steam and reared up to stomp its left hoof against the front bumper. On its right hoof, it wore a man's old leather boot.

Philippe stormed from the car. The driver, old and bearded in a face full of dirt, jumped from the cart and shouted in German beside his horse, who nervously stomped its hoof one last time on the car. Metal cylinders rolled loose in the cart.

"It is the General and his old horse, Gerta," Louis said. "They have a whole cart-full of dragon eggs!"

Everett shivered, recognizing the eggs as old artillery shells, mostly small 75mm rounds, the size of a baguette of bread, all fused and ready to blow. Their worn rotating bands, meant they had been fired. They clumped together but seemed ready to roll apart at the slightest movement.

"What's he doing with that old ordnance?" Everett shouted. "They could explode at any time!"

"He sells them at the Army depot on the edge of Ville Negre," Beatrice said, climbing from the car as Philippe slammed his hand onto the cart and shouted at the grizzled old man who nervously re-adjusted the shells.

"Boche! Collaborateur!" Philippe shouted.

"He is not. Sigmund is a démineur," Beatrice insisted, "a proud démineur! He only digs up unexploded bombs and shells to make a living. He knows how he will die. You seem to want to accelerate the inevitable."

Beatrice comforted her father, Sigmund, who stood grimly by the nervous horse, Gerta.

Philippe reached into the cart and held a shell in his shaking hand before dropping it.

"Sister Beatrice, Philippe's medication?" Annette asked.

Beatrice pulled the opium bar from her purse.

"Do you have a pipe too?" Annette asked.

"I left my old one in the glove compartment," Sigmund said. He stepped to the Mercedes, looking twice at Everett.

"I refuse to smoke from your pipe," Philippe said, and with a quick turn on his heel, he cursed his way to the old French reserve trench.

"Where is Philippe going?" Everett asked Beatrice.

"To the tuilerie, eventually. There are but three ways from here. Follow Rue Gambetta for several kilometers then turn right onto the lane to the tuilerie - that is the long way, or take the shorter path, as Philippe will do, along the Reserve Trench that Sigmund cleared, to Lac Noir then a few paces to the tuilerie."

"What's the third way?" Everett asked.

"The shortest way is along the hypotenuse of the Front-Line Trench - straight through the Zone Rouge, which no one has ever been foolish enough to enter since the Great War."

"Philippe will probably spend the night at Lac Noir again," Annette said. "It is a shame Madame Lambert is not here for him and it is too late for his hydrotherapy. He will need his medicine tonight."

"Does that stuff help?" Everett asked, wondering why Doc hadn't prescribed it for him.

"It soothes him, but perhaps, too much," Annette said with an ache in her voice. "It leaves less to love."

"I will put the opium inside Everett's bag in the trunk," Beatrice whispered to Annette and Everett. "Louis might find it my purse and think it was chocolate as Everett did."

"Sherlock Holmes would know the difference," Louis said. "When Father smokes opium, he imagines seeing a giant fish in Lac Noir."

Gerta took a step backwards, disturbing the cylinders.

"The mere mention of that lake makes her nervous," Sigmund said.

"It makes you nervous too." Beatrice wrapped her arms around Sigmund and kissed his forehead. With her hand, she soothed Gerta's nose. The mare's tail ceased to twitch.

"There, there, old Gerta," she said, bending down and loosening Gerta's boot.

"It is sore," Sigmund said. "I have exhausted your ointment from last month."

Beatrice stood to search her purse and found the tin of ointment she had used on Everett's hand. She placed it in Sigmund's palm.

"Make it last, make it last," Beatrice said.

She showed Everett the shrapnel wound at Gerta's ankle, a deep cut that would never completely heal, but not bad enough to lose her leg.

Sigmund lathered Gerta's ankle. He looked up to his daughter and smiled, "No more ointment? Does this mean you are not returning to Indochina?"

"I have not completely decided, but try to make that last." Beatrice patted her habit, wrapped in paper on the car seat, then glanced to Everett.

"This is the American whom Madame Lambert said would be coming. Monsieur Taylor, Everett Taylor, this is Sigmund Fischer, our General Allemand."

Beatrice's father nearly tripped on Gerta's boot, trying to stand. Everett stepped forward and stooped down to shake hands.

"Russell?" Sigmund said, looking up to him.

Everett shivered at the mention his of father's name.

"My old friend, Russell!" Sigmund said to Beatrice, in French with a strong German accent.

"No, sir. I'm his son, Everett - Everett Taylor."

"Oh, yes," Sigmund said, out of breath from the encounter.

"Évariste, you say? Russell, named you Évariste?"

Beatrice stepped between them.

"Sigmund, why not let me walk you back home where you can relax. Everett will be staying with us in Madame Lambert's tuilerie until she arrives. You can talk tomorrow."

"But my little beauties are getting anxious," Sigmund said, pointing to the cart. "I need the money."

Everett was taken aback and wondered exactly how a hermit like Sigmund, came to be Beatrice's father and how Sigmund seemed to know his father, Russell, by sight better than he.

"Can't you defuse these?" Everett said.

"Indeed, the depot pays me more if I can twist their little heads off," Sigmund said, more relaxed, as he pointing to one. "Once a year, I bring a few stubborn ones, like these, in one big trip rather than risking it each week with one or two. These small dragon eggs will not bring much."

Everett touched a fuse, warm from the sun.

"No! Stand back." Sigmund said, startling Gerta a little. "We must be on our way. When we are finished at the depot I will send Gerta along, as always, back down the trench to the tuilerie."

"Very well Sigmund," Beatrice said, kissing him on the forehead again. "Louis, will you please help the General lace Gerta's boot?"

After Louis leaped over the side of the Mercedes, Beatrice explained to Everett that her father cleared the Reserve Trench when she and Philippe were young so that they, Madame Lambert and Gerta, might all walk safely between Sigmund's dugout and the tuilerie where they lived.

"Sigmund must love you all very much to have done all that," Everett said. "Philippe has never visited your father's home?"

"The last time was after the last war, when he was released from prison," Beatrice said. "He lost his arm to an unexploded grenade while taking Gerta back home after visiting Father in his dugout. Philippe thought the trench was safe. He has not ventured that far up the trench since."

"I'm sorry," Everett whispered so only Beatrice could hear. "For some reason, I thought Philippe might be in prison during the war, because his arm was defective."

Beatrice grasped Everett's collar and brought his ear, rather rudely to her mouth.

"No!" Beatrice whispered harshly, "Philippe was a communist, like his father the painter, did Mother not tell your Doctor friend?"

Beatrice pulled him so close that her tooth nicked his ear lobe. He grew more suspicious of Doc Hershey's motive, otherwise Doc would have prepared them more.

"What Philippe lost in prison was his manhood, not his arm," Beatrice said, then became nearly silent - a side of her Everett hadn't seen before, a side that abhorred ignorance.

He thought of how the last war robbed so many of their innocence and vitality, but at least Beatrice kept an aura of womanhood as a nurse and a nun, albeit a faux nun. Maybe jealousy was why Philippe was still so angry and upset, he thought.

Annette seemed to understand they were talking about her husband. She seemed anxious to return home and motioned Louis to return to the car. He jumped into the driver's seat.

Beatrice plucked Louis from the seat and set him in the back alongside Everett as she sat next to Annette in the driver's seat and started the car. Gerta blew through her nose then relaxed as Sigmund readied the reins.

Beatrice engaged the clutch and smoothly shifted into gear. The big Mercedes crept past Sigmund. Louis waved as Sigmund gently prodded Gerta, leading the rattling cart. Everett watched nervously until both the cart and the horse disappeared behind them.

"Just when Sigmund thinks he has cleared danger from the Reserve Trench - he finds more, especially in the spring when the frost brings them up," Beatrice said.

"You would think he would rich by now," Everett said. Beatrice just shook her head.

"Make it go fast," Louis said.

Beatrice, without checking with Annette, downshifted and with a big burst of black smoke, gained speed. Wind unfurled Beatrice's hair. Annette grimaced as though she in were in charge of a busload of restless children.

"Yes, Sister Beatrice. Yes! I like it when you drive," Louis said, begging Everett to hoist him high. "We are in your hands - angel's hands - we can really fly now!"

The car barreled along Rue Gambetta, shooting through a tunnel of trees. To the east, the woods went deep and dark as they disappeared into the foothills of the Vosges. Along the west side of the road, a small bare plot of land lay covered with dull colored leaves, brightened only by the low light of the late afternoon sun, untouched maybe since being plowed in the fall.

Annette complained to Beatrice that Philippe had lost his temper last month with a farm hand and now he had to do the spring planting alone. Beatrice stopped the car along the small patch. Annette frowned at their little garden.

"Annette, I know you are worried that there is not enough money," Beatrice said. "Philippe's few paintings and disability check may not be enough, even with Madame Lambert returning to nurse the wounded in Strasbourg - perhaps I can find work at the hospital in Ville Negre."

Everett was about to mention that he had money, but then he recalled how the conductor refused his help.

"That is utterly impossible in Ville Negre," Annette said. "We can manage. Philippe can still hunt and fish."

"But Father never brings anything home," Louis said.

"Where is your respect, Louis?" Annette snapped.

The Mercedes roared as Beatrice double-clutched, ending the squabble. She accelerated smoothly down Rue Gambetta.

Beyond the young trees in the dark valleys along the road, green moss and ivy covered smooth snowdrift forms of eroded craters and trench works. On the backside of the hill, the curvature increased, as Everett expected, so that cannon fire would have passed harmlessly overhead - only an airplane, balloon or that lucky artillery round might have a chance of hitting what they were aiming for – the tuilerie.

Beatrice turned from Rue Gambetta onto a narrow lane that led past a small circular pond with a short tongue of a dock.

"Lac Noir!" Louis pointed out. "Father's quiet place."

"A swimming hole?" Everett said.

"We cannot swim there," Louis said grim-faced and sullen.

Beatrice turned to the backseat to explain.

"Lac Noir is filled with unexploded shells," she said as she slowed the car. "You see, long ago, there was nowhere for Sigmund to dispose of the munitions he cleared, only Lac Noir. He rolled them into its depths for over thirty years. Madame Lambert shared Évariste's pension with Sigmund until the Army established the depot at the end of the last war, then he could make some money."

"Father swims there sometimes, late at night," Louis said.

"You must not get into the water, Louis," Beatrice said.

A long red-roofed brick building appeared in a clearing.

"We are home!" Beatrice said. As they continued the short drive up the lane, she apologized for its dilapidated state.

The huge tuilerie, she said, was built centuries ago with its soaring tiled roof, chimneys, and generous overhangs for winter snow. It was divided into two parts. One part, now empty, was for working the furnaces and the other part was for the owners, the Lambert family, to live. The brick and stone tuilerie crouched like a toad near the woods, only slightly wounded by war, a chip here and a hole there. The Mercedes coasted to the edge of a simple stone patio.

Everett looked back towards the front line of battle they had crossed. He wondered at what point a platoon, maybe with his father, returning at night, might begin to hear the band playing. At the edge of the road? By Lake Noir? Could they hear them from the tuilerie, where, in 1918, his father and the other officers billeted? Where did the band billet? The tuilerie was large, but not big enough for twenty-six young men and their instruments. The place looked now like it must have then - rundown.

Everett turned around, startled by the tapping of Annette's fingers on his knee.

"Welcome to the famous Lambert tuilerie, known throughout Lorraine and Alsace for its tile," Annette said, as they all climbed out. "Until Évariste decided to paint his life away."

"Annette," Beatrice said, walking towards the tuilerie with Louis close to her side, "you know very well that Louis' Grandfather, Évariste, was a communist *and* an artist."

"He was more than that," Annette said, walking behind them, "the Lambert men have this irresistible, instinctive urge to thrust their arms to the sky, only to lose them. Sister Beatrice, show our guest inside. I will wait by Lac Noir. May I take some of your ointment for Philippe?"

"I have given it to Sigmund," Beatrice said.

A concerned frown wrinkled Louis' smooth face as Annette walked away.

"Sister Beatrice, am I to lose my arm like Father one day? His arm must hurt like Gerta's hoof."

"No, Louis. You have a perfectly good arm and the ointment is not for Philippe's arm," Beatrice smothered Louis in a reassuring hug as Everett walked ahead to the tuilerie's door. He pondered how Annette might satisfy a man who lost his testicles.

He waited beneath a glass awning that covered a simple step to the tuilerie. There, next to the door where one might expect to see a house numeral was a placard with a red arrow pointing downwards. Beneath the placard and lodged against the porch, lay a big artillery shell, fused like the ones in Sigmund's cart – but much larger. This one had a name, "Chesterfield", painted in yellow on its side. Globules of water from the roof splashed against its fuse.

Everett reeled backwards in panic, bumping into Beatrice and Louis who just then skipped up to the step.

"Are you feeling ill?" Beatrice asked, as Louis slapped the shell's nose.

"No," Everett said. "Louis should be careful though."

"Louis," Beatrice said. "I have been gone for only a month and already you have picked up that old habit. Even Sigmund, thinks Chesterfield is still too dangerous to touch."

"It is for luck," Louis said. "Grand-père Lambert ran out without slapping it. "Évariste", they say, still stands in the Zone Rouge, like a zombie."

"When Philippe was a young boy attending school in Ville Negre," Beatrice bent to Louis' face, "the other children teased him with nearly the same story about your Grand-père Evariste. It is one of the many reasons we educated you ourselves. Where did you hear it?"

Louis shuffled his feet.

"In Ville Negre."

"What were you doing there?" Beatrice asked.

"Mother went shopping for a new dress when she learned Monsieur Taylor was coming," Louis said. "I was bored and went outside looking for hard rock candy."

"I am surprised Philippe had enough money," Beatrice said.

"Mother was only looking, and so was I."

"Someone in Ville Negre told you the legend of Évariste?"

Louis turned away. Beatrice spun him around, gently.

"Madame Chauchat. She tried frightening me with the story," Louis said.

"Why?"

"I," Louis stammered, "I took some of her candy."

"It was wrong," Beatrice said, "but, Annette should be more careful in Ville Negre and you do know there is no such thing as a zombie. Évariste Lambert is not walking dead in the Zone Rouge."

"I know," Louis said. "But I wish Grand-père Lambert might have stayed home, Sister Beatrice, like General Sigmund, or like Chesterfield here, who looks rather content on the porch, does he not?"

"Yes, Louis. Everything would have been different in Lorraine, minus that one legend."

Beatrice moved Louis through the door with a gentle push while Everett stooped down to examine the giant shell.

"According to Madame Lambert, Évariste was finishing a painting when Chesterfield fell at the doorstep. It was the coup de gras - he had finally had enough, saying he would return to extract the intruder, but he never did after storming the trenches, brandishing the paintbrush."

Everett scraped his shoe on Chesterfield's blunt nose.

"Shells usually go in nose first," Everett said. "It looks like someone tried removing it."

"According to Sigmund, the American's wanted to excise Chesterfield while they first stayed in the tuilerie with Madame and young Philippe. They only managed to invert the shell to examine its fuse before Sigmund told them it was too stubborn. So, Chesterfield stands there with his nose in the air, rather snooty like."

"Chesterfield, that's an odd name for a shell."

"Sigmund called them Chesterfield's after the brand of cigarettes the Americans smoked. I am certain he was exaggerating when he also mentioned that the Americans smoked as many cigarettes as there were unexploded shells lying about. Is it possible they could smoke so many?"

"Sure, but how could Sigmund tell - he was a German on the other side of No-Man's-Land. Was he a deserter?" Everett remembered Philippe calling him a collaborateur, but Everett wouldn't say it to Beatrice.

"Oh, Everett, I thought you knew!" Beatrice said with great surprise. "Sigmund, my Father, like Philippe was a prisoner! Did not your doctor friend tell you? Sigmund was taken in a trench raid by the American's in the Great War."

"No one mentioned Sigmund at all," Everett said.

"Mother must have told your doctor friend," Beatrice said. "Father would certainly know something of this band, although he has never mentioned it."

"Maybe Doc didn't think Sigmund was still alive." Everett passed his hand over the cold, wet nose of the shell and raised enameled lettering, "Chesterfield", feeling much the same as the touch of his father's headstone back in Iowa and Doc Hershey's nameplate on Doc's office desk.

Louis nudged the door open with his shoulder then snatched Everett's bag and tugged at Everett's arm, pulling him inside.

"This is where Grand-mère Lambert sleeps," Louis said, opening a heavy oak door to a large, sparse room.

"It was once filled with a magnificent bed, loveseats and walls of tapestry," Beatrice said. "Mother sold it before the Great War to attend the university while Évariste painted his pottery."

"Philippe and Annette sleep across the hall in Philippe's old bedroom," Beatrice said, leading him out. "I sleep in Évariste's old studio when I return. Louis has this old bedroom, here."

Beatrice pointed to a door. Everett knew it once was hers by the way she fondled the iron doorknob, as though she were about to swing from it again like a child.

"You are to sleep there, Monsieur," Louis said, sliding Everett's bag quickly inside. "I will sleep with Sister Beatrice, like we used to, but first, I am famished."

Beatrice led them into the kitchen where they prepared a plate of cheese, bread, and cold sausage. Louis gorged himself.

"For such a grown-up young man of nine," Beatrice aimed a fork at Louis, "you still eat like the sanglier. After I pour Everett a glass of Riesling, I will take a plate to Lac Noir for Annette and Philippe – if Louis leaves them some."

"I don't care for wine tonight, thank you anyway, Sister Beatrice," Everett said, careful to call her by title in front of Louis and thinking he should keep his wits about himself tonight, sleeping in the tuilerie with Philippe sleeping next to the nearby lake.

He tucked Louis into Beatrice's bed after she left, then, lighting a candle, he walked to the bedroom that was his for the night. In the dim, flickering light, Everett explored the boy's world.

Kites and airplanes dangled from the ceiling, twisting in pirouettes by wind from the open window to the front-line trench and the Vosges. Over the ancient, tattered wallpaper, Louis tacked crude drawings of dragons, warriors and angels. A chalkboard, filled with elementary calculations, hung near his bed. On a bookshelf, lay well-worn books of French grammar, arithmetic, and history. Higher, obviously intended for later studies, were the works of Jules Verne and Mark Twain. As Everett opened them, brittle, pressed leaves fell, having marked pages of illustrations, all in a boy's room much like his own. Enough to keep a nine-year boy content for three or four years.

A splash came from Lac Noir, followed by Annette's pleading for Philippe to resurface. Everett turned an ear to the voices.

"There is nothing more you can do, Annette, until Mother returns," Beatrice said, her voice carrying clear on the slight wind from Lac Noir. "The opium is in the trunk if Philippe really needs it after he finishes his midnight swim."

A few minutes later Beatrice returned with a little knock on Everett's door.

"I'm here by the window," Everett said in the dark room.

Curtains ballooned from the open window as, together, they watched the moon pass behind clouds forming over the Zone Rouge. Everett felt her arm wrap around his waist. She sighed as Philippe pulled himself up to the dock and flapped himself dry, like a dog.

"All quiet on the Western Front?" Everett asked, standing at her side. She put her fingers to his lips and tilted her head to his shoulders. She swayed against Everett's hip to the wave of curtains for minutes until they heard the squeak of the Mercedes' trunk and the scrape of Philippe's hand searching the back for Everett's bag and the opium. The trunk lid slammed shut. Everett leaned out the window. He felt Beatrice's tug to return to their subtle dance.

An hour could have passed, Everett thought, but it was only a few minutes before campfire light and laughter rolled from Lac Noir. Everett shook as flames stretched to the sky, carrying light embers, floating in glowing sparks.

"What is it Everett?"

"Is he burning my father's letters?"

"Dear, no," Beatrice said. "Your bag is there by the door, where Louis put it. Besides, your letters are from Lorraine. My brother would never destroy anything from Lorraine even if it were to get his pipe going."

She kissed Everett politely on both cheeks.

"I have never had a more wonderful time returning home, Everett," Beatrice said.

"You're joking."

"I am not."

"I think I might sleep very soundly tonight," Everett said.

"I trust you will," Beatrice softly as she was about to close the door. "For you may very well be sleeping in the same room as your father once did."

◆　◆　◆

A crack of thunder. He raised his head slightly, waiting for the rain. The smell of pine seeped from the window after another crack. He shook before rising to his elbows. The door to his room creaked. He thought Philippe might have looked in on him just then, but there was a hint of vanilla in the air.

ॐ 5 ॐ
Three Legs

"Your orders, Sir?" The sentry asked rather casually. The sentries this far north were more curious than official, Everett guessed, wondering what they had done to deserve such a duty.

"Orders?" Everett said, "Since when does one need credentials to enter hell?"

He prepared an excuse for not having them as he tapped his rear pocket with feigned ignorance, but the papers were right there, as though a tour guide had planted them before he left.

"Captain Taylor, sir. It says you're going up north of Yangu to help with the identifications. You won't be able to drive the Jeep all the way in, the streets are all - well you've seen it from the air. The big rigs can hardly even get through after all the weeks of bombing and now this napalm stench. I should radio in for someone to escort you through."

"I think I'll be all right, soldier. I know the area, but I'll take this along if you think I need it." Everett reached into the back seat for a carbine.

"You won't need that," the sentry said, "it's mostly all dead down there. Besides, you're one lucky bastard."

The sentry turned and pointed his rifle behind him to a sign at the entrance to the back road Everett had been driving, "Danger - Dragon Eggs ahead!"

"I'd keep your helmet on though," the sentry said, pointing to the two holes in his own, "still a few snipers."

The sentry stuck his small finger inside one, twisting it, like clearing his ear. He saluted then waved Everett on with a paintbrush in his hand.

He drove into the ruts of the main road behind a truck carrying young troops of the Republic of Korea. The road would take the fresh ROK troops to the east, past Yangu and head north where the fighting had moved. If it were not for their round and bewildered faces, he thought they could have been a high school senior football team, all helmeted up and put on a school bus to play the game of their lives.

Everett watched their heads pivot in unison as the truck made a turn above the river. He knew he had come to the spot where he pictured Huan fishing – in her own Shangri-la. Thick plumes of black smoke billowed from below where a bridge had been and from the river valley beyond.

◆　◆　◆

In the low morning light, the tuilerie showed its age with small cracks opening in the ceiling. Everett brushed away small bits of plaster from his bedspread. He walked to the window, not square in its frame. Outside, morning fog lay unstirred on the surface of Lac Noir, a distant fire smoldered near where Philippe slept.

The floorboards in the hallway groaned. Louis whimpered at the door.

"Did I wake you, Monsieur Taylor?"

"No, I've been up for a minute. What's troubling you?"

"Gerta did not come home last night," Louis sniffled. "She usually sleeps outside, beneath your window. I think she is out there dead in the trench."

"But Sigmund made that trench safe."

"Did you not hear the explosion? It came from beyond the General's trench, from the front-line trench, deep in the Zone Rouge."

"That was the horse last night?" Everett thought of the thunder that woke him, but it could have been something worse.

"Yes, poor Gerta," Louis shook his head. "Father sleeps by Lac Noir while Gerta is laying about in pieces - like our neighbor's cow last year - blasted by a seventy-five millimeter shell when she found her way into General Sigmund's trench and wandered through that gate that Father left open again. There are thousands of dragon eggs on the other side. Even General Sigmund does not walk far past the gates."

"I'm so sorry." Everett said as he was unsure how to measure Louis' delusion. "You must care a lot for Gerta."

"I change her boot every night after she comes home from General Sigmund's. I make a dry straw bed for her. I comb her hair. I bring her water and oats. Now she is gone. We cannot even go out to find her parts. They will lay out there for the ravens."

Louis began to cry.

"Now, now Louis, that was only thunder last night. What are these gates exactly?" Everett lifted Louis' chin gently with his knuckles.

"From General Sigmund's trench, there are two smaller trenches, called communication trenches," Louis said. "They lead into the Zone Rouge - to the front line. To keep everyone out, General Sigmund built a gate at each one long ago. Father calls them the gates to hell."

"Louis, that's just an expression."

"I know what Father means, Monsieur. You see, now in the spring, the bombs rise up from the ground like turnips. The gates separate our gardens from hell, where there is only iron to harvest."

"Why would your father want to take a single step past the gate?" Everett asked. "After all, he lost his hand and Gerta her hoof to a grenade out there."

"To search for Grand-père Évariste," Louis said.

"Did you ever want to open the gate, Louis?" Everett asked.

"I unlatched it only once," Louis said. "I will never do that again. I was afraid."

"Your father must have a great deal of courage," Everett said.

"Only when he smokes the opium does Father become strong," Louis said. "I follow him from a distance, but he is never strong enough for more than two steps past the gate into the communication trench. He shakes then runs, leaving the gate open. Will you need to smoke to pass the gate, Monsieur?"

Everett shivered at the thought that Louis also was part of Doc's plan. Yet, when he considered the letters, he knew he might need to summon, if not courage, at least spirits of the dead in whatever form they presented themselves.

"Why do you think I need to enter?" Everett asked.

"You are a jet pilot," Louis said, "a dragon slayer – and it is where dragons live."

"Maybe I need to smoke like Philippe then," Everett said, now looking for a way to change the subject. "Is Sister Beatrice awake yet?"

"No, Monsieur," Louis said. "She hardly stirred once during the night, even when Gerta's bomb detonated - I have never seen her so exhausted. She snores like my poor Gerta once did."

"I think if Gerta were in trouble, Sister Beatrice wouldn't sleep at all," Everett said, turning his nose towards the kitchen.

"That is true," Louis said.

"I smell bread rising," Everett sniffed yeast-laden air. "Do you know how to start the oven, Louis?"

"Of course. I see already, Monsieur - we think alike. We will make Sister Beatrice a grand breakfast for when she wakes. She likes her bread toasted with a thick slab of butter to the side. She dips it into her coffee, then she likes..."

"Let's take it a step at a time, OK?

"OK, a step at a time."

Louis tended the fire in the oven until its coals died down enough to set the bread inside.

"It will be another hour, Monsieur," Louis said, as his eyelids fell like slow drips of a faucet. "I am so tired from worrying about Gerta."

"Why don't you go back to sleep," Everett said. "Beatrice - I mean Sister Beatrice, will be wondering where you were."

Louis yawned. Everett guided Louis, yawning and shuffling in his slippers, back to bed. Beatrice still snored soundly and Louis snuggled next to her and closed his eyes. Everett shut their door quietly. Down the hallway, Philippe and Annette's bedroom door, still open, reminded him that he hadn't heard them return from Lac Noir last night during the storm.

He walked outside onto the porch. A fat drop of water from the roof splattered against Chesterfield's nose. Everett put his ear to the cold metal, listening for movement as a mother might wait for the kick of an unborn child, before he realized how stupid that was. He backed away from the porch, wondering how a family could possibly sleep in the company of Chesterfield, their steadfast guard of dubious allegiance.

He stepped beneath his window to find Gerta's bed of dry un-matted straw, protected by the roof's enormous eave. A hint of a smoldering campfire from Lac Noir filled his nose. Crossing a small log bridge, Everett walked a cow's path through tall grass, sprinkled with dew - not rain. To the east, the sun lay low over Zone Rouge. He found himself looking for alerions, the fictitious little eagles, circling the remains of a three-legged mare. A moan broke the silence, then a sigh.

Near the small dock, a campfire blinked its last ember. Philippe and Annette lay in a heap of blankets against a thin oak. Philippe, with eyes closed, locked his pipe in his metal hand. Annette lifted her head from his chest as the dark water of Lac Noir, boiled for a moment. Flies and moths flittered at its surface. Philippe's pipe clunked against the tree as he tried standing. Annette caressed his face and cooed in his ear until his head slumped forward at the neck. She glanced, sleepy-eyed, to Everett as she fell asleep.

Everett choked as he turned away, knowing it was the sort of love that Huan and he hadn't the time to build together. He followed the narrowing path past Lake Noir, leading into low hills whose slender fir trees carried the warning signs - "Non Interdit".

The negligee of thin woods, attempting to hide the Zone Rouge, instead, attracted him. The low sun floated above the fog-filled and devastated land beyond the bar of trees and warning signs. Beneath the mist, layering the Zone Rouge, an animal ranted, not with the snort of maimed horse, nor the growl of a dog, but a grunt - the grunt of a horned beast.

Everett held his breath as he fled down the path, past Lac Noir. Philippe and Annette must have heard it too, Everett thought as he stepped quickly past the tree where they had slept - the blankets were gone, but the fire still smoldered.

Everett quieted his breathing as he came to the tuilerie, whose brick face basked in gold from the morning light passing over the Vosges. Chimney smoke curled upwards. Chesterfield greeted him at the porch.

Outside, Everett leaned beneath the kitchen window to relax but then heard a rummaging inside. Standing on his toes, he found Louis in the kitchen, reaching for some jars on a high shelf above the icebox.

Pulling down a jar, labeled Café, Louis lifted the lid. "Ahh," Louis sniffed.

Everett waited outside, relieved on one hand, that Louis could simply put Gerta out of his mind while making coffee, but distressed on the other when he considered Gerta's fate.

He stepped inside, past the pile of blankets near Philippe's closed bedroom door, to Beatrice's bedroom. Thinking it might be wise to warn Beatrice first about Gerta's demise and the awful sound from the Zone Rouge, he raised his hand to knock. Louis stopped him.

"Shhh. Sister Beatrice is still asleep," Louis whispered as he dragged Everett to the kitchen to prepare the coffee. "Can you reach Sister Beatrice's special cup, it is on that shelf - always too high for me to reach."

Everett stood on a chair and reached into the dark recess of the shelf for a cup. Instead, he felt a smooth leather pouch - with something heavy inside. As he pulled it out, it slipped and fell to the ground with a heavy thud. A pistol slid from a shoulder holster. Everett held the Lugar in his hands. German-made, he wondered how Philippe could stand to hold it, having possibly had it pressed to his temple by a prison guard.

"Have you never seen a Lugar before?" a voice behind him said sweetly.

"Sure," Everett said. "Why does Philippe keep it?"

Everett turned about on the floor, glimpsing her slender, smooth legs and felt the bottom edge of her knee-length morning coat rub across his brow. As he stood, a scent of woman's powder filled his nose. He sneezed.

Beatrice took a step back, gave little a laugh then bent slightly to receive the pistol from Everett. She wore nothing but the coat.

"It is not Philippe's pistol - it is mine," Beatrice said as Everett handed it to her, "It was given to me for protection. I am quite a good marksman."

She checked the cocking action of the pistol, aimed it at a leaking wooden bucket near the door then slipped it back into its holster.

"A nun with a gun," Everett laughed inwardly.

"Can you please put it back before Louis sees it?" Beatrice whispered while slipping the gun into Everett's hand to set back, out of Louis' view.

"Can you reach that cup on the shelf," Beatrice said after Everett slid the gun in the holster. "And be careful, Évariste painted it. Philippe would hate to see it broken."

He carefully handed her the cup as he stepped down.

"Is that bread I smell?" She asked.

"Yes, Sister," Louis said. "It is nearly ready."

"Why are you up so early, Louis? I turned to hug you in bed and you were gone."

Louis nodded to Everett then told her about the thunderous sound in the night, thinking Philippe had left a gate to hell open for Gerta to stumble past.

Everett stepped to the bedroom window to look.

"Is she there in her bed?" Beatrice asked.

"Not yet," Everett nodded nonchalantly, not wanting to alarm anyone.

"Gerta probably spent the night with Sigmund," Beatrice yawned. "Philippe, when he is ill, makes her nervous."

"While you slept, we baked bread," Louis said.

"It smells so good," Beatrice arched her nose.

Everett laughed as Louis, with eyes closed, stalked the smell of warming bread on the table, sniffing like a hound with his nose angled slightly like Beatrice's. Everett thought of Madame Lambert as he turned to Beatrice, interpolating her elegant nose with age.

Louis stared cross-eyed at the bread near his nose.

"Do you see something?" Beatrice said to Louis, smiling at Everett.

"A mirage, I always look for mirages on the hot bread. I pretend I am lost on a sandy Algerian desert, looking for an oasis. Have you ever seen a real oasis, Monsieur?"

"I don't think so, Louis,"

"Now, Louis, you do this each time I come to visit. Tell Mr. Taylor what you would like to find on your oasis."

"I wish it to be big," Louis said, as his eyes swelled. "Big and safe so I can run in its sand with no shoes. I want it to have lots of cool, clear water in a big lake, so I can drink it and dive deep into it while I hold my breath."

Louis stabbed a simple triangular kite into the butter with a table knife. He spoke in a quieter, more serious voice.

"And when I get there, I want to ride Gerta every morning. I want to hang from a big kite high above her saddle, so I can see that all is well. But she is not coming back."

Louis ran from the table to put his chin to the window.

"Take a plate of bread to your mother and father, I heard them come in, just before Everett returned," Beatrice said, then trying to cheer Louis, "and some lumps of sugar for Gerta, she always returns."

"It was not thunder," Louis said as he disappeared down the hall with the plate.

Everett rose after pouring Beatrice a cup of coffee.

"Where are you going?" Beatrice asked.

"I should check up on Gerta," Everett said. "I think Philippe did leave that gate open last night. Louis is right. It wasn't thunder. It didn't rain at all. I don't want him to find her all. . ."

"Heat lightning, Thor's hammer, another accident at the depot, an impatient shell," Beatrice said calmly. "It happens all the time. I would rather you stay here by me. Gerta is too smart to wander into the Zone Rouge."

Beatrice pointed her coffee cup to Lac Noir. She rocked back and forth with the coffee in her hand, then looking about the tuilerie with disappointment before bringing her attention back to the cup she held.

"This cup is special to me." She held it up, handing it to him to drink.

At first, it looked like an ordinary china cup made on an assembly-line, but then Everett noticed the handle seemed bent, ever so slightly, to one side and the rim varied in thickness almost imperceptibly. A machine would have sacrificed the cup's handmade character for the sake of these imperfections. Along its side was an enameled winter landscape of the snow-covered Vosges, near sunset. Before the snow-laden pines, ran an unfrozen stream where a deer bent its long neck into the water to drink. He ran his thumb across the raised enamel.

"It's too fine to drink from," Everett said, handing it back.

"This is one of two," she said, lifting it to take a drink.

"Philippe's father fired the bare cup when this was a working tuilerie. His father painted this one, Philippe painted the other as a gift for me."

Beatrice gazed lovingly at the little cup.

"Someday this will be Louis' cup."

"If it doesn't break," Everett laughed.

"It had better not," Beatrice set it down carefully.

"She's alive!" Louis's voice cut through the silence from Lac Noir.

A clop of hoofs came up the lane.

Gerta sauntered up to them at the patio.

"Why, Gerta!" Beatrice said.

Gerta raised her hoof to a rock. Her boot strings had come undone. It seemed she wanted to make it easier for Beatrice to tie.

"Dear Gerta, if you only had wings," Beatrice said lovingly to the horse after snugging up the boot. She slapped her rear tenderly, sending Gerta to her straw bed.

"Poor Gerta," Louis said looking back out across the road. "She did not take General Sigmund's trench back home last night; I think because Father left the gate open. She followed Rue Gambetta all the way from the General's deep dugout. It was a long walk."

"I'll massage her foot then," Beatrice said, turning to the tuilerie for her purse and the ointment.

Annette burst onto the porch.

"The drug is wearing off and I have tried everything," Annette said, helplessly. "If only Madame Lambert were here. Now we can only give him his cold bath."

She asked Louis to begin bringing water from Lake Noir for Philippe's bath.

"Again?" Louis complained. Annette scolded him.

"We must calm Philippe in a cold bath all day," she said. "It is all we can do until Madame Lambert arrives."

"I'll help you, Louis," Everett said as he followed Louis towards Lac Noir.

"You are our guest," Louis said.

"I'm your friend."

"I do not want you to see my father like this."

"Philippe would have done the same for me," Everett said.

"You did not lose your hand, Monsieur."

"It's not the hand, Louis."

"I know, Father has no Couilles!"

"He's lost more than his testicles, they've taken his heart," Everett gulped, not wanting to say more to a nine year-old, but Louis's eyes were deep into his own. "It makes him so ..."

"Mad? I want to talk about something else," Louis said.

"All right," Everett let him take his time.

"What was the color of your jet?" Louis stepped ahead of Everett towards the lake.

"Mostly silver, to reflect the sky, but its nose was painted with our sweetheart's names."

"What was painted on your nose?"

"Miss Linda," Everett said, regretting that he lacked the courage to paint Huan's name.

"I have a drawing book full of planes of my design," Louis said as they came to the dock. "I will show you, but I have no jets. It is true that a jet has no propeller, like a boat with no screw?"

"Yes, but it's much different. Do you know how your head moves back when you sneeze? A jet sneezes faster than the beat of a hummingbird's wing, but a jet needs air the same as a propeller does. Jets need to breathe very deeply and quickly."

"Which do you prefer, Monsieur, the sneeze or the propeller?"

"It doesn't matter, Louis. Either one must have a wing that will lift you high in the air."

"Your wings looked like that?" Louis pointed to a hawk circling above the water with its head swiveling to keep its eyes fixed on the two of them at the dock.

A melon-sized bubble broke the water's glass surface a few feet from the dock and the hawk swept its wings back and dove fast to the spot.

"Yes, just like that. You know your jets," Everett said.

"Tre beau!" Louis said as the hawk pitched up at the last second with empty talons.

"We must have spooked him," Everett said.

Everett dipped the bucket into the dark water of Lac Noir. The sun flashed across something large and golden at the bottom and then went dark. Everett nearly dropped the bucket.

"Lac Noir spooked the hawk," Louis said. "We must return for Father's bath, later I can show you my airplanes."

Everett lugged the bucket, glad to leave Lac Noir, as Louis drew his little arms back like a jet, marauding back and forth along the path to the tuilerie and falling behind. At the tuilerie's porch, the bucket strained Everett's arm.

He stared at the big shell, named Chesterfield, stuck against the porch, and wondered if the slanted and perfect words, like those in the letters, were his father's handwriting.

"You do not need to ask his permission," Louis said as he directed Everett inside.

The tart smell of opium filled the hallway. They came to a room at the rear of the tuilerie. Everett expected to hear wild thrashing and wailing from the other side of the door. Philippe's orgasmic tone of pleasure resonated behind the thin door, rhythmically accompanied by the squeak of a pair of rocking chairs.

"Father is smoking more than usual," Louis said.

"Some men prefer their agony in privacy or at least with family and friends. I'll wait here, you take the bucket in."

"It may be some time. Father likes to talk when he's smoked this much, but it is only nonsense."

"Listen to him, even if it is," Everett said in a hush. "I'll wait here a minute, just in case he's upset."

A chair stopped its squeaking.

"Everett?" Beatrice asked.

Everett opened the door to find Beatrice and Annette sitting in rocking chairs on either side of the tub, facing the window. Beatrice held the pipe to Philippe's lips as he turned around to the door with dark sunken eyes. Everett quickly turned his head. Louis passed in front of him splashing water on the floor as he dragged the heavy bucket.

"Louis, set it beside his tub," Beatrice said. "Madame Lambert will be here soon. Is Everett there?"

"Why does the Américain not bring the bucket in?" Philippe droned after Beatrice pulled the pipe from his mouth.

Everett listened outside the door.

"He says a man prefers his agony in private," Louis said.

"I am not the one in agony," Philippe laughed as he reached for the pipe in Beatrice's hand. "He is the one in agony. That is why he is out there alone. Come sit here, young man. I took a step past the gate today. I want to tell you the story of Évariste, your grandfather."

"I have heard it many times, Father," Louis said.

Everett felt his throat constrict, watching Louis lug the bucket to the tub.

"But tell me again." Louis said. He hoisted the heavy bucket and carefully dribbled water to Philippe's toes, "if it makes you feel better, Father."

A threat of tears forced Everett quietly into Louis' bedroom, next door.

He found Louis' notebook at the desk, plump with drawings. He turned to the first page - a sketch of stick people in front of mountains - Annette in an apron, Philippe with a pencil in his hand and Beatrice in her habit with a halo above her head - she held Louis' hand.

He flipped past a few more pages to a drawing of a mechanical contraption with levers, gauges and dials next to a chair with straps and belts. There, a child-like cartoon pilot controlled pulleys, gears and a big pot of boiling steam that shot a thin cloud of steam to push up on a tablecloth tied to the machine to lift it up. Everett opened pages upon pages, filled with variations of the machine along with labels detailing the design and its intended operational features. It didn't surprise him that a young boy, left to his own devices, would dream of flying machines.

The door opened and Louis bounded to Everett's side to pull the book down to his lap. He turned back to the first page.

"Father helped me draw this first one when I was young," Louis said. "He wanted me to draw people, animals, land and the sky. Why would he want me to draw such obvious things?"

Louis leafed through his sketches of airplanes, describing how one year, a design seemed perfect and the next year he discovered flaws and solved each of them one by one.

"You would make a good engineer, Louis," Everett said.

"I would?" Louis could hardly contain his excitement as he turned to the blank pages in the back. "Now, draw the planes you like the best."

Everett sketched the silver wings of his F86 jet, but a thought occurred to him that Louis needed something simpler to understand. From scant memory, he quickly sketched a bi-winged plane of the Great War, pointing out the tail and the rudder that controlled its turn, the ailerons and its stick that controlled pitch and roll, and finally its engine, throttle, propeller and pair of wings.

"Show me what lifts the wings," Louis asked.

"It's an invisible force," Everett said, "I could try to explain, but sometimes even I am astounded by it. Maybe someday you can explain this invisible lifting force better to me."

"Could you make the plane pirouette over and over?"

"Roll's are tricky with the bi-plane - but the jet, that's different," Everett said, twisting his hand to mimic the maneuver. "That F86 - I could roll it all day long!"

"Can you draw your F86 jet?"

Everett took his time sketching, recalling its details and ignoring its deadly cargo.

"No propeller," Louis said. "Incredible!"

"The jet engine's inside the fuselage," he said pointing to what he drew, "behind the air intake here on the nose."

"Was it fast?"

"Almost as fast as sound itself."

"Tres beau!" Louis shouted. "Show me what it could do."

For hours it seemed, Everett twisted and turned his hand and dove while Louis chased him in another jet, pretending to shoot him down. They flew missions over mountains of furniture and Louis' unmade bed, where he conjured river valleys and forests near the Taebeck Mountains. They filled the room with the clamor of roaring guns. He felt happy there in Louis' little room.

"Did your jet, this F86, did it push you back in the seat, like the Mercedes does when Father races it?"

"Especially in a climb, Louis. That's when you wonder, who's stronger
- you or the jet."

"It must be loud inside a jet," Louis said.

"I wear my headgear with the radio and my mask, it's peaceful and the
sky turns darker and quieter the higher I climb."

"You wore a mask? Were you afraid of gas?"

"It carried oxygen. The high air is thin and cold."

"This jet you drew, the F86," Louis said, "the nose looks like a shark
and behind it, the holes look like gills."

"Machine guns, three on each side, and what recoil a fifty caliber
bullet this size makes!" Everett held up his small finger.

"Yes, recoil - it is the bullet pushing back with a certain force against
your hand," Louis said. "I have used the Lugar before."

"The enemy loved their cannons, but we loved our guns," Everett said.
"I could make the whole jet shake when I blasted away with all six."

"The enemy mounted cannons onto their planes?" Louis asked.

"They were tiny shells, not like Chesterfield, but if one hit, you have
to jettison."

"What do you mean, jettison?"

"You call on the radio, flip the safe and arm switches by the seat, wait
for the canopy to blow off, and squeeze the jettison trigger. Then it's like
you've been bucked from a wild horse and you watch it running away as
you slowly fall to earth."

"You must have a parasol."

"The parachute?

Louis nodded, his eyes swelled with awe.

"It opens automatically," Everett said. "But the big white parasol
shows the enemy exactly where you are. Unless a helicopter rescues you,
you're a prisoner."

"Have you ever done this jettison?"

"No."

"You have never been a prisoner?"

"No, but I lost a good wingman once."

"Is a wingman like a Valkyrie?"

"No, he's just a pilot who watches over you so you can fight without
being afraid of getting hurt."

"Who watches over your wingman?"

"Nobody."

"You must feel sad to lose your friend."

"But my friend loved flying as much as I did, and flying that F86 was like flying one of your own creations in that drawing book. Flying is the exact opposite of being a prisoner."

"I wish Father could fly," Louis said as Beatrice and Annette led Philippe to bed. "Instead, he looks for his father. He needs this hidden force, called lift. When was this lifting the greatest, Monsieur?"

"When I flipped a little switch that released my ton of bombs, I would become briefly weightless and free."

Everett watched Louis' mouth drop open - to be weightless, lifted by a hidden force. He may as well have given Louis a drug. Soon Louis' eyes drooped with his head bobbing at the edge of consciousness. Everett carried him beside Beatrice, who glanced up from a deep snore to smile before dropping back to her pillow.

Everett lay in his room with the thought of Philippe, perpetually expecting his doses from Indochina, and for Madame Lambert to administer her therapy. In a way, he felt relieved that Madame would have no time to work on himself, as he suspected Doc Hershey had intended. Madame too would have no time to tell him of the band or of his father. He would have worried all night if it weren't for Gerta, munching her oats beneath his window, and Beatrice and Louis snoring in the next room, all easing him into a deep sleep.

✄6✄

Philippe

Aman in a jeep approaches a village that, in the sunset, should be water-colored in golden hues. He stops at the hilltop to watch the river snake through the smoking hamlet. He reels at a stench. Above, rise towering plumes of pungent black smoke, burning as an eternal flame. Beneath the hellish cloud lay the remains of the hamlet. Once flowing in the radiant colors of its gowns and enameled wood, it is now a white, gray moonscape, textured with swimming pool-sized pockmarks from bombs. Each home seems to have one recently installed in its backyard.

He drives down to the village, but the contour of the ground is so wild that he's lost in its own knots. Leaving the Jeep, it's quiet, except for the snapping of fires every now and then. He's drawn to the intermittent darkness, to the hamlet's depth he thought he once knew.

In his jet, it would flick by as quickly as a small village would if he were traveling by train. Here, there was not a single feature he could recall, only the gradual feel of the ground sloping to the hamlet's valley. He smells the river and sees it bending, near the backwater, the water's still there – in it, he see's the moon passing behind clouds, but they're not clouds, and it's not even night yet - it's smoke, black and sooty.

The air is thick with decay - thicker by the river where he walks. It's hot. Rats scurry back to the water's edge. He bows and pukes, to no relief. He thirsts and walks carefully down to the backwater, a drink from the water of last year's snowmelt from the Taebeck's would cool him but there's quicksand.

It should be fresh and cool, but fumes of fuel oil, burnt napalm and flesh permeate the air. There's water at his feet, not too cold, in the shallows. Beaver lounge on their backs, not far away, in the rivers current. As they drift past by, he sees they're corpses, covered in a slick of oil that's been holding them together.

He reaches for one at the end of the dock - smallish, a young ROK, probably home on leave, probably drunk. He lifts him up to clean the dark slick from his face. He's light. He's cut off at the waist. Those dark, wide and lifeless eyes stares back as he eases him back into the water. His friend Bender would wonder if he's been baptized. Maybe this was it.

He walks up from the darkness of the river valley to the last of the sun reflecting from the highest peak of the Taebeck's to the east. It is the only thing golden he has seen all day.

After an hour, it's absolutely dark. The moon stays stuck behind thick black clouds. The only light is the flicker of a low blue flame swirling at his feet. A drum of heating oil lays upended and drips blue darts of flames into a pool.

He soaks a broom for a minute in this oil, waiting for a small flame that's been randomly moving about, to return. When it comes, he ignites his broom-torch, but the light only shows the extent of darkness as it crackles, burning the hair on his hand to search. It is all he can do.

◆ ◆ ◆

A backfire of the Mercedes rang from Everett's open window. A sweet soprano voice soared from the kitchen. It had to be Annette, he thought. If anyone deserved to be that happy this morning, it should be Annette for tending to Philippe through the night. Everett, half-awake, followed the smells of baking bread and brewing coffee to the kitchen, expecting them each morning as much as Philippe depended on his opium. Another backfire shot from the front door.

Everett snuck past the kitchen, where Beatrice and Louis noisily rumpled sections of the newspaper. The Mercedes should be racing its engine by now, he thought. He stubbed his toe on the bench beside the door. As he was about to curse, he found the empty holster - the Lugar was gone. A gun shot again as he bolted, in a sweaty panic, to the kitchen.

Annette paused in her song. Beatrice and Louis looked up from the newspaper, staring at him strangely. Annette continued singing as they continued to read. Everett wondered if he were walking in his sleep.

"Didn't you all hear that? It's Philippe!" Everett said as he ran to the door.

Standing beside Chesterfield, Everett was awestruck that Philippe's family, even Beatrice, the Pasteur's angel of mercy, now seemed so callous and cold as to sit idle, knowing Philippe lay out there with a bullet in his brain. Nothing made sense.

"Laissez-faire," Doctor Hershey would say. "Let it pass."

"What is it, Everett?" Beatrice said.

"He's lying dead out there, past the gates of hell, isn't he?" Everett said.

"Probably so."

"How can you be so matter of fact?"

"Everett, Philippe's father has been dead for a long time."

"I'm not talking about him, I'm talking about Philippe. He's out there bleeding to death."

"What on earth would cause you to say such a horrible thing, Everett?"

"He's taken the Lugar, hasn't he?"

He stood rigid, still not letting her too close, but close enough to feel Beatrice's chest heave slightly. Her arm forced him into her side, soft and warm, the same as when she rested against him on the train.

"Oh, Everett!" Beatrice said. "It is a good sign. Annette has gotten Philippe back into his morning hunting routine. Who knows, perhaps later he will take Louis fishing. Come inside, the bread is ready - you must be famished."

The shot had come from the Zone Rouge, beyond Lac Noir, not the woods behind the tuilerie where Everett might have chosen to hunt squirrel. Beatrice's eyes, green and marbled with slight dark streaks radiating from large bottomless pupils, held him for a moment. He looked straight into one. She blinked so slowly, it felt like a magnificent door opening to welcome him inside.

"Would you like to join them for mass in Ville Negre?" She whispered as she ushered him into the kitchen. "It starts soon and I must change into my habit."

Everett nodded, "No." He was about to remark on the nun masquerade and that the shot came from the Zone Rouge, but then Louis stepped inside the kitchen as she left to dress.

"Maybe your father just might bag some game," Everett said.

"Father has never killed a thing with that little gun." Louis stuffed his mouth with bread.

"Louis, save some for Sister Beatrice," Annette said, as she poured coffee. "You should have more confidence in your father's hunting. He taught you, did he not?"

Louis went silent.

Everett complimented her on Philippe's recovery.

"I have certain charms that arouse him, but only briefly," Annette said, running a finger beneath the shoulder strap of her brassiere. "Madame Lambert resurrects him for longer periods with her special therapy. When she finishes in Strasbourg, perhaps she can spend more time with him."

"I was hoping to get a chance to speak with her," Everett said.

"What is it you wish to know?" Annette said, dangling her shoe from her toe.

"Charms are not enough," Beatrice said as she stood at the door in her habit, so tightly drawn around her face than only her emerald eyes and her long and beautifully crooked nose shown. "For what Everett needs to know, only Madame's Lambert's trance will do."

"Sister Beatrice, why do you never enter the church in Ville Negre?" Louis asked.

"She has her own church, Louis," Annette said with an understanding look to Beatrice. "I have told you before, she goes to Donon for her quiet time, to be alone."

"We will not be long," Beatrice said to Everett as they stepped to the car.

She waved as she maneuvered the big Mercedes away as though she had driven it a thousand times. Everett guessed, after spending all that time in Indochina, packed with people and aboard the Pasteur and its full complement of wounded, that she could use some time, if even a few hours, alone. He thought about how much he liked being alone, but not today – not now. He wanted to be with her on that peak.

"Pop!" Everett stepped towards Lac Noir, where another rang; still not believing that Philippe was hunting. Instead, he imagined Philippe was cursing himself for missing the mark. Everett stood motionless, knowing how upset Philippe must be for needing another shot. A shot to the stomach would have been Everett's first choice.

He waited several minutes- then again, "Pop, Pop," coming from the Zone Rouge. "Pop. Pop. Pop."

"Oh, my God!" Everett imagined how frustrating Philippe's last few minutes on this earth must be, trying to reload - and with that hand.

"Pop."

He raced past the lake, over the bridge, and through a thin line of trees to the Zone Rouge.

Another shot - muffled as though fired into a pillow.

He rushed to the edge of Sigmund's trench where a curl of white gunpowder smoke rose. A squeal. Another shot, deafeningly close.

A sickly wheeze rose from the trench where, Everett guessed, a self-inflicted gunshot finally punctured Philippe's lung after failing several times to hit the stomach, the heart, or the head.

He waited for another, final breath, as it seemed Philippe had found his quiet place at last, but then another wheeze. He inched forward, hoping the Lugar would be empty. It was one thing to kill in wartime, but quite another to kill, even for mercy, in a time of peace - or so he argued to justify his lack of courage.

Everett slid over the slight rise of the parapet, the lip of the trench, into the long deep and dark furrow. Where he expected to find the wire and barbs of his father, his hand felt the short soft grass of spring.

Slipping down, Everett landed on top of something soft. He shrunk in horror that it was Philippe's chest, yielding one final belch and groan. As Everett carefully stepped to the side, he leaned down in the shadow for Philippe. Everett felt hair, mixed with warm blood and the last quivering of a tiny chest.

As his eyes adjusted to the low light, Everett saw he had his hand on the belly of a good-sized pig, which lay dead now on Philippe's chest.

"God almighty - what happened?" Everett said, rolling it off with his foot.

"I thought he was dead," Philippe said, laughing a little. "I intended to heave him over the parapet when the beast stirred to life and pierced my leg with his tusks, you see here?"

Philippe lifted his bloodstained trousers like a slightly wounded matador.

"They are very cunning, Monsieur - in the trench he had me at a disadvantage after I fell. He sat victoriously on my chest and snorted, ready to run his tusks through my throat, but I had three rounds left in the magazine."

"You're lucky you didn't put a slug through your heart, Philippe."

"Luck, Monsieur? No, even though I killed the thing with two shots, he lay so heavy, I could not move. The other bullet was indeed for my heart; otherwise, the bastard's brothers could have arrived and eaten me alive. The only thing left of me would be my own clean white bones, like Father's, out there somewhere. If the boar finds fresh meat, they can run fast and free here in these trenches indefinitely. Can you lift my little friend up onto my shoulder, if you please?"

"I think we should get out of this goddamned trench right now, Philippe - before they come!" Everett's heart thumped so loud he thought Philippe might hear it.

"Are you a coward?"

"I don't like pigs," Everett said. He hoisted the brown, bristle-haired pig and threw it up over the top, then reached back for Philippe.

Philippe first held out his phantom arm to Everett, who reached for it, not quite knowing what to do. Philippe handed Everett the Lugar before letting Everett take hold of his good hand to pull him up.

Everett hoisted Philippe from the trench then Philippe reached down for Everett with his hand to help him up.

"Aren't you going to field dress it first?" Everett asked as Philippe draped the boar across his good shoulder.

"Unlike in your country, Monsieur, here we use everything. For example, the intestines and the blood we use for sausage. Besides, if I were to clean him here, his little cannibal brothers would have his parts for lunch."

Everett helped tilt the boar up across Philippe's back until its hoofs hung limp around Philippe's shoulder. They walked the road in silence, glancing to each other occasionally. Everett caught himself, staring into the boar's lifeless eyes then quickly turned away.

As they strode for Lac Noir, Philippe began whistling. Everett could not believe it was the same man as last night. Philippe paused at the dock.

"I understand you are looking for a band?" Philippe said.

"My father's regimental band from the Great War," Everett said. "Your sister believes they probably died in the Zone Rouge."

"My sister? Beatrice has confided in you a great deal, I see," Philippe said, "but she probably knows no more about this band that I do. Do you really think your father would be so cruel as to send musicians out there?"

Philippe pointed far past Sigmund's nice clean trench towards the Vosges.

"I don't remember much of my father," Everett said.

"You were named for mine," Philippe said, letting the boar sag to the dock's edge.

Everett paused at the thought then followed behind Philippe by a step.

"I'm told Évariste died when you were young," Everett said. "You probably don't remember much either."

"True," Philippe said, cleaning his muddy boot on the boar's hide and tapping his chin with his metal hand as though deep in thought. "However, Mother taught me of Father and the Duello, a code which he lived and died by. You see, my father was named for the French mathematician Évariste Galois. The man, at the young age of twenty, died in a duel over a woman, he had an unloaded pistol. The night before, Évariste Galois created his most beautiful mathematics – in the same way my father finished his painting before charging the enemy with his brush."

Everett considered for a moment that Madame Lambert had planted a subliminal suggestion in Philippe's mind recently to the affect that Évariste was merely a brave man for a painter and that Philippe had embellished the rest while under hypnosis. If Everett couldn't find this band soon without her, Madame Lambert might do the same to him. He liked his truths, plain and free of mind-altering distortion.

"I know you're still searching for him out there," Everett said. "Take me with you. I could help you past that gate."

"Now you must think I am the coward. You need not bother," Philippe said as he lowered the boar into the quiet face of Lac Noir to wash. "Your band is down here, with the remnants of war. I see their instruments, twisted and gnarled, but still with its brass gleaming beneath the water as they sit alongside the shells."

"Do you ever hear them playing?" Everett asked, measuring Philippe's degree of sanity.

"I suppose you think I hear them playing Handel's Water Music," Philippe said then heaved the soggy boar towards Everett. "I suppose too, you think I discovered a whole section of violins and cellos there as well?"

"I'm sorry," Everett said with the boar settling coldly against his foot. "It's just difficult to believe the whole band is at the bottom of Lac Noir, maybe a piece or two, but not the whole band. Did you actually see him bury the band there?"

"As a child," Philippe said, "I watched the old General fill Lac Noir with the metal he cleared from the reserve trench. He cleared it so that he could walk the trench anytime to be with my mother. He told me Lac Noir was haunted by a giant fish and not to swim there."

"But Madame Lambert and Beatrice never mentioned the band at Lac Noir?" Everett nudged the boar away from him with his shoe, towards Philippe. "Maybe you just now decided to create the band for me."

"Mother and Beatrice never swam there." Philippe snared the boar by the leg and hoisted it onto Everett's shoulders. "Now, after a fine dinner at the tuilerie tonight, you will be leaving in the morning – yes?"

"As you wish, Philippe," Everett said, now thinking that room in Ville Negre above the Chauchat's brasserie would serve him better, considering Philip's volatile state, were it not for his concern for Beatrice and even Louis and Annette.

Walking to the tuilerie, Everett let the boar down and dragged it by its leg, not wanting to bloody himself. He felt Philippe's wary eye.

The approaching Mercedes shifted gears.

"They worry for you," Everett said. "They might not worry so much if you let me have that Lugar."

"They like to worry," Philippe said, handing Everett the Lugar before swinging the boar to a butcher's table.

Everett stepped backwards towards the tuilerie with the gun as Philippe raised a cleaver, high over the boar.

"Tell them you have found the band," Philippe said.

"But I haven't, I only have your word for it." Everett took another step. "Besides, I want to know what happened to them. I was hoping Madame Lambert would come soon to tell me."

"Mother will merely tell you what you want to hear." Philippe hacked the pig's head cleanly off. "Now, go tell them we will have boar tonight for your Bon Voyage. They will be surprised."

"Where is Philippe?" Beatrice watched Everett slide the Lugar back into the holster and set it next to the cup on the shelf.

"At the side of the tuilerie, cleaning tonight's meal."

"Father caught that big fish in Lac Noir? It was really there?" Louis asked.

"No, he shot a boar today in Sigmund's trench," Everett said as his mouth mysteriously watered for the taste of fish.

"A piglet must have rooted under a gate," Beatrice said. "Poor little thing."

"Little?" Everett said then shook for a second. "It's the size of a four-year old child!"

"You see, I told you," Louis said. "Father must have left it open."

"Are you cold, Everett?" Beatrice asked as she glanced at the hand he had burned in Marseilles.

"I'm fine," Everett said.

"Triste Américaine," Louis said beneath his breath.

♦ ♦ ♦

Everett knew his French wasn't perfect at dinner that night. Everyone seemed to slow their speech for his benefit. Maybe it was the opium haze hanging in the dining room from Philippe puffing away at his pipe. The dinner wasn't going too well.

Annette reminded Philippe that the boar was tough and needed to soak another day or two in the marinade. Everett briefly considered feigning illness to avoid tasting it.

"Slice it thin and sear it in the pan," Philippe barked as he handed Annette the bottle of the liqueur called, Mirabelle. Philippe demanded they all drink. "I understand Americans like their meat nearly incinerated. Here, use this for your fuel."

Philippe poured Annette a glass for the meat, then made sure the rest of the ether-like Mirabelle circulated around the table. Louis got a spoonful that he tried to spit out, but Philippe insisted he drink it. Everett drank his down, and then secretly took what Louis couldn't drink of the flammable drink. Under its influence, Everett thought, Philippe began speaking from his nose in a way seemingly designed to annoy Everett.

A flash of light and a short scream came from the kitchen as Annette set the boar in flames with the plum liqueur. Everett rose to help, but Beatrice shot him a glance, signaling that it was Philippe's table, his house and his boar after all.

"I think, Monsieur, you would rather have fish, yes?" Louis said.

With that, Philippe abruptly stood, waltzed through the kitchen and out the door. Everett rose to follow him.

"Let him go, Everett," Beatrice said.

A splash soon echoed from Lac Noir. Everett stood again, but Louis grabbed his hand.

"Father is probably wrestling that big fish he says is there," Louis laughed. "Lac Noir has only, Le Gardon, a tiny fish."

"Louis!" Annette snapped from the kitchen. "If your father says it is there, then it is there. Now, please pour more Mirabelle for Monsieur Taylor, as your father wanted."

In a few minutes, Philippe returned soaking wet. No one seemed surprised. Everett guessed it was Philippe's own version of hydrotherapy. His mechanical hand clutched a small brass tube, torn and flared-open at one end with a half-dollar sized cup at the other. He brought it to his lips.

"A nozzle - for a Bidet perhaps?" Louis laughed, as Philippe tried blowing – it seemed clogged.

"It's a tuba mouthpiece!" Everett said. "There's something caught inside."

"Tre bien!" Philippe said as he handed it to Everett, dripping water from his shirt across the table.

Everett held the cold, brass mouthpiece between the tips of his thumb and index finger and aimed it to the lantern to find a small, white obstruction, an inch inside.

"A petite escargot?" Everett said as he tapped the metal on the table. He bowed slightly to Philippe.

"Perhaps Annette can fry it up in celebration," Philippe said, taking a drink.

"I did not know escargot lived in Lac Noir," Louis said. "What do they live on?"

With another tap, a small, yellowish tooth dropped. Everett held it for a moment – a human tooth, a boy's tooth and in a second, the name of his father's tuba player, written in his father's hand came to him - Stephen Collins. Unable to hold it without trembling, Everett set it rocking on the table. Philippe reached his dripping mechanical hand across the table and flicked the tooth, through the open door, outside.

"From your father's regimental band?" Beatrice said, tilting her head in sympathy.

Everett nodded, wondering how he could finish his father's letters.

"Indeed! This calls for a celebration," Philippe reached beneath a shelf for a bottle of cognac. "I have found what you have come for," Philippe smiled.

"Your father was here, here in Lorraine?" Louis asked.

Everett nodded.

"Long ago, Louis – during Sigmund's Great War," Beatrice said.

"And, Louis, it too was the Great War of your Grand-père Lambert, the great Évariste!" Philippe said as he uncorked the cognac with his teeth.

"You came for your father?" Louis asked. "I thought Sister Beatrice was finally bringing a soldier home to stay."

"Louis, pour our guest and me a very tall glass, to toast his good fortune and departure," Philippe glared at the mouthpiece that Everett rolled around on the table.

"But Father," Louis said, spilling cognac on Philippe's pants, "there must be more at the bottom of Lac Noir!"

Philippe swatted Louis, hard across his backside for the mistake, and then batted the mouthpiece from Everett's hand, onto the floor. Everett reached down to pick it up.

"Philippe!" Beatrice snapped. "You have drunk and smoked enough."

"Monsieur Taylor has come to speak to your mother about what happened to the band," Beatrice said. "Now let us sit and eat!"

Everett gave Louis the mouthpiece to examine. He buzzed his lips into the cup until Philippe snatched it. The table quieted.

"I see you have removed your habit." Philippe said smugly, running his hand through his wet hair. "Is this for the benefit of our guest as well?"

Meat sizzled in the pan as Annette stood in the doorway guarding its flames. The foreboding smell of bacon filled the air. Beatrice's face, earlier bright with hope, limped and sagged as the prospects of having a nice dinner at home vanished. Everett wanted to hold her.

"Louis, will you please put the Cognac in the cabinet, Philippe has had enough," Beatrice said.

Louis hammered the cork into the neck of the cognac bottle with a sharp chirp. Philippe turned at the sound.

"I am not finished!" Philippe said, then swatted Louis' arm with his mechanical hand. Everett rose to restrain Philippe from hitting Louis a third time but Annette, bolting from the kitchen, grappled her husband forcefully from behind, but with care. Beatrice guarded Louis behind her back where he breathed in stuttered and painful gasps.

Smoke rolled from the kitchen. Everett quickly strode to the pulsing red and orange glow from the stove. Flames leaped towards the ceiling's wooden beams. As Everett smothered the pan in water from a bucket, Philippe cursed.

From what Everett could make out of the hysterical French insults, Philippe cursed them all for restraining him in his own home, accusing them of turning the tuilerie into a prison camp. Annette reminded Philippe of Louis, cowering behind Beatrice. Philippe called him what Everett thought might be French for bastard, but he wasn't sure.

When Everett had the fire out, he returned to find Annette and Beatrice carrying Philippe to the bath. A crash of china came from the shelf near the front door. Beatrice let Philippe slump to the floor. The door slammed shut. Gerta neighed and Louis was gone.

Everett took Beatrice's hand and slowly led her through the shards of her delicate cup, smashed onto the floor.

"Louis must have taken the Lugar – to keep it from Philippe, thank goodness," Beatrice said with her hand to her heart. "He will ride Gerta to Father's tonight in the reserve trench."

"I'll go for him," Everett said, taking a step past the doorway. He hesitated as Philippe ranted at Annette.

Beatrice's eyes followed the trace of Louis' flashlight wandering down the lane, catching Gerta's nervous tail wagging in the distance.

"It is so dark tonight," Beatrice said. "He will have difficulty even with the lamp and Gerta."

"Will you be all right?" Everett asked quietly, so as not to disturb Annette's calming voice to Philippe.

"If only Mother were here," Beatrice whispered. "I have never seen Philippe strike Louis with that hand before. You and Louis must stay at Father's dugout until Mother arrives to help, Sigmund will understand."

"But you and Annette are in danger," Everett said.

"No," Beatrice laid her head against Everett's shoulder. "You had better hurry now, dear, before you lose sight of Louis' lamp."

'Dear?' Everett focused on the word and her lips while stepping backwards from the porch.

"Mind your step, dear," Beatrice said as she grabbed his shirt then tugged him back to her side. She pointed to Chesterfield waiting silently where he was about to step. The curious ornament taunted him with a brassy smile etched across its worn and weathered face.

"I'll find him, Brunnhilde" Everett said.

"I know you will," she said.

She kissed him, not with a peck, but with a long and dwelling kiss that left a taste of vanilla along the inside of his lips. Her eyes sparkled in the dim light. She turned to run to Annette, closing the door, leaving him in the dark. He couldn't believe he called her Brunnhilde.

He turned to the dark night as Louis' light panned Lac Noir then, near the trench, sank as though swallowed into the ground.

⅋ 7 ⅌

To the Front

The moon tucked itself behind a thick bank of clouds. Everett nearly called out for Louis, but stopped. The thought of returning him to the tuilerie and Philippe's uncontrollable hand smashing Louis' young soft face, was unimaginable. He didn't know how to tell Louis – it was no longer safe to live in his own home. Louis would keep running in the trench, away from danger.

He turned on his heels to search for the flicker of candlelight in the tuilerie – nothing but darkness all around. A few missteps could send him headfirst into Lac Noir, or feet first into a trench. He turned on his heels, unsure if it was a full turn or not. Rather than feeling disappointed that his hopes of finding the band were fading, he strode instead in silence forward, searching for Louis and his light.

A loud clap struck water to his left.

"Louis?" He whispered towards Lac Noir, thinking Louis might have slipped.

Nothing. It sounded more like the slap of a huge fin against the water than either Louis or Gerta falling in. He slowed cautiously, knowing he could soon stumble into Sigmund's trench. Crawling, he searched with his hands for the opening.

His hand glanced across a depression in the soft soil - the stamp of Gerta's boot and hoof – deep and fresh. He followed them as the ground gradually sank into Sigmund's trench, dark - no different from the night sky above. The cleaned-out trench, which by day appeared garden-like with its trimmed grass and segments of Byzantine-like traverses, now felt incomprehensible along the bottom.

Gerta's old hardened prints, along with those of man and boar, mottled the floor. Their crusted edges broke apart in his hand as he grasped them to move. In his father's day, a man would have walked on raised wooden planks, called duckboards, beneath which flowed water, excrement and worse. By now, the boards had turned to powder and melded into soil.

He followed the prints another yard on his knees then felt the grass of the firing ledge at his left. It would face north. He was crawling in the right direction but he needed to catch up with Louis and Gerta. He pulled himself up, braced by the ledge until he could stand. His right hand leaned against the tall earthen trench wall, opposite the firing ledge.

There, up high, he felt a horizontal groove, cut most likely by Louis dragging a stick along the wall as Gerta carried him high on her back day after day. He stood on the ledge ready to run while Louis and Gerta, unseen, plodded along at the trench's bottom somewhere ahead.

Looking out over the top of the parapet into the dark, he imagined riflemen standing beside him, lined up with their bayonets waving like scissors at the sky, waiting for a whistle to send them over the top. Not too far ahead ran the dancing light of Louis' lamp before disappearing. He stood maybe six or seven traverses, or zigzags, behind Louis.

Taking a few careful steps along the ledge, he found it uncluttered and strode on the carpet of grass thinking of the years it took Sigmund to clear the trench of danger. He quickened his step, following the zigzag turns gently to the right and left on intervals of about fifteen steps. Over the top, he caught sight of Louis' light again, far down the trench. Moist air rolled from the parapet to his face. It was going to rain soon.

He stopped to dry his sweating face and catch his breath. Looking out again, he found Louis' lamp – a speck of light, swinging like a lantern on the caboose of a train. Abruptly, the trench bowed to the left and the ledge disappeared beneath his feet. He fell to the bottom, deeper and darker than before.

He groped for the ledge and, not finding it, turned around and around on his knees in the dirt for Gerta's steps. Remembering Doc describing the layout of trench-works, he guessed he sat at the junction to a communication trench, which intersected the reserve trench and ran straight and deep into the Zone Rouge. There ought to be a gate here, he thought, as he crawled. It had to be somewhere very close now.

Thunder rolled long and low, far off in the Vosges, rumbling up through his knees embedded in the earth. As he lurched forward, a wooden beam slammed his forehead – the gate. He raised his arm to stop it from rebounding and felt his hand scrape across a sharp metal sign - he imagined it read "Gate to Hell".

He reached up with his left hand for the smooth grassy firing ledge, but found only the tall earthen walls opposite the firing ledge. He must have turned around after his fall.

On his knees, he turned back around until his right hand met the tall wall again. Instead of finding Louis' playful line carved in the wall, his hand followed horizontal lengths of insulated wire with its cracked hard rubber cover, crumbling in his hand. After a few steps, the wire led to a timber then turned slightly to the left before straightening again for several more yards. He pulled his way to another timber, slipping on an unexploded shell that must have rolled down from the parapet. He tried to remember its location, knowing Sigmund must have missed it, but it was too confusing to reconcile where he was, exactly.

He pressed on, jabbing his shoes on the sharp metal thorns of war while thinking of Gerta or Louis stepping on that shell - he would remember to tell Sigmund about this too. With a few more slips, it was clear, he didn't need to pinpoint them - they were everywhere.

He pulled the wire in quick time, turn after turn until he thought to reach down for Gerta's prints. He was relieved to find hoof prints, but they seemed almost too small for a horse. Nearby, his hand felt the cold form of another shell and more small prints.

At each slight bend he encountered more debris. He pictured Beatrice's father grooming the trench with more care near the tuilerie rather than the vicinity of his dugout. Sigmund's home must be close by and judging from the debris, Everett didn't expect much when he got there.

The strand of wire bent sharply to his right around the corner, past another timber. He tried standing but could only crouch beneath a tangle of vines and overgrowth. No one had set foot in this place for a long, long time.

"Sigmund, you've got a lot of work to do!" He own voice gave him company, knowing Louis must certainly be out of earshot by now.

He guessed that Philippe must have frightened himself, as Louis said, and left the gate open an inch. Louis, riding on Gerta's back, wouldn't have fallen but he should have closed the gate. He winced at the thought that Louis had intentionally opened it, just in case Philippe was following. It wasn't opened that far though, just a crack.

"Just enough for me to crawl inside a communication trench," he laughed.

"Where are the duckboards?" He knew if he were this far inside a communication trench that he should feel rotted boards breaking at his feet like soggy crackers.

He bent down and found the compost of soft, rotted wood turned with soil into a paste, patterned in hundreds of small hoof prints.

"Boars! Smart, like pigs," he shouted as he imagined herds tearing up duckboards, forcing their victims to plod through muck like them rather than to run on wood to escape.

He felt relieved that Gerta and Louis would have had passed the gate to their far left without entering – Gerta would know better, she could probably even smell boar.

He fell again, this time into soft moss rather than soil. He pried the vines away as he stood and found the firing ledge again but now littered with loose soil, an overpowering smell and curious debris that he explored with his hands.

A vertical timber, treated in creosote, rose from the foot of the firing ledge where he crouched. As he stood, his head thumped against a crosspiece. At first he thought it must be another sign, like a billboard, erected to insult the enemy in their trenches not far away, but what he felt as he explored its length, was more like rusted chicken wire.

Breaking apart wherever he touched it, smooth bones fell to his hand from the wire bag that had bound a man to the cross. He examined their shapes with his hands. A whole man's bones, head to foot, lay clumped mostly at the bottom. Pieces of work like this, he knew, could only exist in a frontline trench where no man, since his father, would ever again visit.

He cursed his father for obeying a code of cruelty that only animals lived by. Had his father beheaded the man too? He hadn't seen the man's skull. He explored the strange metal sack in darkness, bound to the post, soaked in creosote so the rotten stench wouldn't interfere with his father's hardtack and coffee.

The skull lay at the height of Everett's shoulder, drooping backwards in the bag above the parapet so the enemy could see it. It felt smooth, except for where the nose, eyes, and ears had been. There, in middle of the forehead, Everett's finger slipped into a perfectly round hole and opposite, at the back, he found the exit hole. It was odd, Everett thought, for the enemy would have practiced putting hundreds of rifle rounds into it, propped up like that.

As Everett reached for the cross' arm to ease back down, his hand found wrist bones surrounded by the wire mesh, still in place. Protruding from the bones through the wire was a thick stick, at its tip he felt bristles bound with a ring-sized band of rusted metal. He now held a brush. He nearly fainted as he realized the man entombed vertically, the one he had his arms around, was the one named Évariste.

He felt relieved to know his father and his men hadn't done this – it was the French and it was an honor. He plucked Évariste's brush loose and slid it into his single back pocket. The bristle itched against his skin beneath his shirt.

Of the monuments he and Beatrice had passed by in Lorraine, all tall and white, perpetually adorned in bouquets and etched in proud epithets – this one, this scarecrow, sprang to life. The bent and broken, Évariste, was raised on the post by men who admired a simple man's angry spirit. Not a man angry with the enemy for invading his country, for this part of Alsace and Lorraine had traded loyalties many times; neither would Évariste have charged for a communist ideal. The brush-wielding display of anger at the enemy for having impregnated his porch with Chesterfield and interrupting his last work of art, that cup perhaps, must have enthralled his comrades. The enemy too, must have been impressed, as there was but the one bullet to the skull of the man, Évariste, left alone to lord over the Zone Rouge all these years at the edge of Lorraine

Lightning shattered his reverie. Phantom electricity surged through the wire. Everett lowered himself from his namesake. A light flashed in the sky.

Far to his right, over the top, Louis' light disappeared around a bend. Everett decided, to reach them, it would be faster following the frontline trench to the next communication trench than to backtrack. He would need to remember where he found Évariste, he thought, but then who could possibly understand.

Slugging his way through the dense vegetation, following the wire, he counted the bends of the trench abruptly vacated thirty-five years earlier. Everywhere, lay broken wooden ladders, decayed wooden crates, rotted backpacks, rusted tin plates and canteens. There were trench knives, bayonet scabbards, discarded hob-nail boots, thousands of dulled bullets inside hundreds of unspent rifle clips, ammo boxes, and even more spent rifle shell casings scattered about like dirty hailstones.

He trudged on, wiping spider webs. Slick runners of young vines wrapped around his neck like tentacles. He caught, though, glimpses of light to his right where Louis and Gerta plodded in the reserve trench, nearly parallel to him.

At the eleventh turn of the frontline trench, the wire led to a wooden box that he pulled from the ground. Inside was a phone. A reflex brought it to his ear. A flash of lightning lit the sky as static crackled from the receiver.

"Who's there?" Everett asked.

Angry at his own stupidity, he tossed the phone down and stormed off several paces, ripping at the vines lashing his face as thunder clapped overhead.

Lightning illuminated the depths of the frontline. He jumped as best he could to the crumbling firing ledge to peer out towards Louis. He hoped he might dash to Louis – but in the brief flashes of light, barricades and wire between the two trenches prevented such a breach. The ledge crumbled under his weight and broke apart. He fell to the mossy trench's floor where he felt the fresh hoof tracks again.

He sat on the trench's soft carpet, hoping Louis and Gerta made it safely to Sigmund's before the storm. He could do no more.

A slow warm trickle ran down his hand. His burn wound bled again. He groped for something to hold and found the wire that guided him to this spot. As he tried standing, lightning flashed. The strand of wire glowed for a moment in his hand. Nothing here seemed safe to touch anymore. Lightning again. His eyes widened as the sky quaked above. He stepped up to what was left of the eroded firing ledge. He found Louis' light moving slowly in Sigmund's trench.

Rotted sandbags, he used to grip to hold him up at the parapet, broke apart like puffballs. The ledge again crumbled as though he were standing on the crust of a soufflé. Moldy burlap dust caught his nose as sand spilled to his feet. He held back his cough not wanting Louis to find him in a worse state than Philippe. He hadn't come to France to be nursed.

His foot slipped off the cylindrical base of an artillery shell. He landed on his seat then draped his arm around the large shell and rested his head on a broken sand bag. He thought of Beatrice's warm breath and vanilla kiss to keep warm. He rapped the shell with his knuckles as though it were

Beatrice's knee, laughing at his absurd situation as his blood slicked the shell's metal skin. He closed his eyes to listen for Louis, a shot from his Lugar, Gerta's whinny, or an explosion, but all he heard was the rustling of leaves and soon would come the cool wind that stirred them.

The wind never came. The rustle turned to a ramble, something on the ground, not in the air, drove it. He slapped the shell and held it tight to sit up. The clap of his bloody hand against the shell rang down the trench. It was quiet for a second before something rambled low to the ground. He held his breath to be quiet. Warm droplets of blood seeped from his hand through his pants leg where it cooled and jelled. Over the pounding of his heart came a grunting and squealing.

"A goddamned boar!" he screamed, imagining its elephant-like tusks and saber-like teeth.

With a clattering of tin cans, snapping twigs and the patter of short powerful legs, the beast ripped and tore its way up the front-line trench. Everett bolted and soon found a good trench ladder to go 'Over the Top'. He climbed up quickly, breaking its rotted rungs.

The boar's hoofs clicked and slipped over the big, blood-coated shell that Everett had rested on, one traverse back, no more than ten yards away. The boar fell hard, huffed and snorted.

A moment later a disgusting slurp and opened-mouthed munch, rose from the spot below. He pictured the bull-sized boar so ravenously hungry that it would lick anything in sight. It occurred to him that the beast was acquiring a taste for his blood.

"You pig!" Everett shouted from the elevated safety.

The boar ceased licking and began bludgeoning the shell with its tusks, gouging metal against bone and bone against iron. He wished it were his fist slugging the big mean kid, Schmitty, for having told him that lie so long ago about his mother, eaten alive by pigs. As the boar rammed away at the shell, he laughed at its futile attempt to explode the shell.

"Bull Roar!" Everett shouted into the dense, still air. "It takes a fuse!"

The boar below, in response, raised its hollow jabs at the shell's mid-section, to the more metallic and bonier blows to the shell's nose.

"Father?" Louis called out nearby, to Everett's right.

How terrified Louis must be, he thought, thinking Philippe was in pursuit. He followed the light as it swung quickly behind him over the moonscape of No-Man's-Land.

The boar stopped its attack, at either Louis' voice or the light panning over the trench, then retreated a few paces backwards, waiting for a good lunge. If everything stayed quiet, he hoped Louis would just turn around and leave.

"Father?" Louis said, closer this time and with more surprise than fear, knowing Philippe could never venture out this far into the Zone Rouge.

Everett cautiously peered over the parapet into the long dark trench for the slightest glint of light from a boar's eye. Relieved, he sighed into the misty, starless night. A fierce squeal pierced the respite.

His breath, alone, seemed enough to stir the beast to life as it adjusted its offensive stance, sucked its hoofs from the soft mud preparing to charge. It swaggered back to the shell and with a series of chinks to the fuse, resumed its relentless, murderous plan.

"You smart son-of-a-bitch!" Everett cursed as he quickly stepped backwards, deeper into the Zone Rouge, leaping into a bomb crater filled with thickets. He kicked at the thorny bush until something grabbed his foot, then the other.

"Damn it!" he shouted. The boar stopped then stomped forward, below where he lay in the crater. It waited a few seconds then with a sniff of the air, the beast began rooting at the trench's wall next to him.

At first, he thought it was nettles stinging his legs, but then he felt the cold, rusted wire with its barbs biting through his pants. Lightning crossed the sky. Louis should be at Sigmund's by now, Everett hoped.

The wire organism rattled each time he wriggled, like a giant metallic squid pulling him down a little more, stinging him with its poisonous tentacles, flipping him on his back. The slightest twist of his wrist excited the wire and those attached to it. With each tug and ring of the wire, hundreds of rattles came to life outside the crater, traveling beyond, well into No-Man's-Land, announcing his intrusion with trip-wires. The boar froze at the sound.

He jerked the wires. With a panicked snort, the boar fled a traverse forward. A few more tugs and he frightened it forward even more. He dragged himself up to the crater's lip with the wire still locked around his shoulders and back. He inched along, noisily dragging his iron parasite to the edge of the trench with the boar scuffling away, forward.

"An awesome, but awkward defense," he chuckled to himself, dropping down into the frontline trench and pulling at the long train of wire. Guessing that Louis and Gerta had made it safely to Sigmund's by now, he began his long walk back to the tuilerie. The wire loosened, strand by strand, behind him.

He stubbed his foot on the shell then knelt to feel its marred metal skin. In a staggering show of lightning, he could see where the boar had licked it clean. Looking up to pulsing clouds, he found Louis' light up the trench.

"Father?" Louis said, from the frontline trench.

"Louis! There's a boar running around up there!"

Everett heard a grunt, and soon a loud crack and squeal. A beam of light panned upwards. Smoke drifted through the steady light.

"Monsieur? Is that you?"

Everett tried calming his voice.

"Yeah, just me," Everett said. "You killed that big boar with one shot?"

"Of course," Louis said, shining the light to Everett still snared in his wire.

"I came to help you, Louis, but now it seems I'm rather tangled up here." Everett pulled at the wire, with its barbs sunk deep into his skin. Louis' lamp illuminated him from behind and Everett quickly removed Evariste's paintbrush from his rear pocket to the front, jabbing him in the groin as though to remind him of Evariste's unusual demise.

"Stay still!" Louis ordered, sliding the Lugar back into the holster around his chest, "I will undo you – it seems attracted to you."

"You thought I was Philippe, didn't you?" Everett asked as Louis began to work. "You must have been frightened."

"I thought perhaps Father might have smoked and drank so much that he finally came past the gate for Évariste," Louis said.

"Does he hit you often?" Everett asked, as Louis untangled a wire at his shoulder. In Louis' light, he noticed smudges around the boy's eyes and streaks where tears had streamed to his chin and dried.

"He is upset that Sister Beatrice was not wearing her habit at the train station. I think she still looked like an angel. What did father mean when he said she removed it for you? Is she no longer an angel?"

"Ouch!" Everett said as though a wasp had stung his back.

"Keep still. There is a barb clinging to your back," Louis said. "I will take care of it while you talk."

"Philippe is confused, that's all. Beatrice has seen much of war in Indochina. Maybe she thinks she's not clean enough to be an angel anymore. Are you about done?"

"Stay still, Monsieur. You call her Beatrice. Is she not an angel to you?"

"She's more than an angel," Everett said.

"Very much more, Monsieur," Louis said while pulling the last barbed-iron thread from Everett's pants where it threatened his inner thigh, "Now there, you are free! I left Gerta at the gate of the next communication trench – she must be worried. We are in the very heart of the Zone Rouge. You ignored one of the gates that was clearly marked 'Accès Interdit'. Are you possessed?"

"The gate was opened a little. It was dark – I bumped my head then lost your track and that big boar was following me too." Everett handed Louis the light and twisted his head back towards the trench. "My hand was bleeding. You see, I have a fear of pigs."

"My friend, the American jet pilot, is afraid? Follow me." Louis turned forward with his lantern, creating long eerie shadows as they stepped over sharp debris. The stab of the paintbrush into Everett's thigh tempted him to move it to the rear, but he might drop it.

Louis pulled the overgrowth aside, snapping branches back to Everett's face. Louis trudged forward a few traverses until he stopped to cast the light to his foot, where something, once alive, now steamed its last essence into the thick, humid night. Everett could not believe what he saw.

"Was he that small?" Everett said, staring at the dead boar, no larger than a toy terrier. He took a step or two back to judge its true, but once fearfully imagined stature.

"Monsieur! Stop!" Louis shouted, aiming the flickering light at Everett's foot. "Now, *that* , you should fear more than a petit sanglier," Louis said, slapping the lamp against his pants until it pulsed bright. At their feet lay a milk-can sized canister encased in a rusted, crepe-like skin of flaking metal.

"Gas!" Louis said.

"You sure?" Everett asked. He knew exactly what it was, but was curious about how much Louis had known of the gas cans. Soldiers wearing boots, masks, and coats of rubber, once poured noxious fuming liquids into the large round cans. They would then slip it, along with a small boosting charge, inside a slightly larger mortar barrel, probably still buried in the ground not far away. He wondered what crime deserved such a duty.

The light flickered again.

"The General taught me."

"I wonder what kind of gas is inside, does it say?" Everett removed his shirt and wiped the canister clean to read.

Louis shrieked as he aimed the light to Everett's back.

"Monsieur, you have cuts all over your back. Sister Beatrice should see to them."

"I'm fine." Everett said. "Shine the light on the canister."

"It will not tell you what it keeps inside. General Sigmund taught me to use my special gift," Louis shone the light to his pointed, but surprisingly little, nose. "There are no other markings, only its perfume – try your American nose."

Everett focused his nose along its length, sniffing, as though the old canister were a stinky Munster. He detected a faint but pleasant smell.

"Fresh cut grass, no?" Louis said.

"Yes, Louis, it does. Like the grass back home, how could you tell?"

"It is phosgene, Monsieur. I can smell it from here."

Everett held the flashlight closer to the cylinder. The warmth of the light seemed to make the skin glisten and boil. The lamp's alternate dimming and brightening made the canister appear to breathe.

"Monsieur! There by your hand, is another!" Louis trained the light on a shell, upright, after rolling long-ago into the trench from above. He brought his eyes within inches of the fuse to examine its markings.

"I correct myself, Monsieur. It is only a 155." Louis raised a puzzled eyebrow. "This one is quite harmless."

The technology of fuses had improved since the first world war, Everett thought, reflecting on the time-delayed fuses used in Korea – small vials of acetone, which on impact would break and begin to eat away at layers of Plexiglas delaying the fuse from igniting the high explosive. These munitions were of the Stone Age. Everett pictured a thin, fragile, rusted thread of iron being all that suspended the fuse from its deadly purpose in life.

"I think you should stand back, Louis. The thing has been waited all these years to get some attention."

"Not this one," Louis said. "General Sigmund taught me, ones like this will never explode."

"Inert?" Everett asked. Louis looked confused.

"Without power, duds – impotent," Everett said.

"It has power, Monsieur. It lacks only brains to detonate."

Bad fuses, Everett guessed.

"Lift me up to the parapet, if you please, Monsieur."

"Be careful," Everett said as he boosted Louis up. "What are you looking for?"

He hoped it wasn't Évariste.

"Eggs!" Louis said over the clap of thunder. A slight wind picked up as Louis turned his light to a ladder. "Come see."

Louis raised the light up high so they could see over the parapet. The meager lamp flickered across a small cemetery plot of what seemed like small, toppled headstones.

"Dragon eggs!" Louis gasped. "A whole nest of dragon eggs – just as General Sigmund said there would be."

As Louis steadied the lamp, it was clear – the closest stone was made of iron.

"All duds?" Everett asked. Louis nodded.

Everett glared in disbelief at a grouping of unexploded artillery shells, thirty or forty duds, not far from where he had fallen into the crater of No-Man's-Land. Louis slanted his dimming beam of light across a field so thick in wire, that it resembled a raspberry patch – the light, as dim as it was, found cluster after cluster of the duds.

"Look at them all!" Louis gasped.

One or two duds, Everett understood, considering the engineering and production standards of the Great War, but not hundreds, not thousands and certainly not German duds all in one place. They would have looked like Christmas tree ornaments in their new metal jackets, sticking in the mud.

"I must tell General Sigmund - he collects them, the duds as you say – but never out here. Perhaps tomorrow he will finally come past the gate too."

As they climbed down, Everett's foot crunched on a canister. He knelt down to it and cleared the mud with his shirt. A sharp, pungent odor caught his nose. Louis slapped the light as the battery ran down to examine Everett's shirt, stained in yellow.

"Mustard!" Louis said. "It leaks badly, we must go."

Everett snapped his shirt free of dirt and was about to slide his arm inside the sleeve when Louis stopped him.

"This mustard is not the same that you spread on sausage," Louis said pointing to the stain. "The General said the essence of mustard will burn worse than melted wax on your skin. I am afraid your shirt is ruined."

"I'll leave it here to mark the eggs," Everett said.

Lightning and thunder erupted over the Vosges.

"Dragons! The Zone Rouge, General Sigmund said, is teeming with their nests, ripening more each year. Follow me. It is about to rain, we could drown. There are so many dangers."

Cold wind funneled down the trench as Louis swaggered ahead of Everett, swinging his light, pausing occasionally to stare at bizarre sculptures of twisted metal from ruptured fortifications, long dead trees broken in half, shadows of posts and wire near the parapet and more dragon eggs covered in moss and mud - a boar's perfect wonderland.

After several traverses, Everett hoped they might be coming to Sigmund's trench.

"Louis, slow down. Did the General have a name for this awful place?"

"Hagen's Trench," Louis turned around to say, "Accès interdit - teeming with dragons there and there," he pointed with his lamp to vague, irregular forms behind them. "They fear my light. Is it not marvelous! Here at my foot is yet another egg. Stand clear while I bury it at sea."

Louis turned his back to Everett, clamped the flashlight in his armpit, spread his legs and waited while looking down to his feet where the light steadied on a partially exposed gas canister. In a few seconds, a glistening stream of urine etched Louis' steaming mark, fizzing like acid, into the old metal.

The cold, damp air and the sound of the spray took Everett's mind away from their predicament. Instead, he focused on his own expanding bladder.

"If you've finished with him, toss me the light," Everett said, playing along. "He needs another good dousing!"

The flashlight came somersaulting high above the trench, blinking out at times. He caught it with one hand, shook it to life, and stepped to the shell.

"Keep the light trained on him, Monsieur. When it mesmerizes him, you can send him to hell with your blast."

"Glad to!" Everett said as he, like Louis, turned away to tempt the thing, staring at its metal cylinder embedded in the wall, dripping and steaming with Louis' pee. The exposed flaked metal skin of the canister, already laid bare by Louis, seemed like the face of an old wrinkled man, yet beneath the rusted iron case, Everett sensed a potent, pent-up force.

"Any time, Monsieur," Louis said impatiently. "It might rain before we reach General Sigmund's dugout."

Everett's bladder seemed like it might pop. Glaring at the dragon egg, so old and helpless, waiting for a decent death, he wished his bladder were big enough to kill the whole nest. He relaxed and quickly put this one out of its misery.

"Target destroyed!" He tossed the light back to Louis and snugged up his pants. The paintbrush stabbed his scrotum, Everett thought, as punishment for the desecration.

"Well done, Monsieur! The dragons are lamenting."

"What do they say?" Everett discretely adjusted the brush.

"I do not speak reptilian very well, but they cried."

"Good!" Everett huffed out a good laugh.

Louis pointed out hazards with his fickle lamp as Everett followed him past several traverses then turned sharply right. After twelve turns, they emerged from Hagen's frontline trench into the next communications trench.

"Where's this one taking us?" Everett asked.

"Away from the front," Louis as he wiped his forehead with his sleeve, "I think."

Everett turned back briefly to the dark scar from which he had stolen the paintbrush from Evariste's hand. It was no place for an artist and Philip was right, Everett thought, the Zone Rouge was no place for a band either.

"Are you sure this is the way?" Everett asked.

"Sure. This will take us to the General Sigmund's trench," Louis said. Everett liked the way Louis used 'sure' with such confidence. He felt the lamp at his back.

"Your wounds look terrible. You need an injection – soon."

"Tetanus?" Everett said laughing. "Oh, I think I'll make it, Louis, it doesn't hurt much. And my jaw hasn't locked up yet."

"Good," Louis said with a deep and serious tone. "It is another ten minutes to where I left Gerta by the last gate."

"Your parents must be worried," Everett said.

"You must never tell father where we have been," Louis said. "He is waiting for the courage to look for Évariste, past the gate, by himself."

"What do I say about these?" Everett poked at the wounds on his bare back, chest and neck from the barbed wire.

"Show them to Sister Beatrice, she will not tell." Louis laughed to the side. "She will thrust her needle into your derriere like a sword. You will promise her anything for her to remove it."

"I don't trust nurses," Everett said, surprised at his own serious tone.

"She is much more than a nurse," Louis said, stopping as lightning struck behind them. "She is Sister Beatrice, my saint - my Jeanne de Arc, my Valkyrie!"

Everett imagined Beatrice's green eyes, vanilla breath, her touch and her beautifully crooked nose, drawing his scent deep into her lungs while she bent down to scoop him up to sit alongside her saddle on her powerful white-winged steed. He felt a little better about her being more of a nurse than a Valkyrie.

Louis returned to his dogged pace towards Sigmund's trench as the paintbrush, in Everett's front pocket, threatened to rub him raw. To their left, lightning scrolled horizontally across the foothills of the Vosges in a vibrant white-indigo coil, followed a few seconds later by thunder tearing slowly across the sky. The lightning stuttered above the clouds while thunder rolled like long passages of timpani. Spectacular pink clouds ignited above them.

A marble-sized pellet of hail struck the thin metal of Louis' light, hitting so hard that Louis nearly dropped it.

"Dragon spit! This is not a good sign," Louis said, flicking the lamp with his wrist to the side while the flashlight, by accident, showed Louis covering his mouth, erupting in laughter.

"A dragon?" Everett shouted above the clap of nearby thunder. "Why, if it's one thing I hate more than a boar, it's a dragon. Spit on your hand, you say? Why that dirty, filthy, bat-winged bastard!"

"The bastard!" Louis shouted.

Dragons seemed more natural here than birds, Everett thought, as Louis swaggered ahead of him along the bottom of the trench, taking charge and having fun pointing out fictitious creatures in the mud of the trench walls with his light.

Rain to the north, hammered the wires of No-Man's Land like a harp. It pattered against the lush overgrowth of Hagen's Trench behind them, sending its liquid discharge to flow downhill through the communication and reserve trenches and perhaps to Lac Noir.

A rivulet ran between Everett's feet and in time, turned dirt to mud, mud to muck, muck to slop. Louis swung the fickle flashlight from side to side.

"Mind your step, Monsieur."

Louis strutted while directing his lamp at half-submerged shells, tips of wire, rusted bayonets and debris as they moved past a few more traverses.

The flashlight dimmed, came to life, and then went out. Darkness filled the trench as Everett stepped to Louis.

"Can you make it work again, Monsieur? I think we are going to need that light," Louis said, now more seriously.

Everett reached for Louis' arm. Finding it slightly shaking, he followed it firmly down Louis' hand to the cold aluminum case of the flashlight - it seemed to calm Louis. Everett lifted him up, not wanting Louis' shoes to fill with the water rising in the trench.

"It's done for," Everett said.

He cocked his arm and hurled the lamp into the Zone Rouge, relieved of having Louis discover the brush and of Everett having to describe the gruesome detail of Évariste, hanging to rot on a post with the brush in his hand.

"I'll carry you," Everett said. "Climb up on my back and watch for dragons," Everett said, shifting the brush at last to his rear pocket. "Still have that Lugar?"

"In my holster," Louis said. "My eyes are already adjusting to the dark. I see dragons, they are everywhere."

"You're just getting tired, Louis," Everett said, nearly tripping in the dark over a metal spear on his first step. The rivulet of water from the approaching rains turned the loose dirt into a thick soup that tried sucking his boots off with each step.

"We'll find a place to rest," Everett said. "It won't be long before the rain will be on top of us."

Everett stepped forward with Louis on his shoulders.

Water inched up Everett's legs, carrying leaves from last fall. Annual torrents would have washed all the garbage from long ago wars downstream towards Lac Noir unless it was heavy like dragon eggs, tubas or trombones, or a man, unless secured to a creosoted post with wire.

With each step, Everett understood that only a mad man would order a band to this part of the front, unless they traded their instruments for stretchers and went out for the dead. He reached back to his back pocket to feel the brush's bristle. It was real – no one had come for Évariste. Who would want to re-intern a God, he thought.

A few paces further, Louis slumped to the side to sleep and nearly toppled Everett, trying to keep upright as a light, cold rain fell.

With Louis asleep on his shoulders, Everett swiped the walls of the trench looking for those special hovels where he knew soldiers, under his father's command at the front, must store, food, shelter and ammunition to live for weeks. Thunder roared like cannons and lightning arced across the Zone Rouge. A sheet of rain crawled towards them.

After a few bends his hand felt a thick, brittle curtain, smelling of tar and oil – a dugout.

"What is it, Monsieur?" Louis mumbled, half-asleep.

"A store of some kind, probably not any bigger than a bear's den," Everett said, examining the size of the entrance. "We need to get up out of this water."

Everett stuck his head inside - it was amazingly dry. He knocked on the corrugated steel that reinforced the thick earthen walls and ceiling, laced with corrosion and cobwebs, but solid. His hand grazed a large wooden shelf, waist-high, with depressions hollowed out and filled with thirty-five years of debris. Towards the rear of the frame, he felt a row of smooth metal ovals, each the size of a small ostrich egg.

He shook one off and found the pin, still in place. It was an earlier grenade, French maybe, and smooth, not textured with the familiar small rectangular patterns that made fragmentation, and therefore death, more efficient.

Everett juggled the steel bulb in his hand, imagining young Philippe playfully pulling the safety pin and Gerta wisely setting her hoof on the arming lever until even the most patient of beasts must take a step. The explosive weight, Everett judged, would be sufficient to sever a horse's hoof and a boy's thin arm. The grenade slipped from his hand and rested again in its wooden coffin.

"What is it Monsieur? Food? Wine?" Louis yawned.

"Nothing, Louis." Everett said.

He swung Louis inside then crouched next to him in the small, but well-preserved cave. Louis' wet matted hair lay cold against Everett's bare side. He cradled Louis' head and covered his small ears as rain splattered hard in the flooding trench outside.

Soon, hail plopped into the water as the storm, passing overhead, sent its volley against the opening's hard tar cloth cover, thumping like a deranged woman beating a carpet on a line. As the hail turned to cold rain, Everett imagined what a rolling barrage of cannon fire in his father's time must have sounded like. He lifted up a bit to remove the paintbrush with its short stubby bristles, still irritating the barbed-wire wounds at his waist and back..

The rolling barrage would have infuriated a quiet artist like Évariste, Everett thought, but not Louis – he slept through the whole storm.

ಐ 8 ೮

A Deeper Dugout

Everett lifted the heavy cloth cover as the storm subsided. The thick dark clouds had already passed over Lac Noir, the tuilerie and on to Ville Negre to the south. A dull-gray new moon ran behind a veneer of clouds.

He let the cover drop and leaned back. He ruffled the brush's hair with his fingers while Louis snored and the water outside trickled away. The boy, Everett thought, was good with a pencil and drew wonderfully detailed aircraft, unlike the fine artwork of his grandfather, Évariste, or his father, Philippe. Stroking the brush, he wondered if the engineer inside Louis came from Annette's stock instead of Philippe's.

Louis licked his lips, dry from snoring, and produced a suckling sound as he cuddled in his sleep next to Everett in the safety of the dark quiet cave.

Everett weighed the chance of Philippe apologizing to Louis for striking him. It seemed as remote as stopping the Great War from beginning in the first place. Once the metal hand had swung, it was as though two great duels had begun - one between father and son, the other between Gods and Giants.

"No Gods or Giants," Everett mumbled to himself, "only dragons and boar."

A terrible wooden clapping shattered his thoughts. Everett jumped and hit his head on the metal ceiling. Louis sat up.

"What was that, Louis? It just scared the Sam Hell out me. My hands are trembling, can you feel them?" Everett held them out.

Louis turned an ear down the trench.

"General Sigmund and his gas rattle - he can make it roar!" Louis said. "He used it to wake soldiers in gas attacks."

"It could wake the dead," Everett said. He tested the trench with his foot. "It's muddy, but I think we can go."

Outside the dugout, the sky was clear. A final gust of wind from the Vosges carried the smell of pine. The rattle roared down the trench again. A few traverses to their left, a rhythmical march splashed with a strange and staggered stride.

"That is my Gerta!" Louis said. "But she would never come past a gate. She must be in General Sigmund's trench."

"You mean we're only a few feet from a gate?" Everett said. "Climb up on my shoulders and take a look."

Cuts reopened on Everett's back as Louis scrambled up.

"What is it?" Everett said. "Quick, I can't hold you up much longer."

"It is her!" Louis said, jumping down.

Everett stood on a large rusted ammunition box to see.

A beacon, panning occasionally above the trench, caught something in its beam. A white mane flared, several traverses away. Behind it sailed a red scarf. Everett felt ill for a moment, until he realized it was Beatrice's long hair, undone in the wind and not a Valkyrie. Gerta hobbled in front of her.

Louis bolted to the gate. Everett stopped him.

"What's the hurry?" Everett said. "You might step on something."

"If I can get to the gate quickly," Louis said in short breaths, "I can say that I was waiting there all night for you. I would be in serious trouble if they knew I went in."

"Go ahead, give it a try," Everett said. Impressed with Louis' white lie, he let him loose. Louis shot like a bullet towards the gate, a few traverses away.

Everett sauntered down the last few traverses, trying to give Louis time to make up a good story. Turning the last traverse, he felt Louis clinging to his legs.

"Monsieur," Louis sighed quietly. "It was wrong for me to leave you. Sister Beatrice would say that I have broken a code of honor."

"That's alright Louis," Everett whispered as they laid low.

Ahead at the gate in the light shone from behind, Beatrice walked past then Gerta, who stopped briefly and rolled her big brown eye towards both of them, cowering in the dark like criminals.

"They think we were lost ahead, in General Sigmund's trench, Monsieur," Louis said. "Shhh, here comes the General now. I want to surprise him!"

"I don't think that's a good idea," Everett whispered, as Sigmund stood close by.

Louis clapped his hands with a pop. The lantern fell. Sigmund dove to the ground and gave the rattle a quick warning crank, as though by instinct.

"General Sigmund?" Louis asked, swinging the gate and finding Sigmund crouching along the grassy ledge. "Are you all right?"

Sigmund's astonished face shown in the light as he thrust the shaking lantern towards the gate and dropped the wooden, cage-like gas rattle.

"Meine Fratz!" Sigmund shouted as he reached for Louis' arm to help him up.

Sigmund's terrified face melted into a grin as he boosted Louis onto his shoulders. He gave Everett a curious look then slammed the gate closed.

"Louis?" Beatrice said as she pulled Gerta around the bend. "What on earth were you doing in there?"

"We expected you hours ago, before the storm," she said as she ran to him. "You have been in the Zone Rouge all this time? Let me see you."

"I am fine. You should see my friend's back though," Louis said. "He needs an injection."

"Where is your shirt, Monsieur?" Sigmund said. "There is a lady present."

"Sigmund, I have seen the backs of many men," Beatrice said. Everett felt her strong hands gently probing around the cuts in the dim light.

"First your hand, now your back – does it hurt?" Beatrice said, as Everett felt the warmth of her breath at his back.

"Only a little," Everett said.

Her vanilla breath poured from her mouth as she inspected his neck.

"Thank you," Everett whispered. "I thought you would stay with Philippe?"

"Madame Lambert came to the tuilerie by taxi, moments after you left," Beatrice said quietly. "She began administering her therapy to Philippe at once. After he was deep under her trance, I gathered your bag then raced the Mercedes to Father's dugout to wait for you and Louis. When Gerta came alone, we came looking – I was so afraid."

Sigmund gave the gas-rattle a disturbing twist.

"Sigmund gets nervous being this close to the Zone Rouge at night," she said.

"That is because there are dragons and boar running wild," Louis said as he withdrew the Lugar from his holster. "We found the nests full of dragon eggs, General Sigmund – just like you said there would be. Monsieur left his shirt to mark the spot - they are beginning to hatch!"

Louis spun the pistol and slapped its magazine.

"Louis, put that away," Beatrice said. "Dragons are not real."

"Oh, but the boar is," Everett said. "Louis saved me from one with that pistol."

"And the dragons, too!" Louis said. "How many did we kill, Monsieur?"

"That is enough." Sigmund grumbled as he approached from behind with the lantern. Everett felt its heat moving up and down his back.

"Those are barbed wire wounds," Sigmund said. "No one has been to the front line here since 1918, Monsieur, not even me. I thought you had only wandered up this communication trench, seen the danger and turned around, but to set foot in Hagen's trench is tempting fate."

"General Sigmund, Gerta is getting tired," Louis said. "Can we walk her down?"

Beatrice spun Louis around and walked ahead with Gerta at Louis' side.

Everett took a step, until he stopped – snagged from behind.

"Uh, uh," Sigmund whispered in Everett's ear as he tugged at the paintbrush in Everett's pocket. "Not just yet, Herr Taylor."

"Follow Gerta down to her bed by the Mercedes," Sigmund called out to Beatrice and Louis. "She knows her way in the dark. The door, below, is locked. So come back up when you have finished with Gerta, We will wait for you at the topside opening, here. I want to speak with the American."

A door at the bottom of a trench, Everett imagined, could only lead to hell. He felt the paintbrush lift from his back pocket.

"Try not to be long, Sigmund. I should look after Everett's wounds."

Sigmund waited until Gerta's tail flicked past the traverse. Everett's excitement grew at the prospect that Sigmund might want to talk in private about the band and his father.

"It appears you have half of France in your back pocket, sir," Sigmund said, bringing the paintbrush up close in the light. He rolled it like a fine cigar.

Disappointed that Sigmund focused on the brush rather than the band, Everett turned to grab the brush from him, but Sigmund gripped it like the hand of a child about to fall. Everett realized then that Sigmund knew all about the legend of Évariste.

"Why did Louis not mention this?"

"I didn't tell him. He's too young to understand the circumstances."

"I know," Sigmund said, in a voice, kinder than Everett expected. "I see you have inherited your father's sensitivity."

Everett burst out with a cynical laugh.

"Sensitivity? Do you know where my father left Évariste's bones hanging?"

Sigmund ran the bristles across his fingers.

"Of course, where the first communication trench meets Hagen's trench, but it was the French who put Évariste's courage on display," Sigmund said. "Is he still posted?"

Everett nodded with a grimace of disgust.

"Why do you let people think Évariste is lost if you knew where he was?"

"For the same reason you did not tell Louis," Sigmund said as he moved the lantern across Everett's shoulder. The heat ignited the pain from the cuts, bleeding again.

"Those barbs must hurt," Sigmund said. "There is only one place where there is that much wire, Monsieur. To stumble into the front-line-trench is one thing but to walk into no-man's-land, the very heart of the Zone Rouge, you must be insane."

"Those gates are flimsy," Everett said.

"I will lock them, tomorrow," Sigmund said, eyeing the paintbrush in the lantern light, "to keep the curious out."

"You will not mind if I keep this," Sigmund said as he slipped the brush into his own pocket. "There is no need to tell anyone what you have found."

"I didn't come all the way to France for a paintbrush," Everett said.

Everett felt a firm grip on his shoulder.

"My daughter informs me that you saved the young girl in Marseilles, but Louis, it appears, saved you," Sigmund said. "We must be getting back. I prefer being close to my dugout after sunset."

Everett, surprised that Sigmund referred to Beatrice as his daughter so soon, moved forward at Sigmund's prodding. After a hundred yards of easy walking in the clean trench, a train whistled twice in the distance, from below, as though they stood on a hill.

"The last train from Schirmeck is coming into Ville Negre," Sigmund said.

"I didn't know there was a train to Ville Negre," Everett said. "Beatrice and I could have taken it yesterday, instead of Philippe having to drive. We might have avoided this whole mess."

Sigmund stopped. He raised the lantern high above the parapet and looked ahead.

"Good. Let us walk slowly and quietly," Sigmund said. "They are taking Gerta down her path to the right that leads down the hillside towards Rue Gambetta. I want to make certain they are far enough away so that Louis does not hear what I am about to tell you."

"What? That your daughter is no angel?" Everett said.

"Now, you listen to me!" Sigmund said, his face bearing an ugly and stern wrinkle. "It is difficult to speak to you like this, as you remind me so much of your father. Beatrice did not return wearing her habit this time."

"She wears it for protection, she said."

"Woman, especially beautiful women, will wear the most awful clothes for that purpose. Madame Lambert, for example, wore the black mourning veil for months after Évariste's fatal charge," Sigmund said. "She feared that her own countrymen might take advantage of her. She wore it again when the American's came. It was only after they left that she removed it for me."

"You were captured by my father. Why would she remove it for a prisoner?"

"I was a shattered, trembling man the day your father and his men departed," Sigmund said. "Something terrible happened the night before. Madame Lambert brought me solace, not with her therapy, but with her love."

"Beatrice was conceived that day?" Everett said. "Out here?"

"Brunnhilde, indeed," Sigmund said. "Our daughter fell in love with a German too. It must run in Madame Lambert's blood. She donned the habit to escape."

"I've seen her passport – she had help."

"The kind German officer saw to it that she got out safely," Sigmund said. "There were a few people in Ville Negre who wanted her killed."

"The Chauchat's?"

Sigmund spat up over the hill towards the screech of grinding train wheels coming to a stop in Ville Negre.

"Beatrice, wearing the habit up-close, normally takes the train to Ville Negre," Sigmund said. "I cannot even call my own daughter by her real name."

Sigmund handed the lantern to Everett to check on Louis, Beatrice and Gerta.

"Climb up on top," Sigmund said. "Tell me where they are."

Everett pushed himself up over the back parapet and stood on a small patch of tall grass. The bright distant lights of the train station at Ville Negre dimmed one by one as passengers disembarked. Halfway down to Ville Negre, along the steep slope of the hill, the station's lights eclipsed smoke from the tuilerie's chimney, coiling upwards. A corner of the world kept safe by its geometry and distance, connected by Rue Gambetta threading north up to the high plateau, cut with trenches and laced in wire on which they perched.

Everett swung the beam down the hillside from the trench. It flashed against the Mercedes, parked below. Louis and Beatrice turned up to wave as they tied Gerta to the chrome bumper. Everett trained the light on them as they climbed their way back up.

"Are they down there?" Sigmund asked.

"They're coming up, now."

"You must never mention the name Brunnhilde again or I fear she will again wear the habit and return to Indochina," Sigmund said. "The countryside beneath the hills of Dien Bien Phu must look like the Zone Rouge by now."

A car sloshed through mud, flashing its headlamps and blasting its horn. Not more than fifty yards from where Everett stood on the firing ledge, the car left the hill's crest, airborne, with its engine revved high, over the same road that Philippe had taken from Rothau.

"Le Général!" hollered the young drunken revelers towards the dugout. "Le General Allemand!" they shouted as the car dove down a steep grade towards Ville Negre.

"Kids?" Everett said, turning to Sigmund.

"Yes," Sigmund said. "At one time they shouted it to annoy me, I am sure – but now, I think, they just want to see if I am still alive."

Sigmund helped Everett down, pointing to a ladder next to the dugout's entrance.

"Climb up, if you wish," Sigmund said. "It is quite a view."

Everett climbed up then dipped the lantern's beam of down the foothill's slope, where divots, creases and a few craters marked the artillery's history of near misses.

"Where, exactly, are we?"

"We stand on the grassy top of my deep dugout," Sigmund said. "This is the top of my world, at the very edge of the Gods' great chess board, on the leeward side of hell."

Below, Beatrice lectured Louis on the dangers of the Zone Rouge as they marched up from where they bedded Gerta next to the Mercedes.

"Step down now," Sigmund said. "I hear them coming. Hand me the lamp."

Sigmund swung the beam down the slope, flashing the Mercedes' chrome grill and Gerta's white coat. Walking up the path towards them were Louis and Beatrice, with Beatrice still reprimanding him for entering Zone Rouge.

"Yes, Sister Beatrice - never again," Louis repeated.

Beatrice and Louis entered the trench, panting, out of breath. Her green eyes met Everett's as she hooked her arm around his elbow.

"Did you and Sigmund have a nice chat?" Beatrice said.

"Indeed," Sigmund answered before Everett could clear his throat.

Sigmund shone the lamp to his right. A huge tarpaulin framed a side of the trench. Pulling it aside, Sigmund revealed the entrance to a dugout – a step up, then a step down.

Inside, a single electric bulb glowed at the bottom of a long flight of wooden steps, twenty feet below. Timbers, sturdy and well maintained, held the high walls and ceiling of the stairway tunnel. The light bulb swayed from a wire at the bottom step, due to their footsteps. Sigmund knocked on the door in some sort of code, "Ta-da, Ta-da, Ta-da", then carefully twisted a tarnished brass knob. Everett gave Beatrice a curious glance.

"An old habit from his war, when one never knew what he returned to," Beatrice said softly.

"Wilkommen," Sigmund said. He pushed the door open and showed them inside.

His tall frame bent slightly beneath the low ceiling of the deep dugout. A fireplace sputtered to life. He set the lantern on a pine-surfaced table next to a Parcheesi board then stepped to the right where the fireplace cast an orange glow. Walls of bulging wooden planks and logs held the earth in place except for tiny piles where it had fallen to the hard-packed dirt floor. The air smelled of ripened potatoes, mushrooms and of the old man himself.

A wooden clock, with its shattered watch glass, hung on the wall. Everett thought it should be close to morning, but it was only six-fifteen.

Sigmund showed them past a crude kitchen to a sleeping room off to the side, separated with a red-beaded curtain that Everett guessed was Madame Lambert's attempt long ago to soften their harsh subterranean nest.

"Louis looks tired from saving our American friend," Sigmund said to Beatrice as he tossed Everett a pair of pants. "Perhaps you and Louis should go to sleep while I speak with Russell."

"His name is Everett, Sigmund."

"I apologize, but he looks exactly like his father – it takes me back in time."

"He must be getting tired too - of your war stories," Beatrice said. "I need to clean his wounds."

"All I need is a good bath," Everett said, hoping it alone would stop the pain on his back and shoulder, growing irritated at the fuss over him and wanting to find the band.

"I will tend to Everett," Sigmund said. "I have my own kit."

"God no!" Everett thought to himself of Sigmund crafting Gerta's foot.

"You only have the sulfa drugs and hypodermic I gave you for your work, Sigmund," Beatrice said. "You have nothing for the pain."

"Ach! Russell never needed anything for his pain," Sigmund said.

"Well, Everett is not this Russell," Beatrice said. "Just look at his back, he's going to need more than just a little of your Jagermeister."

"It is far better than what you give Philippe." Sigmund said. "Far better too, than your Madame Lambert's trances."

Louis stepped to Sigmund with a raised eyebrow and asked, "General Sigmund, what is a trance? Is Grand-mère not bathing Father tonight? He might need me. Do you think he is asleep yet?"

Everett's throat choked, suddenly thinking of a touch and a smell of a man's face – the one named Russell. He thought of Louis as Philippe might come into his darkened room in the middle of the night, to touch him with a cold metal hand. He now knew more of Philippe than Russell, his father.

"A trance is like sleep, Louis," Beatrice said, leading him to bed. "Madame will plant a sweet idea in your father's head for the night to sleep on."

"Perhaps Madame should marry Svengali," Sigmund said.

"Perhaps Madame should hypnotize you," Beatrice said.

Bedsprings rang. "Good night, Monsieur."

"Good night, Louis."

Beatrice returned and smiled to Everett. Her face, drawn and tired from a war in Indochina and now, he guessed, from attending to him, Everett waved her to bed with Louis.

"Don't let my screams keep you up," Everett laughed.

Beatrice winked then returned to the bedroom.

"I am serious, Monsieur," Sigmund said. "You may wish you had Philippe's opium curse by the time I finish with you."

"I never touch the stuff," Everett said.

"And neither do I," replied Sigmund.

"It is on the mantel above the fireplace," Beatrice yawned. "Mother – er, Madame Lambert, wanted it out of the tuilerie in case she needed to call an ambulance – the police usually accompany them."

"I'll save a few grams for Philippe," Everett said as Beatrice disappeared behind the brief tinkle of beads into the bedroom. "Good night, Brunnhilde,"

"Brunnhilde?" Louis said.

Everett turned cold as he sensed Sigmund breathing down his back.

"I asked you not to use that name," Sigmund snapped. "Now, come this way."

The old man snatched the opium and led Everett to a room, pulling a curtain closed.

A Victrola phonograph stood like a brown bear on its haunches off to the side, aiming its silent trumpet up towards the center of the room. A stove in the corner, glowed dull red, simmering a teapot and dimly lighting the room. A hand-painted cup, with the tiniest pastoral setting, rested on top of the Victrola. Sigmund set the opium beside it.

"Philippe painted it, copying his father's last cup when he was young. He brought it here for Beatrice, the one time he visited my home."

"He was quite an artist. What a shame ..." Everett stopped as Sigmund firmly gripped his arm and moved him to a short stool by the stove.

"He still is. Kneel down and bend over this stool and hold that cup out."

"Why?" Everett asked.

"As I remove your barbs, I prefer not to step onto the rusted thorns."

Everett felt the warmth of the lantern as Sigmund examined his back, up-close.

"Mmm, very bad," Sigmund mumbled. "Never trained to fall onto the wire?"

"I was in the Air Force," Everett said.

Sigmund's bent-over shadow stretched across the tall, varnished wooden panel of the Victrola and up the wall behind, reaching to a bag on a shelf.

Sigmund rummaged through the bag, pulled out a long stainless steel tweezers and dropped it in the boiling pot.

"Madame thought I might need this one day for shrapnel, given my line of work.

"For Christ's sake Sigmund, it's not that bad, is it?"

"Dozens of rusted barbs have broken off under your skin. I assume you were given tetanus shots before Korea, but these need prying out. It will hurt. I see I must now ruin my favorite meerschaum pipe with Philippe's opium for your sake. Do not scratch your wounds. I will be a minute. I need to ask Beatrice how it is done."

After returning from the bedroom, Sigmund stepped to the Victrola where he prepared his long stemmed pipe. Biting a tiny corner from the dark bar of opium, Sigmund kneaded the black tar with his fingers and dropped it into the bowl.

"It's like a big booger," Everett said, pointing to his nose.

"Worry not. It is only a speck." Sigmund sunk a flaming match into the pipe's small white bowl that soon flared in his face.

The pipe trailed a curling white thread of smoke as Sigmund swung like a priest casting out demons with incense. He filled the room with the smell of burning flowers as he drew from it, stoking it until its ember dimmed. He offered the pipe to Everett.

"I don't need that," Everett said. "The barbs are only like little slivers."

The pipe shook.

"You will. My hands are not all that steady anymore," Sigmund said.

"Only a puff," Everett said.

Everett drew hard, nothing. A tiny cinder fell to the floor as he tipped it.

"I apologize for dwelling on the first pipe," Sigmund said, stepping to the Victrola. "I was always curious how this affected Philippe. It needs another load."

Sigmund tore a corner from the sticky black bar and rolled it into a larger pellet. He turned around and touched a long straw into the belly of the stove. Withdrawing it in an elegant orange filament of flame, he painted a line of light from the stove to Everett's face and the pipe, like an altar boy reaching to light his first candle.

The black tar boiled alongside the flame in the bowl until the opium ignited in a yellowish glow. Sigmund lifted the straw that had done its work and flicked it once to put it out. His eyes glistened as they focused, like a chef's, on the bubbling flame in the pipe. He drew the smoke into his lungs time after time until his eyes briefly rolled back into his head.

"That is much better," Sigmund said, admiring his blaze.

He extended the pipe to Everett, this time with a steady hand, like a conductor's baton, waiting for the orchestra's eyes after raising it for their attention.

Out of courtesy, Everett took a short quick draw and found it not as sweet as the smoke's aroma. His tongue recoiled and throat gagged at the strange chemical taste. He held the pipe out to Sigmund.

"It takes several draws, I am just now feeling its calming effect," Sigmund said, turning the pipe back to Everett. "Keep it alive while I busy myself on your back."

The towering shadow of Sigmund moved to the stove. He picked up the boiling pot, whose white steam curled dark against the shadow and set it to Everett's side as Everett took another drag from the pipe. Sigmund lowered the lantern to within a few feet of Everett's back and fueled the mantel until it glowed white-hot. The wounds awakened as Sigmund soaked them with a steaming cloth.

"The opium doesn't affect me at all," Everett said, closing his eyes at the pain.

"Take another draw," Sigmund said.

As he did, Sigmund's words came from across the room rather than above him where Sigmund stood. The brightness of the room shone transparently through Everett's closed eyelids. The deep-dugout became soft, quiet and white with snow falling in large flat flakes as Sigmund tossed cotton balls to the floor.

This last puff seemed to be working. He concentrated on the wall's animated shadow, the steel tweezers chattering like castanets as Sigmund clicked and poked, his shadow dancing to the Victrola and back, countless times for opium.

"Does that old thing even work?" Everett asked, recalling how the hiss, pop and glow of his wingman's new tube amplifier, on cold and snowy Korean nights would fill their Quonset, near the runway, with warmth and the sounds of Charlie Parker and Miles Davis.

"That old thing, as you call it, is your father's, and of course it works," Sigmund said. "I keep it polished and well-oiled."

Everett twisted his head to stare at the gooseneck arm resting to the side of the turntable. He tried conjuring an image of his father turning the crank to spin the wheel, but all he saw was Sigmund's shadow draped across the wooden machine.

"What is it doing here?" Everett asked. "It would think that the needle would be skipping out of the record's groove with all the artillery thumping up on your roof."

"Like the clock, your father's Victrola was in the tuilerie during the war," Sigmund said. "He had it shipped where they trained, but when the time came to attack, they dropped everything, including me. I brought it with me when I later moved below ground. Madame Lambert and I grew rather fond of the Victrola and your father's old records."

"I didn't come to France for my father's recordings, I came for the band."

Sigmund snapped the tweezers next to Everett's ear.

"Jesus!" Everett yelped as though a yellow jacket set its stinger deep into his back and pumped hot poisonous acid into a nerve.

"The barbs are deeper than I thought. Do not move," Sigmund said, dipping the tweezers again into the steaming teapot.

Against the wall, Sigmund's shadow reached into a back pocket, extracting something – a knife, Everett thought – a Damascus bladed dagger. Sigmund dropped it with a dull thud into the cup Everett held. It made a soft, wooden sound. Everett stared at Évariste's paintbrush with relief.

"Take one last draw," Sigmund ordered as his tweezers prodded what felt like a fishhook, sunk deep into his back. "This barb is about to surrender."

"What's with the brush?" Everett said.

Sigmund tugged on the bit of metal in Everett's back until it yielded its grip and an ocean of calm flooded over his body. The opium nauseated him at first, but now it flowed in his blood, spreading like a warm salve of camphor.

"Philippe may have the same sense of relief when he sees that brush?" Sigmund said. His tweezers clutched a small rusted bloodstained shard. "He is as desperate for his father's remains as you are for this band."

"Hold that cup out," Sigmund said, then dropped the barb to rattle in the cup.

Everett looked glumly into the empty pipe bowl, expected nothing but more pain.

"There is much more, I am afraid," Sigmund said.

Time blurred, as Sigmund continuously replenished the bowl and the cup slowly filled with metal barbs. It could have been an hour. It could have been two. Everett swore the clock's hands had swung a full circle through the night, but it still read six-fifteen.

"Évariste wore ordinary clothes," Sigmund said after the pipe grew cold and dark. "Overalls, a sweater – it was cold that spring, and his black beret. All that would have rotted, through the years of rain and snow, and his bones, picked clean by ravens and boar."

"How do you know all this?" Everett asked. "You were too frightened, I'm told, to have seen him like I did."

Everett felt Sigmund probing deeper for a barb that he said remained and which, like fish in a lake, may be there or not. He sensed the tweezers approaching a nerve.

"I could use a little more opium," Everett said, "if you please."

"I observed the French through my telescope, paying respect each time they passed Évariste," Sigmund said. "They would straighten his beret after a storm, or prop an arm or leg that wandered from his proud and natural stance, or tighten his belt buckle as he thinned out each week."

"Beatrice thinks Madame Lambert is still waiting for Évariste to return," Everett said. "He was going to remove Chesterfield."

"Sometimes, a fairy tale is all that holds a family together," Sigmund said.

Sigmund's tweezers found a sensitive spot. Everett jumped.

"I'll need more opium."

"It is unfortunate that I must give you this for the pain," Sigmund said, as he rolled another ball between his palms and dropped it into Everett's pipe. "I rather enjoy it now, and we will not be getting more unless Beatrice returns to Indochina."

Sigmund held Everett's hand with the pipe. He wiggled a flaming straw over the black tar until it turned to lava and flared to life.

"Aren't we saving some for Philippe?" Everett asked.

"There is enough, besides, Madame Lambert is caring for him and soon, if I can convince her that Évariste has been found, she will be mine. The brush and his bones might convince them that Évariste has returned. I was rather hoping you might fetch him for me, Évariste – that is."

"Back into the Zone Rouge? Bull roar!" Everett said, rising up only to feel Sigmund's old leathered fingers gripping his neck. Everett stewed for a second, wondering if Doc Hershey knew the mess he had gotten him into.

"Bull roar - you say it just as your father did," Sigmund sighed.

Everett twisted on his knees.

"I apologize," Sigmund said. "I should not have asked you the favor. Please, take the last of the pipe. My daughter will be furious if you were to suffer before you died."

"Aren't you being a little melodramatic?" Everett managed to say before briefly passing out as he watched Sigmund's hunched shadow on the wall examining his back.

"The last ones, near your neck will be quite painful," Sigmund said with a touch of sympathy Everett hadn't heard before. He tapped Everett's head to get him to inhale.

Sigmund clicked the steel tweezers as he exhumed the barbs. They dropped like hailstones into the cup as he worked his way around Everett's lower neck.

"I have come to the last bit and it will be the worst," Sigmund said with a jab of the hot steel tweezers. "Perhaps in the morning, while I lock those trench gates, you might feel well enough to return to the Zone Rouge and exhume your namesake."

"Fat chance, General," Everett said, raising his head.

"That was unkind, sir," Sigmund said. "Try not to move."

Everett felt the skin around his neck pull away as Sigmund struggled with the barb. He relaxed as he heard the last barb hit the edge of the cup. Sigmund cleaned him with a cool, moist cloth soaked in perfumed medicine then patted Everett's shoulder.

Everett took a short draw on the pipe and felt the small punctures in his back and neck seal shut. Sigmund handed him the cup with a quarter-inch layer of barbs at the bottom, rattling as though they were babies' teeth. Everett explored the cup's fluted shape and texture, trying to focus on Philippe's miniature painting.

It was like Philippe's father, Evariste's work - but better. A family in Lorraine lay picnicking along an olive green river, lacing orchids and violets between their toes. The foothills of the Vosges lay covered in blue forests beneath a blue sky. Giant white storks circled the treeless, rounded balloons of the Vosges before soaring to their chimney top nests along the Rhine. Parents strolled shoeless before fat, naked babies, crawling and squealing in the tall grass. It all moved and came to life in the tiny painting between his hands.

Everett felt the cup rise from his hands as Sigmund carefully lifted it.

"It is the Lorraine and the Alsace as we all wanted them to be," Sigmund said, as he raised the cup. "Still quite beautiful, there are parts, like the Zone Rouge, that appear, strangely enough, like your backside. I will find something to cover you."

Sigmund stepped into the bedroom. Beatrice's familiar snore came from behind the bedroom curtain as Sigmund re-emerged, carrying Everett's bag.

"Good. They sleep soundly," Sigmund said, opening the bag. "Beatrice brought your bag from the tuilerie. Do you have a clean shirt inside?"

Everett sat on his knees and was about to stand as Sigmund held the stack of letters in one hand while searching the bag with the other for a shirt.

"Only underwear and socks." Everett reached for the letters but Sigmund held them back, flipping the stack with his thumb at the addressee corner.

"Somewhere in France? Hmm," Sigmund said. He held one closer to the lantern. "These are quite old and brittle."

"Stop! They're mine," Everett said, turning up to speak. The back of his neck itched as though he had the pox. Sigmund handed him the letters.

"Thanks," Everett said. He brought the pipe to his lips and sucked for relief.

"They were from the AEF, American Expeditionary Force – not your Air Force," Sigmund said. "They are from your father - my friend Russell, are they not? How many?"

"Twenty-six," Everett said, coughing to the side of the cold, burned-out pipe.

"That cough," Sigmund said, "it is your father's."

"I don't remember him," Everett said.

"How can one not remember his own father," Sigmund said.

"Doc Hershey may have told you," Everett said, surprised Sigmund didn't know. "My father died when I was nine. He probably told you that I have nightmares of my war."

Sigmund tugged at an ear, and then cleared his throat.

"I am so sorry, Monsieur – I did not know. I have not heard from Doctor Hershey for over thirty-five years, I have nearly forgotten him," Sigmund said. "But these letters, your father should have posted them then."

"They are letters of regret to the families of the dead. My father didn't finish any of them," Everett said, relieved to know Doc Hershey hadn't meddled, at least with Sigmund. "That's what I've come to do, the way my father would have wished. Madame Lambert was to have helped me."

"Do you mind if I read a few?" Sigmund asked, as he dropped another ball of tar into Everett's pipe and touched a flaming straw to its surface. "Perhaps I can assist."

"Doc never mentioned you, only Madame Lambert," Everett said.

"I am certain Doctor Hershey believed I died long ago, at the hands of the French or my own men," Sigmund said. "He often visited your father for that awful cough. I would cook them both a fine dinner, but the Doctor always blamed me for that cough. Your father never did."

Everett handed the letters back to Sigmund then coughed as he took a draw or two, catching himself nodding ever deeper to his knees.

◆　◆　◆

He jumped, thinking a bee had stung his hand. The pipe lay hot against his wrist as Sigmund tucked the last letter tenderly into its envelope. Sigmund's old, sagging eyes each held a teardrop.

"Madame Lambert will be of little help with these old letters," Sigmund said.

Everett stiffened and groaned from the sudden movement that awakened his wounds.

"You know them? Do you know this band?" Everett said.

"Stay, still," Sigmund said as he reached into his shirt pocket and opened the small tin of salve he had used on Gerta's hoof. "I must apply this to your back."

The smell of camphor, the same as Beatrice had used on his hand, met Everett's nose and startled him awake. It radiated heat through his raw back as Sigmund worked it into the cuts.

"What happened to the band?" Everett asked.

Sigmund's strong hands melted. His palms lay cold, like dead fish against Everett's back.

He handed Everett a clean grey woolen shirt from a chest. The overpowering smell of mold caught Everett's nose. Empty stitch marks, like ghosts, appeared where military patches and pins once adorned the shoulders and lapels. Sigmund helped him wiggle inside the right sleeve.

"There you are, son," Sigmund said. "Now, I should think another pipe and a little music is in order before we retire, yes?"

Before Everett could respond, Sigmund brought a flaming stick to the pipe. Everett tried to stand, but the old man's hardened hands tightened around his wrist until Everett succumbed to the pleasurable smell of the smoke.

Sigmund threw down a few woolen blankets on Everett's cot next to his own then pulled a record from the Victrola's wooden chamber and set it spinning.

"Wagner's Tannhauser Overture," Sigmund said as the French horns called from deep inside the Victrola's long trumpet stem. "Not a band, but an orchestra."

"Wagner," Sigmund said reverently. "Our trenches were even named for the characters of his Opera - Brunnhilde, Kriemhilde, Hagen, and of course Siegfried - the best trenches the world has ever seen."

Violins and cellos called for the horns to come closer into the room. Sigmund held the paintbrush like a baton to conduct.

"I must be on Mars," Everett said.

"An excellent choice of planets, indeed," Sigmund said. "You have come to the proper place, now the music will carry us to the correct time - there, now do you hear it?"

The crescendo of horns swelled. Trumpets heroically entered the room, bold and brave. It moved so quickly, with a phantom melody that never really appeared.

Minutes later it settled into an ending as best it could, built on a majestic tone. Everett expected the melody to reappear at any minute, but it didn't.

"Did my father enjoy listening to it?" Everett asked.

"Not much," Sigmund said. "It was my record. It was the only thing your father allowed me to take with me when I was captured."

"What did father like to hear?" Everett asked.

"He liked something livelier," Sigmund said, kneeling to the Victrola's belly.

Sigmund extended his long boney arms to the far reaches of the Victrola's wooden chest and carefully removed a thin black hard-rubber platter from a cardboard cover.

"Ah, here it is," Sigmund said. "Wagner's Tannhauser March - one your father's favorites."

Sigmund set the arm down on the spinning record. The needle scratched four times, Sigmund counted them on his fingers, before the brass tuba blasted from the wooden horn.

"Stephen Collins. He is setting the foundation for the march," Sigmund said. "Oh, how I remembered his young face with that tuba coiled around him."

Sigmund sat on the cot next to Everett, closed his eyes and drew from the pipe that Everett handed him.

"You knew him?" Everett asked as though they just passed a young Stephen Collins on the street.

A section of trumpets took the lead and soared with such pronunciation that the notes, staccato yet bold, might have been sung rather than buzzed through a small metal pipe.

"Indeed," Sigmund's voice, crimped from holding a lungful of opiate-laden air until he burst. "And there is the trombone – Crabshaw, Jim Crabshaw."

"You know this band?"

"All of them. They play Wagner's march as though they were German."

The horn section carried on in a triumphant blare. The trombones and saxophones bent and shaped the tones to their liking. Flutes and clarinets gave some class and ornamentation to the driving martial theme punctuated with drums and a flurry of snares and rim-shots.

Sigmund reached for his back pocket and found Évariste's brush. He stood to conduct the last of the march until the music faded away in scratches to a dull, grinding halt.

"The names were mythical for so long," Sigmund said.

"The names are real. I know where their families lived in town," Everett said. "They played Wagner's march so well because many still spoke German in their homes."

"They were haunting names from the past," Sigmund said. "Like the names of imaginary friends of ones childhood."

"Do you know why my father couldn't finish the letters?" Everett asked.

"Russell's regiment went on the attack and never returned this way again," Sigmund said as he stretched for the smoldering pipe beside Everett. "That night was the last I heard from him. I am not surprised he carried all those letters, I am certain he intended on finishing them between battles. That is the sort of man your father was."

"If he was that good, why didn't he finish them?" Everett asked as he kept the pipe at arms length from Sigmund.

"Ach," Sigmund turned his head to spit. "You know how these wars all acquire a life of their own, you have been in one. Your father's regiment probably went through so many replacements in the next few months, that he would need a whole staff just to write letters home. He would never allow a stranger to write a letter either – that was your father, all right – to a tee – as he would say."

"I want you to tell me about the band as my father would know them - who they were, and how they died," Everett said. "I want to finish those letters."

"Why?" Sigmund asked. "You certainly are not thinking of posting them, after all these years – are you?"

"I only need to finish them," Everett said. "I feel close to my father in those letters."

"You have had too much to smoke. I cannot believe Doctor Hershey would recommend that as a treatment for your nightmares," Sigmund said.

"He's sent me here to visit Madame Lambert for that, he trusts her," Everett said. "But I refuse to have anyone poking around my skull. Instead, I might probe her about these letters if you won't tell me."

"If you wish to keep something hidden, you had best be careful around Madame Lambert," Sigmund said.

"Bull roar!" Everett said.

"What a splendid expression," Sigmund said as he lifted the pipe from Everett, stoking it, and was about to take a drag, but handed the pipe back to Everett, full of fire.

"Madame Lambert's hypnotherapy was never successful on me," Sigmund said, "at least, from what I am able to recall of her attempts."

Everett's hand reached, helplessly, to the bowl, boiling in smoke. His lungs ignited as he took in a half-breath and coughed uncontrollably, bending at the knees. The spasms opened tiny cracks of coagulated blood covering his wounds. He shivered slightly before the drug draped loosely over the inferno in his chest like a cool, soft silk sheet.

"I need to know about the band, Sigmund. You must know how they died."

"I am certain, I do," Sigmund said. "Someday, I may find the courage to recite the awful fact just as someday, I might wander by accident into Hagen's trench and retrieve Évariste Lambert. After that, I may have enough courage remaining to ask for Madame Lambert's hand. But for tonight, I prefer the safety of my deep-dugout as I have for the last thirty-five years."

Beatrice's snoring in the bedroom drew their attention.

"It is a comforting sound, yes?" Sigmund said.

Everett nodded, wanting her head next to his again, rocking against him as she had done on the train.

"That is where the courage lies," Sigmund said. "Beatrice cannot stay long in the Lorraine. I am afraid she will return to Indochina."

"Why? Dien Bien Phu is lost," Everett said. "Why would she have to leave the Lorraine?"

"Because it is not safe here for her," Sigmund said, "and besides, Beatrice has fallen in love."

Everett's heart sunk inside his chest. He undid a button of the woolen shirt to breath.

"If she's fallen for a Legionnaire from that bar, the Port-du-Chien, I'm happy for her then," Everett said with a note of finality.

"Are you blind, man?" Sigmund grunted.

"Not yet," Everett said as his eyes slid backwards into his skull.

"Good, because my Beatrice is in love with you," Sigmund whispered.

"She's in love with me? Did she say that?" Everett imagined the opium logic at its deceptive best.

"No, but I have seen the way she looks to you, the way Madame Lambert does to me," Sigmund said. "It makes me feel good inside."

Sigmund rubbed the warm white meerschaum against his leathered cheek as though the pipe's bowl were flesh.

"How does your back feel?" Sigmund asked, handing Everett the pipe and walking to the Victrola. He carefully placed the record into its paper shell.

"Better," Everett said. His eyes grew heavy. "Doc Hershey would be impressed."

The bubbling tar popped in the pipe as Everett tasted the bitter smoke at the back of his throat. He set it down, thinking of nothing other than the deep gentle snore of Beatrice.

"I am certain Doctor Hershey did not expect you to follow Russell's footsteps into the Zone Rouge for the band, I apologize for not having it cleared. Tomorrow, in return, I shall allow Madame to tour my memory for the twenty-six stories of your letters."

Everett waited a moment for the pain in his back to return and listened for the pattering of boar on the roof before saying what he expected Sigmund wanted to hear.

"I'll go for my namesake's bones in the morning, if you just lock up the damned trenches for good."

"Perfect," Sigmund said as he turned to the comforting sounds of Beatrice and Louis traded snores. He smiled and, with a nod, drifted asleep. Under thirty feet of soil and filled with echoes of Wagner, the deep dugout felt like the safest place on earth.

౮౨9౧౮

Evariste

A man with a burning broom stands by a smoldering hamlet. He swings at an invisible fluttering or flapping as though a bat or phantom is attacking him. He's been swinging the flaming broom all night. Now, before dawn, he sits down, exhausted.

He sits lotus-like, eyes closed, beneath a soot-blackened sky with the torch raised high and slowly fills his lungs through his nose and holds it, searching for his lover's perfume. But the summertime air, here in the Taebacks in the year, 1953, of our Lord, should carry the only perfume of a true communist – sweat. There is something else.

He pierces the silence with a blasting cough and hack, for the air is full of mayfly stench and napalm, preserving the dead in boiling creosote, as his hand becomes one with a torch. Too bright to bear, too hot to hold, he grips it firmly in his hand.

♦ ♦ ♦

Light ebbed orange and yellow beneath his eyes. Everett raised his brow to the flame of a candle on a table beneath the clock. It was six-fifteen. The door creaked then opened. A hazy sliver of daylight spread across the floor. He smelled something burning.

Sigmund stood with his back straight against the door's jamb, smoking his pipe – tobacco today. His head arched up to bask a side of his whiskered face in the light, spilling down the steps from the dugout's opened door above.

A dirty, oily bag rested at Sigmund's feet. It clanked as he kicked it. Bedsprings squeaked from the next room. Beatrice first yawned then sang. Everett couldn't believe his ears as she screeched 'America the Beautiful' in a key only American Indians would appreciate. Sigmund kicked the bag again before putting his pipe away.

"The voice could wake the dead," Sigmund said. "She sings like Madame, like a drunken lark."

"God, my head hurts," Everett fell back into the cot to his pillow.

"Up and at 'em!" Sigmund said kicking the bag again. "Your father, in the tuilerie, always woke me that way."

"What?"

"The call to charge, over the top, with fixed bayonets," Sigmund said. "We could hear the American's yelling that as they came towards our machine guns. They learned later to be more quiet."

"You slept in the tuilerie with my father and his men?"

"Why yes," Sigmund said. "He always rose early, anxious for me to prepare breakfast. 'Flapjacks and bacon, Up and at 'em, Ziggy', your father would say - knowing it was my men he wanted me to charge - such a sense of humor he had."

Everett swung his legs from the cot after Sigmund kicked it, good-naturedly.

The cuts in his back itched as the shirt rubbed against them. A few bled through and fused with the fabric.

"We must go before they ask too many questions about our quest," Sigmund said, tipping his pipe to Beatrice's room.

"Oh, yes," Everett said, "the quest. I was afraid you would remember that."

"Up and at 'em!", Sigmund said. "I will lock these chains around the trench gates while you fetch me Évariste's bones."

"I've enlisted as a grave robber," Everett thought to himself, wondering what else he agreed to during the night.

He scratched where the woolen pants itched then pulled them up snug around his waist, tucking the grey shirt inside. In the dim light, the stitch marks on the sleeves and lapels, retained the outline of a German regiment from some past war.

"I didn't sleep well," Everett said, as he staggered up the steps behind Sigmund into fresh air and blinding light.

"You did not sleep at all," Sigmund affirmed. "I listened to you twisting and moaning on the cot, as your father did - worrying about his men. You must have been dreaming of the band."

"It's just these itchy old clothes," Everett said, not recalling a dream at all. He reached to open the door to trench above.

"Wait!" Sigmund flipped the cover of a small peephole and looked outside.

"It is all clear," Sigmund said. "Now, I doubt my friend's old uniform kept you stirring. You had enough of my opium to put even Gerta to sleep."

"Do you mind if I stand on your roof to look around before we get started?" Everett asked. "I need a pilot's view."

"Be careful," Sigmund said. "The sun is dazzling."

Everett pulled himself up to the roof above the trench. His eyes felt like someone sandpapered them during the night, but as they moistened up, a vista bloomed around Sigmund's deep dugout. He faced the morning sun over the Vosges.

He stood on a grassy bluff with his back to the trench. The cool air, scented with fresh green grass and pine from the Vosges, quickly purged Everett's lungs of the moldy, stale air of the deep dugout below.

A valley flattened to the right. Over his shoulders, the immaculate reserve trench ran its stitch of zigs and zags in a straight line to the distant glint of Lac Noir. Smoke rose from the tall chimney of the tuilerie on the far back slope.

"Annette must already be baking bread for Philippe and Madame," Sigmund said. "It is a good sign - Madame succeeded. Gerta has even returned to the tuilerie."

The Mercedes' chrome sparkled from below where the path had led Gerta from Sigmund's trench. She was gone.

Not far from the Mercedes, her empty cart sat parked along Rue Gambetta. The road and the train tracks led straight to Ville Negre, with its rising columns of chimney smoke and a church spire.

Further down the slope, Everett found the outline of a road, branching to the right towards the tuilerie. Without the Mercedes, it would be a long walk along the road unless one followed Sigmund's trench. With daylight, came the logic of the lay of roads, the town, and the trenches.

"Let's get going," Everett said. He caught himself stomping his boot on Sigmund's roof. "Sorry."

"Save your father's sensitivity for Hagen's trench," Sigmund said pointing back down the trench. "Évariste's remains lie along the very spinal chord of the Great War."

Everett envisioned the Great War playing out on a chessboard as Sigmund suggested last night. Except this was a folding chessboard, creased at the frontlines, all resting above the valley floor on a tabletop. He thought of Chesterfield and turned again to the tuilerie and Ville Negre where artillery long ago spilled from the table.

Before they stepped down, Sigmund pointed out the veins of the communication trenches striking out from Sigmund's cleared trench towards the front. Everett could see the masses of wire in No-Mans-Land in the distance, like fire-ant hills, where he had fallen during the night.

"We must first lock those gates," Sigmund said.

Everett helped Sigmund step down into the reserve trench then hopped in. The firing ledge, green and lush, glistened with dew. He could lay his head on the ledge's turf and could not find a single protrusion of wire, brass, iron or bone.

"The old man turned the hellish reserve trench into a promenade," Everett thought to himself.

Plump sand bags, restored along the parapet, lay neatly stacked to their proper height, so that one would have to stand on his toes for the top of his helmet to show. A sturdy ladder leaned against the bags. Except for the muddy bottom, where wooden duckboards should lay, the trench almost seemed ready to withstand an attack. Sigmund wrapped his hand around Everett's arm to help himself up to the firing ledge.

"You spoke in an Asian tongue last night," Sigmund said after they had walked past a few traverses. Everett stopped.

"Korean," Everett said. "I learned enough to curse."

"I did not know that Koreans wept when they cursed," Sigmund said, pushing him forward. "Keep moving."

Everett bit his tongue.

"The one whose shirt you are wearing," Sigmund said, "he would sleep on the same cot and tell me in the morning that I spoke English during the night."

"Was he taken prisoner by my father, like you were?"

"No, it was the last war, during the occupation," Sigmund said, stopping to take a breath. "Manfred was a German officer in charge of Ville Negre who would visit and sit by my fire to listen to my old stories of the Great War."

"Did Manfred tell you what you spoke of in your sleep?"

He scratched where the old shirt rubbed the wire wounds around his neck, yet Sigmund said nothing and increased the pace down the trench.

He asked about his father, Russell, by name, to break the silence as they stepped over Gerta's fresh hoof prints and arrived at the gate nearest the dugout.

Sigmund dropped the bag with a clank, dumping a length of chain to the ground. The links were longer than a normal chain - all very clean.

"I was the same rank as your father, a Captain," Sigmund said as he wrapped the chain around the gate and the pole where it latched. "But he still kept me chained that first night to the leg of the Victrola, what a waste of my men's treasured Gunter chain."

"What's that?" Everett asked.

"My men were miners," Sigmund said. "Your Doctor Hershey did not tell you? The Gunter chain measures distance in the mines."

Sigmund found a lock in the bag and snapped it shut.

"One more gate and we are done," Sigmund said. "Step lively."

"Father handcuffed you with your own chain?" Everett asked.

"I told Russell, 'How impolite! You do know I could break this delicate wooden leg from your Victrola and escape, this was to be a quiet sector after all.' Your father said, 'We came to fight, not to sleep!' When Dr. Hershey visited the next day, he spoke with him to have me unchained."

Everett carried the bag of remaining chains as Sigmund lit a match for his pipe. "Do you think my father was mean?"

"No, but he did not understand the unspoken arrangement here," Sigmund said as he walked and rekindled his tobacco. The smoke carried a hint of opium.

"Arrangement?"

"An unspoken truce between sides in a stalemate," Sigmund said. "We were each accustomed to hearing ten-thousand artillery rounds by sunrise, for maximum effect, before battle. After we realized the stalemate, our notion of maximum effect became ten rounds at precisely ten AM, fired with a minimum charge. They would plop harmlessly into the mud of No-Man's Land out there where you walked last night."

Sigmund pointed his pipe up over the northern parapet of the reserve trench to the French front-line trench.

"The French abided by the understanding – just short of mutiny, that is, until the American's came. Your father was only following orders when he disrupted our peace with the trench raid that captured me."

"The tuilerie, although protected by the slope of the hill from artillery, was susceptible to a reprisal for that raid and I insisted that Madame and Philippe leave immediately. She refused, still waiting for Évariste's return, although he had been posted out there for a year."

Sigmund aimed his pipe to the gate just ahead. It had swung open again.

"Is that when you fell in love with her?" Everett asked.

"It was her commitment I loved first," Sigmund said as he peered over the parapet. "Madame told me she could not marry me while her husband was missing - a remarkable woman, after all these years. We must hurry. Philippe steps to the gate each morning while he hunts."

"And you, like Philippe, can't step past that gate to bring the man home?" Everett asked, pointing to the gate. Beyond, the first traverse of the communication trench, from which Everett and Louis emerged last night, ran to a sharp corner like a dark and ominous closet.

"Our artillery must have driven Évariste insane to have run down the communication trench with that paintbrush," Sigmund said as he pointed past the dark bend towards the front-line of Hagen's trench, his arm noticeably shaking.

"There he lies," Sigmund said.

"He doesn't lay, he stands," Everett said, "although his bones are a little fragile these days."

Everett took a deep breath as though he were about to jump into the sea, thinking about the trenches he and Louis had passed through.

"Do not worry about boar in the daylight," Sigmund said as he emptied the bag of chains and patted Everett on the shoulder to send him through the gate. "But do watch for dragon eggs. The sun tends to warm their juices. I will wait until you return before I lock the gate."

"How will I hold Évariste?" Everett asked, stepping past the gate. "He's bound up in pieces."

"Put this at his feet as you free him," Sigmund said as he flung the empty bag over the gate to Everett. "Perhaps he will simply collapse into the bag."

"After all these years Évariste should weigh no more than this," Sigmund said as he kicked the chains on the ground. He shook his head from side to side, raising the corner of his mouth in a regretful arc.

"This trench really frightens you, doesn't it?" Everett said.

Sigmund stared down the communication trench, past the gate.

"The Vogelscheuche standing his post is what frightens me," Sigmund said, hunching his back and flapping his arms loosely.

"Évariste – a scarecrow?" Everett said.

"Indeed," Sigmund said. "In exchange for you gathering him to free Madame Lambert of her vows, I must gather twenty-six long-buried souls in twenty-six haunting little stories for you."

Sigmund looked up with a hint of a smile and placed his worn hand on Everett's head.

"Put this in the bag as well, after you gather him up. I want the old boy just as he stood. Off you go," Sigmund said as he flipped the paintbrush to Everett and relit his pipe. "While you excavate him, I must consider how Évariste is to be delivered to Madame."

♦   ♦   ♦

The communication trench, in daylight, looked like an old municipal dump, cluttered and overgrown with weeds. As his eyes adjusted and focused, the features of the Great War reappeared beneath the thin crust of dust, moss and loose soil eroded by the wind, rain and snow.

The telephone wires along the walls could guide him as they had last night if he needed them. Yet, it would difficult managing the bag-full of bones on his return. By walking carefully, he didn't need the wires at all in daylight.

The frightening trench he had stumbled into last night, today, took on definition and character. A mortar tube, bent in half; an Indian motorcycle, metal re-enforcing panels for dugouts, rusted and half-buried. Dragon eggs and shells, in the daylight, lay everywhere like squirreled away nuts – some showing the tip of their fuse and others, the grooved edge of their corroded copper rotating band, green with age.

Peering over the parapet, the random tangles of barbed wire that gripped him during the stormy night, took on patterns. A strand of rusted wire, when pulled up, led to two, and two to four, multiplying geometrically. The gang of sharp-tentacled squid that attacked him at night, now stretched quietly in sculptured waves of wire, forward.

Vines, that he swore he had ripped and shredded in his blind dash at night, now gently blanketed the communication trench, bandaging every trace of his nocturnal steps. The carpet of moss thickened towards the front-line trench, a few more traverses away.

He leaned against the soft green mat of the communication trench wall to rest, thinking of Beatrice's soothing stroke on his burned hand. He felt it here too, at work on the land, torn by war. If only Beatrice's salve could rejuvenate those dark, burned husks of napalm inside his head and clear his nostrils of the soapy smell of his freshly loaded bombs. He straightened up, as his nose twitched uncontrollably.

A sharp, pungent odor from the next traverse crept in a thin jaundiced ribbon at his feet – "Mustard!"

Closing his eyes, he straddled the poisonous stream while breathing through the elbow of his shirtsleeve. He pictured the canister, in the front-line, that Louis had urinated on, now emitting a slight hiss, spewing its foul breath, far beyond the bones. He ran his fingers down the side of the trench wall to feel for the telephone wires that had saved him before.

He found them and tugged at the taut strands. Though now blinded, he felt confident in finding Évariste, and of coaxing him into falling neatly into the bag, as Sigmund suggested. He edged forward a few more traverses and felt the wires in his hand bend sharply to the right, as before. His nose sensed the poisonous vapor turning left where, he guessed, unseen dragon eggs must be hatching. He dropped the telephone wire, knowing he stood in the front-line trench with Évariste nearby. A buzz droned along the trench floor.

"Locusts?" Everett wondered.

He uncovered his nose, expecting a concentrated mustard cloud, instead a waft of cool putrid air passed down his nostrils. The buzz rose from the floor. As he opened his eyes, a swarm of breeding black flies darted about his ears, and circled his head in a dizzying blur, taking aim at his pupils. He quickly closed his eyes and swung his bag wildly, striking every other blow against Évariste's mesh tomb – bones fell like soft sandstone as they accumulated at the bottom of the wire basket.

After a minute, the flies tired and settled down near the floor. As Everett opened his eyes, Évariste, who had for so long stood his post, now lay in a heap at the bottom of the mesh. At his feet lay the tiny dead boar.

Everett guessed a small gash along its belly from Louis' random shot, sent it scurrying from its cannibal brethren to hide beneath the looming Vogelscheuche of Évariste in his full glory.

"Pigs may eat everything," Everett thought, stepping around the boar's carcass with newfound sympathy, "but black flies always eat what's left."

Everett pulled a bone, a tibia, from the bundle. He dug a shallow grave and delicately nudged the boar into the hole, and slowly covered it with dirt and moss, giving the flies time enough to leave in pairs rather than a swarm.

He carefully broke the rusted wire mesh at the bottom, letting the bones fall freely into the bag. When he finished, he set them aside and cleaned them against his pants, before laying them into the bag.

He found the skull with the two eye sockets he had felt the night before, filled with dirt. He knocked it against his hip and found the third hole, squarely in the middle of the forehead - a perfect rifle bullet-sized circle. Sifting through the debris, he found a metal belt buckle.

He put it all inside the bag and, before leaving, tamped the boar's grave, protecting it from raven's, flies and brethren boar. A decent grave for such a determined creature, Everett thought as he turned around and stepped from the front-line into the communication trench.

Skipping with delight over exposed shells and wire, he lifted the bag to his shoulder knowing that soon Madame Lambert would sift through Sigmund's head in return for the treasure he had found.

Approaching the last bend of the traverse, before the gate, a loud clang of chain against metal and wood shattered the quiet of the trench. Everett wondered, as he rounded the bend, why Sigmund was having so much trouble locking the gate.

There stood Philippe, at twenty paces, behind the gate's bars on his toes, anxiously looking at him as though Everett were a long lost brother. Everett stepped into full view. Philippe's face sagged. His hands clasped the back of his head as though a terrible bell had sounded.

Everett took a few cautious steps forward and peered around for Sigmund, but he was gone. It occurred to Everett that Sigmund had solved the delivery dilemma and that made him angry, or at least disappointed, in the old man's ways.

Philippe stood still, staring at the paintbrush sticking from Everett's bag. Everett guessed the brush, at the top of the shouldered bag, from a distance, must have appeared as Philippe's father's ghost approaching in the sunken trench. Everett slung the bag low to his side and offered Philippe the brush through the bars of the gate.

Philippe dropped to his knees and, with his hands cupped through the gate, accepted the worn-out brush as though it were the body of Christ.

"My, oh my!" Everett thought. "What a head job Madame has done on her son."

Everett tried tossing the bag full of bones over the gate, but it stood too high – he didn't want them to spill disrespectfully in front of Philippe. Instead, he handed the bones, one by one, to Philippe through the bars until Philippe had them stacked in a neat pile. Everett found the belt buckle and dropped it into Philippe's palm. Philippe rubbed it to a dull shine against his pants. His face, a moment ago, so blank and cold, now reddened with joy as he reached for Everett's hand through the gate. A warm and tender grip surrounded Everett's fingers.

"Allow me to help you over, Sir," Philippe said. "I am forever grateful. How can I repay you?"

Everett handed the bag to Philippe after climbing over the gate, meant to keep, it seemed, only children away.

"Tell your mother, Évariste has returned," Everett said.

Philippe carefully placed his father's bones in the bag and topped it off with the brush, all the while glancing to Everett as though the bag held Lazarus.

"We have waited so long for you to come. Merci, merci beaucoup," Philippe said, head bowed and backing away to the tuilerie.

After Philippe disappeared around a traverse, Everett sighed in relief as he strode back towards the deep dugout, amazed at how Madame Lambert had so quickly transformed her son. He skipped along the firing ledge grass, humming the tune he had come to know, feeling rather proud of himself too, for his hand in Philippe's remarkable, albeit strange and tenuous recovery. He clapped his hand free of dirt and bone dust. He knew he had fulfilled his end of the deal with Sigmund in which Madame Lambert could apply her now proven, mesmerizing abilities to release the details of the band and that night from Sigmund's head.

As the new lord of the Zone Rouge, he had Sigmund as his prisoner, yet all he wanted was a warm, vanilla-scented breath at his neck.

Everett caught a whiff of tobacco smoke as he rounded the last traverse. There, near the deep dugout stood Sigmund at the next gate to Hell, smoking and pacing off distances measured by the length of a chain. He half-expected Sigmund to go into hiding after leaving him, literally, holding the bag for Philippe. Everett crept up behind him.

"Pony up!" Everett hollered then quickly stepped back as Sigmund nearly swiped him with the chain.

"I do not like being surprised, especially here," Sigmund said.

"I don't like surprises either, Sigmund," Everett said.

"What do you mean, 'Pony Up'?" Sigmund asked. "Those were not the bones of a horse hanging from that post."

"You owe me twenty-six stories for that bag of bones," Everett said. "You think you're clever, Sigmund, but soon, I'll see how you stand up to Madame Lambert's inquisition about the band."

"I was afraid you might say that," Sigmund said as they moved to the oiled tarp, half-covering the dugout's entrance. A corner pin, holding it, had worked its way out.

"Philippe seemed almost serene," Everett said. "Madame Lambert must be good at what she does. What will she do with her husband's bones?"

"I hope she will bury them quickly," Sigmund said, smashing the pin into place with his boot then re-hanging the tarp. "I will then ask her to live with me forever here, in the deep dugout. I would hate to arrive at the tuilerie to ask for her hand and discover Philippe had reassembled poor Évariste on the porch."

"You worry too much," Everett said. "Do you really think she'll refuse such a persistent Bosch as you?"

"She will first put me under her spell," Sigmund said. "Then she will tell me I am an old fool, but then she will say, 'Yes'. Madame, however, might not enjoy living in my dugout. I am already measuring for improvements she might want below."

"Why don't you live in the tuilerie, with the rest of them?" Everett asked. "There's plenty of room. Why did you ever move to the dugout after my father left?"

Everett felt a jolt at the bottom of the trench. Overhead, a low rumble quickly developed into an earth-shattering crack, shifting the loose dust along the parapet in rippling pulses that subsided as the roar dissipated.

Everett scrambled to the roof of the dugout as a tall black cloud rose beyond Ville Negre.

"It is the depot, beyond Ville Negre, detonating unexploded munitions." Sigmund said, looking at his watch. "It is Ville Negre's de facto town crier – 10 AM every morning except Sunday."

"It is safer here than in the tuilerie." Sigmund spit a stray bit of tobacco up, back over the parapet. He lifted the heavy gas cloth to enter then leaned to Everett's ear, "Besides, Madame still keeps her paramour, Chesterfield, at attention by the tuilerie's door."

"That big artillery shell?" Everett asked.

"There are thousands more, like Chesterfield, resting in the Zone Rouge." Sigmund gestured back over the parapet with his pipe. "I am quite nervous around the tuilerie with Chesterfield there, he is a stubborn one."

"That reminds me, I need to finish some work," Sigmund said nudging Everett forward. "Beatrice and Louis must be having their breakfast. Why not join them below?"

Sigmund brushed Everett's gray woolen shirt free of dirt.

"Say, just a minute, Sigmund," Everett said, holding Sigmund. "You look fresh as a daisy and I look like hell and, by the way, that's exactly where I went for you this morning. Because you suckered me into delivering the bones to Philippe, I'm going to need to tell them; soon the news will be all over town. Now, I'm going to have to lie to them about Évariste's unusual pose."

"There is no need to mention that," Sigmund said. "Now, remember to use the code on the door, Louis might think it is Philippe after him. I have more work to do below."

Sigmund stepped down Gerta's path.

"Where do think you're going?" Everett asked.

"I need to make some money," Sigmund said, ambling down the far slope.

"The old fart," Everett thought. "He's bailing again!"

ಬ10ಆ

Donon

Today Philippe seemed saner than the old man who sold unexploded munitions, who lived in a bunker dreaming of a woman waiting for her husband to return from the dead.

Just as Everett considered that Sigmund might have put that rifle bullet through Évariste's skull and was now escaping, Sigmund turned abruptly, before reaching the Mercedes. He disappeared into the side of the hill to the sound of a creaking door.

Everett ducked inside the dugout's entrance, stomping his boots clear of mud on the wooden steps to the deep dugout. He rapped on the heavy door, 'Ta-da, Ta-da, Ta-da'.

The door opened a crack. A blue eye, wide, young and glistening, stared.

"It's only me." Everett said.

"Monsieur? Oh, Monsieur you are just in time!" Louis panted, as Everett entered. "I need your help. Where is General Sigmund?"

"He says he's got some work to do, below, I guess. What's he up to?"

"He keeps the depot busy," Louis said, sniffling. "I am afraid General Sigmund cannot help me, he does not like being disturbed while he works. You must help instead."

"What is it?" Everett asked.

"It is Sister Beatrice," Louis said.

"Is she alright?"

"She left a note. She has taken her bicycle to the Donon. There is a wolf!"

"Little Red Riding Hood?" Everett asked. "That's just a story, Louis. Whoever told you it was real?"

"Father did," Louis said. "There is a big bad wolf waiting for Sister Beatrice whenever she returns from sea."

"Why would Philippe tell you such a thing. Besides, you're a big boy now, nine years old."

"Father does not want me to hike the Vosges, near Donon," Louis said. "Father once told me Sister Beatrice's crucifix keeps her safe. I stopped believing in the wolf, but today, Sister Beatrice is without her cross and you need to save her – now."

Louis took Everett's hand and pulled him across the dugout.

"Where are we going?" Everett asked. Louis led him to the bedroom to another door Everett hadn't seen during the night. It was open. The metallic clash of tools and chains echoed from below.

"To the Mercedes," Louis said, pulling Everett and stepping down a long flight of stairs. "You must drive it to Shirmeck and Donon."

"Why don't you come too?" Everett asked.

"I fear wolves as much as you fear boar," Louis whispered as he approached a partially opened door near the bottom. The pathway widened. Ruts, from Sigmund's cart wheels led to the door from outside. Louis stopped at the last wooden step and put his finger to his lips.

"Shh, the General is at work in his secret room, he usually keeps it locked," Louis whispered. "We must be quiet."

Louis stepped past a sliver of light from a room behind the half-opened door. As Everett peeked inside, the wooden step croaked. Sigmund, stooping over a long wooden workbench, looked up at the noise as Everett ducked back before returning to work.

A large electric bulb, under a broad metal dish, illuminated the room. The bench looked like a butcher's cutting block where saws had long ago left their marks, darkened by blood having soaked into its crosscut grain. Behind the table, a full set of wrenches, chisels and hammers hung neatly from a board. Sigmund, with a large wrench, stepped back to adjust his stance. Everett swallowed hard at what Sigmund was working on, twenty feet beneath where they had spent the night.

A big artillery round lay on the bench like a chubby child, strapped in chains. Sigmund gripped its nose with the giant wrench. It slipped.

Everett jumped as the wrench hit the floor. Sigmund spun around.

"Manfred?" Sigmund said.

Another shell swung slowly in chains above the bench.

"Oh, it is only you," Sigmund said. He polished the metal projectile with his shirtsleeve. "How did you find your way down here? I thought Beatrice would have breakfast for you."

"Louis is here," Everett said.

"I cannot believe a nun could leave you hungry after all that work," Sigmund said with a nod of thanks to Everett.

"Sister Beatrice took the bicycle to the Donon," Louis poked his head inside the shop. "Monsieur must save her from the wolf!"

"Fairy tales again, Louis?" Sigmund said.

"She is without her crucifix this time," Louis said.

"Sister Beatrice was always more of a Valkyrie than a nun, Louis. Wolves are frightened of Valkyries – not nuns."

"General Sigmund believes in fairy tales too," Louis said to Everett.

"Touché, Louis," Sigmund said. "Monsieur can take the car but first I need him to help me unscrew this fuse. Sister Beatrice will be safe for awhile, wolves hunt at night."

Sigmund handed Everett the wrench.

"Louis, you should go outside." Everett frowned at the huge shell, some ten inches in diameter.

"There is no need for worry," Sigmund said. "I know what I am doing – I have done this hundreds of times. I will hold it still while you turn the fuse."

Everett carefully gnashed the teeth of the wrench into the corroded metal of the fuse. He motioned Louis again to step outside, just in case, but Louis only moved in closer.

"Louis, go outside, it will make Monsieur feel better." Sigmund wrestled with the twisting shell in the chain. "Now, put your weight into it, man."

"Are you sure?" Everett said.

"Trust me," Sigmund said.

Louis stood at the door with his fingers in his ears. The fuse screeched like a hawk before breaking loose. Everett twisted off the conical head then carefully placed it on the bench, hoping no one noticed his trembling hand.

"Danke! I see we are all still here!" Sigmund laughed. He pulled a rag out of the bench drawer. Everett reached for it to dry his sweating forehead, but instead Sigmund used it to clean out the threads of the shell where the fuse had been. He then tore a corner from the rag and crammed it deep into the fuse-well, above the explosive.

Sigmund grabbed a mallet and a chisel from the board. He set the chisel's edge to dig into the thread's pitch. Everett turned his head as he saw what Sigmund was about to do.

"Come now, Monsieur! You must know that it requires more than a spark to ignite TNT. I placed the cloth on top for your convenience. I have yet to have one explode."

"You've already de-fused it - why do that?" Everett looked over his shoulder.

"An idiot, you call a nincompoop, might try twisting a good fuse into the well," Sigmund said. "It is my signature, watch."

Sigmund tapped the threads with the mallet to score a starting mark then smashed the chisel through to finish the job.

A satisfying smile grew across Sigmund's face as he examined the permanent furrow plowed into the metal of the now impotent shell.

"There! That will fetch me a few Francs," Sigmund said.

"How much would Chesterfield bring?" Everett asked.

"Not as much. He does not come fitted with one of these," Sigmund juggled the fuse in his hand. "Chesterfield is a stubborn one."

"Is that like Chesterfield's brain?" Louis asked.

"Yes, Louis. However, ones like this are rather dumb," Sigmund said. "Chesterfield's brain, though simple-minded, is quite reliable."

"I found grenades back in the communication trench last night," Everett said. "Why don't you sell them?"

"The grenades simply do not bring me the money I can make from selling these large unexploded artillery rounds," Sigmund said. "Especially when I bring them to the depot, un-fused and clean so they can be safely driven across France to detonate at sea."

"What about ones like Chesterfield?" Everett asked.

"They are destroyed on site, at the depot," Sigmund said.

Sigmund gave a friendly slap to the shell hanging in chains then pulled it over the bench top.

"I need to work, I need the money," Sigmund said as he lowered the large bomb to the bench and adjusted the wrench around its nose.

"But, General, you and Gerta took the cart to the depot yesterday," Louis said.

Everett shrugged his shoulders as Sigmund looked to him for guidance, knowing Louis would ask why Sigmund needed more money now. Everett rehearsed it in his head. Sigmund: I need money to improve my home for Madame Lambert. Louis: Why did Grand-mère not move in before? Sigmund: She was waiting for her husband, Évariste, to return and remove Chesterfield. Louis: Why did Grand-père Évariste never come home before? Everett: He was bound to a post in the Zone Rouge, like Christ.

"Last evening, while our American friend was looking for you, he stumbled onto your Grand-père Lambert," Sigmund said.

"Monsieur, you did not tell me," Louis said, looking to Everett, with blue, tear-swollen eyes. "The whole night, you knew?"

"It was dark Louis, I wasn't really sure if..."

"Did Grand-père Lambert look like me?" Louis said.

"He is not a zombie," Sigmund said. "Everett found his bones. Your Grand-père Lambert was a proud man standing his ground, just like the paintbrush legend. And because Evariste Lambert is coming home, the world around here will be quite different."

"Will Father be better now," Louis looked to Sigmund. "Will I be safe?"

"Perhaps," Sigmund said as he knelt down to Louis. "I can now ask your Grand-mère Lambert to marry me. She will stay here, away from Strasbourg and be closer to your father to help him as she did last night."

"Uh, General Sigmund, sir," Louis said, glancing into the dark corners of the dugout, "Grand-mère Lambert does not like this place."

"Not to worry, Louis," Sigmund said, wiping his brow. "I will turn my deep dugout into a palace for Madame, but it will take money. These two big ones will help pay for it and her ring."

Sigmund wrapped the chains around the other un-fused shell, raised it a foot with the pulley and dragged it along an overhead rail from the ceiling towards the rear of the room.

"But, General," Louis said, "the depot will not pay you enough for even a small ring with just these two."

"Sigmund, last night, Louis and I found a whole field full of duds in the Zone Rouge," Everett said. "I know you don't like to go out there, but I'll help you, if you do."

"Monsieur, if you please." Sigmund moved behind Everett and parted a gas cloth on the wall to reveal a pair of large doors. He swung them open and pulled a thin metal chain to turn on a string of lights.

"Voila," Sigmund boasted. He introduced rows upon rows of neatly stacked artillery shells. Rusted but cleaned, they stood at attention like a

well-tanned regiment of dwarf robots, round and squat with their pug-
noses straight, all robbed of their fuses.

"O La-La, General! You have more than enough for a ring!" Louis
gasped.

"Enough to start another war," Everett said.

"It is the last of my cache, barely enough for Madame Lambert's
tastes," Sigmund said. "Louis, run outside and find my wheelbarrow."

"It is too much for Gerta and her poor foot," Sigmund said, straining
his neck waiting for Louis to disappear. "The Mercedes was always so
much more efficient."

"You've loaded up the car before?" Everett loosened the collar,
cinched-up at his neck. "You drove an enemy's staff car during the last
war?"

He always pictured Huan's Japanese father in Korea shoving a
Samurai sword clean through his business suit rather than submit to the
Communist occupiers. He guessed his face pretty much showed his disgust
at Sigmund. Sigmund looked down, stunned, as though shot through the
heart by a comrade. He turned his face.

"A worthy blow," Everett thought, for here was Sigmund, albeit a
hermit, thriving on the residues of war. Ready to chastise Sigmund for
driving the Mercedes, and about to remind him what Sigmund's dear old
American friend, Russell, would have said, Everett stopped short. It struck
him, that his father might have simply told Sigmund to enjoy the spoils.
Yet again, he had no idea of what his father might have said at all.

The outside door nudged open as Louis appeared with the
wheelbarrow.

"Louis, why don't you go start the Mercedes for me," Everett said.
"Sigmund was just telling me a few war stories – you've gotten an earful
already."

"No," Louis said. "I want to hear about General Sigmund, when he
was young."

"I think you should...," Everett started saying.

"He is a most curious boy," Sigmund said, "like his father."

"Go on then, when you were young," Everett said, thinking of Louis'
father, Philippe, as more consumed than curious.

"It was not more than a few years ago that I drove the car each week to
the depot," Sigmund said.

"I'm surprised you've lived this long," Everett said, thinking of the French resistance, then of the danger. "I mean, removing unexploded munitions from the trenches."

"You do not understand, I only removed certain ones," Sigmund picked up the fuse Everett had removed. "Read its markings to me."

Everett caught it after Sigmund tossed it to him.

"Dopplezunder - Frankfort," Everett said.

"And you are certain, Frankfort and not Essen?"

"Dopplezunder - Frankfort," Everett repeated.

"Good, I am right. You see, all the Dopplezunder fuses made in Frankfort that lay here are bad - faulty setback - duds as you say. I was the production engineer."

"You screwed up the whole batch?" Everett asked.

"General!" Louis put his hands to his knees, dropping his jaw in disbelief.

"Precisely," Sigmund said. "You must wonder how the image of the efficient German machine is maintained - I will tell you, those that "screw-up", as you say, are sent to the front. It is best for all concerned. Do not forget this, Louis."

Sigmund plucked the fuse from Everett's hand and hurled it into the dark corner of the cavern.

"How did the projectiles here get fused with them?" Everett asked.

"It was merely one of the many ironies of war," Sigmund said. "You must understand. I am almost ashamed to tell it."

"Go ahead, this is the sort of thing I was looking for," Everett said. "But, Madame is still going to cross-examine you."

"Very well, then," Sigmund said. "I had been inspecting the progress on our digging. When I finished, my men and I came out into the dark, all black-faced and exhausted."

"Weren't the German dugouts and trenches deep enough already," Everett said.

"We came from the beneath the ground. They were not trenchers, but tunnelers! I led my men out by a step, quietly into the dark trench and ran straight into a pair of boots. By their height, I knew it was an officer. "Over here!" he said in English, American style. I discretely signaled my second in command with my hand to go back, knowing he would disperse my men in the many tunnels in which we labored. Before I could say a word, I felt the steel of your father's trench knife at my throat."

Louis' head jutted from his shoulder towards Everett.

"Your father came to kill General Sigmund?" Louis asked. "There were tunnels?"

"Everett's father later told me that his men in the trench became suspicious when their morning coffee rippled on their cook stoves," Sigmund said. "He led a patrol and found me, black and dirty, and bound me with my own chain. Our machine guns rattled behind me as he led me away. Your father never discovered the tunnels, only me."

"Why tunnel?" Everett asked. "You could have just kept lobbing these big ones over the top."

Everett slapped the shell with his hand.

"The target was not the front line, but rather the reserve lines, the headquarters in the tuilerie and rear support areas in Ville Negre. They sat on such a slope, as you have mentioned before, that only a massive shelling might destroy them and if not, there were always the tunnels – worked on for a year by my predecessors. I made certain they were never quite finished."

"Louis, you said you could drive the Mercedes. Why don't you go get it started for me," Everett said, not wanting Louis to discover that Sigmund was not only a collaborateur, but a saboteur as well. "I still need to take care of that wolf."

"The tuilerie and Ville Negre – you were about to destroy them, General Sigmund," Louis asked, not listening to Everett, "with everyone who lived there? Even Grand-mère Lambert, even my father?"

Sigmund trembled once and then composed himself in front of Louis.

"Even them, Louis. So, er – uh," Sigmund struggled, "I located a few bad lots of my fuses and trucked them in. After days of firing into the tuilerie and the Reserve trench to no effect, I realized I must have produced thousands of bad fuses. That is why I only defuse certain ones."

"Why do you even bother removing the fuses when you know they were duds to begin with?" Everett asked, looking at the rows of un-fused projectiles in the cavern.

"I never told your father or the French that the fuses were bad," Sigmund said. "I would be considered a traitor, and there is nothing worse than an enemy who knows that."

"And of course," Everett added, "with that unique signature of yours, they would pay you more at the depot?"

"Naturally, they are always surprised to see me alive."

"General Sigmund, does this mean you are rich?" Louis asked. "Will you buy a new chateau, a big one - one in America?"

"I am thinking of a place in Ville Negre," Sigmund said. "I need a little more money for that and the dugout."

"I'll give you some, Sigmund," Everett said. "I don't want you blowing your head off just yet, you owe me something first."

"Nonsense, Louis and I will wheel my stash outside," Sigmund said. "When you return with the car from Donon, we can start loading for the depot. Now go, before Sister Beatrice decides to return to Indochina again."

"Before the wolf devours Sister Beatrice's heart," Louis said.

Sigmund brushed Everett's borrowed shirt clean. He straightened the gray collar, rubbing his thumb across the stitches where insignia had been torn.

"My little Valkyrie's heart is only broken," Sigmund said as he opened the outer door that led to the gleaming Mercedes sitting alongside Sigmund's rickety cart.

Everett found the starter, the pedals for the accelerator, clutch, brake, and the shift lever exactly where one would expect them. With one turn of the engine, the car came to life in a deep rumbling purr. It was, he knew, a Mercedes after all.

He drove down the lane, until it rose to meet Rue Gambetta and the end of Sigmund's trench, where Philippe nearly smashed Sigmund's cart when he first arrived. He turned north towards the hills and Schirmeck. The land to his right, cleared of war, stretched as far as he could see. He rumbled over the bridge, passing the last of the frontline trench. To his left, behind stands of slender beech trees, some posted with signs, lay the Lambert property - "Access Interdit."

The high forests of the Vosges and the small mountain of Donon lay ahead with long valleys stretching to each side. He figured, even with the few hours of head start and Beatrice's strong physique, she couldn't have gotten too far. The road twisted and turned as he drove higher in the hills past Schirmeck, leaving the railroad behind.

He wondered, knowing the train could have traveled from Schirmeck to Ville Negre, why Philippe couldn't have picked them up at the station in Ville Negre - it seemed closer. Maybe it was the name, Ville Negre, "Black Village", that upset Beatrice. The road narrowed. Everett focused on driving the big car up and around the ever-tightening turns and cutbacks as the road coiled upwards. He looked for her resting along the road or beneath a tree, as the hill seemed more like a mountain now.

Below, wound the road on which he had just traveled. The line of the Western Front lay bordered in patches of tilled farmland and green meadows dotted with white Vosgienne cattle. The small dark stretch of the un-reclaimed Lambert property with its trenches, wire and craters insulted the beauty that surrounded it. Lac Noir, a brief shining dot below, soon vanished into the war's blemish. The vista changed abruptly as Everett swung the car into a sharp cutback then turned up onto a road that, Sigmund mentioned, led to Donon.

He must have missed her somewhere behind, Everett thought, as only a superwoman or one driven by a passion stronger than flesh or muscle, could endure such a bicycle climb.

The maze of tall, narrow trees staggered the sunlight and nearly mesmerized him. A pinecone bounced from the windshield. A low branch sprayed the Mercedes with the smell of spruce and fir. Another cutback led into a forest of beech and pine running up along steep hillsides. As the car begged for a lower gear, Everett imagined Beatrice taxing her bicycle further, filling with her lungs with the sweet and cool morning air for such a passion.

He thought of Huan and how she walked into the fire of a war that her parents had tried to save her from and how she fought for her beliefs. He knew she would have done the same for their child. Huan could have been from Domremy-La-Pucelle. Beatrice could have been from Domremy-La-Pucelle. It was what he loved about the two.

A lumber road angled up the hill through a dark and dense forest. The car bottomed out in ever-deepening ruts as he climbed higher along a ledge, of thinning trees. A valley, quilted in cultivated green and yellow patches, spread far below.

The Mercedes was out of its league here, he thought, as he tried keeping its large frame on the road, now a serpentine dirt path. At its center ran a narrow groove, cut straight and true, where Beatrice's bike tires had rolled.

As Everett tried keeping the car from stalling, he thought of how powerful Beatrice's legs must be, legs of a bear would be needed up here, not those of a nurse or a most passionate nun.

Her trail ended near the bottom of the narrow, wooden track where sleds, which Beatrice had called schlitts, could unload lumber and firewood onto trucks. Beatrice's bicycle lay near the lower end. He shut off the noisy engine and climbed out into a bright blue morning sky, quiet, except for the slight wind, whistling through the tall, slender pine.

"Beatrice," he called, anxious for her voice. Nothing.

He stepped on the rails of the schlitt's track and followed it, winding through stands of trees, up the hill, climbing over a bridge and stream then up another steep hill until it leveled off near the crest. He stopped to catch his breath. As he looked back down the schlitt track, what seemed like a mile had only been a climb of about three hundred feet.

Piles of timber lay ready for splitting, loading, and sliding down the mountain on the schlitts that, when empty, looked like a small horse-drawn sleigh. The loaded schlitt, before him looked more like a humpback whale on hockey skates. The schlitt, ten-feet long and loaded with a stack of cut firewood three feet wide and six feet high, sat locked into the track by a long timber alongside a low seat at the very front. The mass of timber towered above and behind the seat where would sit, according to Beatrice, a massive and stubborn woodsman who would ease his schlitt fearlessly down against his muscled and hairy back.

Trees groaned. Towering white clouds formed in the pale sky. He hiked towards the summit on a soft bed of needles beneath tall growths of pine. He watched his step as the rugged ground turned to large slabs of rock and boulders of soft sandstone, carved with hundreds of initials of century-old explorers and lovers. Sunlight nurtured a grove of saplings below. Between large, rotting stumps of an old forest, harvested long ago – he stepped down. Young trees bowed in a constant wind towards a short and narrow spire near a cliff.

The distant marker, the height of a small man, overlooked the valley to the east. Closer, he noticed a crossbar with red markings, possibly a border marker or another Zone Rouge warning sign. He found instead, a simple rusted iron cross, marking a grave.

Vines covered the inscription. He knelt down and pulled the green mass to the side to read, "Manfred Wolff - Démineur". The rest of the inscription, he struggled to translate from German; - A Captain in the German Army; born in 1910 in Saarbrucken, Germany, died in 1946 in the Vosges. Everett read it again, the single narrow line so carefully chiseled into the soft iron, probably from Lorraine and forged with coal most likely from the fields of the Saar Valley to the north. He ran his fingers across the letters as though it were in Braille, knowing it was Sigmund's young German friend of the last war.

He wondered, like Évariste's bones, had this man been properly collected? Had he died digging up a shell from the Great War, or maybe slicing a knife blade under an anti-tank mine his own troops planted in the last war? As he stood, his shirt caught the rusted crossbar and ripped trying to hold him as though Manfred wanted to him to stay and chat.

He turned, leaning against an outcropping of rock, as shadows of clouds behind him creep slowly from Lorraine over Alsace where he now stood. He imagined that Manfred must have stayed on Donon, where it was quiet and he could behold both Germany and France in peace. Manfred must have truly believed that work will make you free, to volunteer as a démineur. One last dark blotch crawled over the Vosges to the other side of the valley towards Germany, leaving him cold in its shadow.

A song pierced the silence. A powerful, yet sorrowful voice wailed, it seemed, from the sky. It could only be Beatrice, he thought, recognizing the healing song from the spa with its errant pitch and meandering tempo. His cheeks, warmed with a gush of blood. He whistled, climbing hand over hand up the rocks to the strengthening voice. There she was.

Beatrice lay on a large stone slab that seemed designed for that purpose with smooth round stone pillows, warm with lecithin, yellow and green. She cupped her hand over her eyes until Everett moved to cast his shadow across her face.

"Manfred?" She licked her lips.

"No, Beatrice - it's just me," Everett said as he sat down beside her.

"Oh, Everett," Beatrice said, touching the shirt where it had been torn.

"I can take it off if it bothers you," Everett said.

"No, just sit with me." Beatrice turned away to the sky, royal blue and dotted with cotton white clouds rolling east towards the Rhine valley.

"Were you singing for him?" Everett turned towards the grave.

"I was singing for you," Beatrice said as she glanced at his hand, carefully pulling him down to sit.

Everett felt a warm glow wash over his face.

"I was singing to wish you luck with this band you came here to find," Beatrice said. "From the dirt on your hands it looks like you have been busy already this morning."

"I have a feeling I'll soon know what happened to them," Everett said, then told her of delivering Évariste's bones to Philippe and of the deal that Sigmund had made.

"I'm impressed with what Madame has done for Philippe," Everett said. "He's fairly straight today. I can't wait to see what she can release from Sigmund's head for me."

"Why did you come to Donon rather than stay for Mother?" Beatrice asked.

"Louis was afraid you might run into the Big-Bad Wolf," Everett said.

"First, Father frightens Philippe with stories about Lac Noir and Hagen's trench," Beatrice said, "then, years later, Philippe frightens Louis about the Big-Bad Wolf. You must be special to Father, for him to allow you to enter Hagen's trench. I never understood why he lacked the courage to look for the bones himself."

Everett shrugged, not yet ready to tell her why Sigmund had guarded them all from viewing the grim state in which he found Évariste today.

"Come sit closer and look up there - that is my quiet place," Beatrice pulled him down to sit and waved to a rectangular arrangement of stone below the peak of Donon. "It is a true Roman camp. You must have a quiet place back home, yes?"

Everett told her of the cemetery on the hill overlooking the river in Iowa where Indians camped.

"You should feel at home here, Everett. According to legends, we are sitting on a sacrificial stone where Druids gathered long ago from Gaul and every part of the world. If I had not been dreaming of being Jeanne de Arc or Florence Nightingale, I would dream of joining the secretive religious Druids. I always wanted to be small - like an elf."

"I would think that someone known as Brunnhilde would require a larger frame" Everett said, "something more worthy of a Valkyrie."

"The patients aboard the Pasteur and the men at the Port-du-Chien, believe I am worthy, Everett," Beatrice said as she rolled a few stones down the hill. "And, what did you dream of in your quiet place by the river?"

A warm wind ran through the tall pines. The distant train, the peal of a church bell, the echoes of war around him - all suddenly hushed by this whispering wind.

He closed his eyes, feeling Beatrice's warmth as she nestled beside him and lowered her head to his shoulder, calming him with slow, deep breaths. A minute passed; it could have easily been five. He shuddered as his Korean nightmare ran before him in daylight, not in shadows, but behind translucent eyelids reddened from the sun. It played out fast, spilling out as waves into the fields below. Blood rushed in currents to his groin.

"I imagine that after Father helps you with the story of this band, you will be leaving alone?" Beatrice asked. "That is to say, I mean, if you discover their bones you will not be returning home alone?"

"I like it here," Everett said. "Here with you."

Beatrice dug her head into the space between his shoulder and chest.

"Are you certain? You need to know that living with a Valkyrie can be difficult," Beatrice said, with a vanilla-scented chortle to his ear. "You can see how Mother's missions of mercy taunt Father so."

Everett laughed, loving the way she was and realizing his affection for her wasn't only physical, but grew more as he understood the depth of her idealistic devotions. There was not one like her in the whole world, anywhere, not anymore.

"Look, there's something you need to know first," Everett said.

He sat up beside her as a cloud obscured the sun. Across the distant valley, lightning flashed, followed by muted thunder.

He described the nightmares. He told her of Huan. She squeezed his hand gently, but, when he told her that Huan might have his child, she nearly crushed it in anger. They turned to look up as lightning struck the top of Donon with a single deafening crack.

"Thor is not pleased and neither am I!" Beatrice said.

"You don't understand," Everett paused, off-balance. "I want to find my child more than anything in this world."

"Then why are you here in Lorraine at all? Why look for this band?" Beatrice said as she stormed downhill.

"For the same reason you sail to Indochina," Everett said, trying to keep up with her pace, "for lost souls, souls my father might have saved."

"My dear Everett, those souls in Indochina are not lost, but wounded. You cannot very well get on with your life by trying to patch together your father's lost fragments."

"Don't you see?" Everett stopped. "That's all I have left. The fragments are right here in Lorraine – I can feel it. Someday too, I'll be whole enough to return to Korea to look – somewhere in North Korea. How could it be done now – it would be suicide."

Beatrice straightened her overalls and undid her long, red hair. "I am taking the schlitt."

The way she stomped her boots was enough to convince Everett that she was serious. Clarity overwhelmed him.

"Beatrice, that's crazy! You're not strong enough."

"I am stronger than you know!" Beatrice's voice bellowed from the rocks. She hurled herself downhill towards the clearing.

When he caught up with her, she was sitting on the schlitteur's bench beneath the stack of wood, loaded high onto the schlitt. Her arm worked frantically at loosening the pole that locked it in place.

"Beatrice, you'll get hurt!"

He jumped aboard the small bench-like seat and gave her a little push to settle in. She pushed him off and sent him rolling down the hill. When he climbed back, she had loosened the pole and jabbed it at his stomach. The schlitt budged forward across the timber, growling like an abrupt bowing of a string bass, then stopped. Beatrice strained as both of her legs took up the load. She turned bright red from holding her breath.

Everett slid in next to her. He planted his feet firmly against the cross-timber next to hers. As he relieved her, he understood her real strength. He felt humiliated as the massive sled pressed into his back, inching down, in ever-increasing fractions, ignoring his resistance.

The pressure at his back doubled, while his legs, which only a second ago felt so strong, now tensed and buckled. His face muscles twitched. The schlitt worked at trapping his foot against the wooden tie. He gnashed his teeth.

"You need to take a step and move - sometime soon I would say," Beatrice said calmly. "I suppose that if you want to lose that foot, I could stitch it back on later."

She sat with her legs crossed casually and hummed as though she were knitting. It angered Everett enough, that he stubbornly held his ground. He turned to glare at her.

"If you don't soon lock it in place with that pole, Beatrice, I'm just going to jump off and let it go."

"It will be all the more fun to ride down then," Beatrice laughed, "alone, like in one of your jets."

"OK, then. I suppose someday they'll find our bones still wedged against this stupid thing, like I found . . .," Everett stopped then grunted as Beatrice adjusted herself in the seat, purposefully nudging the sled.

"I cannot believe you went into that horrible place again?" Beatrice said. "You must have a death wish!"

Everett told her of the proposal with Sigmund, hoping she might change her mind about returning to the Pasteur. His hamstring muscles knotted. He motioned his head for her to put the pole back in and lock the schlitt into the track. She turned away again.

"You are a most stubborn man, Everett. Sitting there like Atlas with the whole world on his back. You remind me of my Manfred, refusing to leave after the war so he could clean up after it. And you, so desperate for the past that you would have Mother exorcise this band from my father's feeble mind, so stubborn, all of you."

"Stubborn?" Everett grumbled. "Returning to Indochina for the last wounded Legionnaire is stubborn. I don't want you to go."

The schlitt trembled as though the wood shifted or the ground itself had shook.

"Oooh," Beatrice smiled. "Manfred is telling us to get moving, there is only room on this mountain for one grave – his."

The strain quickly overpowered Everett's back. A hamstring muscle cramped and his legs bent at the knees. The schlitt seized his foot – he had to take a step.

"I'm going to need some help here, Beatrice. This thing's got a mind of its own!"

"A schlitt expressing its free will?" My dear Everett, you, of all people, should know the sled is a prisoner of gravity."

She took his arm and put it on her lap. She caressed it. The schlitt took control.

He tried jamming his leg, every three feet, at each timber crossing, yet the schlitt moved on like an ice floe - slow and determined. Beatrice held her hand out to touch the vines and flowers as the schlitt crept downhill.

"Father must have wanted you to come to Donon," Beatrice said. "Well, I tire of those trying to save me. First, my Manfred begging me to wear the habit and changing my name to Sister Beatrice, then the men of the Pasteur, liking my old name Brunnhilde, so strong and eternal, and now you. I am not one who needs to be saved; it is you – all of you."

Everett turned to her, thinking it was something only a Valkyrie might say.

The wayward schlitt hammered across the track's ties.

"Let's just see then." Everett said, raising his voice above the schlitt's racket.

He swung his legs to her lap, and let the schlitt have its way. The sled seemed, truly, to know where it was going, accelerating down a straightaway after turning a sharp corner. It carried them, barreling down to the little bridge above the creek's ravine.

"I do hope you are not trying to kill yourself," Beatrice said. "You are never going to die, my dear Everett."

Her breath, warm and moist, spilled from her mouth. Everett fantasized a life, reborn again, and again, in the arms of a Valkyrie. She held his hand as the schlitt picked up speed, bouncing from the wooden side pegs that held the cross timbers in place.

"Like Manfred, back up there on Donon?" Everett asked.

Beatrice kissed the cuff of Manfred's shirt, and then kissed Everett's hand.

"I used Manfred, at first, to save Philippe from prison, before I fell in love with him. Part of Manfred lives in Louis, you see."

The sled wobbled in its track before shooting over the bridge. Everett wrapped an arm around her and held on tightly to a side as they slid down a steeper slope. Through the valley in the distance, chimneys, here and there, lifted white smoke into the sky.

Everett opened Beatrice's hair near her ear.

"Manfred was blonde, like Louis?" Everett asked.

After hearing his own question, Everett remembered Beatrice saying Philippe had lost his manhood. Now, he knew it was well before Louis' conception. Beatrice gave him a puzzled look, as though he should have known it all along.

He felt not only helpless, careening down the slope with a ton of lumber at his back, but like an idiot next to Beatrice.

"It hurts Philippe to look at him sometimes," Beatrice said.

"Promise me you won't return to Indochina. It's not safe, not even for Brunnhilde." He said over the creaking tracks.

The schlitt bounced and lifted before settling back onto the track. He knew from walking up earlier that it would turn sharply at the next bend before rocketing down the last slope, too late to jump.

"I would imagine, my dear Everett, that Brunnhilde would prefer to ride out to sea in a burning ship," Beatrice smiled as the wind tugged her hair back. "An accidental death on a runaway schlitt, for a proper Valkyrie, just would not do."

Ahead, the track looked as though it might drop off the edge of the world before the turn. He gripped her tight as trees flashed by. Off to the side, ahead of them, a plump bed of straw lay, conveniently placed, Everett guessed, by a relative of a deceased schlitteur.

He turned her head to the straw then pushed her out then quickly leaped after her towards the straw, hitting his head on a stump as he rolled. He wasn't fully conscious when he heard Beatrice crawling though the straw to his side. She straddled him. His elbows sunk into the straw mat as he lifted himself to her.

"I need you close to me," Beatrice said as she undid the strap to her overhauls and guided his hand like a kingfisher deep inside. Around the turn of the track, the schlitt crashed into the Mercedes with a distinct crash, as though it were a ball, striking bowling pins.

Everett jumped to see the car's chrome gleam in the sun as the perturbed Mercedes, inched backwards down the hillside of the road. Beatrice gripped his hair.

"Let his Mercedes go!" Beatrice begged. "Let it go!"

The dull thud of the bumper, hitting a tree, echoed in the woods. The rock felt warm at his bare back. Her hair parted before the hot noon sun as he did, let himself go.

◆ ◆ ◆

They found the Mercedes resting against a small stump at the edge of the road, saving it from bounding over the cliff. Everett, behind the wheel with Beatrice asleep at his side, glided the Mercedes down the Donon in a slow spiral. The world spun - the Saar River valley to the west, the Rhine River Valley between the last northern peaks of the Vosges and the spine of the Vosges to the south. Placid Lac Noir, gleamed to the west.

"Philippe thinks there's a giant fish there," Everett said. "No doubt, one was sent by Neptune to guard the band I'm looking for."

"When I was young, the other children at school teased us that our Lac Noir was haunted." Beatrice gathered her hair into a ponytail and tied it with a boot string she had broken while ripping her boots off earlier. She turned away to look back towards Donon for a moment before turning to gaze at the dot of glistening water in the distance - Lac Noir.

"Those boys came one night, lurking around the tuilerie for the lake," Beatrice said. "Mother was ready for them with her broom and a few stern words."

"Ready to cast a spell before heaving them into a boiling caldron, I suppose," Everett said, trying to picture Madame Lambert.

"She told them the blinding truth - that it was not safe around the tuilerie. It was the very first time Philippe and I had ever heard that. Mother swung her lantern beneath Chesterfield's nose and told the boys that they could be very well be standing on one just like him at that very moment - beneath their shoes. Most of my brave classmates fled like deer."

"A few defiant ones remained. I remember not feeling sorry for them. They walked towards Lac Noir after a school of small fish splashed. Mother ran ahead and cut them off. She held the lantern just under her chin so that she really did look like a witch. Do you think I look like a witch, Everett?"

"No, Brunnhilde," Everett teased. "Does your mother look like one?"

"That night she certainly did," Beatrice shook her ponytail. "Philippe and I stepped outside in our bare feet to hear her cackling. It was in the fall. It was cold and foggy and the wet leaves clung to our feet - I wanted to go inside, but Philippe had to hear her - 'And just where do you think you are going!' Mother boomed at them by the lake - it frightened even me. The leader was not taken in, 'We are not afraid of you - you old witch. We are going to wake the General now!'"

Everett noticed Beatrice staring down at the little rectangle of the Lambert's land below. She spoke as though she were talking to someone still there.

"Mother shook the boy's shoulder with her free hand, she said - 'The General? - What on earth do you mean, young man?'"

"The boy said, 'The nervous old man - the General - the one who sleeps in the ground like a mole back down the trench - the one who jumps at the clap of a hand.'"

"It was then that Philippe and I knew who the boys were talking about. We had thought he was a hermit who lived on top of Donon; we never realized that the General lived so close. We even made him jump once or twice when he passed by leading his horse and cart through town. I felt sorry for him, but clapped along anyway."

A corner of Beatrice's mouth twitched. Everett held her close as he thought of the irony of Beatrice discovering her father at the same age that Everett remembered losing his. The car's engine, which had hummed like a tenor's bass voice while she spoke, sputtered then stopped with a slight quake.

"That was a long time ago, Beatrice - you were just a kid." Everett tried catching her eye, but she stayed focused on the spot of brown land below Donon that lay not reclaimed.

"That night," she went on, "Mother told me that Évariste was not my real father. We never returned to school. I never set foot in Ville Negre again, until I first returned from Indochina in the habit."

She squinted towards Sigmund's burrow, hidden from view on the slant of the hill. "We visited him often afterwards. Now, each time I return, I notice how much smaller the Zone Rouge seems and how much older Mother and Father have become. I am glad you found those bones when you did, for soon the grass and moss would be covering it all. But still, Mother would have never forgotten Évariste's promise to return for Chesterfield."

"I sure hope she's over Évariste' by now," Everett said as he started the car. "You should have heard Sigmund talk about proposing to Madame. Like a frightened little boy asking a girl out on his first date."

"Were you not frightened as well, when you were young?" Beatrice asked, with a kiss to his cheek.

"I didn't have a big brother." Everett felt her pull away slightly.

"Could you please drive me to the tuilerie," Beatrice said. "I must see Philippe. It is best you not come inside. If he is well, as you say, tonight Mother and I will return to the dugout with dinner. Perhaps then, Father will allow himself to be hypnotized for the stories."

Along the way, Beatrice described her brother's malady - noting that it didn't start with prison - he had always been morose and Everett felt relieved knowing Louis might not suffer the same. At the tuilerie, Everett stopped the car long enough for Beatrice to jump with a quick wave. It satisfied him so, that it was only a half-mile later, he wondered if it were his last vision of her - a turned head, a flick of her hand.

‫11‬

Disposals

Rue Gambetta's hard-packed clay shimmered in the noon heat as Everett drove to Sigmund's dugout. He thought of the twenty-six letters and how his father couldn't finish just one. He thought of his own child, now six or seven years old, an Amerasian, castaway to the Demilitarized Zone to live in the land of the hermit. Turning the Mercedes from Rue Gambetta, the Zone Rouge loomed above the plain, laying like a giant, sleeping on its side.

Everett switched the engine off and coasted down the lane to the dugout's lower entrance. A neat row of un-fused shells, all rusted 210's, lay like ripened melons in the yard. Louis sat in a wheelbarrow nearby, pretending it was a jet. Sigmund rolled the last shell with his boot heel. He opened a canvas stretcher by the invalid shell, waving the Mercedes forward as though it were a MEDEVAC.

"You look tired, Monsieur," Sigmund said. The old man's arms, although thin and boney, bulged with turbid veins above his lean muscles. "Is she still determined to return to Indochina?"

"I'm not sure," Everett said.

"You did not leave Sister Beatrice alone on Donon, did you?" Louis asked.

"I dropped her off at the tuilerie, to see Madame Lambert about your father."

Sigmund tapped the shell with the tip of his unlit pipe.

"How is Madame? How did she look when she saw those bones?"

"I didn't see her," Everett said. "Sister Beatrice said I should stay away for now."

"She has a sense about such things," Sigmund said, groaning as he budged the harmless shell. "Did you happen to mention that I wish to propose to Madame?"

"Yes. Sister Beatrice will walk Madame here tonight – they'll bring dinner." Everett bent to the stretcher to help.

Sigmund's rough face blossomed in a broad beaming smile as they carried shell after shell in the stretcher, standing them in the rear seat of the car while Louis counted them. The Mercedes, after several minutes work, sagged like Gerta's back. Sigmund stopped to wipe the sweat from his forehead.

"You seem full of energy this afternoon, Everett," Sigmund said. "Did you take a rest on Donon?"

Everett kicked the Mercedes' ever-flattening tires.

"One more - that's all it will hold, Sigmund," Everett said, not wanting to tell Sigmund how truly rejuvenated he felt.

Everett bent his knees and grabbed the handles of the old stretcher as Sigmund rolled the last shell onto the old fabric. Sigmund smiled and lifted his end. The two parallel wooden poles along each side of the canvas creaked and bent as the 210 slowly rose.

"The old boy is as heavy as a boar," Sigmund groaned. "I would imagine he would not measure up to the behemoths you dropped - no?"

Everett squeezed the handles to hold the stretcher motionless at his waist, looking down at the dull shell Sigmund had cleaned. A gash from the wrench ran across the smooth metal - like a grin. He nodded to Sigmund, hoping the quick gesture would satisfy the question, but Sigmund tilted his head sideways waiting for an answer.

"Yours had to be at least twice as paunchy as the old boy here," Sigmund said. "What, perhaps two-hundred kilos?"

Everett set his end down, not thinking, until he felt the shell slide in the canvas to rest against his foot. Sigmund set his end down.

"Well?" Sigmund asked.

Sigmund bowed at the other end, bent still at the waist, his head tilted up, and waiting. He smiled as a bead of sweat ran to his jaw. Everett judged it was an innocent question and lifted the stretcher.

"A quarter ton of high explosive," Everett said as Sigmund picked up his end. "I flew with two - one under each wing."

"Did you give the bombs names, like Chesterfield?" Louis asked.

Everett hadn't noticed that Louis was paying attention then shrugged, not wanting to say much. He got back to work while Louis, from the depths of the wheelbarrow, recited a long list of names of children.

"Several years ago, they taunted him at school in Ville Negre," Sigmund said. "Philippe brought him home for good, but Louis has grown. He should return to school."

As Everett and Sigmund walked the stretcher to the car each time, the names of his bombs came to Everett in a chronological flood. The addressees of the most hated came first, Stalin, Marx, Mao, followed later by the names of his own commanders, bullies and every mean dog of his youth. Towards the end, they scribbled the names of their sweethearts and wives on the big bombs. Like the nose art on his jet, he remembered he had chosen "Paula," a girl of his childhood. The name, "Huan", he wanted to use then, would have raised questions of loyalty on the flight line.

"It wasn't a gentleman's war like yours, Sigmund."

"Did you hear that, old boy?" Sigmund said to the shell. "He calls you a gentleman, but you have never been a gentleman, have you - my cold cylinder of death. At least you will be sleeping beside your friends here after your last party, Hah!"

Between them, the stretcher's taut fabric closed around the last shell and swung from side to side like a hammock beneath their legs. They hobbled, Everett guessed, like a pair of hemorrhoid-ridden men. Everett backed into the car with his end of the stretcher, about to hoist the shell onto the top of the stack when a small rip of canvas he'd been watching developed into a running tear, accompanied by a lightening in his arms.

"Everett, watch your feet!" Sigmund warned. "The big shit is splitting his britches! You will have to get under him and push him up." Frustrated, Sigmund peered into the sky, raising his hands for mythical assistance. Louis came running.

Cold dark iron filled Everett's hands and with it, an angry strength he hadn't known. He grimaced and with a mighty push sent it to the top of the stack. The shell bounced and settled oddly with its un-fused nose tilted up like a pig's snout to the wind.

Sigmund slapped it.

"He wants to feel haughty, one last time. By God, Everett, I swear if he had legs and arms that he would cross them and if he had eyes that one would be wearing a glass monocle, and if the arrogant prince had a voice, it would command us to drive him back to his castle. Well, my old boy, we are taking you and your friends to hell. Ah! If you only had ears!"

"I want to go to the depot for once," Louis said, "to see them all go to hell."

"Come inside now Louis. There is much you need to begin to prepare for tonight's meal while Monsieur and I are gone."

"You never let me go, General," Louis said.

"The depot gave some their 10AM ride to hell already, Louis," Everett said. "I'd like to see it, myself."

"I will speak to the guards," Sigmund said, "perhaps later today they will detonate some of Chesterfield's old friends for our American friend. Your young ears are much too sensitive, Louis."

"I need some papers from the dugout," Sigmund said, as he escorted a balking Louis back inside. "Could you please ask our stone-faced passengers for their tickets?"

Everett checked the shells, making sure they wouldn't shift around. Not that they would explode, but that they might sail from the backseat at an abrupt turn that could send them, car and all, back to the Zone Rouge.

Sigmund returned with the black bag that containing his surgical instruments. He tossed it into the trunk.

"You don't expect an accident on the way to the depot, do you?" Everett asked, half-jokingly.

"No, I expect everything to go perfectly, like the Great War. Hah!" Sigmund wiped his forehead on his sleeve and started the car. Everett turned around to steady the 210's with his arm around the last one they loaded.

Sigmund drove slowly up the lane then turned right onto Rue Gambetta that would lead south through Ville Negre then on to the dépôt. Although the Mercedes was huge, the weight of the shells on the rear axle lifted the front end of the car into the air with each bump in the road, yet Sigmund drove faster.

"It's only past noon," Everett said above the engine's roar. "What's the hurry?"

Sigmund pointed to a train in the west. It seemed on a collision course.

"Half the town is on that train, from the Victory in Europe holiday in Epinal."

Sigmund opened up the throttle. The rear wheels dug in under the weight and threw up clouds of dust. The train kept to its schedule, only a few hundred yards away.

"So?" Everett asked.

"They are not accustomed to me driving the Mercedes recently, especially loaded with my little beauties back there at this late hour," Sigmund shouted. "And you - you look a great deal like Manfred in those clothes."

"Are we going to make it?"

Sigmund cut back on the accelerator. The car's hood lowered like the bow of a speedboat coming to port as they approached a crossing. The train's engine cut in front of them as the car skidded to a halt up the slight incline before the crossing. The car's hood rose and the shells settled back into the seat, except for the one Everett still embraced. The passenger's faces flashed by, peering from the windows as the train slowed into Ville Negre.

"Everett, in the trunk is an old army blanket - do you mind covering them," Sigmund said. "This car, with me driving, is enough to cause a panic, let alone the 210's - not everyone knows they are un-fused. Cover their eyes as though they were not yet alive."

Everett opened the trunk and found the blanket beneath Sigmund's half-opened black bag. As he pulled the blanket, the bag tilted and opened wide. Inside, piled to the bag's lip, lay rows and rows of neatly shuffled Franc notes - thousands of them, Everett estimated. He quietly flipped through a single stack wondering how many shells it represented.

"Schnell!" Sigmund shouted, "They are becoming curious."

The last train car rolled by slowly, just as Everett returned. In the open doorway stood a big, older woman standing beside a short fat man. Everett had seen them before.

"Damn!" Sigmund grumbled towards them.

"The Chauchats?" Everett asked.

"Do you know that woman?" Sigmund slapped the steering wheel.

"She and her husband tried boarding the train that Beatrice and I took to the baths - Beatrice didn't seem to like them."

"The old tart, Chauchat, prefers Germans," Sigmund said. "She was always trying to seduce me, until the Gestapo came to town - they were younger."

"Is that why Beatrice doesn't like her?"

"Oh, there is more." Sigmund said, still eyeing the Chauchats.

"I know about Louis. I know about Beatrice and Manfred too," Everett said as he straightened Manfred's shirt collar.

"I thought as much. Did Beatrice also tell you what happened after Madame Chauchat's Gestapo lover left town?"

"They loved the same man?"

"God, no man!" Sigmund huffed. "Manfred was a regular German army, like I was in the Great War. When the Gestapo left, Madame Chauchat turned to me."

The train vented steam.

"She seems like she gets what she wants. Did she get what she wanted from you?" Everett asked in a voice louder than he felt comfortable using.

"No, but there was a penalty for my stubbornness," Sigmund shouted as the whistle blew. He leaned to Everett's ear. "When Madame Chauchat could not have me, she informed the Resistance that Beatrice was carrying Manfred's child."

"How would Madame Chauchat know?" Everett asked as the last car rolled by.

"No one knows for certain," Sigmund said with a stutter as the Mercedes straddled over the rails. "I would guess Manfred informed the Gestapo to help secure Philippe's release from prison."

"He was a caring man, like yourself and your father," Sigmund said as he nervously patted his front pocket for his pipe. "Manfred did tell me that when the Gestapo first arrived, looking for communists, Madame Chauchat suggested they search the tuilerie – I know you think me vain, but the woman was vindictive for not having me. I have business yet to attend to with Madame Chauchat. I wished I had Philippe's opium just now."

"I think you should keep your wits about you," Everett said.

The train snaked ahead of them to Ville Negre.

"You remind me so much of your father." Sigmund checked his teeth in the mirror, spit in his hand and straightened his hair. "He had, how do you say, common sense."

The tallest feature of Ville Negre, a church steeple, towered above all else. The car backfired along a narrow street lined with three-story buildings. The Mercedes' staccato note played against the walls of stone. A few tall, green-painted shutters opened. Heavy wooden doors swung open. A few citizens stood beneath their awnings. Everett thought, so close to the front, they aught to be made of wrought iron, rather than ornate and colored glass.

Most of Ville Negre's citizens seemed to have moved to the railway station. Sigmund explained that they came to greet returning family and friends from a festival and to fascinate themselves with pairs of thin parallel strands of steel rails, woven into France.

Sigmund followed Rue Gambetta to the railroad station - the second tallest structure in town. The French flag hung limp from a pole rising from the station's elegant white stone peak. A gust set it flying straight back in vibrant colors of red, white and blue.

A crowd of passengers and greeters milled about the street in front of the Mercedes, visiting and hugging each other. Some complimented Sigmund on the car and seemed pleased that he wasn't leading nervous Gerta and the dilapidated, shell-filled cart through the village. Another gust lifted the blanket that Everett had thrown over the bombs. The crowd hushed as they examined the heavy back seat passengers. Sigmund pleaded with people to step aside.

"Oh, Sigmund, Mon Cher Démineur, Mon General Allemand," Madame Chauchat called out as her husband stood with their luggage.

Sigmund shifted uncomfortably in his seat and raced the engine. He rose slightly as Madame Chauchat approached his side of the Mercedes.

"I have other business, Madame, but perhaps later over lunch sometime," Sigmund said, arching his head to the rear seat. The Mercedes lurched as he tapped the accelerator.

Everett felt the shell lift. Sigmund worked the clutch and gearshift as the car picked up speed. He twisted the wheel to veer from hitting a fountain at the center of Ville Negre and followed Rue Gambetta south of the village.

A smile of contentment swept across Sigmund's face as he downshifted for a turn and the car responded smoothly. Everett felt the shell lean from the turn, then sway back comfortably as the shells beneath settled into the seat.

"Just what sort of business do you have with Madame Chauchat?"

Sigmund scratched his head.

"I sometimes provide the village my services for free, especially when they know the Department of Demining will condemn their property after one of their children stubs their toe on the fin of an aerial bomb in their backyard, or another 210 or worse. When they hear my horse and cart coming down their cobblestone road to their home, they gather their family and go to church until I have finished my business. They leave a box of beer and bread on the porch for my work. For the special lunchtime service I will someday provide her, Madame Chauchat will leave me more than that – much more."

"You're not seriously going to screw up our deal over a cheap old tart like Madame Chauchat? What about your proposal tonight to Madame Lambert? Are you nuts?"

"You are overly protective, like your father," Sigmund said. "A simple affair, there is a monster in the yard by the vamp's house, with a fuse – a Dopplezunder made in Essen, very dependable. Her husband, Henri, refuses even to clear the weeds around it. Each time Madame Chauchat lusts for my bones, I remind her that she should spend more time at home with the Dopplezunder, it would be less expensive than me!"

Sigmund roared and then turned onto a narrow road, south of Ville Negre. Everett felt like he'd read a whole book and hadn't understood a word.

They approached a bizarre rise in the land, like a small inactive volcano about a hundred feet high and round as a small glacial lake. The road gently coiled up the hill beneath a crown of oak trees, behind which could be seen a tall barbed-wire fence with lights every few hundred feet focused to a hidden center somewhere below. They passed a sign, "Halt! Militaire Zone Rouge, Access Interdit". A sentry drew his sidearm then slipped it back into the holster around his chest when he noticed Sigmund at the wheel.

"Viola', we are here!" Sigmund proudly slapped the wheel of the car and drove right on past five covered military trucks lined up alongside the road.

Below, lay a rock quarry or rather a large water-filled gorge. They pulled over to let a truck coming up towards them pass by. Everett twisted to its dusty wake to look. The last of the trucks carried a banner warning of danger. Piled against the steep walls of rock slept hundreds of bombs just like Chesterfield, dropped off for disposal. Men in uniform approached the car.

"Wow!" Everett said, not knowing what to say after seeing what looked like a spot of hell placed in the middle of paradise.

"I shall do all the talking here, Everett – if you do not mind. They are not accustomed to strangers."

"Bonjour Professor Fischer!" A soldier waved Sigmund out of the car. They spoke for a minute before another walked ahead then motioned them to move forward.

"He tells me he prefers Gerta and my cart, but he understands I am growing old and knows this car will make my life easier - not necessarily longer - he said, but easier. He always asks me, do I have a cigarette? I always point to my cart. The 210's we named Chesterfields, the 75's Lucky Strikes, and the aerial bombs, Camels. I tell him, like today, I have Chesterfields - and does he have a light?"

"He asks if I have any perfume, Eau-de Mustard, Eau-de Chlorine, or a splash of Eau-de Phosgene? I always ask him why. Do I stink? You see, they put gas bombs, projector canisters, and other Dragon eggs on the bottom layer of a stack of bombs to vaporize."

"The soldier asked about you," Sigmund went on. "I told him what you were doing here. Wave as we drive by, he will like that. You may be the last American he sees."

As they drove past the soldier, Everett automatically saluted. The soldier saluted Everett, then looked at the 210 on the top and said in nearly perfect English, "Welcome to hell, Mr. Shesterfeld, Sir."

Ahead, another soldier held a cigar box on top of a clipboard, He handed it to Sigmund for his signature.

"Here is the best part of my day," Sigmund said as he signed a paper attached to the clipboard. The soldier counted off several Francs as he placed them one by one into Sigmund's hand. Sigmund dragged his thumb across his neck, indicating that the shells were defused. The soldier noted it and doubled the money. Sigmund handed half back. The soldier looked confused.

"My grandson is still sleeping and missed the morning show," Sigmund said with a wink. "Could you be so kind as to rouse him shortly with a bang?"

The soldier laughed as he handed the money back to Sigmund then motioned to a pair of soldiers standing by stacks of munitions, each larger than a schlitt fully loaded with wood. The soldiers guided Sigmund towards a partial stack, with a layer of 210-millimeter shells near the top. Everett helped them lift the dead weights from the back seat to the stack as Sigmund described the other layers of bombs.

"Are they going to do it?" Everett asked.

"With an honest soldier, one never knows," Sigmund said.

The Chesterfields filled out the last of the layer of 210-millimeter shells. Above, a few layers of 75-millimeter shells, then a layer of mortar rounds, then land mines. The last layer would be an icing of plastic explosive and detonation cord. The foundation would be reserved for the perfumes - phosgene, chlorine, or mustard gas shells.

Sigmund pointed to a bundle nearby as a huge crane lowered it into the deep water of the quarry for underwater detonation.

There, Sigmund explained, the upper layer explosive's shrapnel would slow by the drag of water and the blast would set off the lower layers, until finally with so much heat, that it burned off the deadly gas at the bottom. They were still perfecting the technique, using relatively small, fused stacks here at the dépôt, according to Sigmund. They planned to explode even larger ones at sea along the coast in the future, but they would be mostly un-fused – like the ones Sigmund delivered yesterday in his cart.

"There's more?" Everett asked.

The crane turned about after setting the bundle in the water. A guard whistled to Sigmund to move along.

"Always more," Sigmund stuffed the money into his shirt pocket then circled along the rim of the quarry. He stopped just past the entrance gate beneath an oak tree.

Everett looked back down the road that led to the water. Soldiers moved in a quick step up the road. They approached the guard who they passed earlier. He quickly glanced at his wristwatch and motioned them to move faster. A siren wailed from a tall pole at the rim of the quarry. The men ran until they stood just outside the gate. The siren changed pitch. Sigmund counted, slapping his hand against the side of the car.

"Fünf. Vier. Drei. Zwei. Eins!"

The ground shook beneath the car. Sigmund grasped the car door handles to restrain himself. Loose rock tumbled from the sides of the quarry around them. Dust lifted from ledges and fell back down to rest. Trees shook birds from their limbs, acorns fell and insects took flight. In a second, a roar came from below, deep in the quarry's water that had muffled its sound at first, but now failed to contain the blast's fury. Taking Everett's breath away, it shot into the air like giant red and orange geysers.

Both water and fireball bloomed and seemed to hang high at eye level until it fell. When he could breathe, the air carried a dry smell that Everett knew was the smell of hay or grass, followed by a stringent smell of burning oil.

Sigmund coughed, engaged the clutch, and spoke but Everett couldn't hear a thing except a ringing inside his head. He felt dizzy. It became dark.

After the smoke cleared and his ears stopped ringing, Everett looked around. It smelled awful around him.

"It was terrible was it not, Everett?"

"Why didn't you drive further away?"

"You looked exactly like your father, Russell, when he first came under attack and took in so much gas. Men still cough. You must certainly remember him coughing, when you were young."

"I'm a blank," Everett hacked over the Mercedes' doorframe. "Can't we get out of here?"

"I think you need a beer," Sigmund said, racing the engine.

∞12∞

Proposals

In Ville Negre, Sigmund turned off Rue Gambetta to a narrow cobblestone side street. He stopped the car in front of a two-story brick building with a wide railed-off patio - Chauchat's brasserie. Prospective diners examined the menu on the wall. He honked the horn several times until the door exploded open. Madame Chauchat waddled out to the car.

They argued for several minutes in German. Everett guessed that it was Sigmund's way of approaching women, who found him attractive. Sigmund held his hand up, counting his fingers - something about money. Madame Chauchat would turn as he counted, to see if anyone was still listening. She puckered her mouth to form a kiss and pressed her hands at the side of her enormous breasts. At last, they agreed. Everett wondered why Sigmund would risk such an amorous adventure on the day of his proposal to Madame Lambert.

"I told her you want to be seated up there," Sigmund pointed to a cement balcony perched out above them with a table and metal chairs. Not chairs ornately scrolled for a delicate person, but big, thick wrought iron thrones. Madame Chauchat motioned Everett into the brasserie.

"Up there, Madame Chauchat always served the Gestapo so they could keep an eye on things," Sigmund said. "Manfred and I always ate inside where it was dark and too noisy to be overheard."

The streets filled with people. Everett thought it strange for a weekday afternoon. They flowed past the brasserie, down Rue Gambetta and clustered in the park like lost sheep.

Sigmund handed Everett some money from his pocket and motioned him inside.

"Order a beer for me too, though I might be gone some time," Sigmund said. "I have serious business to attend to."

"You're a crazy old fool, Sigmund."

Everett climbed the stone steps to the balcony and sat down, letting the sun warm his face, wondering if Beatrice might inherit her father's infidelity. She was loyal to Manfred - could loyalty and fidelity be two different qualities?

As he took his first deep clear breath of the past ten minutes since the blast, he gazed across the red-tile roofs to the south, towards the dépôt. There, the tall black cloud still drifted towards the village that having feared the Great War, now feared the destruction of its endless aftermath.

Below, he watched Sigmund put a pipe to his lips and start the car, waiting for Madame Chauchat. Her husband Henri rushed to the car. He seemed to be warning Sigmund, but then curiously shook his hand. Everett had to remember that France was famous for its civility, even in matters of the heart, to explain it. Sigmund, alone, then drove north, against the crowd and up the street, now simmering with people. Most waved as they realized it wasn't Philippe behind the wheel, but instead, the haggard and bearded old man they had grown accustomed to seeing lead Gerta and his old cart of bombs through town. Sigmund spoke with a few then drove further north along Rue Gambetta, then off to the left. The crowd sighed, as they gave the sign of the cross.

"What's Sigmund up to now?" Everett wondered, half-believing he was leaving town for good to escape Henri's wrath or maybe to avoid fulfilling his promise to Everett.

A few spotted Everett perched high above them. Everett couldn't understand why they paid much attention. Maybe he looked like he conducted the whole, untimely affair at the depot, but then he remembered that he wore Manfred's shirt.

Madame Chauchat's small husband, Henri, crouched covertly at Everett's lone balcony table. His overpowering scent of lavender nearly bowled Everett over as the man nervously twisted the tip of his handlebar mustache with one hand and silently produced a tall mug of beer in the other. Without a word, he disappeared, in a vaporous wake of cologne.

The warm beer tasted unlike any he had ever had - hopped and slightly bitter, but flavorful. The skunk-smelling foam tickled his nose and cut the lingering stench of burned mustard from the depot as he licked the foam from his upper lip with each swig.

He was surprised when Madame Chauchat appeared at the top of the steps, out of breath, holding a tray of bread and more beer as customers below clamored for her attention. She looked past Rue Gambetta from the balcony, wringing her pudgy fingers in her apron.

After an hour, customers again filtered out to the street. They crowded at the intersection of Rue Gambetta where Sigmund had disappeared. A thunderous applause pealed against the hall of stone-faced buildings. Everett clapped, drunk, not knowing what was happening at all.

As Madame Chauchat appeared with yet another tray, a shot rang out. Madame Chauchat dropped the tray and hustled down the steps. Everett peered down, to find the German staff car backfiring. The Mercedes' rumbled to a stop, below.

Sigmund removed his bag from the trunk. He held something in his other hand, tossing it up and down like a baseball. More arguments with the Chauchat's inside before Sigmund finally appeared – he guzzled the last beer before sitting at the table with Everett.

"I thought you bailed," Everett said, "but it looks like you just played some ball. What is it, cricket, or is that a croquet ball you have in your hand?"

"Demining - A most dangerous sport," Sigmund said.

Everett focused on the object in Sigmund's hand – a huge fuse. He rolled it in large circles on the table until the Chauchats both appeared. Without a word, Madame Chauchat tossed a three-inch stack of new Francs on the tray.

Sigmund, from the balcony, looked over the wall into the side yard where a garden of hops grew in vines along a stone fence. Everett eyed the fuse up-close.

"So, you finally found an Essen fuse that was a dud?" Everett asked.

"Straight from the monster's jaw in their yard. I feel like Odin himself today," Sigmund said, giving it another twirl. "A golden tooth, is it not, Madame?"

The Chauchats nearly tumbled down the balcony, fleeing.

Sigmund tossed the fuse against the stone fence. It erupted in a thunderous crack, sending shards of granite into the yard. He opened the bag and crammed the money inside.

"At last, I have enough for Madame Lambert's hand," Sigmund said, as they left.

They drove north along Rue Gambetta. Sigmund pointed to the huge bomb he had defused at the Chauchat home.

"I cannot wait to see Madame Lambert's face when she sees the ring I am about to buy from that bit of work," Sigmund said, wrinkling his forehead with his wide grin.

Everett sensed he was equally delighted with his newfound courage to neuter a monster bearing the wrong fuse type.

Sigmund brought the Mercedes to a stop next to a bank and grabbed his black bag. "I never trusted banks much, but I need to prepare a transaction. While I do, you can get me an appointment with that barber over there."

He aimed the bag at a shop, just reopening after lunch. "A decent shave and haircut are a small reward for such a grand day, no?"

"Not a bad idea at all," Everett said. "I think I'll reward myself first though."

"Good! Said it with the same élan vitale as your father," Sigmund paced off, with his bag swinging, towards the bank.

The old barber sat in the big swivel chair, smoking a cigarette, behind a newspaper headlined with Dien Bien Phu. He rustled it in despair then glanced up as Everett stepped inside the open door in the sunlight.

"Manfred?" The barber said, squinting to see.

"No, Monsieur," Everett said as he ruffled the shirt along the collar. He started to explain until the barber stopped him.

"Ah, you are the friend of our Démineur Fischer!" The barber said, then proudly referred to Sigmund's removal of the Chauchat's monster as though Sigmund were an old baseball player who had come out of retirement, just to slug a homerun in their back lot.

"A shave and haircut, if you please," Everett said.

The barber brushed off the chair and dropped his cigarette to the floor, briefly igniting a ball of hair.

"Pardon, Monsieur," the barber said as he snuffed it with his foot. "I myself have become immune to its stench after all these years."

"I'm OK with that," Everett said, surprised that the smell that lingered like bad cheese in his nose since Korea had vanished. "My name is Everett, by the way."

"Yes, we know – after our great Évariste, the one you have recovered from the field today," the barber said with even greater pride as he wrapped an immaculate white apron twice about his thin frame. "The whole village knows."

Everett slipped for a moment in the leather seat, not quite certain how to deal with his sudden fame. The barber propped him up and twirled Everett's seat towards the window to display, leaving him alone for a moment. It was enough time for a sizeable crowd to form at the window, all clasping their hands near their hearts, mostly citizens younger than Sigmund, and a few older women.

The barber returned with a hot steaming towel, folded it over Everett's face and let him soak. It felt so good having everything drain, as though sucked into a divine poultice, into that hot towel. As it cooled, he thought of that crowd outside, probably still watching, and not a Frenchman in it the age of his father. He recalled the statistics of the Great War and of a generation lost - but still, there should be a few standing there to honor the Great Évariste.

He felt the towel being unfolded then smelled the fragrance of talc near his nose as he realized, those Frenchmen, the Poilus would never, in a million years, dishonor themselves by telling a civilian of the true state the Great Évariste had attained on that post.

The barber spun him around then dabbed soft, lathered cream on Everett's face. Tall and lanky, he folded in half at the waist to work on Everett's stubble. With a fancy flurry of the blade, he was done.

"Une coupe?" The barber asked. "With a name like Everett, a French style haircut would be quite popular here today with the citizens."

"Just give me what Sigmund gets," Everett said.

"Le Americain," the barber regretfully moaned as he reached for a large pair of shears and began to hack away.

When he finished, he spun Everett to the window again. His hair looked as though it were cut around a bowl and his sideburns had all but vanished - just as Everett expected Manfred would have wanted it cut, not an American cut at all.

Sigmund smiled as he appeared at the door wearing a new suit.

"I look like Manfred, huh?" Everett asked, standing from the chair, grinning.

"No, you look like your father," Sigmund said. "No hair, no lice, he would say."

"General Fischer, your seat is ready," the barber said. "The usual?"

"The same as my old friend Russell here," Sigmund said, pointing to Everett. "Madame Lambert always liked his looks."

After the barber finished, he swept up a pile of hair that could have filled a mattress. Sigmund rewarded him well for the harvest.

All the way along Rue Gambetta, north towards the Zone Rouge, Everett complimented Sigmund on his new suit, smooth face and handsome haircut. Sigmund glowed, as the sun set behind a bank of dark clouds on their return to the deep-dugout.

"I hope your dashing new appearance isn't enough to charm Madame Lambert from getting what I need from you," Everett said, reminding Sigmund of the possibility that Madame Lambert might put him under a spell. A speck of rain fell to the windshield.

"You are like your father, no patience at all," Sigmund said, rather too confidently for Everett, as rain sprinkled.

ಜ13ಜ

Madame Lambert

The awesome plateau, into whose side the dugout burrowed, loomed ahead like a huge cloaked wizard lying on its side, napping. The dugout's chimney smoke vented from a small hole in the earthen wall. It crept up the slope to the fog-filled trenches and merged invisibly beneath a tarnished silver sunset. A scent of burning oak was the only evidence that someone was living inside the ridge, halfway to the top. Everett filled his nose with the campfire scent, blown to him by a westerly that once spilled phosgene, mustard and chlorine gas from the plateau of war.

"I don't see Gerta," Everett said, stopping the car next to the dugout's big lower door. "Maybe those bones weren't a good idea. Maybe Philippe took a turn for the worse. Beatrice and Madame Lambert might be spending the night with Annette again, to help."

"I know you are anxious for Madame to help me tell you about the band," Sigmund said. "But truly, I am more anxious about proposing to her. They could be on their way right now with Gerta."

"Let's go up to the trench," Everett said. "Maybe they're at the door."

They walked in the light rain up Gerta's path to Sigmund's trench. No one was there. Sigmund flipped up the gas cloth and they climbed down the steps. Everett rapped his knuckles on the door, 'Ta-da, Ta-da, Ta-da'. In a few seconds, it opened a crack. Louis' big blue eye looked Everett over.

"Who goes there?" Louis said, practically choking to hold his laughter. "You look like a foreigner."

"He is, Louis," Sigmund said as he rubbed Everett's haircut from behind.

"And who, exactly, is that speaking? He does not sound French," Louis demanded, still chuckling. "Step out from behind, or I will shoot!"

Everett let Sigmund move to the door.

"He looks like a foreigner, too," Louis said.

"He is, Louis. He is," Everett said as he mussed-up Sigmund's new haircut.

Louis held his side, laughing as he let them in.

"Saboteurs are lurking about. One must be suspicious," Louis said. "There was a big explosion this afternoon."

"Maybe someday General Sigmund can take you to the depot and watch them go to Hell," Everett said, "that is, before all the shells are dug up."

"Not in Louis' lifetime," Sigmund said. "What is that wonderful smell?"

"I have been cooking, as you asked," Louis said, opening the door. "But, Grand-mère and Sister Beatrice have not returned. Father must be having a bad night again."

"It's only six-fifteen," Everett said, looking at the old clock on the wall.

"But, it is always," Louis said, and then stepped to the door as a tiny clattering of heels tapped down the wooden dugout steps.

"Ta-da, Ta-da, Ta-da," rapped the code, like a judge's gavel, against the door.

"It is Madame Lambert!" Sigmund said. His hand fidgeted as he reached for the door, behind which came the domineering voice of an old woman.

"Bonsoir, Bonsoir!"

A black cloth glove slipped into the door's opening. The woman, large like Beatrice, entered backwards. She wore a black beret and a black cape whose red velvet lower fringe was wet from the walk. She scraped mud from the shiny black shoe she had knocked on the door. She held crockery.

"You honor us, Madame," Sigmund sniffed around the bowling-ball-sized jar. "You have even been so kind as to bring us something for dinner?"

"Philippe sent his boar," Madame Lambert said, turning around. "I finished marinating it in my special sauce. He was so pleased to have his father's bones."

Everett was stunned by her resemble to Beatrice, the same large frame and red hair, only more blanched and thinner than Beatrice's. Her emerald green eyes sparkled in the lantern's light like Beatrice's as she scanned the dark earthen home, with the clinical look of a inspector rather than with Beatrice's kind and accepting blink.

Madame swung the jar to Beatrice to set in the kitchen, Everett followed her. She cracked open the lid and passed it under Everett's nose before sliding it inside the oven. He felt especially adventurous tonight, as though he too had changed, and took a deep whiff, hoping he might actually like boar now. Instead, he reeled from the powerful stench, sour and pungent as a week-old sock.

"At least you tried it," Beatrice whispered, noticing his suffering. "I thought a great deal of the courage it took you to return to find Philippe's bones – I am so sorry for what I said, about leaving your child."

"It's nothing compared to what Sigmund must do in return for those bones," Everett said. "Do you really think he will let your mother hypnotize him?"

"I dare say that Father is already under her spell." Beatrice laughed then kissed Everett and was about to do it again before he noticed Madame Lambert running her glove across the face of the clock, leaving a clear trail. She snapped her finger free of dust.

"Madame Lambert," Sigmund said as he tipped his head, "I am pleased you came. I hope you find my trench still to your liking. Allow me to take your beret."

"No!" she said, as Sigmund lifted it slightly.

He discovered the beret was still pinned to her hair. Sigmund nervously tried replacing the pin, but the small bun of hair unfurled in his hand.

"Je suis désolée, Madame." Sigmund let it fall. "You have such beautiful hair. I do like it like this."

"I do not!" Madame Lambert bunched her hair, quickly re-pinning it as Sigmund silently winced and cursed himself for beginning the proposal so clumsily.

Madame Lambert handed her hat to Louis.

"Oh, Monsieur Taylor?" she said, gazing at Everett in the corner of the kitchen while ignoring Sigmund. "You are as handsome as your father who, I understand, was kind enough to name you for my late husband, Évariste."

"I've been looking forward to meeting you, Madame," Everett said, "Doctor Hershey sends his regards."

"My, you sound so much like Russell as well," she said. "I am so sorry he is gone. I am pleased that the kind doctor encouraged you to come here, to my Lorraine."

"I apologize for being detained," Madame Lambert said as she carefully looked for Louis nearby. "Sister Beatrice and I were very busy, helping Annette. You see, the thrill of finding those bones changed the course of Philippe's therapy. He is now exuberant. Tomorrow, Louis should return home to the tuilerie with us."

"But I feel safe here, Grand-mère," Louis pleaded.

"Nonsense," she glared at Sigmund. "How can a person possibly live in this filthy hole on the verge of erupting so near to the Zone Rouge?"

"I must say, Madame, that Philippe sounds fit," Sigmund said, ignoring her insult. "Your abilities have matured greatly - 'âge certain', as they say in your language."

Everett discreetly jabbed Sigmund, then silently mouthed "âge certain, or certain âge." Sigmund again cringed at his attempt to impress Madame Lambert. He forgot the difference, in French, between indicating that a woman was approaching maturity rather than indicating, as he did, that a woman had definitely attained it.

"Due to my age, old Boche, it took longer than I planned to rebuild Philippe's confidence," Madame Lambert said as Louis helped her out of her cape.

She glared at Sigmund then handed the cape to Louis.

Louis draped it across his shoulders and ran to the bedroom, pretending to fly.

"I see there is at least one gentleman in this macabre chamber," Madame Lambert said to Sigmund.

"I am sorry, Madame," Sigmund said. "I expected you too might be pleased to have your husband returning home."

"As a skeleton?" Madame Lambert roared.

"But Madame, I always assumed all this time, that you were waiting for something," Sigmund said.

"Oh, you are a foolish old man, Sigmund - it has been over thirty-six years! I was waiting for you, not him," Madame Lambert said.

"But," Beatrice said, "was Évariste not coming home someday - to remove Chesterfield from the porch?"

"I know the legend grew in the Ville Negre about the Great Évariste, charging with his paintbrush - but he was a high-strung and ill-tempered man most of the time. He was not a God - he left us standing on the porch with Chesterfield, after all," Madame Lambert flared her nose towards the kitchen.

Everett noticed how cold and quiet the room became, and how Madame seemed startled and regretful at what she had just said.

"I suppose I do still miss my walk along the trench at night with Évariste," Madame Lambert said. "It was a touching place for them to bury him."

Everett glanced to Sigmund, who nodded his head, and lipped – 'not a word about the post.'

"Be seated," Beatrice said. Everett sensed irritation in her voice. "The boar is still being warmed, but the entree' is now ready to eat, compliments to Louis."

"Oh, I do love a wild boar," Madame Lambert said, nudging Sigmund over with her substantial hips. "You will not mind if I sit beside this old one then. Give a lady some room, if you please."

Everyone laughed, including Sigmund. Beatrice shot Everett a promising look, hinting her parents might become comfortable with each other after all.

Everett helped Beatrice pour the aperitif, "Framboise Royal" - raspberry champagne, tart and sweet. The thick liquid smeared the side of the glass as Everett swirled it by the thin stem and listened to Sigmund and Madame.

Madame Lambert boasted she had once cast a spell on the bomb, Chesterfield, still wedged against her house - just to keep it asleep. Sigmund insisted that if Madame believed so much in her magical gifts, why then, did she not attempt to dislodge it herself. Their bickering continued unabated above the clattering of china in the kitchen as Beatrice served the entrees. She ladled Louis' mushroom soup into their special bowls, and broke open fresh baked bread flavored with anisette. The arguments ceased when Everett popped open a bottle of wine next to Beatrice.

"Is it going OK?" Everett asked quietly.

"Yes, until Mother mentioned Chesterfield," she whispered as the others ate.

"I am so pleased with this soup, Louis," Madame Lambert said, lifting a spoon to her long, inquisitive nose. "Where did you find such flavorful mushrooms?"

"Up there," Louis pointed towards the door leading up to the trench.

"I am surprised, as Sigmund has cleaned his trench so thoroughly," Madame Lambert said, "but then there is so much decay in the Zone Rouge for mushrooms to grow, all those poor young..."

Sigmund's spoon fell from his fingers into the soup. He grimaced after he spat a big slice of mushroom onto his plate.

"Madame Lambert!" Beatrice said. "You know very well that mushrooms grow on tree stumps, not bones!" She held Sigmund's nervous hand until he could manage the spoon for his soup.

When Sigmund finished, he pushed himself away from the table and snapped his suspenders, drawing Madame Lambert's attention.

"The woman loves to make me appear uneasy amongst friends," Sigmund said. "She knows there a certain things I vowed never to speak of."

"Do you remember what that is, dear?" Madame Lambert said, folding her napkin as neatly and calmly as her voice.

"There, you see – she has done it again!" Sigmund said, looking for his pipe.

"Well?" Madame Lambert laid her napkin to align with the perimeter of the table.

"Of course not!" Sigmund huffed through the empty pipe in his mouth, stepping to the mantel. "I must bow again to your unique abilities. Where is Philippe's elixir?"

"I have it, Sigmund," Beatrice said as she brought in clean plates for the next course. "Perhaps wait until after dinner, when Louis has gone to bed."

"Is General Sigmund going to propose to her soon?" Louis whispered to Everett.

"They're like a pair of squirrels," Everett laughed quietly. "They like to fight before they go off together."

Louis nodded, with a grin, that he understood as he and Everett helped Beatrice prepare the next course. The conversation between Madame and Sigmund escalated.

This time Sigmund sat back and listened as Madame Lambert remarked on his home, how it smelled like a dungeon, how she noticed Sigmund walking more crouched lately because of the dugout's low ceiling - all not fit for human life. She pulled a femur, lodged into the earthen wall.

"How long have you lived in this ossuary?"

"Thirty-six years. You know very well, Madame," Sigmund said. "I will take that, if you please – new construction."

Sigmund plucked the bone from her hands and tossed it under a table where he had collected a small pile.

"You are too stubborn to move out, Sigmund. Just look at your complexion – your face is turning the color of a white pasty grub."

Beatrice shook her head to Everett in disappointment. She rose and walked back to the stove to tend a pot, boiling over.

"I have fashioned the earth to my liking at last, Madame," Sigmund said. "I thought you at least might approve."

He explained, he widened the windows to bring in more light, replaced the rotting gas protection cloth above the dugout with a new one. He also dug the floor down deeper over the years to give him more headroom and space to move around in and, in the process, was always finding more bones.

"It is almost too big for me," Sigmund said. "Even with Louis and Sister Beatrice here, it is still quite large."

"It is big enough for all of us, even Monsieur Taylor," Louis said.

"Tomorrow you will return to the tuilerie with us, Louis," Madame Lambert said.

"Father must never strike me with that hand again," Louis said.

The room lay silent, except for pots boiling over. Louis ran to the kitchen.

"Madame, Louis must have some assurance first," Sigmund said.

Madame Lambert sighed and shrugged her shoulders.

"Very well," Madame said, turning to Beatrice. "Those bones rejuvenated Philippe instantly, did they not?"

"It was remarkable," Beatrice said, stepping into the kitchen. "He did not need opium today, and he walks with a slight bullish stagger that Annette is rather fond of."

"The tuilerie will be safe," Madame Lambert said. "Although this hole of Sigmund's is quite safe it is quite filthy, even for a young man, like Everett."

"Why do you not remove your socks and spend the night, Madame," Sigmund interrupted. "Feel for yourself how I have improved even the floor. I remember a time when you enjoyed its mud oozing between your toes. Now it is as smooth and solid as the wood and tile of the tuilerie itself."

Sigmund reached down and ran his hand along the floor to tickle her ankle. She closed her eyes to sigh a brief whisper of pleasure but then quickly crossed her arms and resumed her gruff demeanor.

Beatrice emerged from the kitchen wearing a large white apron and, tapping a glass, said, "Hors d'oeuvres, and bread, compliments of Louis!"

She hoisted a plate of goose liver pate and bread above their heads.

"I like you in that apron, it looks like a habit," Louis asked. "But where is your habit? I have not seen you wearing it at all, Sister Beatrice."

"I no longer need one, Louis."

"Thank God," Sigmund said. He kissed Beatrice as she set the tray next him.

"I too, liked your habit," Madame Lambert said, "and your nursing gown as well – you look superb in a white uniform – not a wife's apron, of course."

"That is enough," Beatrice said.

Madame Lambert shifted the conversation to Dien Bien Phu after explaining she had not raised Beatrice to become an ordinary woman.

"She must return," Madame Lambert said as she looked to Everett. "I trained her to be a nurse and the Pasteur is an honorable calling even if the war is lost."

Sigmund downed a small glass of the plum liqueur, Mirabelle. Again, Everett declined after inhaling its ether-like aroma. Sigmund's face reddened.

"That is for me to decide!" Beatrice snapped her apron, shooting crumbs into the air as she returned to the kitchen.

Air whistled through Sigmund's yellowed teeth in a deep breath as he controlled his anger. He waited until Beatrice was busy tending the stove.

"Madame, enough!" Sigmund said, "Our Sister Beatrice is over thirty years old now. Do you want her remain a widower like you for her whole life?"

"Louis, why don't you and I go into the kitchen," Everett said.

"Why?" Louis said. "They often quarrel like that, as though they were the only ones in this little room."

Everett drew the curtains and walked Louis to the kitchen. Beatrice turned from the blue tile oven with a plate of boar meat in her hands, then seeing Everett motion towards the curtain, set it on the stove.

"The meat will keep," Beatrice said.

"Sister Beatrice, were you the last angel to leave Indochina? Is that what a widower is?" Louis asked. He turned his head so he wouldn't miss the muted shouting behind the curtain.

"No, Louis," Beatrice said. "There are many good nuns there still, real angels, though I fear for them now."

"Louis, even the real angels are leaving that part of Indochina now," Everett said. Beatrice scowled at him for a moment.

"Can angels be afraid?"

"Anyone can be afraid, Louis," Everett said.

"Not you, Monsieur. You fly jets," Louis said. He turned his ear again to the other room. "Oh, they are quiet now."

"Are they progressing?" Beatrice whispered to Everett as Louis parted the curtain slightly.

Everett moved her hair away from her ear and whispered, "I think they're deciding your future."

"But Sister Beatrice is an angel," Louis said. "Only Gods tell angels what to do."

Louis returned to the curtain to listen and watch.

"They turned the lantern down," Louis whispered. "There is only the light of the fireplace, but I can see enough - O-La-La-La-La!"

"Louis, please close the curtain." Beatrice said.

Everett reached over Louis to close it, but he couldn't resist looking. He turned the kitchen lights down and tugged Beatrice by her apron to the curtain.

"Why is General Sigmund on his knees?" Louis whispered.

"Shh," Beatrice said.

The light from the fireplace caught the ring's large diamond facets and sparkled in Madame Lambert's wide and watery eyes. Sigmund whispered words in her ear. Tears ran down her plump red cheeks. He gave her a nervous kiss on the forehead and moved his head far enough back to look into her eyes and waited for her to speak.

She pulled Sigmund to her and whispered something that made his hands shake. She helped him slide the ring onto her thick finger.

Everett felt Beatrice's arm wrap around his waist. She bent down to Louis and whispered into his ear, "Beautiful, yes?"

"Look at it shine," Louis said.

"Not the ring, Louis," Everett whispered.

"What then?"

Sigmund closed Madame's hand in his and turned to Louis with a shy smile.

"Please, come in," Sigmund said.

"See my ring," Madame Lambert said, "sent straight from the heart of my brave Démineur - Ziggy."

Beatrice sprang from the curtain and smothered them both in kisses. Madame Lambert touched the corner of Beatrice's apron to her daughter's eyes.

Everett grasped Sigmund's hand then kissed Madame Lambert's dazzling ring. As he was about to say something in the way of a toast, a tiny bell tinkled from the kitchen.

Louis entered the parlor carrying the plate heaped with chunks of Philippe's boar.

"Voila! La pièce de résistance." Louis lowered his nose to the steaming plate.

"I am famished!" Madame Lambert said. "You must be starved, Monsieur."

She took the plate and passed it beneath Everett's nose.

"But, Grand-mère, Monsieur does not," Louis said, and then stopped as Everett waved him off. He was going to try again.

The boar meat, drenching in a thick marinade, fumed an acrid smell. His forehead beaded sweat and his stomach knotted. He flashed a jaundiced glow as his throat constricted, but managed a polite smile.

"Let me serve my friend," Louis said.

Everett was relieved as Louis carved off the tiniest shred of meat and laid it inconspicuously at the edge of his plate.

"I remembered, Monsieur," Louis whispered.

Everett discretely buried it in mushrooms and nibbled at the potatoes.

After dessert, Louis tipped in his chair as Sigmund sipped from his hot cup of coffee in a loud, vacuuming sound.

"I want to fly, Monsieur, like a rocket," Louis said.

"Louis, you only imagine you are flying," Sigmund said. "That is far different than the astral traveling Madame Lambert achieves on her broomstick."

Sigmund jostled Madame Lambert with a shoulder. She blew him a kiss in return.

He lifted Louis by the back of his trousers so Louis could pretend to fly, and then carried him to the fireplace where they sat down on a chair together.

"I am hoping Sigmund will, at long last, leave this old musty dungeon," Madame Lambert said to Beatrice.

"I like it here, and so will Louis," Sigmund said. He ran his hand across the wall, crumbling its soil and stiff dried moss in a light patter to the floor.

Everett shrugged his shoulders helplessly to Beatrice.

"But Sigmund," Beatrice said, "the Zone Rouge is too dangerous a place for Louis."

"It is the safest place on earth," Sigmund said. "I sometimes still hear my old friends digging behind these thick walls of soil."

"The band?" Everett asked.

"No," Sigmund said. He put his head to the wall and closed his eyes.

"Sigmund, you promised Everett that Madame could put you under a trance."

"It is futile," Madame Lambert said. "He still refuses to speak about what happened to the band that night. He came to know each of them over the weeks in captivity. I have tried putting him a trance, but nothing. In my practice, I have seen grown men believe they could fly like birds, not Ziggy. He would just sit there until I brought him out."

Louis turned from the fire he had been coaxing with a poker. His eyes went wild.

"Put me in a trance! I want to fly!" Louis said.

"I remember my promise," Sigmund said, turning from the wall. He grew quiet.

After a minute of listening to Louis begging for a trance, Sigmund walked to the Victrola and opened the storage door beneath the turntable. He filed through his old brittle records and removed the one Everett heard before - the band.

Sigmund carefully removed the record then cranked the turntable.

"You always play Wagner, how dismal!" Madame Lambert bristled.

"Madame Lambert, would you care to dance?" Sigmund begged, tilting his head.

"But it is Richard Wagner," she said. "Have you lost your senses, Old Boche? We cannot foxtrot to Wagner. Turn the record over – that is what I want to hear!"

"It is turned over, Madame, for your pleasure," Sigmund said as he twisted the Victrola's trumpet to face the room, set the needle onto the spinning record then reached for her hand.

Everyone bent towards the Victrola's trumpet to a series of scratches, and then a long crescendo of a snare drum as a band of cornets, trombone and clarinets introduced a lively rag. Madame Lambert's eyes ignited, her face curved with a smile of years long gone. A thin, tinny-like voice sang through a megaphone, - "Come on and hear, Come and hear, Alexander's ragtime band."

"Oh, Ziggy!" Madame shouted.

Sigmund grabbed her by the waist and swung her once, then lifted her slightly into the air as she kicked her thin feet backwards. She lifted her long black dress to the calves of her legs, lined in purple spider veins, and then pulled a long pin from her hair to let it swing. She followed Sigmund's steps to the music as he led her around and around the small room in a dizzying blur. They looked at nothing else in the room other than each other's eyes as they sang along to the music blaring from the Victrola's trumpet, "Come on along, Come on along to Alexander's ragtime band,"

Louis followed them around the dugout, reaching his hand up for a turn to dance. Nothing could stop them, not even Louis trying to break in.

Everett felt Beatrice's arm wrap around his back, along his waist. He held her hand as they watched Sigmund and Madame Lambert spin and twirl. As the music ended, Madame Lambert stood on her toes and kissed Sigmund on the lips for a very long time. Sigmund stood dumbfounded until she did it again. He kissed her and showed her to her chair then stepped back to the Victrola and set the record spinning for Louis to dance with Beatrice. Sigmund sat with Madame and watched their daughter and grandson dance. He soon drifted to sleep against Madame Lambert's chest.

When the music finished, Louis clapped near Sigmund's ear. Sigmund jumped.

"Louis!" Beatrice said. "General Sigmund does not like being surprised like that."

"I want to see them dance now," Louis said, pointing to Beatrice and Everett.

"But, I can't dance," Everett said. Louie looked at him in disbelief.

"Here!" Beatrice slid her arms behind Everett while Sigmund cranked the Victrola again. She followed him wherever his clumsy feet led. He led her through clouds.

Minutes later, the repetitive scratch of the needle on paper forced them to look away from each other to the revolving black disk slowly winding down inside the Victrola.

Sigmund lifted the Victrola's arm, removed the record and slipped it carefully into its paper jacket. Before he placed it in the drawer beneath the turntable, he brushed the cover with his hand and patted it as though he was putting a baby to sleep. He stopped a small tear from dripping down the corner of his nose.

"What is it?" Beatrice asked her father.

Sigmund, with his hand twisted up, signaled the end of the conversation. He turned to the door and pulled his boots on.

"I am sorry for clapping before, General Sigmund," Louis said.

Sigmund rubbed Louis' hair then found the pipe and stoked it with tobacco before opening the door up to the trench. He closed it behind him quietly.

"I have never been able to bring more out of him about that night," Madame Lambert shrugged in disappointment. "I hoped Sigmund would be more open after playing that music – he has not played it for a long time, it was that band, you see."

"Madame, did you ever happen to hypnotize my father?" Everett asked.

Madame Lambert became even more somber, as though someone had mentioned a stillborn child, long buried. She turned to look at the blank wall of dirt and timber. Silence stunned the small room, disturbed only by the snap of a burning log in the fireplace.

"I'm sorry, Madame, I shouldn't have asked." Everett said.

"No, it is quite all right," Madame said, "I was only thinking of the first time I met your father - it was in the base hospital in Epinal before he returned to the tuilerie. You, no doubt, know he was severely gassed."

"My father never really recovered, from what I'm told," Everett said. "Doc Hershey couldn't do much for him."

"Doctor Hershey tried his very best to help him during the war. He knew of the techniques I had been using with our own soldiers and called for me to help. Your father wanted to get back to fight."

"Do you mean Father didn't want to be sent home?"

"Your father could have been sent home, but he insisted on returning to the sector of Ville Negre. Doctor Hershey wanted me to determine if Russell was delirious or had a death wish before he made his recommendation."

"When you hypnotized my father, was he delirious?" Everett asked.

"Normally it would be confidential, but since your father has passed on, I can tell you no, Russell was not delirious but he did have a wish - and not a death wish. I remember it quite well, actually. He wished to return home to his girlfriend to tell her he would fight in a great and final war. He wished to tell her they could have babies after and live safely in his farmhouse in Iowa. Oh yes, and he wished all his men the same fortune. What a wish! Such a sweet man."

"I wish my father was that brave, Monsieur," Louis said.

"Philippe is brave, Louis," Madame Lambert took Louis' hand. "You are old enough now to know that when the Gestapo, having kept records from the first war, came to the tuilerie - they asked where the communist was hiding. They came looking for Évariste, not knowing he was long dead. Instead, Philippe thrust his hand upward more quickly I am sure than any 'Sieg Heil' they had ever seen. Philippe has the same principles as his father, Évariste."

"Principles?" Louis asked.

"They're codes we live by," Everett said.

"Like the Duello, Louis," Beatrice said. "Only instead of one God against another, it is one God against them all."

"Why would Father hit me if he has these principles?" Louis said. "I am only one small boy."

"Things happened to your father in prison, Louis," Everett said. "Someday he might tell you."

"Why does General Sigmund not talk about that night?" Louis asked.

"It's probably just a promise he made to himself," Everett said.

"But he promised," Louis said, "that Grand-mère was to put him in a trance. I want to be in trance, Grand-mère. Can you put me in one? I worry for the General."

"Louis, Grand-mère knows what she is doing," Beatrice said.

"But I do! I do worry about General Sigmund. What if he gets stuck in a bad dream?"

"Louis, I would never take him somewhere in his dreams he does not wish to go," Madame Lambert said. "Trust me."

"I will not trust you until you put me into a trance – I want to see for myself – it is my principle!" Louis folded his arms and stomped his feet.

"Very well, just a little one," Beatrice said.

"Here is what I will do, Louis. Do you like the boar meat we had for dinner?" Madame Lambert pointed to the pot still warm on the stove.

"Oh, yes Grand-mère! I could eat it all night."

"Very well, then when I bring you back from the trance, you will not like boar – it will taste like the worst thing you can imagine."

"Impossible! Grand-mère, try something easier for you."

Everett watched as Madame Lambert swung her new ring on a thread with its colored light moving about the room until Louis was under. Everett was amazed that it took less than a minute to work on Louis.

She implanted the suggestion and brought Louis back in a matter of minutes.

"Louis?" Madame Lambert asked.

"Grand-mère, are you going to put me into a trance now?" Louis asked.

"Oh, but I did."

"No, Grand-mère. I was only sleeping and it has been a fine day. I think I would be stubborn like General Sigmund, if you tried to put me under a spell."

"Louis?" Madame asked. "Would you like a warm slice of boar from the stove?"

Louis ran to the stove, lifted a large piece of ham with a wooden spoon then placed it on his tongue and chewed. The expression on his face changed from delight to horror as he spit it out and ran to the washbasin.

"You see, Louis – how it works?"

Louis shot her a puzzled look then smiled as he ran to the door, "I think I hear General Sigmund now."

A dull thud sounded against the door, too light for a boot, too heavy for a hand. Sigmund cursed at himself outside the door. Louis helped him inside as Sigmund rubbed a blemish on his forehead.

"Oh, Ziggy, are you hurt?" Madame Lambert asked, "You really should not smoke that horrible tar that I made Philippe give up."

"I was not smoking opium!" Sigmund said. "It was a mere slip. I need to replace those rotted steps. Your palace still needs some minor work."

Sigmund sat in his chair, scratching his chin, by the fire next to Louis.

"You will enjoy her spell!" Louis said. "It was like sleeping! She can help you remember the story, General Sigmund."

"Madame Lambert always had me under her spell," Sigmund rubbed Louis' head. "In spite of that, I have never mentioned what happened that night in 1918."

"Why General?" Louis asked. "It could be no worse than what Father saw in prison."

"Philippe was never a traitor," Sigmund said, "as I was to the Kaiser that night."

"Louis, why not go into the kitchen and have a nice plate of boar," Beatrice said, "while it is still warm."

"It only tasted bad that one time, Louis," Madame Lambert said, "The General's story might not be good for a little boy to hear."

Louis stuck his tongue out in a feigned gagging sound.

"If Louis is old enough for the Duello, he is old enough for this," Everett said. The cane seat of his chair strained and squeaked as he tried getting comfortable.

"Why not sit with Everett, Louis. I think he would like it," Sigmund said.

Everett lifted Louis up and sat him down on his lap. He wondered if Louis noticed his pensive look or his short apprehensive breaths as Sigmund tossed a log on the fire and began. Sigmund drew with his finger in the coating of dust on the floor in front of the fire.

"You must understand the geometry of the frontier," Sigmund said while he drew a long pair of lines with his fingers. "It is much more detailed than this of course, but this side of the ridge is German, the other French, they stand on the crest of this hill."

Sigmund used both hands, pretending to gather up dirt to make a hill. He swung his hand a few feet behind the French line, down from the hill and tapped the floor.

"The tuilerie stands here, far to the rear on the back slope, nearly out of range," Sigmund snaked his small finger near the tuilerie, "and here is the stream feeding Lac Noir."

"You forgot Lac Noir," Louis said as he drew a small circular dot for the lake.

"Lake? Try not to interrupt me, now," Sigmund said. "We bivouacked in the tuilerie, sitting by the fire," Sigmund tapped the spot with his pipe. "Russell was standing right beside Madame Lambert. Her hair then, like my, er ah – like Sister Beatrice's – was red and full of life. Russell's lungs sounded much better. I apologized again for sending over a volley of our gas projectors, it hurt him so."

"You threw dragon eggs?" Louis asked.

"Everyone threw eggs, Louis," Everett said.

"Russell had taken me prisoner a few months before in the trench raid," Sigmund went on. "We were both of the same rank. After he removed my chains, we agreed to dispense with formalities. He discovered I could cook and we became great friends."

"Didn't my father try to interrogate you, in all that time?"

"We were officers! Russell did finally ask, in a casual sort of way, about our attack plans. I think he did this for his own conscience and I told him he should know better than to ask me that."

"You could have been shot if you were ever returned," Everett said. He noticed Louis twist uncomfortably.

"Precisely," Sigmund said. "It was then I decided not to escape. I liked it there at the tuilerie with Madame, little Philippe, the Americans and their band. My, that band could play! They played each night at 6 PM, sharp, as your father would say. Before I was captured my men and I, in the German trenches, looked forward each night to a polka or two."

"I asked him what he thought of our artillery barrages near their headquarters in the tuilerie over the several days before he captured me."

"Your father laughed and laughed and coughed that cough of his."

"Why was Father laughing?"

"It was those fuses I was telling you about," Sigmund said. "After I was sent to the front for that manufacturing infraction, by some fortunate blunder they had that whole bad batch of fuses sent all the way from Frankfort by train, truck and mule to here," Sigmund pointed to far north of the German line, "to my artillery batteries a few kilometers to the rear. The fuses had followed me like a swarm of harmless bees – Ha!"

"A few hours before sunrise, each of four cannons of each battery was ordered to fire four rounds a minute for thirty minutes, then cool down for an hour before repeating throughout most of the day – it went on for five or six days. New barrels after the fourth day and the old barrels returned. My superiors in Frankfort expected to find them well-worn."

"But your infantry was counting on you to beat up my Father's outfit pretty good before they came over the top," Everett said.

"I was hoping after the fifth day, someone other than me would report that our shells were impotent," Sigmund said. "That way we could call off the attack and we all could listen to the band play for the remainder of the war, but Frankfort never bothered to look or ask – they were so confident in their grand design."

"I would have shot you if I had been there!" Everett said. Louis shuddered.

"But your father would have said the same," Sigmund said, "exactly as you put it so crudely just now, I knew him. But, I am trying to tell this story you desire so much, so Louis too can hear it without getting too frightened."

"I guess I know these things happen," Everett said, knowing his pilot friend Bender would have done the same.

"Your father's men certainly did," Sigmund said. "Russell said, for days, his men came out each time we fired, just to watch them plop into the mud!"

Louis chuckled.

"We always had trouble targeting the tuilerie from that range. After my capture, I watched our rounds landing short and to the side and not once getting one to drop in beside Chesterfield there by the porch – to keep him company."

"Chesterfield is a lonely one," Louis said.

"We have had enough of Chesterfield, Louis," Madame Lambert said. "It haunts poor Philippe, and I must say, I do remember the cannons' terrible roar."

"That is correct, Madame," Sigmund said. "After several months of being captured, our cannons grew fiercer, day by day – but still with no affect on the tuilerie. Then one night, the cannons boomed continuously, 'Whiz, Bang!' all night long – they had found a good lot of fuses. Your father remarked that I should have produced more bad ones, then laughed and coughed. It made no difference – the tuilerie could not be touched because of its unique location on the geometry, here, near the Vosges."

Sigmund tapped the spot on the floor with his pipe.

"I asked him what date it was – your father was supposed to keep it secret as well – but, he said June twentieth. I think he thought it would do no harm to tell me, considering all the duds that rained down before."

"But, my mind went wild when he told me the date. I stayed outwardly calm because I did not want to frighten him or Madame or little Philippe - I asked him again - he said the same date."

"What was happening?" Everett asked.

Sigmund started speaking, but covered his mouth with the back of his dirty hand.

"What is it, Sigmund?" Beatrice asked as she came to his side.

"It was a secret," Sigmund said, looking to Everett. "I kept it for all these years, even when Manfred first walked down those steps in those hob-nailed boots, wearing that shirt. I was afraid he had come from Germany to interrogate me, to see if I had ever told anyone. He just wanted to visit. I never told him, either."

"Who is Manfred?" Louis asked.

"Never mind, Louis," Madame Lambert said. "Sigmund is stuck, not in a nightmare, but in the past. Let me see what I can do."

Madame Lambert loosened the ring from her finger and fished out a string from her pocket.

"No," Sigmund said. "It is not that at all. If I were to say anything then, it would compromise my miners' lives. I never told then and I am still afraid to tell now."

"You promised Monsieur Taylor," Louis said.

Sigmund twisted his head left and right as though asking permission or forgiveness from phantoms of the past. He finally sighed as turned to Everett.

"I could not tell Russell, you must understand," Sigmund said touching Everett's shoulder, "but a plan, conceived in Frankfort, was in place long before I had been sent to the front. If the headquarters in the tuilerie could not be taken by artillery fire, which it had not due to the backside slope of the hill the tuilerie rested on, then the plan called for burrowing a tunnel beneath it and to be filled with tons of explosives."

A nearly imperceptible tone of pride carried in his voice.

"My men had been digging it for months before I was captured," Sigmund said. "I knew their schedule - like the trains, they would not be a minute late. They dug one whole length of chain each day, no more no less, day after day, from here straight to the tuilerie."

"Stop now, Sigmund - that is enough," Madame Lambert said.

"All this to kill Grand-mère and my father along with the Americans?" Louis asked as he sketched a straight line, running from the German side to Lac Noir. "But General Sigmund, even the German's cannot tunnel beneath a lake. You could see it from the Vosges."

"There was no lake then, Louis, only the stream," Sigmund said.

"Still," Everett said, "it would be tough tunneling under a stream."

"Frankfort's grand design included pumps and huge tubes to evacuate any water," Sigmund said. "Headquarters convinced me it would work, but after my capture, while visiting the band quartered along the stream, I learned how truly deep the stream ran. My men, beneath them, would never be able to pump that much leaking water out."

"Good. So you didn't need to warn my father in the tuilerie after all," Everett said. "If you had, the German's would have shot you for treason if they ever found out."

"Not quite," Sigmund said, this time with a more solemn voice, lacking the boastfulness he had used to describe his men digging. "I knew Frankfort would choose a secondary target. They would not alter their attack schedule, either – June twentieth at six PM – everything had been arranged to maximize the confusion, so bodies could not be recovered until morning's light."

"I can't see there would be anything of value to destroy before the tuilerie," Everett scratched his head.

Sigmund recovered the small spot, marking Lac Noir, with dirt.

"I am trying to tell you that Lac Noir did not yet exist," Sigmund said.

Louis raised an eyebrow to Sigmund.

"You remember, do you not Madame?" Sigmund asked.

"You once asked that I forget, Sigmund," Madame Lambert said. "The band's bivouac of big tents sat on the very spot, next to the stream where they would clean the bloodied stretchers on which they carried the dead and wounded during the day. At night, the band would play as though the day had been so lovely and grand."

Everett, at first, felt dismayed that his old peaceful image of the band gathering around Lac Noir at night with lemonade, no longer fit - but pure horror soon displaced his simple discouragement. He felt like covering Louis' ears, but held off as Sigmund continued.

"You listened to the band play there each night?" Everett said. "Knowing exactly when they were all going to die?"

"Yes," Sigmund said as he glanced away from Louis' stare. "I had hoped the war would end before that, but it went on and on and in that time I came to know those boys in the band as well as my miners."

"Ziggy, if you had only told me," Madame Lambert took a few steps towards him, but he held her back with a simple look. "Everyone said it was a very large and lucky cannon shell. I would have understood why you never wanted me to mention the band or Lac Noir ever again."

"It was matter of honor," Sigmund said. "I could not betray the men I had toiled with beneath the earth anymore than you could have deserted the memory of your Évariste."

"The Duello?" Louis asked Everett.

"Not so much as man against man, but as a man against many powerful Gods," Sigmund said.

"The twilight of love, Louis," Beatrice said as Sigmund nodded his approval. "Louis can certainly listen to the rest."

"So, I drew Russell into a game of pinochle shortly before 6 to keep him away from the band outside, where we normally went each night. He hesitated until I wagered a fish dinner. The mention of fish attracted Madame, Philippe and several officers who would be sharing the meal if I won. We played as the band tuned. I had to hold back tears as I listened to each boy test their instruments. The tuba, the trombone, the flutist, the drummer - all of them I knew by name, each one playing a few bars of their favorite tunes – you know the ones, Russell."

Everett, somehow, felt good that Sigmund mistook him for his father.

"Your father and I, then the rest of his men, turned towards the band. It had grown quiet as it does when the conductor steps to his podium and raises his baton."

Everett felt Louis shake again. Although he trusted Sigmund wouldn't become more graphic in the violence, he held Louis tight, ready to cover his ears.

"How many pounds of explosive do your jets carry?" Sigmund asked. Everett felt Sigmund's eyes by their slant, not a mean slant but a sympathetic one.

"A half-ton," Everett said. Beatrice translated for Louis.

"I know how much a half-ton is," Louis said in awe. "It is ten Chesterfield's."

"As the clock struck 6," Sigmund continued, "I folded my pinochle hand and I remember pushing little Philippe's head beneath the big oak table, he began crying. Nothing happened, no rumble, no roar. Everyone looked at me so strangely. I let Philippe up."

"The clock. Perhaps it was broken then as now," Louis said, pointing to the clock on Sigmund's wall, still at six-fifteen. "Why do you keep that old broken clock?"

"I watched it tick that night, Louis," Sigmund continued. "In my mind, I pictured my men scrambling back into the tunnel to replace a damp fuse. I watched it tick for fifteen minutes, until it shook loose from the wall as the power of eight full tons of explosives, not a pound more or a pound less, erupted beneath the band at precisely six-fifteen that night. I stole the clock from the tuilerie, so I would never forget."

Everett felt Louis shake after Louis calculated on his fingers.

"One-hundred and sixty Chesterfields!" Louis said.

"What few glass panes left intact in the tuilerie came like shards across the room, then the roar," Sigmund said.

"The blast was horrific!" Madame Lambert said. "Poor Philippe trembled like a leaf beneath the table."

"Everyone joined Philippe, not knowing it was over," Sigmund said. "I walked to a shattered window and, as the smoke cleared, watched the stream rush into the crater where the band stood a second earlier, all twenty-six of them, and beneath, my miners, my boys."

The band. Everett imagined how his father must have felt, ordered to march off after the explosion, then days later trying to write letters to their parents, coming from the same little part of Iowa as he. How could he possibly describe the earth opening its mouth and swallowing a whole band of twenty-six.

Everett couldn't remember his father at all, let alone anything his father might have mentioned to him about any of the band. He covered his eyes with his scarred hand.

"Why not let Grand-mère help you, Monsieur?" Louis said.

Everett, although shocked at how quickly Madame had transformed Philippe, felt strong next to Louis and Beatrice, he knew he would need to sew every thread from the rags of his memory into a deceptive coat for Madame Lambert to admire, just to keep her outside that part of him that could take him back into Korea. He felt good - better than he expected.

"You can try, just as Doc Hershey did," Everett said, "but I'm afraid you'll be disappointed, Madame. I would hate to ruin your evening. What do I have to do?"

Madame Lambert removed her ring as Sigmund rolled his eyes in doubt.

The big diamond's facets scattered a rainbow from the low light of the fireplace. Madame's deep, comforting voice and the smell of vanilla on Beatrice's breath, when she kissed him, distracted him from the ring until its captivating swaying, inviting him to dance.

Everett followed the harmonic motion of the diamond, twisting in the light by a string. Madame's baritone voice counted down, as the fire swirled a blue flame around the coals, "trois, deux, un".

Everett stared at his father's Victrola. The trumpet, shaped with six sides, the cabinet trimmed with ornate inlays of green enamel on varnished wood, all patterned with water stains, chips and gouges – it breathed and sighed. The trumpet pivoted to face him.

A log in the fireplace, once a glowing ember, erupted in flame. Pine-scented vapors hissed from a fissure of boiling sap. The purple light ran across the room to paint the Victrola in an invisible ink that appeared when he stared long enough. The wooden machine's feet, carved in lion's paws, bent at its toes, digging its claws into the dirt floor. The Victrola pounced to land in the far corner of the dugout in a single, bounding leap.

◆　◆　◆

He heard his grandmother calling and didn't think it strange at all.

ଊ14ଓ

A Good Night's Sleep

The boy worked feverishly by the back door untangling fishing line. Only a few yards remained. The soft tumble of potatoes, rolling into a bowl, came from the kitchen. His grandmother finished peeling them for tonight's special meal.

"Everett," she said, snapping a towel to get his attention, "are you finished with those poles? Russell will want to take you to the river before it storms."

"Dad's late this year," he said, "and it hasn't rained for weeks." He wiped sweat from his forehead, losing his place in the knots.

He had fun yesterday when he brought both poles, his and his dad's, up from the storm cellar. He practiced casting the line, with its big lead sinker, deep into the yard until dusk. That's when the line ran off his reel and he took his dad's reel, instead. It felt awkward, so he switched the rod to his left hand. He practiced casting until its line ran off too. His grandmother always got grouchy when he played with his dad's things, never his dad.

He spent the night trying to untangle the lines, then tossed in his sleep to a nightmare in which raccoons dragged his dad's pole to an oriole's nest too high to reach. In the morning, he found the line still snarled but less so than he feared. He spent most of the morning straightening his own line.

Now, he had the line snug on his dad's chrome reel looking just like he left it last year - with the hook dug into the cork handle and tied to the line stretching to the tip of his dad's tall pole. He clicked a red and white cork bobber on to finish it.

"Not many nine-year olds could do that, Everett. Where's the army tunic that Russell wears fishing? You didn't loose it, did you?"

"Dad's shirt? It's in the chest, I'll get it." He ran outside then down the storm cellar steps.

Everett's grandmother reminded Everett that the chest once held his dad's army spats, boots, bayonet, gas mask, papers, and the shirt. Now, all that remained was his fishing gear, some papers and the shirt.

Last year, 'Mean Schmidty', the school bully, swiped the spats and boots after Everett had worn them to school and left them unattended in the hallway. The bayonet lay on a high shelf where his Grandmother placed it after she caught Everett honing its blade on a stone, sharpening it to poke Mean Schmidty a good one. Everett never touched the gas mask – it frightened him. The mask disappeared after one of his dad's visits.

He opened the lid. The skunky smell of the khaki shirt overpowered the aroma of the cedar chest. He buried his face beneath a sleeve. Passing his nose over the stink of dried fish scum and bait, he found his dad's scent of shaving cream, mustache wax and medicine. He buried his nose in the cloth.

The sun glinted from the shirt's dazzling pins, still tacked to the collar; a pair of crossed-rifles, a US insignia, and a pair of pins his grandmother said were captain's bars and his father's regiment number.

The drab shirt's only dash of color was an arched patch on the tip of the shoulder. He let his fingers dance over the rainbow patch before stepping back inside to the kitchen.

The water pump sucked, deep and hollow, as his grandmother worked its wooden handle above the kitchen sink.

"Let me do that Grandma, you'll faint again."

"That was a whole week ago, Everett. I'm not about to let this old pump get the best of me again, not today anyway."

He cleared the tackle box from the chair by the table then jammed his hands into his pockets as his grandmother attacked the handle again, and again. Folds of skin beneath her arms waved and wobbled at the end of each down stroke, still no water.

She tried five times then steadied herself at the sink for a moment. Everett pushed a chair close behind her, knowing she always worked too hard when his dad would come home. Out of breath and with her hand over her heart, she collapsed into the chair. Through her thin vein-lined skin, he felt only delicate bone as he held her little head like one of her precious salt and peppershakers.

Beads of sweat trickled through rays of her silver-white hair, gathered in a bun at the back.

"Did it come undone, Everett? Your father always likes it in a bun."

Any other morning, she would hide her beautiful hair beneath a scarf, this morning it was in a bun. She had powdered her face until she sneezed and stopped, wiping it clean. She was as excited as Everett was about his dad coming and asked Everett if her hair was out of place as she slumped in the chair after struggling at the pump.

"Just a little, Grandma," He tucked a few strands of her hair back behind her ear. "It looks really nice now. I'll get you a cool cloth before you get up."

He wiggled a chair to the sink to reach the pump then clung to the handle with his right armpit. He hung with his feet dangling above the chair. Slowly, the handle yielded to his weight.

On the eighth pull, water gushed from the pump and spilled into the large white-enameled metal bowl filled with peeled potatoes.

He moistened her towel and gently daubed her forehead until she took it.

"You're such a good boy. Your father's coming home from the hospital, this time for good." She kissed his forehead then squeezed his hand as she stood. "Doc Hershey's spending the night, too."

"Good! Now, Dad and I can fish every day."

He wondered why she called it a hospital today. It was always the Sanitarium before - the place for soldiers to rest until they felt better. He hoped to take his dad, if he was better, into deeper water for bass.

"What's Doc going to do here, Grandma?"

"He's going to cook fish - the way he and your father did during the war."

"I didn't know bass lived in France, Grandma."

"Not bass, carp," his grandmother said. "Your father is going to fish from the bank for that big carp today, the one he always releases."

"I want bass!"

"I'm sorry Everett," his grandmother said. "There's to be no more wading in the river anymore. The hospital said your father is supposed to get plenty of rest."

"But I already dug up crawlers for the bass."

"Carp can eat anything, Everett. Go out on the front porch now and wait for them."

He sat on the step with his elbows on his knees and his chin jammed into his hands, thinking about all that line he untangled for nothing. He stared to the far tunnel of cedar trees over the winding gravel road, waiting for the dust to rise, waiting to ask his dad all those things he promised himself to remember.

"That Indian arrowhead he found near the river - where did the Indians go? The airplanes in the sky - why didn't they fall? The rainbow patches - could he take one off for himself? The gas that Doc Hershey said had made his dad sick in the war - his teachers told him it wasn't a natural element made by God, like hydrogen and oxygen - who was the man who created phosgene? And why, after all that, was it called a Great War?" He made himself dizzy, wondering if there would be time to ask him everything this time.

A white plume of dust rose above the trees. A black car emerged and drew up close.

"Here they come, Grandma. I can see Dad."

The long black car, covered with white powder, glided gently to a stop near Everett's feet. Before the window fully lowered, a familiar, raspy voice called out from inside, "Do you have our poles ready, Ev?"

Everett wondered why his dad called him Ev just now. Before, it was always Everett. His dad's smile though, was always the same when he came home, always wider than the one he smiled during Everett's and his grandmother's weekly visits to the Sanitarium. His grandmother said his dad saves that smile just for them when he comes home. She knew his dad didn't want to smile too much when they visited him in the Sanitarium, because of the respect he had for the other men there who didn't have families to see.

"Sure, Dad. I've got the cup of fresh night crawlers under the porch - just like always."

Everett saw his dad pop one of those mints he always carried as Doc Hershey opened the door, a foot away.

"Let me give you a hand, Russ," Doc Hershey said.

"Bull roar!" Everett's dad bolted from the car.

Everett felt the grip of his dad's taut arms hoisting him high, holding him close to twirl and watch the world spin. He shot Everett a loving look with his eyes - moist and glistening in the low morning sun. A perfect bull's eye, Everett thought, striking his heart.

All Everett wanted was to stay in his dad's safe and comforting arms and to read his smiling eyes, knowing he had time for questions later. Abruptly, his head twisted away from Everett. He felt his dad's chest stir, rising and falling like a wild bird trapped inside.

"It's his emphysema," Doc Hershey said. "Maybe you should set him down, Russ."

"The emptyzema, Dad?" Everett said. He knew what came next. "I thought Doc fixed that for you."

"Oh, Ev, I'm so sorry," his dad said, then gently held Everett away, carefully setting him down on the porch. Everett took a few steps towards him, but his dad held his hands out to keep Everett back.

He watched his dad bend to cough, then rise to fill his lungs, again, and again like a toy soldier winding down. Everett caught the deep odor of his dad's breath, undisguised by mint, more like mushrooms.

Doc Hershey helped Everett with his dad up to the screen door where Everett's grandmother stood with the towel to her mouth. She cried as she wrapped her frail arms about her son's sagging shoulders. His dad seemed smaller now and she held him longer than she had ever held Everett.

His dad looked up, wiped her brow and brushed her thin hair with his fingers. He rested his head on her chest and breathed easy. She hummed into his dad's ear then kissed it, putting him to sleep for a moment. Everett never remembered his dad ever doing that before, sleeping against her like a child.

Everett's dad opened his eyes then led her into her bedroom to lie down. Too much excitement for them, Everett guessed.

Doc Hershey dragged Everett's Dad's rocking chair to the back door, sat down and lifted Everett to his lap.

"What's the matter, Everett, your Dad? Don't worry. I'll give him something so he can fish today."

"But we can't take any bass," Everett said. "Grandma said we can't go wading. Maybe later Dad will feel better. Tomorrow maybe?"

"No, not tomorrow, Everett."

"Now Dad and I have to just sit on the bank and wait for that carp you're supposed to cook tonight."

"Who says?"

"Grandma!" Everett said, surprised he didn't know.

Doc Hershey, his eyes always full of mischief, this time seemed sad as Everett looked up to him.

"Do you know what your Dad would like? He would like to go fishing today with you, and in his favorite spots."

"But, Grandma?"

"Everett, all of his favorite spots - Do you remember where they are?"

"Sure thing, Doc," Everett said. Doc's eyes twinkled again, the way Everett liked.

"I'll settle things with your grandma while you two get ready for bass," Doc said.

His dad wore the fishing shirt, crammed with extra leaders, sinkers with lures and spinners pinned to the front, a bobber in one pocket and their sandwiches in the other. Everett thought he looked magnificent, but laughed.

"What's so funny, Ev?" his dad said.

"That shirt would never fit Doc."

"It did once," his dad said.

He winked to Everett as they marched in step, side by side, to the river. His dad teased limestone dust from the tree leaves with his tall pole. Everett held the shorter pole at his shoulder like a rifle.

At the river, his dad pointed to a line of bubbles rising like pearls in a calm pool by the bank.

"The old carp, Ev. He likes to eat when we do. Try your luck while he's hungry."

"They're no good to eat," Everett said. "Grandma tried before, we just fed them to the cats. Bass, that's what I like - battered up and fried in the pan, you know."

"Listen, son. What I like best about fishing is waiting, and there is nothing, believe you me, like waiting for a carp. The only thing you have to worry about in this whole, wide world is your bobber. If you lay it in just right, he will swim up and nibble for a while, then take it down. Here, take my pole."

Everett baited the hook with a twisting worm and cast it where his dad pointed. The crawler, with the red and white cork bobber flying behind it, looped around in the air then landed with a little splash right on the spot. He let the sinker take it down then took up the slack in the line, watching his bobber slide back over the spot.

His dad stood over his shoulder, saying nothing. Everett was mesmerized, looking only at the clouds and the blue sky reflecting from the shimmering water around the spot.

Everett thought he saw it go down once then pop back. He took up more slack in the line with the reel.

"Let him play with it, Ev. We've got all day."

Everett loved the voice - rough, but with a kind tone. His dad had given him this same advice dozens of times before on the quiet river. Everett waited.

"He'll take it down when he wants to, Ev. Then he'll run hard, like he's just sneaked a cookie."

Everett watched the bobber. His dad hummed a tune.

Everett looked up at his dad's face after the tune ended, expecting him to be pointing to where the bobber already was moving fast. Instead, his dad was looking intently towards the swifter water in the main channel where the bass lived.

The line got his attention and tugged him hard, bending the rod towards the water. Everett trapped the line, paying out, with his thumb against the rod. The bobber ran fast beneath the surface. The reel clicked as it worked to slow the advancing line.

"OK, now set the hook." His dad said, still looking away to the bass, "Reel him in slowly. Don't give him more line now."

Although Everett didn't like eating carp, he liked to catch them because they gave a bit of a struggle and enjoyed their heavy pull. After a minute of play, they felt like a boot on the line, not much fun. This one was no different. In a minute, he reeled the fish up in the weeds along the bank.

The carp rolled its eye towards its pouted lips where the hook's eye stuck out attached to the line.

His dad showed him what he already knew - how to remove the hook, and then how to coax the carp's pursed lips open to accept the pointed metal end of the stringer. He threaded it down its throat towards its wide-opened gill where the metal point finally appeared.

He looked up to his dad just before he pushed the point through the metal loop at the end of the stringer to snug it tight up against the carp's scummy skin.

"Let's go for bass now," Everett said, "in your spots."

"OK, but bring our carp along so the dogs don't get at him. And keep moving him so the river can still run through his gills."

His dad removed his boots and socks and set them beside a boulder near the bank. Everett set his side by side. In the river, the carp floated behind him as they waded upstream towards faster water. Its gills waved slowly.

After a few minutes the gills nearly stopped. The carp rolled to its back. Everett pulled pliers from his pocket and was about to rap its head, when his dad turned.

"What are about to do, Everett. Kill him?"

"He's hurting, Dad."

"No, he's just running out of oxygen in his river, that's all - like falling asleep in your own bed. Now, if you had ripped its lips or guts for the hook - that would be different. I'll take him now."

Everett grabbed his dad's leg for support as they waded into colder and faster water where bass might linger in deep holes. The feel of his dad's leg gave him confidence.

"Ev. Come stand next to me on this other side. I want you to remember where this hole is - an old one I forgot about. Can you feel it with your feet? Don't worry, Ev, I have you. Can you touch bottom yet?"

"Got it, Dad."

Everett felt the mud squish between his toes.

"Do you remember where all the other holes are?"

"Sure, Dad."

"Good, don't forget."

They went further and deeper than ever before. The water came up to his dad's waist and Everett's chest.

"Climb up now, Ev, it's getting deep."

His dad lifted him onto his shoulders. Everett ran his hands over the rainbow patches on his dad's shirt to feel the colors again. They had a name.

"Roy G. Biv," Everett said, "Why that name, Dad? I forget."

"Red, orange, yellow, green, blue, indigo and violet - just like they're laid out in the rainbow, Ev."

"I like my name, Ev, a lot better than Everett. Where does it come from, Dad? I get teased at school."

"Everett is for, Évariste - a brave French painter who was lost in the Great War. It's a proud name, Ev."

Everett straightened up, feeling famous now, on his dad's shoulders.

Not far away, a fish flipped into the air then slapped back into the river – a bass. He felt his dad turn towards it, trudging against the powerful tug of the river.

"Dad, it's getting pretty deep now."

Then Everett felt the eruption in his dad's lungs. The emptyzema was having its way with his dad again. Still his dad didn't cough and continued to move slowly in the water. It knocked again, as though the disease knew someone was home but not answering the door. His dad stopped and leaned forward a few degrees. His dad's face looked contorted in the swift water, letting go a bucking cough. Everett heaved and swayed. His dad held him tight.

"Dad, let's go back downstream to the bank for our sandwiches. We can take some bass tomorrow, you'll see."

The boulder shimmered baking hot. Everett sat, tying his shoes, wondering how Doc might cook his carp. His dad walked up the ridge, pausing to pant and catch his breath before the summit.

"Ev, we'll have lunch up here, but I need a push."

Everett led his dad by the hand up a gentle path to rest on the exposed roots of a lone silver maple, looming over the river like a watchtower and shading the family gravestones. After a minute, his dad told him to sit for a while as he walked over to the grave of Everett's mother. His dad cleaned the stone with a handkerchief. Everett kicked at puffballs on the ground.

"Let's walk over to the Indian fire-pit where my old company used to camp," his dad said, briefly startling Everett. "We'll have lunch there now."

They came to a circle of small rounded boulders from the river. Everett stirred the ashes made by those men who had looked for work - the ones his grandmother let camp there, the ones his school friends called bums. He sat by his dad, eating his sandwich and watching the wind lift the ashes out across the river wondering where those men of his father's company went.

Just as they finished eating, his dad barked a cough down the river valley. He stood to cough again and walked to the edge of the limestone cliff overlooking the river.

"What are you doing, Dad?" Everett asked. He didn't like his dad standing so close to the edge with that cough.

"I was just thinking. What day is it, Ev?"

"It's 1937, Dad, the middle of June already."

"No, Ev. What day of the week?"

"Wednesday."

"Woden's day and tomorrow is Thor's day - do you remember that story, Ev? You tell it to me this time."

His dad leaned his back against a tree and reached for Everett, letting him fall back gently to rest against his chest. Everett ran his fingers lightly across the patch on his dad's shirt as though it were an old sore. His dad softly sighed.

"It's hard to remember," Everett said.

"I know, Ev. Make up a story then. I just want to hear your voice - it's different now, deeper. I like its sound."

Everett took what he remembered from the old story where Gods and Giants liked to pick fights, snakes and dragons breathed fire, wild boar patrolled and swords killed only what they were made to kill and beautiful ladies waited with their children for the fires and smoke to clear so they could find their men again. He bent it around until it made some sort of sense.

"That's pretty good, Ev," his dad said, then after taking a short breath, "how will you end it?"

"Is it your emptyzema, Dad?"

His dad produced a blast of coughing then a high-pitched wheeze to vent his lungs. The empty, water-pump sound made Everett shiver with fear.

"No, not this time, son." His dad's eyes closed.

Everett closed his eyes too and put himself there in that place his dad had once spoke of, a place far away where it wasn't safe. A place where one world ended and another might begin. A clash where all the rainbows spilled together into darkness until a band started to play music that everyone knew.

"Did you learn the story from your dad too, Dad?"

"I learned it while Doc and I were in France, from a German friend of mine."

"The Final War?" Everett asked.

"No, only the last one," his dad said. "My friend taught us how to cook carp too - blue carp."

"But Dad, our carp's not blue."

"He will be soon!" His dad laughed all the way home.

Doc Hershey stood near the door, speaking to Everett's grandmother. Their voices hushed as Everett came to the steps - something they didn't want him to hear. He flopped the big carp onto the wooden steps just to let them know he was there.

"Everett got himself a big one," his dad said as Everett gently slipped the stringer from the carp's gaping mouth.

"I'm not cleaning that thing," his grandmother said.

"I think she'd like one of Sigmund's big marinated rats!" Doc Hershey said with a smirk then unsheathed his knife and slit the carp's belly wide open.

"Don't get too carried away with your knife, Doc," his dad laughed. "The head and scales stay, remember? Give those guts to Ev. He'll bury them by the tomatoes."

"Yuck!" Everett said as he gathered the innards then carried them at arm's length to the garden patch.

Everett hadn't heard his dad laugh like that for a long time.

"Come over by me, Ev," his dad said as Everett returned.

Everett's fish lay at the edge of the sink. He wouldn't have known it was dead if it weren't for those big fixed eyes staring back at him. Everett lifted his fish, about to slick off the thick gooey slim of its skin.

"Uh, Uh, Ev." his dad said. "That's the good stuff. Open him a crack so I can load him up with salt."

Everett pried the carp's underside open as his dad sprinkled a handful of salt inside. His dad nodded his head and puckered his lips, indicating it was enough salt, then held a big bowl beneath the fish as it began slipping from Everett's hands.

"Now we'll give him a little bath," his dad said as he covered the carp briefly with boiling vinegar. He drew Everett back a few steps, as though the carp needed some privacy. In a minute, Everett inched his way back up to see.

"He's still not blue, Dad," Everett said.

"Give him time, Ev." His dad rubbed Everett's head with his stinky hands.

"Aw, Dad!" Everett said.

The back door flew open. He heard Doc whistling.

"One for the carp and three for the musketeers!" Doc Hershey juggled four bottles of white wine.

"But Russell can't," Everett's grandmother said.

"I prescribe Riesling tonight," Doc said, "from the Vosges, for medicinal purposes only, you understand."

Everett's grandmother stepped to the back porch as Doc uncorked and emptied a half-bottle of wine into the boiling vinegar. A chemistry experiment, Everett thought.

"Stand back!" Doc Hershey said as he lobbed onions and lemons at the carp then blessed it with laurel leafs.

"Doc thinks he's Merlin tonight," his dad said. "In a way, he is. Are you sure you're not turning it into gold, Doc?"

"Blue," Doc Hershey said, taking a swig from the bottle.

"Make his gills move again, Doc," Everett chuckled.

"No. I can only make him blue," Doc said, about to cover the carp in boiling vinegar and wine.

Before Doc Hershey covered it, the carp's eyes stared at Everett, looking as if it might come to life. Doc Hershey helped his dad to the porch to drink while the fish cooked.

Everett's grandmother scolded his dad for drinking, but then stopped. She told them of his dad's first big fish – a bass. How helpless she had felt when a bone caught in his throat.

"I forced bread down Russell's little mouth until it took the bone," she said. "I thought I lost him then."

It was quiet and Doc poured more wine. Doc spoke of Mexico, where beer was never cold and Pancho Villa never found, where Doc first met his dad. Everett sat enchanted, never having heard this before about his dad, who always seemed so out of breath. After Doc stopped, it quieted again.

Doc looked to Everett as if it were now Everett's turn to say something about his dad. Everett felt strange. He didn't have all those stories like Doc - just fishing and now the blue carp.

Everett's dad set him on his lap, humming that tune again. Doc Hershey sang too, even Grandma knew the words. "Come on and hear, Alexander's Ragtime Band - Come on and hear, it's the best band in the land." It went on and on until the carp boiled over in the kitchen.

"Come on and see," Doc Hershey slurred the words.

Over dinner, Everett gorged himself at the small table, with tomatoes and cooked potatoes bathed in butter and with the carp dipped in horseradish. His dad poured a glass of wine for him, then more fish, more wine and more stories.

After he could eat no more, Everett felt his head bobbing just above the table, high enough to look the carp in the eye. Only its head remained. While listening to the others sing that song, over and over, he imagined the carp's lips moving too. He decided he was drunk on the blue carp.

Everett's head was so heavy on the pillow that he couldn't raise it when his dad came in and gave him a minted kiss. He felt the mustache graze his cheeks and tried reaching for his dad's bare chest, grooved with scars. The shirt, flapping on the porch rail to air out, sent him into the deepest sleep he had ever known.

He would tell his dad in the morning of his first dream in color where the carp, he named Roy, was bluer than indigo or violet - bluer than blue.

◆   ◆   ◆

"Rain!" Everett snorted as he climbed from bed in the morning. Heavy drops splattered on Doc Hershey's big black car outside his window.

The farmhouse groaned against a gust of wind.

Everett's bones popped as he stretched in the moist river air singing through the backdoor screen. A kettle whistled endlessly on the stove. He staggered through the empty kitchen towards the porch steps where his dad liked to drink his morning coffee.

Doc Hershey walked slowly behind his grandmother up from the river towards the porch. She must have fainted again, Everett thought, as she leaned against Doc in the rain.

In the corner by the door, Everett's left hand grasped the tall pole, ready to go. His dad's shirt which had hung on the rail, now lashed about on a step, stuck on a nail where it snagged in the wind.

He ran towards the river until Doc Hershey stopped him. His grandmother's eyes filled with tears. He never saw her cry like that.

"Your dad's fishing - alone today," Doc Hershey said. He knelt down to Everett. "He's gone for that bass, you see?"

"But he forgot his shirt and he took my little pole, and it's going to storm," Everett said, as Doc Hershey stopped him again. He had never seen Doc Hershey cry, ever.

"He's left them for you, Everett."

ଞ15ଔ

Renovations

Everett woke with a cough. The air smelled like a smoldering room, thick with soot, yet layered in a tinge of sweetness. Sigmund rocked in his squeaking chair, teasing a lantern's flame with a straw until it burst into a yellow tongue of fire.

The room glowed in a haze as Sigmund ignited a small pellet of opium in his pipe. He returned to reading a letter from Everett's stack. Everett moaned as he checked the clock. It was 6:15, as it had been for thirty-five years.

"We had a small fire last night," Sigmund said. "The old oven rusted through and tossed sparks onto my floor rug. The others took the Mercedes to the tuilerie for the night. I hope you are not expecting bread and coffee again."

Everett stared in disbelief at the rusted oven door in the kitchen. It lay like an up-ended turtle on top of a singed rug. Sigmund had let him sleep right through it.

"I can tell that you miss the dope as much as I miss coffee and bread," Everett rubbed his eyes. "Why are you smoking that stuff so early in the morning."

"I am fulfilling my end of the promise," Sigmund said. "I need a little help at first, especially with this Crabshaw fellow from the band – it is most painful."

Sigmund dipped a fountain pen into an inkbottle, about to write on the letter.

"Don't do that!" Everett stepped towards the rocking chair in his underwear. "What do think you're doing, Sigmund?"

"What Russell should have done," Sigmund said.

"He left that for me to do." Everett grabbed the pen and sat at the table beneath the lantern with the letter. "This trombone player

Crabshaw, Jim was his name, you tell me what Dad thought of him and I'll write it down."

Sigmund thumbed through the stack of letters.

"This will take some time," Sigmund said, puffing on his pipe. "First of all, Jim played the drums – not the trombone."

"Dad wrote that he was a trombone player."

"That is because your father, even at his young age as an officer, knew that a parent would want to know their son as he was, not what the war made him."

"Christ, Sigmund, I can't very well write them that just because war is hell, it forced their Jim to switch instruments."

"No, you cannot, and you also cannot write them that their young Jim went out for the dead one morning after a nighttime gas attack. Your father found him gasping for a breath without his mask in a crater still filled with phosgene. Russell, his lungs already poor, gave his mask to Jim. Neither of them ever breathed a full breath again. Jim could only play the drums from then on."

Sigmund took another puff then turned to Everett who had listened to every word and began to scribble. "What is it you are writing, Everett?"

"How Jim, after the long cold march to Neufchateau in the middle of winter, led the band into town. How cold his mouthpiece must have been, putting it to his lips and blaring his favorite solo piece. I'm sure both of you, Norton and Matilda, have heard him play it a thousand times at home - 'The Atlantic Zephyr'. The crowds who lined the streets for us went wild, we were so proud of him."

"Very good, Russell – very good," Sigmund said. "What of Jim's demise – what will you say to them?"

Everett filled the pen then scribbled, "I regret to tell you that all twenty-six young men of the band, including your Jim, perished instantly on the night of June twentieth in the line of duty as they performed the regiment's favorite song, 'Alexander's Ragtime Band'. A subterranean blast, although coldly calculated by the enemy to send our boys to the inferno, instead sent the band's souls to our dear lord in heaven where they now rest in peace. The enemy, if they had taken the very hearts of those of us who still stand, could not have hurt us more deeply. Sincerely, Capt. Russell Taylor – AEF, 1918, Somewhere in Lorraine."

"Very good Russell," Sigmund said.

"Only twenty-five more to go," Everett said as he fanned the letter to dry. "Do you think we can finish them today?"

"Tomorrow I will help with another," Sigmund said as he wrapped the opium in the foil. "It may take days, possibly weeks while preparing my home for Madame, which she calls a dungeon and now this fire."

"Bull roar! You promised."

"Yes, Russell." Sigmund shuffled through the letters. "But that promise has rather made you my prisoner."

"I must have said something awful to Madame Lambert last night," Everett said, thinking of Korea. "And you keep calling me by my dad's name."

"Madame made us swear, but I can tell you what you said in your spell was not awful," Sigmund said as he kicked a chest near Everett's cot. "There are more of Manfred's clothes here for you - working clothes."

"I could get killed wearing these to Ville Negre again," Everett said.

"We will work here today. The Zone Rouge is not very particular about the uniform a man wears," Sigmund said. "We can work without distractions. Madame Lambert decided it would be best for Louis to be with Philippe and Annette. They left in the night after the fire."

"Where's Beatrice," Everett asked, still thinking he might have divulged his war madness.

"She was helping me with the stove when she overheard Madame Lambert mentioning to Louis that it might be good if Louis took Philippe fishing in Lac Noir. She left with them."

"But there's nothing worth catching."

"You remember nothing of your spell?" Sigmund asked.

"Nothing," Everett blew into an envelope to open it.

"It is a pity, I cannot tell you," Sigmund said. "Now, put those letters away."

As Everett bent over his cot to slide the letters into his bag, his stomach rumbled, a low hungry note.

"Beatrice promised to bring us cake this morning. She will meet you half-way down the trench in a few minutes, but first you must see these." Sigmund reached into a drawer and pulled out his plans for the dugout's renovation.

Everett followed Sigmund's calloused fingers over the pages, some yellowed with age and others burned with new spots of ash from his pipe.

They called out every step – as if a recipe for a magical concoction designed to please Madame Lambert.

With Everett's help, he would carve out room for her things. They would bring sunlight into the dark dugout, bring in running water for a sink and a bath and now most important, to fashion an old field-kitchen into a proper stove and oven – one that wouldn't set the house on fire.

Everett though, suspected that no matter how much Sigmund could make the deep dugout feel like a home, she wouldn't be happy. Madame Lambert was not a cave dweller but a vital social cog in the region of Alsace and Lorraine.

"Those are romantic plans you have here, Sigmund, but," Everett said, hesitating as he realized Sigmund could never live above ground.

"I know what you are thinking," Sigmund said. "Madame needs a place to convene with her colleagues to discuss Freud, Janet, and Jung."

Sigmund turned to the bedroom door, where a faint pounding rose from the workshop door below.

"Beatrice?" Everett asked as they walked past the workshop to the big doors below.

"No, that is a rather harsh knock for her." Sigmund pulled a trench knife from a timber near the door. "Wait for the code."

Sigmund looked relieved when, at last, he heard a hammering at the door, 'Ta-da, Ta-da, Ta-da'.

"Who is it?" Sigmund asked.

"Me, General Sigmund. Father and I have something to show you."

Sigmund swung the big door open and there stood Louis holding one end of a stringer and Philippe, with his mechanical hand, holding the other. Between them swung six small rock bass. Philippe gasped briefly at the sight of Everett in Manfred's clothes then relaxed as Louis tugged the stringer.

"Le gardon!" Louis said. Philippe proudly patted Louis' head with his good hand.

"Louis informs me that you dislike boar, Monsieur – I am so very sorry," Philippe said. He loosened a small fish from the stringer and tossed it to Everett. "I hope you will enjoy Le gardon instead, it is delectable."

"Thank you, Philippe," Everett said.

The fish, still alive, squirted from Everett's hands to the floor. Everett picked it up and slid it back onto the stringer.

"We just don't have a decent stove to cook it with," Sigmund said, motioning them into his workshop. "Come inside, Philippe. It has been a long time since you last visited."

"Nine years, General Fischer," Philippe said, lifting Louis up onto the workbench. "Mother delivered Louis right here, not much bigger than a howitzer shell then. Look at him now."

"I thought I was born in the tuilerie," Louis said.

"Er, uh, Philippe," Sigmund stammered, "I was just showing Everett my plans for the dugout."

"Why not live with us in the tuilerie?" Philippe said. "Your dugout is still so dark and confined."

Strain crossed Philippe's face.

"The tuilerie was Évariste's home, not mine," Sigmund said. "I imagine Ville Negre will soon be fashioning plaster around his bones to form a statue or shrine."

"Annette told the postman about the bones," Philippe said. "Late last night, a committee did come to the tuilerie for that very purpose, they even wanted the paintbrush."

"Hasn't he been standing long enough?" Everett said.

Sigmund turned to Everett, shaking his head, reminding him, silently, not to say more of Evariste's unnatural pose.

"Did you give them the bones, Father?" Louis asked.

"Of course not, Louis," Philippe said as he adjusted the spring on his arm. "I crushed his bones into meal and spread them around the roses in back."

"Yuk!" Louis said. "I dug fishing worms by those roses today."

"Évariste is gone, Sigmund," Philippe said. "I would be honored now to share the tuilerie with you."

"I am sorry, Philippe - there are still so many memories in the tuilerie," Sigmund said. "Besides, I have enough money to buy the brasserie from the Chauchats - your mother can meet her friends there for coffee - perhaps you might feel like managing it."

"She still will not like living here," Philippe said.

"Why not a contest?" Louis said. "General Sigmund can fix the dugout so Grand-mère will like it and Father can fix the tuilerie so the General will like it. On the wedding night they can both decide where they want to live."

"That's not a bad idea, Louis," Everett said.

From above, came a faint knock. The code rapped softly.

"That will be Beatrice," Everett said, forgetting her title.

"Sister Beatrice?" Louis said.

"We need to start cleaning the tuilerie." Philippe reached for Louis. "And to clean the Le gardon for dinner."

"Can we fish later in the afternoon?" Louis asked, leaning into the big outside door with Philippe. "I want to catch that big one you say is down there in Lac Noir."

Louis tossed the stringer of fish into the Mercedes' trunk then Philippe lifted him to his lap in the driver's seat. Louis steered the Mercedes onto Rue Gambetta and disappeared.

Everett turned to Sigmund, "Madame Lambert's hypnosis has worked miracles on Philippe, or maybe it was the bones."

Inside, at the upper door, came "Ta-da, Ta-da, Ta-da", soft and unhurried..

"Or simply a good day for fishing," Sigmund said he unlatched the door for Beatrice.

She cradled a small brown bundle of cake in the crotch of her elbow.

"I took a small bite on my walk," Beatrice said, glancing towards the kitchen and laughed. "I hope the cake has not cooled, Father's oven has deserted him."

Her laughter, like her odd singing, filled the dugout with warmth. Sigmund chortled into his pipe, raising sparks. Everett reached for the cake as it was about to fall.

"I will take that," Sigmund said, coughing. "You two take your little walk in my trench. I need to get busy fixing this old hole after I have something sweet to eat."

"No more opium, Father, please?" Beatrice said as they left.

"It has to last you twenty-five more days, Sigmund," Everett said.

"Twenty-five letters, I know." Sigmund ducked and disappeared into the dugout.

Beatrice smiled from the corner of her mouth and after a few traverses, hopped up to the firing ledge to look out over Zone Rouge. She tossed her hair to the side.

"All this rubble, wire, craters and devastation must seem like an amusement park to you," Beatrice said, dragging her finger along the parapet, dislodging a rifle shell casing.

"What do you mean?" Everett asked as he jumped up at her side. He thought of the trance. He thought of the details he might have described. "Can't you tell me what I said in the trance?"

"Only that I wish you might stay longer than twenty-five days." Beatrice said. "Is that considered an especially long holiday in America? I suppose you will be leaving then?"

Everett breathed a sigh now knowing he hadn't said anything about Korea before.

Beatrice took his hand and sent her tongue darting between his fingers.

"Ach!" She turned away, reeling and then laughed. "Your hand smells like fish. You have not gone fishing with Annette already, have you?"

Everett, stunned by her jest, sniffed it himself.

"Louis and Philippe just left with a stringer-full of little fish," Everett said, explaining that Louis, like Sigmund, made a deal or rather a contest to see where Madame and Sigmund would live in twenty-five short days.

"Sigmund's clock is ticking." He kissed her. Beatrice's tongue played against his teeth like a xylophone.

"A most unpredictable clock," she said, "like one of Father's fuses."

"I have a long fuse." He unfastened one of Beatrice's straps. She covered his hand with hers.

"It is not a good time of the month for that," Beatrice said. "Just hold me."

Everett did for a long time, then squeezing her, said, "I need to get to work."

"You see, you even sound like Father. I feel like a drive to Donon now," Beatrice whispered in a long stream of vanilla-scented breath. "I can get the car from Philippe."

"I really do need to get to work," Everett said as he pinched her buttocks and smiled. "Tomorrow? Same time?"

The contest was on. Sigmund's daily pipe produced the words of Everett's father to another family, long gone, in Iowa. As Everett mastered his father's penmanship and sentiment, he discovered how his father sang, how he ate, drank, slept and stank. How he could turn cowards into heroes and rotate his men in combat to share the blood, except for the band. The sorrow in Sigmund's voice as he also described his own men, the miners, lent color to Everett's ever-deepening daily glimpses into his father's heart.

He understood now, how his father loved those boys and kept them from harm. For his men needed their music to remind them of home - a safe and soft world, filled with sounds of larks, loons and songs of love, songs that Sigmund's miners, too, longed to hear after clearing the soil of Alsace and Lorraine from their ears.

After Everett penned Sigmund's daily opium-induced insights of the bandsmen, Sigmund would guide plumbers and carpenters, insisting they follow his drawings and plans. They gulped at the task he was paying them to do. Everett, laying down the pen, helped them carry the new stove and bathtub from their truck, up the back steps. German's, even now, couldn't have engineered a better dugout, Everett marveled - Madame Lambert just might like it.

Everett, wanting to remain impartial, helped Philippe around the tuilerie, repointing cracks in the ceiling, the stonewalls, and trimming the rose bushes that somehow sprang to life. He loaded Gerta's cart with everything Philippe could find of Évariste's, - things that might make Sigmund feel uncomfortable to live in the tuilerie with Madame Lambert.

Out went Évariste's easels, his red hammer and sickle armbands, clothes, dried bottles of paint, half-finished canvases and porcelain, all settling to the bottom of Lac Noir.

Everett tried persuading Philippe to accompany Sigmund to the brasserie in Ville Negre where he might begin to learn the Chauchat's business.

"Chauchat's? The collaborateurs!" Philippe said, wanting nothing to do with Sigmund's generous offer.

Sigmund learned Madame Chauchat's business only after Everett agreed to accompany him as protection against her. Her husband, Henri', instructed Sigmund in the art of the maitre d' - the foods, wines, the staff, and the proper greetings he would need to know to host Madame Lambert's social gatherings.

Sigmund looked magnificent in his new white uniform. Madame Chauchat, from the kitchen, leered at Sigmund's tall figure, from his top hat to his old boots that he insisted on wearing. "O-La-La!" Madame Chauchat would call out after Sigmund was out of sight.

After more than three weeks, there remained only one day in which to complete the dugout for Madame Lambert, that is, if she chose to leave the comfort of the tuilerie. Only one letter remained to be finished, Stephen Collins – the tuba player. Everett impatiently loaded Sigmund's pipe as Sigmund shaved.

"What's keeping you, Sigmund? Are you trimming nose hairs for your wedding tomorrow?"

"I am afraid you must wait until the day after the wedding for me to finish the letter," Sigmund said, stepping out half-shaven. "Tomorrow night, Madame Lambert will crave for my bones. If I smoke today, tomorrow night I will be worthless. I hope you understand."

"It's been thirty-five years, what's another day."

♦   ♦   ♦

Everett waited at the communication trench's gate for Beatrice to come with his daily kiss and cake. She was late today. On the other side, even the most devastated sections of the Zone Rouge lay cloaked in thick green moss, soft grass and a dense jungle of vines, leaving no trace that he had ever walked there. He draped his arm over the gate into the Zone Rouge and shook it hard. The lock felt tight, he felt good.

He wondered what Sigmund might say the next morning about Steve Collins. He wondered what he might do when he finished that last letter, wishing, in a way, there were more.

From No-Man's-Land, rang a chink against heavy metal. A stone arched high, towards the front, followed by Beatrice's voice.

"Louis! Stop throwing those into the Zone Rouge," Beatrice said. "Are you trying to get them all to explode?"

Everett trotted to greet them.

"Sister Beatrice wants to kiss you," Louis said. He hopped up onto the firing ledge and pushed his cheeks together to form a fish-like mouth.

"Louis!" Beatrice said.

"How can you tell?" Everett asked. Beatrice grinned and turned away.

"She sings to herself, her face is rouge and she does not hear a thing I say," Louis said.

"I do listen," Beatrice said.

"What have I been saying all this time then?" Louis cocked his head and smirked. "You said nothing, all the way here."

"My dear Louis, you were talking about how different you and Philippe are. How your father is neat and you are messy, how he is slender and you are thick-muscled, like me. How Philippe never wants to leave the tuilerie and you always run away. You see, I listen to you."

"You did not mention what I said about Everett, our friend here, that I think he wishes to go home."

"I heard you, Louis," Beatrice said. "But that is for him to decide, when he wants."

"Everyone seems able to read my mind," Everett smiled, but felt uneasy. "Madame must have left it wide open that night."

"Only a crack," Beatrice said. "But, enough for me."

Everett felt only a little better about the trance.

"What about your contest, Louis?" Everett asked. "Have you brought this lovely angel along as a referee?"

"Please, not in Louis' presence." Beatrice smiled.

"You see, Monsieur? Sister Beatrice is turning red again. You can take my angel home with you, but first you must tell me how you will take care of her - what will you do in America?" Louis said.

"Louis!" Beatrice said.

"I have a small farm, Louis, but too small to make a living. After the war, I was in school about to graduate in Aeronautical Engineering, the study of flight."

"You will fly airplanes for a living?" Louis said.

"I was thinking about teaching," Everett said. He realized it was the first time he ever considered it.

"I hate flying now," Everett turned to Beatrice. "But, a Valkyrie might carry me back home on your winged Gerta."

"I do not fly anymore either," Beatrice laughed.

Everett touched Beatrice's chin and he wondered again, what he said during the trance. Beatrice looked at him carefully as though looking for a crack in a crystal glass.

"While you kiss, I will turn my head," Louis said.

"No, Louis. We have much work to do, remember?" Beatrice said. "We have come to help finish preparing the dugout while Philippe finishes the tuilerie."

"Grand-mère is like Father," Louis said, "so neat."

"How is Philippe?" Everett asked, walking a few paces towards the dugout. "Did you two catch any fish this morning?"

"Le Gardon?" Louis said. "No, today Father dropped his line in the lake and stared at the water like it was a mirage. 'Move the worm around so they know it is there,' I asked him. Father got up and left to clean the tuilerie again. I think he is afraid Grand-mère will choose to live in the dugout and not the tuilerie. It seems like someone must lose. Father, Grand-mère or General Sigmund. Is marriage like the Duello?"

Beatrice raised an eyebrow and shrugged her shoulders.

Louis looked to Everett and said, "If you and Sister Beatrice were married, I think you would both win."

"She would lose her wings, though," Everett said, glancing towards Beatrice to see if he should have kept quiet.

Louis brought Beatrice's hand to Everett's palm. Her fingers clenched Everett's in a tight and sweaty grip.

"I think you and Sister Beatrice should get married."

"Beatrice might want to return to Indochina, Louis."

"My work is done there," Beatrice said, "just as yours is nearly finished here in Lorraine with those letters. Perhaps we might fly to Korea one day."

"I would like that very much." Everett turned to her glistening eyes. Reflections of moss near the parapet, melded green to her emerald iris. A blink washed away a tear.

Everett's throat seized. He swallowed, relieving a sudden dryness. Beatrice turned to the Zone Rouge and sniffled. Happiness spilled from her breath. More tears.

"You see, now you have made her cry," Louis said. "Ask her – she will say yes, like Grand-mère Lambert. Ask her now."

Everett's face flushed warm and red. Standing next to her in the trench, his legs turn to jelly. He understood why men drop to their knees to mumble those few beloved words.

He ran the years across her face. Only wrinkles formed around her teary smile and she was still beautiful. She smiled at him now, as he knelt down.

"Beatrice, I love you. Will you marry me?" Everett asked in a voice still caught in his throat.

"Of course," she said, kneeling to him. "But I need to marry you right here and now."

"Not in a church, Sister Beatrice?" Louis said.

"This is the church," Beatrice said. "The Zone Rouge. Promise me your undying love before all these lost souls."

"I do, Beatrice. I do." Everett stood and held her.

"It is done then," Beatrice said.

"A kiss," Louis said, "then it will be done."

Her shoulders drooped. Her lashes rose and fell. As Everett touched his lips to her cheek, she glanced to Louis.

"Turn around my young man," she said, lips parting.

Everett wrapped her in his arms. Her breath poured, sweet with vanilla, folding into his, dissolving borders and maps of Yangu and Dien Bien Phu. Their tongues danced on the roofs of their mouths and when they tired, they braided into one and lay like two lovers on a flesh colored beach.

"Are you married yet?" Louis asked after a minute.

"Yes, Louis," Everett said as he looked to Beatrice.

"Indeed," Beatrice said, "And that is our little secret. We don't want to upstage the wedding tomorrow."

"Why can they not be married just like you are?"

"We are all married in our hearts, where it counts," Beatrice said. "I do suppose we should post our marriage banns though. It will make the journey to the New World easier."

"But you must post the notice at the Mairie in Ville Negre," Louis said, "just as General Sigmund and Grand-mère did over a week ago. Can you keep it secret that long?"

"We can make the arrangements and post the marriage banns in Remiremont," Beatrice said. "That is where my official residence has been, at the convent."

"If everything is ready for their wedding tomorrow, we can drive to Remiremont yet this morning," Everett said. "I have my birth certificate in my passport, here in my pocket."

"Can I see?" Louis asked.

Everett unfolded the document for Louis.

"St. Clair?" Louis said. "You were born in France, Monsieur? You may not even need a passport. The village is not far from here."

"No, Louis," Everett laughed. "Many towns in Iowa have French names, like Marquette, Dubuque, even Des Moines. The French explored Iowa long before it became a state and was named for Native Americans – back when it was still called the New World."

Louis examined the document with an official's eye.

"I see you are marrying an older woman."

"Not that much older." Beatrice straightened her hair.

"Russell - that was your father," Louis continued reading. "Helen - was your mother? What was she like?"

"She died when I was born, Louis."

"There is no one left for you in Iowa?" Louis dropped the birth certificate in the trench, his mouth gaping open.

"Only my old friend Doc Hershey and the land I grew up on." Everett picked it up and folded it into his passport.

"Why do you not stay here in France?"

"I want to go to America, Louis," Beatrice said, knotting her arms around Everett.

"In Ville Negre they say, people go to America because it is like running away from home," Louis said. "Why are you running away, Sister Beatrice?"

"To follow home the one I love, Louis. You see, it is not like the Duello at all."

"Can I come?" Louis begged. "I will miss you so much."

"Perhaps Philippe and Annette might send you to study flying," Beatrice said.

"I want to go, now!" Louis pouted, leaving the trench.

"I wish you could come, too, Louis," Everett said, as they walked from the Zone Rouge to Lac Noir. "This a pretty dangerous place to live, except for Lac Noir here."

"Louis, why not show Everett where le gardon feed while I go inside the tuilerie," Beatrice said. "Philippe promised to catch plenty for tomorrow's wedding dinner. Remember, not a word to Philippe about Everett and myself. I will return shortly with my papers for the wedding banns."

Everett followed Louis onto the dock, extending only a few feet over the deep pond called, Lac Noir. Everett felt uneasy and off balance trying to imagine, that beneath this flimsy shimmying dock, once stood a large tent that, each night, pumped the night sky full of waltzes and ragtimes.

He lost himself in the lake's clarity. The stream flowing through, from west to east, caused deep and undulating waves - the lake's only motion. Below, the current wasn't strong enough to dislodge the iron, brass and steel cylinders of war that gravitated, over the years, to the lake's navel.

"Can I tell General Sigmund that you married Sister Beatrice?" Louis asked as he skipped a round, flat stone across the lake.

"I should have asked Sigmund's permission for Beatrice's hand," Everett said. "That's how it's done in America."

"In Lorraine, once must ask permission of the father," Louis said. "General Sigmund is like a father to Sister Beatrice, is he not?"

"Indeed," Everett smiled.

"Besides, the General wants you to marry her," Louis said. "It will make him very happy."

"Alright, you can tell Sigmund while I drive Beatrice to Remiremont, but no one else. I don't want to spoil their fun."

A distant metallic blow shattered the quiet lake as Philippe's hand struck the Mercedes' chrome grill. He gripped a fishing pole with the other. He smiled as Beatrice chided him.

"Will you tell Father that Sister Beatrice is no longer a Sister?" Louis whispered.

"Maybe," Everett said. "Quiet now. Not a word yet, OK?"

"OK," Louis said then moved cautiously to Philippe.

"Bonjour, Everett," Philippe said as he handed Louis the fishing pole. "I shall enhance the brasserie's menu for tomorrow not only with my own boar, but with le gardon from my own pond – I know you dislike the boar."

"That's kind of you, Philippe," Everett said.

"Le gardon swim with the band," Philippe said. He bent down to the water to look. "Their red fins follow their leader, the great one."

Louis nodded his head to Everett in disbelief.

"Father, there is no giant fish living there – only old rusted shells, grenades and dragon eggs that Le gardon play in."

"Everett, I wish to thank you for helping me," Philippe said as he stood, ignoring Louis for a moment. "I have ordered Madame Chauchat to prepare a room for you above the brasserie tomorrow night after the wedding dinner."

"But Father, Grand-mère's room will be open in the tuilerie. He can stay with us." Louis said.

"It is proper, Louis, that Everett and Sister Beatrice not share the same roof." Philippe glanced to Beatrice, catching up. "What has overcome my sister lately?"

"It is simple Father, she needs ...," Louis said before Beatrice interrupted.

"Yes, a bath. I am in need of a bath," Beatrice said as she snatched Everett's arm. "I need a long, comforting bath like you, my dear brother. We are off to the spa!"

Everett slowed the Mercedes along Rue Gambetta as they came upon Sigmund walking beside his cart. Gerta hobbled, with the empty cart in tow, towards the tuilerie.

"I hope this is the last that Philippe needs Gerta," Sigmund said. "He needs her today, I need her tomorrow."

Gerta's tail flipped nervously from side to side. Sigmund slid his hand up along the bridge of her nose.

"Philippe is hauling a few last things to dump into Lac Noir, nothing heavy," Beatrice said.

"Gerta still gets nervous when she walks by that lake," Sigmund said. "Before the depot existed, she would help me haul shells there to dump."

Sigmund bent down to open Gerta's boot.

"Is Gerta going to make it?" Beatrice asked.

Sigmund opened a tin of salve from his pants pocket. The menthol caught Everett's nose just as it had on the train. He recalled how rejuvenating it felt when Beatrice applied it to his burned hand.

"Of course she will make it." Sigmund slathered the joint where the hoof, fashioned from wood, met Gerta's toughened flesh at the ankle.

"I remember when Philippe would still let me do this to his arm," Sigmund said as he closed the tin. "Where is he?"

"Fishing in Lac Noir with Louis, for your wedding dinner," Beatrice said.

"Poor Philippe," Sigmund said as he finished tying Gerta's boot. "Even Gerta senses Lac Noir has more shells than fish. He had better shoot another boar for the Chauchat's to cook."

As they left, Gerta rolled her big brown eyes to Sigmund, welled-up in tears of appreciation.

After an hour's drive, they came through Remiremont to the convent, whose bells had just rung eleven. The square building with Mairie embossed into the high stonework, stood next to the convent.

"It's not too late to get married in the church," Everett said.

"Far too late, dear. Drive on past," Beatrice said. "And the Mairie will not be open until after lunch. Drive to the spa. I really do need a bath."

With no road signs directing them to the Bain de Guerre, Beatrice pointed the way from memory. The doorman slept under a tree as they arrived. Beatrice quietly disappeared into the adjacent bath.

Everett disrobed and slid into the warm pool on the men's side of the bath as Beatrice sang. He soon drifted into sleep to her lovely, but odd, warbling.

He woke to the sensation of his skin shriveling and another voice, inside his bath, singing, then pausing, waiting for Beatrice to join, but her voice had been silent for some time. Everett recognized the voice, high and scratchy.

It was of the old German soldier he had heard before, the one who knew Alexander's Ragtime Band so well. After the song, the man floundered, blindly searching for the exit rail. Everett caught his arm and steered him from the bath. The elfish, withered man covered his left eye.

"Salt?" Everett asked, as he placed his hand on the old soldier's forehead. "That smarts. Let me have a look."

"Amerikanisch?" The old man asked.

"Ya," Everett answered.

As the old man slid his hand away from his eye, he exposed a crater where long ago, a big, steel blue eyeball once nested. The old man toweled himself dry then dressed as he whistled the tune again.

Beatrice stood on the marble steps, dressed in her sweater and pants, soaking her face in the ruby light from the ceiling. Everett helped the old soldier from the room. The old man found a black velvet patch, strapping it quickly across his socket as Beatrice appeared.

She took his hand and ushered him to the side, where she spoke in German for a time.

"His name is Otto. He says we look like we are already married."

"Ask him if he'll be our witness," Everett asked.

After Beatrice asked him, the old man rocked on his heels and proudly snapped his suspenders.

Everett drove back to the Mairie in Remiremont, listening to the old soldier in the rear and Beatrice in the front, humming the tune.

Inside the massive white and pink stone building of the Mairie stood impressive towering cabinets and labeled drawers. A clerk walked while sipping her cup of coffee and reading a newspaper, still full news of Dien Bien Phu. She walked straight to a drawer and blindly retrieved a form.

She unfolded their papers on the table and donned an official-looking black robe bearing no cross, medallions or tassels. After languishing over Everett's passport, she fussed with Beatrice's. The clerk's tongue nervously tapped the roof of her mouth. Her hard soul shoes shuffled obnoxiously inside the large cavernous hall.

"You didn't give her your papal passport by mistake, did you?" Everett asked quietly, playfully elbowing her waist.

"Shhh, it is my birth certificate - the other me," Beatrice said as the official handed them back and gave her the banns to sign.

Beatrice signed her full name 'Brunnhilde Fischer'. Otto looked surprised.

"Deutsch?" Otto asked.

"Alsacien, Lorraine, French, and German," Beatrice said in German.

Otto stood on his toes, whispering to Beatrice.

"Otto comes from the Saar to bathe each month," Beatrice said. "He is spending the night at the convent. Do you mind if I help him walk there?"

"I'll meet you with the car," Everett said. He watched as the two slowly walked towards the convent.

Beatrice held the old man's arm after he nearly fell at the entrance steps. They spoke later for several minutes. She hummed as she bounced into the seat next to Everett.

"How does he know that song?" Everett asked.

"Perhaps he was captured by the American's as well, I did not want to ask," Beatrice said. "I have invited him to the wedding. He looks so thin and pale. Father might enjoy his company, he so misses speaking German."

"Do you think that's wise," Everett said. "After all, Sigmund believes in his heart he's a traitor. I have a feeling that's why Sigmund doesn't bathe in the spa."

"What harm can it do? They are both old soldiers."

"Maybe back then Otto was sent to kill Sigmund," Everett said, "so he wouldn't divulge the tunnel's existence."

"The German's would never have sent such a frail little man for that evil task."

"Back then, Otto could have been a big barrel-chested schlitteur," Everett said. "Back then, there was a code."

"The Duello?" Beatrice said. "I think not. I will send Philippe to gather poor Otto tomorrow. You need rest, dear, plenty of rest."

He turned on the headlamps of the Mercedes as the sun set over the plains to the west. He felt Beatrice's head slowly inch from his shoulder where she rested to his lap where she snored, fast asleep in the fresh, pine-scented air.

As he drove up the lane to the tuilerie, his headlamps wakened Gerta, standing by the porch near her cart, loaded with trash. Beatrice woke as the Mercedes came to a stop.

"Philippe has been busy cleaning, I see," Beatrice said as she yawned and stretched. "I hope it does not become a compulsion - that would be a bad sign."

Everett walked her to the porch where Chesterfield's nose shined in the yellow candlelight from inside the window.

"He has even polished Chesterfield," Beatrice lamented.

"We all want a new beginning," Everett said as he kissed her. "A new start, like Sigmund and Madame will have tomorrow. Bonne nuit, Mrs. Taylor."

"Bonne nuit, mon chéri'."

He drove without headlamps beneath the bright three-quarter moon before stopping by Lac Noir to get out and to dwell on her dreamlike words. The dock groaned and squeaked as he walked to its edge. The water lay still, except for the moon's waving reflection. He turned again to the tuilerie. Gerta nickered a song. The light of Beatrice's window dimmed.

"Bonne nuit, mon chéri'," Everett said to the tuilerie.

A bubble burst softly just beneath the dock. "Lac Champagne," he said. "What good fortune do you have for me?"

Another bubble, followed by a swirl. He dropped to his knees and searched the dark water. It gurgled. Something wasn't right.

In his mind, he formed the image of a rusted fissure opening up along the welded seam of a projector's tube of mustard gas, but his nose would be already on fire if it were. Another bubble burst. A whorl of water spun near his face. He sniffed for phosgene and its notorious grassy smell as the water boiled.

In a few seconds, he judged, there wouldn't be time enough to stand. The whole pond would erupt in a violent and hellish gush of pent up energy, gas and heat of unfulfilled battles. Then it stopped.

His hand, near a post on the dock, snared a line of string running into the water below. It throbbed like a live wire. He plucked it, snapping it tight against the dock, setting it to vibrate like a thick harp string. Whatever Philippe caught today must be huge, Everett thought. Filled with the young lives of his father's regimental band, with Sigmund's black-faced miners and with the character and legacy of the Lambert's that Philippe had stripped from the tuilerie to encourage Sigmund to live with his mother and him, there had to something left alive in Lac Noir.

The Mercedes headlamps penetrated the tall thin line of poplars whose limbs, after thirty-five years of hiding the dead land of war, had grown fragile, like everything in Lorraine, except for the voltage tingling in his hands from that string running into Lac Noir.

ಬ16ೞ
Wedding

Philippe eased the big Mercedes down the tuilerie's lane, towards Ville Negre. Everett, sitting in the rear seat between Louis and Beatrice, discretely smoothed his hand along Beatrice's thigh. Fluttering her eyes, she straightened her short red dress then turned at Gerta's clopping behind them. Madame Lambert, wearing a simple yellow print dress, cuddled next to Sigmund on the cart and straightened his white bow tie.

"A stunning pair, are they not?" Beatrice said.

"He's dapper, that's for sure," Everett said.

"Philippe, your mother is absolutely regal today," Annette said, elbowing Philippe in fun. "Perhaps one day, I might dress like that for you."

With his right hand free of Gerta's rein, Sigmund, raised Madame's dress to her knees and admired her legs, dressed in white hosiery. She spanked Sigmund's roving hand, after noticing Louis' curiosity and straightened her back like a queen in a radiant gown. She straightened Sigmund's tailored suit and adjusted the boutonnière pinned to his lapel. Sigmund swatted the lilac as though it were buzzing with bees.

Philippe twirled the steering knob nervously with his mechanical hand. Beatrice whispered to Everett that Madame Lambert had put Philippe under another trance last night as Philippe then seemed overly anxious – she didn't want him to spoil the wedding. Everett worked his hand beneath Beatrice's dress again, until she rose slightly and sat on it.

"Sister Beatrice, you look marvelous!" Annette said, powdering her face in the rear view mirror and greasing her lips red as they left the cool, shady façade of poplars that masked the Zone Rouge for the hot open road. "How long has it been since you have come to Ville Negre without your habit?"

"Nine years," Philippe answered.

"That is how old I am," Louis said.

"Your mother admires what you have done to the tuilerie, Philippe," Beatrice said. Everett felt her seat move nervously. "It looks as pretty as Annette."

"I cannot imagine why Mother would want to live in the dark prison that the old Boche calls home," Philippe said.

"If it were not for old Chesterfield, General Sigmund might actually like the tuilerie," Louis said.

Philippe grimaced in the rear mirror.

A rank stench swirled up from the Mercede's shiny black trunk, baked in sunlight.

"What is that stink?" Beatrice prodded her brother. "Not another boar, I hope."

Philippe ignored her and blasted the Mercedes' horn as he led the procession along Rue Gambetta to the brasserie where a few people gathered. Madame Lambert held her hand out until Sigmund and Philippe came around to escort her inside. Henri Chauchat, in a cloud of powerful lavender cologne, led guests inside as though he and Madame Chauchat still owned it. Henri glanced twice at Beatrice.

Sigmund's soldier friends from the depot whistled and shouted. It wasn't even noon yet, Everett thought, and they were already drunk. They pointed to a large truck parked far enough away and loaded with munitions too potent, they claimed, to explode safely in the depot. They were to drive them to the sea tonight after the wedding. To sober up, they engaged Louis in a game of Parcheesi at a nearby table.

Philippe escorted Madame Lambert through a cluster of friends from Ville Negre, until she found her colleagues from the university. Madame Chauchat trailed impatiently behind him, trying to get Philippe's attention as Madame Lambert introduced Philippe to her colleagues, informing them of his recovery. Everett noticed them retreat a half step as Philippe extended his hand to shake.

"I do apologize," Philippe said. Madame Lambert's friends then moved in to grasp and admire the hand. Philippe pinched, by accident, one person's finger as Madame Chauchat surprised him by tapping on his shoulder.

"Monsieur Lambert," Madame Chauchat said. "I need to prepare the Le Gardon you were to bring. Did the market guarantee they are fresh?

Our brasserie, I mean, Sigmund's brasserie, is always known for its quality."

"I caught it myself, in Lac Noir," Philippe said proudly.

"Not from Lac Noir!" Madame Chauchat said. "Nothing lives in that water, it is poisoned. The pond is haunted."

Philippe's pleasant face wrinkled to one side and snarled, "There is a fish in the trunk of the Mercedes."

"Only one?" Madame Chauchat matched his ugly tone.

"Go get it," Philippe ordered as he exercised his hand, squeaking and in need of oil. He opened and closed the fingers and randomly twitched the wrist near Madame Chauchat's ear.

"Stop that!" Madame Chauchat said.

Beatrice brought along Madame Chauchat's husband, Henri. She got Sigmund to break away from the Parcheesi game to see why Madame Chauchat was complaining.

"Philippe, perhaps Henri can bring it inside," Beatrice said.

"Who are you?" Madame Chauchat asked. "You look familiar somehow - Brunnhilde?"

"Her name is Beatrice," Philippe rattled his hand. "Now, I already asked you, Madame Chauchat, can you not manage my first, simple little command - get the fish!"

"Just look at all these people and only one small fish, he says!" Madame Chauchat said as she stepped to the car, turning again to look at Beatrice, "Sigmund, you have a lot to learn about operating my brasserie."

"Open the trunk," Philippe said.

Madame Chauchat gasped as she raised the lid.

"Henri, you had better help her," Philippe said.

"What did you catch, Father?" Louis asked as he took Philippe's hand and looked up into his father's confident, squared-off and suddenly handsome face. Philippe grinned. A groan rose from the rear of the Mercedes.

"Make way! Make way!" Henri said as he parted the crowd for Madame Chauchat. She waddled behind him to the door past the soldiers.

"A grouper!" One said.

"No, a prehistoric monster!" said another.

"Large as Madame Chauchat!" Yet, another chuckled, "Run, Henri! It is coming for you!"

"Is this the one?" Madame Chauchat said, with the slimy carp slipping from her hands.

"Russell, can you believe that woman?" Sigmund laughed. Everett felt uneasy hearing his father's name.

"Ha, is that the right fish?" Sigmund said as the brasserie erupted in laughter.

She flipped the behemoth fish onto the floor in front of them. The fish's large, drooping belly looked as if it had swallowed Chesterfield. Everett found himself short of breath.

"It is a Carp!" Louis said. He knelt down to examine its huge head. "How did it ever live in Lac Noir?"

"Carp eat anything. Is that not what you said in your trance, Everett?" Beatrice asked.

"I did?" Everett, dazed by the sight of such a large carp, wondered what else he might have said. "This old boy looks like it did eat everything."

"How do you expect me to cook such a beast?" Madame Chauchat said as she placed her shoe on the carp's head and turned to Sigmund with a helpless look.

"You prefer it blue, do you not, Russell?" Sigmund turned to Everett.

"Blue?" Everett said. He felt strangely ill at the thought of the fish, a ghastly blue.

"Why yes, Everett," Beatrice said, coming to his side. "You had Carpe au Bleu when you were young, do you not remember telling us?"

"He never told me," Louis said.

"You went to bed after dancing that night, Louis," Madame Lambert said. "It was a deep trance, Everett, but I am sure it is harmless now for us to bring the matter up, that is, what it was you spoke of - surely you remember some of it."

Madame waved her large ring in front of him, but Everett already knew. He felt it in the line by Lac Noir last night, the same tautness in the line his young hands had held.

"Yes," Everett said from kindness, and not really recalling anything else. "Now I remember it - thank you Madame."

"Serve us hors d'oeuvres now, Madame Chauchat, and something to drink while we wait for you to prepare Carpe au Bleu," Philippe said. "We have all day."

"We no longer prepare Carpe au Bleu, Herr Fischer," Madame Chauchat said with a sour tone.

"But you served it each Christmas," Sigmund said, "offering it up to the Gestapo with such a grand smile, Madame Chauchat. Oh, the things you did to keep this little brasserie during the occupation. Must I run Henri from the kitchen and prepare it myself?"

"Nein, Hauptmann Fischer," a small voice came from the kitchen.

"Who goes there?" Sigmund asked.

"Gefreiter Planck." The small old soldier smiled from the kitchen, sharpening a butcher's knife.

"Otto?" Sigmund said. "It cannot be. You must be a ghost!"

"Ya," Otto said. "Carpe au Bleu, Hauptmann Fischer!"

Otto dropped the knife, stood at attention and saluted as Sigmund approached him. Sigmund snapped his hand forward to shake instead, and then smothered the little man in his big, leathered arms. They reminisced while stretching each others long drawn jowls, shining bald spots, and instinctively checking for head lice. Sigmund pulled Otto's eye patch down to examine his wound.

"You know Otto?" Beatrice asked Sigmund.

"He's one of my miner's and our cook. The others are all dead. He said the blast spit him out of the tunnel like meat gone bad that night. Ruined his hearing, although he likes the way you sing."

Sigmund continued reminiscing with Otto, but the little soldier patted Sigmund on his back for him to return to his bride while he prepared the dish. It would be another hour or two.

"Step back, Henri. My comrade, Otto, will help you prepare Carpe Bleu and it will be sublime. Madame Chauchat, bring us something to drink."

"I suppose now that you are at last getting married, Mon chéri', you will want champagne." Madame Chauchat said after removing her apron, full of fish scum. She wobbled her ankle suggestively at the end of her chubby leg.

"What do you suppose we should have, Everett?" Sigmund turned to him for his suggestion.

"It's your wedding, Sigmund," Everett said.

"My dear son," Sigmund said. "If you were getting married and your mouth was watering for Carpe au Bleu, you do remember how it is so tart and sour - what would taste good, no - as your father would say - what would go down good with that?"

"Riesling." Everett heard himself say.

"Excellent choice!" Sigmund said.

"Yeee!" Madame Chauchat screeched.

"I want some too," Louis said after poking Madame Chauchat in the rear with his fork.

"Louis! Please, try to be pleasant to her," Madame Lambert said.

"Where do you think you are, little man, Valhalla?" Madame Chauchat snorted.

"This will soon be Philippe's Valhalla!" Sigmund said.

"Yeee!" Madame Chauchat screamed again as Philippe pinched her with his mechanical hand, not in jest.

"The Riesling - all there is. Schnell!" Philippe demanded. Everett sensed the same unnatural sternness in Philippe's voice as when they first met.

Annette came to Philippe's side. Madame Lambert's colleagues exchanged doubtful glances as though they could predict Philippe's extreme moods. Everett wondered for a moment if Philippe's father suffered such a despairing mood before he charged the line with his paintbrush. He glanced to Louis, still playing cards with the soldiers.

Madame Chauchat quickly returned with the wine. Her hand trembled as she poured everyone a glass of the Riesling. Beatrice silently toasted Everett from the far end of the table. Louis, seated between Philippe and Annette, confidently raised his glass to join the toast. Everett's nose filled with a fruity aroma as he brought the glass of pale gold wine to his lips. It sent wonderful shivers through his brain as though he had drunk it before.

After an hour, Everett imagined everyone in the brasserie had become as intoxicated as he was. Louis had vanished into the kitchen to help Otto finish the fish. Just as well, Everett thought, as a drunken Philippe stood on his chair for another half hour captivating the audience with fond childhood memories of clearing the Zone Rouge with Sigmund and how he so enjoyed leading the team of German demineurs to neuter the tank mines, sown throughout the Vosges.

With each drink of wine from his carafe, Philippe described his tales in ever more horrifying detail until he came to the day he lost his arm and Gerta part of her hoof. Philippe glanced at Louis, and Everett knew that even in such a bizarre state, Philippe would not dare mention the day Louis was born when he last visited Sigmund's dugout. Philippe continued to protect the secrets everyone, but Louis, knew. A skill, Everett guessed, one could only learn in prison.

Philippe sat down and, with his thumb, tilted an enameled plate on its edge, in search of its creator's signature. As he tried grasping the plate, it turned a pirouette then wheeled to the floor and crashed. Philippe kicked the shards beneath the table as Madame Chauchat brought him a plain white plate. The crowd, once boisterous, grew quiet until an irritating squeak came from the kitchen.

Otto, with Henri's help, pushed a large rolling table, covered with cloth, from the kitchen to the center of the dining room next to Beatrice.

"Ahh!" the crowd exclaimed as a steamy, pungent vapor seeped from the cloth.

Otto rushed to Sigmund's side, whispered in his ear then leaned back anxiously on his heels. In a slanted wag of his thick hairy eyebrow, Otto indicated to Sigmund and Madame Lambert – it was nearly perfect. Otto shrugged his shoulders, only a few problems.

"Ladies and gentlemen," Sigmund shouted. "Please close your eyes for a minute. I will tell you a story while Otto adjusts his gastronomical presentation. You will not be disappointed."

Sigmund waited until most had closed their eyes. Everett kept his open a crack. Otto worked with his hands beneath the cloth-cover trying to assemble three huge dissections of carp, that whole, was too gigantic to fit into the oven.

"Christmas, 1917 – Do you remember, Otto, near sunset?"

Otto raised his head and nodded, then looked down with disappointment as the carp fell apart once again.

"We were here on the front at the edge of the Vosges, where the sun was ready to set as it is now, only it was cold and clear then. I stood at the parapet of our frontline line with my telescope as the light faded, watching the Americans moving into the French trenches for the first time. I had never seen an American before in my whole life. They looked so young that I prayed they would leave before they all died. Then I heard their band playing and I watched their faces, soon to be torn and scarred, forever eighteen years young and eager - so full of life. It sounded like millions of them singing."

Sigmund turned to Everett. Everett bowed his head slightly.

"My duty was to check their line," Sigmund continued. "My habit, instead, was to observe Madame Lambert, through my lens, walking her son Philippe to the front porch at about this time each night. They would stand at sunset, beside Chesterfield and watch the darkness fill our trenches. I wanted to believe she was looking straight at me. The last glint of sun must have reflected to her from my lens. But, I knew she only wished to find where her husband, Évariste, had perished while bravely charging us with that brush."

Sigmund watched Madame Lambert's eyes fill with tears. Everett couldn't tell if they were for Sigmund or for her husband's memory until she grasped Sigmund's hand.

"I saw it all – I tried telling my men over the sound of our guns that it was only a paintbrush, but to them I am sure it looked like a grenade – a potato masher. The constant roar of our artillery must have been maddening for Évariste to leave such a woman as Madame Lambert alone. She is as lovely and beautiful now as she was then."

Madame Lambert daubed a handkerchief at her eyes. A chair squeaked as Philippe came to her side.

In front of them, Otto, ignorant of the emotions, quickly worked at re-assembling and propping up the carp pieces with his fingers, but it was to no avail. The three blue chunks - the tail, the torso and the head all tottered then fell inside the pan. Louis tugged at Otto's apron – he wanted to try. Otto lifted him up. In a few seconds, Louis had lodged onions up against the carp until it looked like a blue Noah's ark, ready to launch.

Sigmund turned to the fish, took a deep breath then closed his eyes again. Everett watched as everyone, except for Philippe, did the same.

"I can smell the onions, the potatoes and the Carpe au Bleu cooking in its bath of wine and vinegar as I did when Otto brought me my Christmas dinner in 1917. It fogged up the lens as I chewed that first delicious bite and it was then, at six sharp, that the band struck their first brassy note over the ridge."

Otto, bowed his head to the resurrected blue carp.

"Now, ladies and gentlemen," Sigmund said, "please raise your glasses in a toast."

The crowd gasped at the steaming carp – big, fat and blue with its translucent eyes and its opened mouth frozen, halfway through a dumbfounded phrase.

Sigmund touched a fork to his wine glass. He motioned Everett and Beatrice to come alongside Madame Lambert and him and for the others to rise. The brasserie chirped with a moving of chairs as people stood. Sigmund raised his glass to Madame Lambert.

"To my lovely wife, for whom I shall love no matter where she calls home. Louis, before we eat, will you let Madame whisper into your ear, her choice - where she wants to spend the rest of her life with me?"

Louis ran to Madame Lambert, who seemed suddenly withdrawn and torn.

"Oh, Sigmund," Madame Lambert said. "You have painstakingly seen to my wants and needs in your new subterranean world, but I cannot yet choose. Perhaps we should spend a night in each."

"The tuilerie is yours," Philippe said. "Sigmund, I implore you, please, spend the first night there with Mother. I have removed every reminder of my father for you."

Madame Lambert lifted her brows to Sigmund.

"What of Madame's boyfriend, Chesterfield, in his metal jacket by the porch?" Sigmund asked.

"I am certain Philippe has already taken him for a swim in Lac Noir," Madame said.

"Santé!" Sigmund directed a toast towards Philippe.

"Santé!" A chorus of voices responded.

"I am sorry for making the wedding into a contest, Sister Beatrice was right - it is not the Duello," Louis whispered to Everett before returning to the steaming carp in his charge.

Sigmund turned to Otto and Louis standing beside the carp with their glasses - he winked then turned to Everett.

"To my old friend Russell and to his son, my new son, Everett - Santé! Santé!"

Everett was stunned. Silence fell over the brasserie, like a burning fuse disappearing into a stick of dynamite.

"Santé!" The crowd then roared.

"Kiss, Kiss!" Louis shouted above the din.

"We will watch them while we eat!" Sigmund laughed. "Otto, sit with us now - while Henri serves up the carp."

Everett held Beatrice and turned her down in his arms for a long kiss. From the corner of his eyes, he noticed Philippe and Annette with

Madame Chauchat. Philippe had Madame by the throat, until she waved her hands in a hasty agreement. Philippe hustled Annette away.

"Where is Philippe going?" Everett whispered in Beatrice's ear.

"Probably taking Gerta and the cart back to the tuilerie," Beatrice said. "I think the excitement has affected him."

"Maybe I should see," Everett said as he took a step towards the door.

"Let him go," Beatrice snagged his arm and closed her eyes. "Just kiss me!"

"Now, I am famished!" Beatrice said, after another long, lingering kiss.

The meal started civil enough, Everett thought, as Madame Lambert delicately pried a sliver of fish from its blue skin and lifted it to her quivering lips. The soldiers from the dépôt, too nervous for forks, resorted to using fingers as did everyone.

At the end of the meal, their plates lay heaped in long white carp bones and their hands and faces, blue as the fish.

Everett turned an ear to the kitchen where an accordion attempted a few bars of that, now familiar, old tune.

"I want to dance now," Beatrice said. "Like we did that night you told us that wonderful fishing story."

"But I don't dance," Everett said, still curious about what he had said in his trance.

"Take your shoes off. Dance with me now," Beatrice said, placing his hand beneath her hips. "We must stay awake tonight to drive Mother and Father home to the tuilerie. The dugout will be ours alone, for the night."

The Mercedes leaned slightly as Everett turned off Rue Gambetta onto the lane. The gray new moon, high overhead, painted Lac Noir in dull silver light. Beatrice's hair fluttered in the slight wind. Louis sprawled in her lap. Her parents entwined in the backseat, asleep.

Everett turned the Mercedes' slit cats-eye lights off and coasted quietly towards the tuilerie where a candle light flickered on the porch. Louis puckered his cheeks and wet his lips with his tongue. The sound awakened Beatrice, who looked at Louis as though he needed suckling.

"Poor Louis, his mouth is so dry from all the Riesling," Beatrice woke. She looked to the tuilerie. "I see Philippe and Annette have put out a light for us - how sweet."

Shadows folded over the porch. Gerta snorted nearby.

"They are on the porch," Beatrice said. "Do you think they waited up for us?"

Annette held a candle as Philippe hunched over the side of the porch.

"Do you think Father is sick from the blue carp?" Louis said, waking and rubbing his eyes.

"Look," Beatrice said, "Philippe is pulling on something. Gerta sounds nervous. I think they are removing Chesterfield!"

Beatrice reached to the backseat trying to revive Sigmund from his carp stupor.

"Wait right here," Everett said.

"No, Everett!" Beatrice said in a harsh whisper.

"Bull roar!" Everett barked. "I'll be right back."

Everett slowed as he approached Gerta, not wanting to startle her. From a short distance, he peered around her rump to see Philippe tipping the big shell away from the tuilerie wall where it had been motionless for over thirty-five years. He listened as Philippe read the fuse markings. Annette steadied the flickering candle nearby.

Philippe turned to her, looking distraught when he finished. He carefully leaned Chesterfield back into place before taking the candle from Annette's hand. With his good arm, Philippe embraced her on the porch.

"No!" Sigmund cried from the Mercedes.

As Annette placed a kiss on Philippe's lips, they suddenly twisted their heads in unison, Tango style, towards Chesterfield. Gerta blew. Something whizzed past Everett's head. A pang shot from one ear to the other as though his brain were at the sweet spot of a shimmering Korean gong.

A blanket of the warm, white horse hide of Gerta's back surrounded him as he soared on a silent hot breath of orange fire. The horse was but a banshee - no substance or spine to her at all - only her white coat, now a pale, bloodstained, flying carpet. Philippe's artificial arm hovered in mid-air near Everett's head. He grabbed it then rolled out of control.

Moonlit Lac Noir tumbled in his vision - if he could only make it there. He struggled to curl an edge of Gerta's torn hide to form an airfoil to control his fall and, with luck, to acquire some lift. It was no use – he let go of Philippe's arm and held onto the bloody hide like a child clinging to a blanket in its sleep.

The ground spun around the star-filled night sky as he spiraled downward. His ears rang a perpetual tone, a single long note that drummed memory from the brain and music from his heart like a marching band passing in review.

Tall reeds, brittle from the autumn and winter, lashed his burning face. A new growth of grass, covered in evening dew, felt refreshing against his face. He bounced and rolled, tucked into a ball, until his head smacked a boulder. He drew his hand across his shoulder, arms and chest – all in order, then sat up and checked inside his pants then his legs and his feet.

His left toe buckled up at a right angle, his shoes and socks, sucked from his feet by the blast. He laughed. That was it. – A broken toe? The laugh seemed to gurgle from his throat as he crawled through the grass towards the croaking of bullfrogs in the distance.

He stopped every half-minute to rest, breathing through a new place in his throat as well as his mouth. Although he smelled grass and burned flesh, nothing flowed through his nose. Grass turned to reeds and hard ground to marsh as he crawled, weak and shivering onto the dock of Lac Noir. Frogs flipped into the water.

As the dock shimmied under Everett, a tall white crane bobbed at its edge. The huge wings beat damp night air across his face as the bird took to flight over the Vosges. The dock heaved and swayed. He flopped his feet over the edge and fainted.

He put his hand to his head and felt a burnt and fractured cinder. He fainted again. A warm stream of blood trickled to his feet. He dangled them in the water. He fainted again. A rush of Le Gardon nibbled his toes.

He felt like speaking. Not to call out, it was too late for that, but to somehow mark the wind flowing down now from the Alsace to Lorraine with his last breath. He lay like a cold, dim meteorite. He tried murmuring, "Lost. Somewhere in Lorraine."

"Perdu dans le temps", someone replied. The words fell to him, filled with a comforting scent of vanilla.

♦ ♦ ♦

It had been good to hear Doc Hershey's voice several weeks ago on the telephone, but then everything was good while under the laudanum the doctors in Strasbourg prescribed. Everett tried speaking, but produced only a miserable, pathetic mumble, warped by the maze of wire fixed to his jawbone. Tight skin grafts, especially at the corners of his mouth, bound his lips in a puckered, clown-like expression.

Doc did the talking then. He said these doctors in Strasbourg were professionals who could fix his face. They had lots of practice and were right to leave that last bit of shrapnel, being so close to the spinal chord. Doc said the farm in Iowa was waiting for his new family, and then turned away from the phone to cough, asking Everett to come home as soon as he could.

It had taken weeks in the hospital to reduce the dosage of laudanum. Everett was clear enough to think. One day, he waited until only Sigmund remained in his hospital room. Everett mumbled through his harp-like mouth to Sigmund about the one band member who Sigmund had not yet spoken of – Stephen Collins the tuba player.

Sigmund shrugged his shoulders in ignorance. Everett realized Sigmund couldn't understand a single word and motioned Sigmund to give him a swallow of laudanum. It took several minutes to reduce the pain in his hand so he could write a note.

After reading the note, Sigmund took a large gulp from the bottle. Wiping a thread of the wine-colored laudanum from his chin, Sigmund sat next to Everett's hospital bed and waited, before whispering, in his German, guttural tone - Stephen's story.

"Your father tried finding the band," Sigmund said, "but by morning the stream had already filled most of the huge crater the mine had created. They had orders to attack from the frontline, to cross no-man's land without formation like Indians, to pursue the enemy in Hagen's trench – my old line.

"Your Doctor Hershey was rushed here from another unit the next morning. He knew your father well. Doctor Hershey told me what I am about to say. Are you certain you want to hear this? Lift a finger if you do."

Everett raised a finger then a hand and his arm until the pain gripped his shoulder.

"Alright then," Sigmund said. "Your father was in no condition himself to attack because of the gas, month's earlier. He led his men over the top anyway, 'Up and at 'em!'.

Sigmund paused to check for his pipe, and then continued without it.

"They came under relentless machine gun fire from a position I knew well - it was where I watched Évariste coming at us with that brush. Your father had his men attack randomly, at different times and directions, until they overpowered the machine gun and advanced all down the line, cutting my men down with their Springfield's, Tommy Guns, trench knives and grenades."

Sigmund asked him if he wanted something more for the pain, but Everett signaled 'No' with his hand.

"Doctor Hershey, working triage on the enemy, my own men, first came across the tuba," Sigmund continued. "All that brass, once wound so majestically round Stephen Collins, lie there flayed open like a giant leaf."

Sigmund gnarled his hand into a hideous shape to show him. Everett, remembering having seen much worse in Korea, resisted any recognition of the horror. He only smirked, but it was enough movement of his facial muscles for pain to throttle him like electricity.

"Further into the attack," Sigmund continued, "Doctor Hershey happened upon a more spontaneous form of triage – your father was holstering his pistol, a forty-five – still smoking. Beneath him lay half of the young Stephen Collins, blown a hundred yards like you, but with his stomach and intestines exposed, his veins pumping the last bit of blood and a perfect bullet hole – straight through his forehead. You have lost your father's face, of course – but all the rest of you are here."

Everett twisted, uncomfortable in any position. Sigmund walked to his cabinet and returned with Everett's bottle of laudanum.

"Your Doctor Hershey never spoke of this, I see. Such an awful thing to remember," Sigmund said as he corked the bottle with his old and yellowed teeth.

"I should think your last letter should read something like this," Sigmund removed a folded piece of paper from his shirt pocket and read it slowly to Everett.

"I must tell you Mr. and Mrs. Collins, once I suffered a string of fitful nights. A whole squad of mine had not returned from a trench raid, you know these boys - they are from our town. I tried praying, I tried counting the lice I plucked from my tunic, I tried everything I could to sleep without dreaming of those boys crawling out there, not far away, trying to reach our wire and line."

"I thought I was quite mad after that night, until your son, Stephen, began blasting his big brass tuba outside his tent, pounding out forceful arpeggios that rebounded from the tall walls of the tuilerie in a beacon of sound for my lost squad."

"At first, I disciplined your son, as the sound might give our position away, but then I realized the tuilerie was perfectly safe, as it had been for years, due to its slope and range. I asked Stephen then, if he had enough wind to play even stronger and, for the remainder of the night, his low blast carried out across the wire."

"The squad I prayed for reported for duty the next morning, saying only that they followed the horn, that beautiful fog-horn home. I shall miss him, greatly. Sincerely,"

Sigmund paused.

"Captain Russell Taylor, AEF 1918, Somewhere in Lorraine."

Everett, having closed his eyes to Sigmund's painful last words, tasted the chalky red syrup as Sigmund tipped the bottle to his lips. He moved close to Everett's ear a few minutes later.

"Listen to me, before you get too comfortable, I have another proposal," Sigmund said. "You are aware of the storm brewing far across the Rhine to the east? The communists now have your great American power. The giants possess the same weaponry as the Gods and I shall need to line my dugout in lead for Madame. We want you to take our Beatrice and her Louis to America where it is safe. Do you hear me?"

Everett strained to speak and when he tried, his vocal chords produced only an animal's grunt. It didn't hurt to say 'yes'.

"Good," Sigmund said. "You will be happy to know that I have wrestled a few more Chesterfields from the Zone Rouge – enough for a decent first class voyage on the Ile de France sailing from LeHavre when you are ready. Perhaps one day, when this part of the world is safe, you might return my treasures to Lorraine."

Chesterfield's metallic spinal remnants sang a high-pitched chorus until Everett raised his hand 'No', he'd seen enough.

ॐ17ॐ
A New Life

The Ile de France, luxurious and huge, absorbed the crash of waves against its hull while Beatrice and Louis snored in bed. Everett felt every shudder and shake. Seated at a table by the door, he licked sweet laudanum from his lips and lifted the letter, wet with ink. Having tried each of the six nights at sea, he finished writing to the parents of Stephen Collins with the last drop of ink. He forged his dad's name, forcing his left hand to scroll the same cursive style as his father's elegantly slanted words. At last, he held it quivering with his right hand - the bad one.

He sealed the old blue envelope addressed from Somewhere in Lorraine and wrapped it in a ribbon together with the other twenty-five he had written before the blast. The band he, like his father, had come to know all lay lightly in his hand, whole and complete. He set them down, pressing them with the laudanum bottle and feeling confused and depressed as though finishing a mediocre book, wishing there had been more to say, but relieved it was over.

He reached to switch off the lamp when a thin sliver of Chesterfield's iron, lodged near his spine, wiggled and turned. A familiar tingle toyed with his back. In a way, he looked forward to the unbearable pain that would certainly follow.

The Ile de France , old but elegant, groaned like a settling house as it slowed, nearing port. In darkness, he cloaked a ship's robe around him while clutching his cobalt-blue bottle of laudanum. The bundle of letters, sticking to the bottom, came up with it.

Shrapnel crept like an inchworm, close enough to his spine where it would shunt an electrical switch and send torrents of unending pain to his brain. Since Strasbourg he became comfortable with the tickling sensation – this was different, he knew. It could work itself into a real storm, leaving him paralyzed and forever prone on his bed, not in the defiant, erect pose of Évariste, but as a pitiful, living memorial.

Bedsprings squeaked as Louis snuggled against Beatrice from the large first class suite. Everett took the cane from the back of the chair – needing it because, although his legs and feet felt fine, his brain had trouble commanding them. He limped quietly with the bottle tucked under an arm and the letters in his hand to the quiet darkened deck outside. He dragged a deck chair to the rail and slowly lifted his foot to its seat. A door somewhere creaked opened.

He glanced to the second-class deck below. A steward looked up and flicked a cigarette to the pre-dawn light. The eastern sky turned from black to a deep indigo morning. He rolled the cold blue bottle in his left hand and painfully gripped the letters with his right, flapping them against the rails as the ocean sloshed below.

A white gull lifted up and hung briefly in the air next to his head. In the dim deck light, fog-like air rolled over the tips of its wings before the gull banked and turned to dive down to the sea. He raised the bottle to uncork it with his teeth. An orange light flared up behind him. Everett turned slightly, gripping the bottle.

A steward, wearing the ship's standard red blazer with a red cap, lit a cigarette. He sloshed a tall drink as he walked towards Everett. Dragging his hand along the rail, the steward stopped a few paces away in silhouette against the opening morning light. His loose shirttails fluttered in the gentle breeze.

Everett stared below into the frothing sea.

"Good morning, Monsieur," the steward said. "Pardon my untidy uniform, I work second class below deck at night. I came up here to watch us coming to port."

The steward took a long drag from his cigarette.

"I have not seen you since the woman and the boy wheeled you aboard. They spoke English to you. I thought at first I recognized her, but when I called her Brunnhilde she did not respond."

Everett wondered how many ports Beatrice had visited – but it didn't matter.

"If she were, you would be in good hands," the steward said, "although I have never seen Brunnhilde escort a man across the Atlantic before."

The steward's face kept to the shadow, but the voice sounded like André's - the steward on his voyage to Marseilles. Something about the way he wore his cap, too, reminded Everett of André, but it was smaller than André's and something else was different. Everett sensed the steward didn't seem to recognize him at all, but then that was understandable, given his new face.

"That is quite alright, Monsieur. I can see it is difficult to speak. You must be an American with the Foreign Legion returning home from Indochina, or perhaps from Korea – I can tell you wear the LeFort III."

Everett remembered the LeFort III upon seeing a stranger's face in the mirror weeks ago. The doctors in Strasbourg had argued, as he stared at himself then, over whether his face should be a category II or category III. The LeFort categories were devised, they said, by the French surgeon, Rene' Le Fort, in 1901. The III meant his cheekbone separated from the bone behind the forehead and the bridge of his nose was now a trench. They did what they could.

The steward tipped the glass back for a drink. Everett thought the heavy French accent sounded like André, but the ship line would employ many Frenchmen on the leg to and from Marseilles. It just couldn't be André though - the cap was all wrong and his drink was clear with ice cubes, not yellow and neat like André liked his cognac.

"Allow me to help you with your medication, Monsieur. I can see you do not use it often, the opiate has settled at the bottom."

The steward discretely pried the bottle from Everett's hand and shook it hard then uncorked it with his teeth. Everett was shocked as the steward tasted it.

"C'est bon! You need a little sip now, yes?" The steward sighed as though he had just tasted a cold beer. He handed it Everett. "Let me turn your chair around for you to sit and watch the sun rise."

Everett held the chair fixed with his body while he dangled the letters with his right hand over the rail. He snatched the bottle from the steward with his left hand, holding it up to the east where some light shone through a line of clouds. He grunted as he noticed the steward had swallowed more than a quarter of the remaining laudanum.

A klaxon wailed nearby. Everett's leg took a step without his permission, scrambling for another night bombing raid and stunning him so that he dropped the bottle. It spun on the deck, swirling a stream of red-colored syrup until the steward picked it up, hammered the cork in and set it on the chair. The bottle still had enough left for later, Everett thought, bending down some to check.

"Nerves! I know, Monsieur. It was only a siren from shore," the steward said, putting himself between Everett and the bottle. "I often get jumpy too, as you Americans say. I am so sorry it spilt, Monsieur. It must have been comforting to know it was there when you needed it. I once liked cognac, but now I prefer your 7-Up. Here, take the rest of mine."

The steward placed the glass in Everett's left hand and helped raise it. Everett waited for the switch to close across his shrapnel. The carbonation tickled his tongue. He looked up-close at the glass in the dim deck light for his face and found only the dark gray disk of the new moon.

A wind picked up. Everett let the warm ocean air sooth his face as the switch threatened another tickle across his back. He drew his newly burned right hand across his cheeks and, discovering deep fissures, raked the letters through them to produce a pleasurable shiver.

He looked again for the ghost's reflection in the glass and found his father's wonderful smile instead. Ice rattled like loosened bones against his skull until he set the glass down on the deck rail. The wind fanned the letters in his left hand as though he held a live grasshopper inside. He let go.

The steward thrust his arm out and snared the loosening bundle.

"Unusual morning winds," the steward said. He glanced at the return addresses printed on the blue envelopes. "I see the letters are from Lorraine. You must not have had time to post them from France, yes?"

Everett nodded, and then reached for the letters.

"We are at sea, but while we are aboard this ship we are still in France, I can have these posted Paquebot for you," he said. Everett grabbed the letters, pressing them close to his chest.

"Monsieur, beneath the LeFort, you have a kind face." The steward stepped closer to Everett, but Everett turned. "You need not be ashamed. Allow me to remove my hat."

A soft rose-petal nub of an ear lay planted on the side of the man's head, not quite healed. He turned it towards the ring of ship's bells. Everett's face warmed and he wondered if he hadn't blushed.

"Oh, but it is amazing what can be done!" The steward flipped the cap back on, cocking it to the side by habit then proudly straightening it back up. A tugboat's horn tooted a code, shortly answered by another. Everett felt the man's breath against the strange skin of his left cheek as the steward kissed him like an old friend. Everett loosened the letters.

"A whole new face you have, how marvelous!" the steward said.

He lifted the letters from Everett's hand and reached for the bottle on the chair.

"If you can trust me with these letters," the steward said, "I can trust you with this."

He handed Everett the bottle of laudanum, struck a match to a cigarette, and stepped away to his duties with the twenty-six letters locked under his arm.

A sharp jab throttled Everett as the shrapnel found a new nerve to torture. He quickly sunk his teeth into the soft cork. It refused to budge. About to curse the steward, Everett looked up as the sky, shown in steel-blue city light, opened beneath clouds to the west. Fresh morning air coated his throat. Behind him, a mother's song broke through the mist. An immigrant's song, filled with hope, sung sweetly and off-key.

An itch crawled like a bug inside a long deep scar on his face. He touched it with his right hand and found a droplet, warm and salty. More began to flow freely in the strange new brooks of his face.

A skyscraper switched on its morning lights. Window to window and floor to floor, light filled its hollow cavities like a Jack-O-Lantern. One, then ten, then twenty skyscrapers wakened the city with a brief brilliance, overpowering even the low sun basting the spires in majestic tangerine and peach. Everett breathed in the stale air of eight million lungs, ready to go.

A tugboat nudged the ship from below, guiding them straight to a pier with tall twirling cranes. Trains, with lighted passenger cars, coiled through the city like a prizefighter's pulsing veins. The city welcomed the morning, not with a yawn, but a gasp.

The cabin door opened from behind. He elbowed the laudanum overboard.

"Everett?" Beatrice asked as she stepped to him. "Have you been out here all night? Was someone here?"

Everett thought of the letters on their way to addresses, long vacant. His father would be pleased with the band coming home this way.

A light beacon swung around in the distance and fell across Beatrice's long flowing nightgown. Everett mumbled helplessly, as a thundering, and soon, a deafening roar came over their heads.

"A new life? Yes," Beatrice whispered in his ear, holding him close, "I know."

He warmed to her side, marveling at her clairvoyance.

Above them, the belly of a silver beast hurled towards the northeast. With red-tipped wings swept back, it whined with an eerie after-glow from its engines tucked in the wings near its fuselage as it banked into the sun.

"Is that a jet?" Louis shouted as he stood in the cabin doorway, still in his pajamas. He pointed to the disappearing streak.

A gentle spark worked at Everett's throat. Nothing came.

"Everett says it was a Comet, Louis."

"Bull roar," Louis barked. "Even our Lorraine's own, Messier, would know that was a not a comet, it was a jet."

"Bull roar?" Beatrice said. "Where did you hear that? Is that what you would name the jet, Bull Roar?"

Everett nudged her cheek with his and managed a smile.

"No, I would call it a phantom," Louis said. "It came from nowhere."

"Maybe it's like your jet," Louis tugged at Everett's robe. "Is it flying all the way to Korea?"

"Not yet, Louis," Beatrice said as she helped Everett close up his robe, billowing in the wind. "Maybe, one day. Maybe, one day you'll fly a phantom."

"Is New York, where people who run away from home, come to stay?" Louis said. "Even people who are mad?"

A warm, wet and comforting breath fell across Everett's thin new skin of his face then filled his nose with vanilla. He kissed her ear with his parched and tender lips.

"Everett says, it teems with wonderfully mad people just like us," Beatrice said.

The shrapnel tested another site in his spine. Everett grinned delightfully to spite it. He watched as Louis swiveled his head to the skyline then swung his small awkward body in circles with arms swept out to both sides.

As the jet rumbled low to the east, Everett lifted a corner of his mouth, smiled to Beatrice's ear and babbled nonsense - something that only Brunnhilde could understand. Beatrice turned to Louis.

"It's a new world, Everett says. He's taking us to a new world."

"Who does he know there?" Louis asked.

Everett coughed once at Beatrice's neck. She turned to Louis.

"Not a single person, he says. They're all new, just like us."